LOSER'S MEMORIAL

by

Larry Nocella

Other works by Larry Nocella

Where Did This Come From? a novel

It Never Goes Away (short story)

LOSER'S MEMORIAL

by

Larry Nocella

ZERD

IRAQ

2007

I can't remember what I looked like.

I know I was once covered in tattoos, but they're all gone now, my skin blank. I'm trying to re-draw them from memory, but my recall is so splotchy, I don't know if I'm getting them right or just making them up. I don't even know why I bother.

Actually I do.

Those tats were a part of me. Not just physically. They told my story.

Now, no matter how many times I scrape the knifepoint over my skin, the cut seals up and erases what I've done. It reminds me of what they did to you, Dad. You wanted to tell a story, but they didn't want it told, so it was covered up, sealed, erased. Just like you, the harder the efforts to quiet me, the harder I scrape. I'm willing to draw blood, even my own, just to have my say.

At first it was fascinating, the skin rupturing, two ragged edges rising on either side of a red line, the pain distant. If I stared long enough, I could actually see it closing back up, like watching water dry in the sun. No matter how deep I cut, after a while, my blood art disappears, taking my story with it, like neither ever existed.

That chemical weapon or bio-weapon, or whatever it was, messed up me and my crew real bad. Of course I couldn't just die like everyone else. I had to be the oddball. They wanted to screw me up, but I always screw things up myself so both forces cancelled each other out and here I am, some kind of perfect. Now their project is ruined and it's time to start over.

When I say they made me perfect, I mean in a sense. Instead of my body destroying itself with cancer, like happened with the other guys, my flesh repairs itself. We all had our DNA scrambled, but mine got scrambled in the wrong direction. It sounds cool at first, to heal so quickly, but it's hell for a tattoo-freak like me. I don't want to heal. I just want to be me.

In a way, none of this surprises you, does it, Dad? Screwing up is in our genes. It might even go deeper. It's in our destiny.

It's just as well my improvised ink disappears. The drawings are crap because all I have to dig into my skin with is this ridiculous knife.

I wish you could see it. It looks like a prop from some future apocalypse movie. There are holes for my fingers, a resting place for my thumb and spiked knuckles bristling from the handle. The blade is a solid nine inches, a psycho's wet-dream.

Even though my skin forgets, the drops of blood and flakes of flesh pool together on the floor. Hell, I can't even go cleanly. The gore puddle is so large, you would think someone bled to death here, but it's just me, leaking, sealing up, cutting myself, leaking again. It's the only mark I make that stays.

The floor is getting slippery, so I'm going to move across the room, closer to the family I've been staying with.

Oh, I didn't mention them?

I keep my distance because whenever I get near them, my stomach rumbles. It's damn annoying.

Comic book superheroes have crazy powers, but they never have to fuel them. They fly, get shot, lift buildings and more, but you never see them tank up. As for me, the dulled pain and speedy healing doesn't come free. I think it's got something to do with protein. If my body is going to close a wound, it's going to need raw materials.

I read once, I think I did, that the wrinkles in the brain are what make intelligence and memory. The more wrinkles, the smarter you are, the more memories you have. So, just as my skin closes wounds with unnatural speed, I think the kinks of my brain are flattening out, the lobes smoothing over like a dented car popping back to its virgin shape. Hey, great, my skin seals up wounds, but my brain wrinkles are closing up too and that makes my memories fade.

You can't get something for nothing, right?

Yes? No? Well it makes sense to me.

My stomach rumbled again. Time for some human jerky. I walked over to one of the corpses in the corner, almost skating there on my own blood, and I sliced a strip off a dead body's withered brown ass. I didn't think about it, I just did it. Hunger is empowering that way.

I didn't mention the family I'm staying with is dead? Oh, forgot that detail. If it makes you feel any better, I didn't kill them. I found them in this compound, huddled together, probably fleeing from something, dying and decaying for who knows how long.

Wait a minute, you're saying, what compound? Where?

I'm holed up in an abandoned sandstone building in the desert of Iraq.

I'll try to explain later.

While I was chewing on raisin-wrinkled ass flesh, I scraped my sci-fi knife across my head, taking hair and chunks of scalp with it. I knew the job was done when my head felt like a map of smooth shapes and slick wet spots. The wet spots dried as the skin grew back. In minutes, the bleeding stopped and I was bald.

Ready and built for battle.

Nothing was inessential, no hair to grab.

I put the knife in my crotch and thought about it seriously for a long time.

Even after all I've gone through, I can't do it. I know my skin closes up wounds, I know I'm going to die soon, but I'm not willing to gamble with my privates. So the weakness stays. Some things never change, I guess.

Except for my face, I was just about featureless. No zits, no scars, no moles, no hair, no ink. Just skin. Like a mistake the gods never got around to finishing. The stories of scars, gone. Like I was meant to be someone and never became him.

That's partially correct, but I know I am someone.

I am Zerd.

Remember him? I cut into my arm, where that first tattoo was before it vanished. As best I could with my failing memory, I recreated that crazy lizard.

He was once surrounded by art, but I can't remember what. I slid the blade up and down my arm until I remembered a gravesite. A skeleton partially buried, its skull smashed in, bony hand giving the world the middle finger. I remember it, but just barely. Four letters were carved into the capstone. What were they?

I don't know how long I was fishing in my mind before I finally remembered. They could mean more than one thing, but at that moment, they were a sign-off. The same one I planned to use any minute now, when I check out of life: P.S.F.U.

* * *

So, Dad, you're probably asking why.

I understand. You're wondering what the hell is going on.

The short answer is I screwed up. Then I screwed up again over and over and one thing led to another, and here I am.

The long answer will take some explaining.

I don't know much about fighting, except for Steve's rules. Not that it would matter. It's one versus four, and those four have made their livings killing people. I'm realistic about my chances, so I'm going to go out my way. That's why I keep trying to draw the tattoos.

This is the end, Dad.

Right now, I know what they're saying. Their orders are something like, "We need a confirmed kill." They need my dead body, or at least my head. Beheadings are the thing to do to your enemies around here.

When in Rome and all that shit, right?

Bottom line is they want to cover their tracks. I'm not really sure what their master plan is or was, but it didn't include letting me or any of the other guys live, and it definitely didn't include turning me into some kind of speed-healing memory-less always-hungry freak.

When I look out of this brick oven into the white heat of the desert, I see a plume of dust. It's the tail of a monster-size black SUV, carrying four guys I've come to know well.

Why don't they just bomb the place? Because they don't want anyone else involved, probably. Clean-ups like this, closing loose ends like me, that's what these guys get paid to do.

I think you once said something like: You can't know what the enemy thinks, but once you learn his habits, you can guess how he thinks. Something about conspiracy theories, you were saying? I can't remember.

What brought me here is a long story, but I'll try to get to it before my mind goes completely blank.

I'm thinking these thoughts in the hope that somehow, across the world, through some spiritual connection between father and son, you'll hear me, feel me, maybe even dream about my final message to you and only you.

Of course, this is assuming you're even still alive. As for Mom, I've got nothing to say to her. I don't give a damn about her. I haven't since that day.

* * *

They're here. The plume of dust has settled. The black SUV is at rest, the Redfire Corporation logo proud and large on its side. I expected four men, and that's how many spill out, but someone slides over to the driver's seat.

Who's the fifth guy? I'll never know.

These aren't working-class military stiffs. These are the volunteers. Contractors they call themselves, because they hate the word mercenaries. You pay them money and they kill who you want, the enforcers of a rich man's will.

See, Dad? I listened. Your lessons must have gone deep if they're one of the final things I can remember.

These four are the guys you hate, so I'll try to take at least one with me.

Enough babbling. Time is running out and I want to make sure to say I love you.

I'm sorry things turned out this way. I'm sorry I'm going to die across the world from you with so much left unsaid and undone.

I love you because you gave me one thing I've always used, and I'm going to use today for all it's worth.

Fight.

No matter how much the world kicked your ass, you always spat back, even though you lost most of the time.

And I know you love me. I didn't always know that, but I do now. You were a pain in the ass, but you don't really get to choose the way someone loves you, and I guess that's part of the problem.

Here they come.

There's no running for me this time. They would hunt me. There's nowhere to run anyway so this is it, one final battle.

You said something to your class once that hasn't left me yet. You always worried about how young I was, that I would find the lectures boring, but when I sat in the back, I wasn't just drawing. I wasn't always skipping out to smoke pot with your students.

Sometimes I listened. You spoke with force, with belief like a preacher. It was kind of cool. A chill went up my spine then, and as much as I can feel anything, it's happening again now.

"People have a breaking point," you said. "When they've been spit on, stolen from and bruised too many times, they rise up and cannot be stopped, even against overwhelming forces. Call it what you want, but I think it's best described as the will of God."

You paused there, and the auditorium was still. You had us all, what's the word?

Enthralled.

I loved those words when you said them, and I never told you. Of all the things I've done wrong, I might have to say that's my biggest regret. I think you would have been happy to know that, since you probably thought I hated you all the time.

Well, that's it. I need to focus now. I'm signing off. Probably for good.

No. Definitely for good.

That's another thing you taught me: be tough when nothing is going your way and always be honest. Or at least realistic. Fight the good fight, but don't delude yourself about your odds.

How do I know I'm going to die? Well, aside from the four trained killers entering this building that's been my home recently, my life is flashing before my eyes. I always thought it was a dumb cliché, but it's happening. Maybe it's my memories flaming out. Who knows?

On one of those final pathetic visits with Tracy, when I was trying to remember some detail of my stupid life, she said, "Don't strain to remember the bad times, remember only the good times." I'm not sure I buy that. The bad times sucked, but at the end of my life, they're a part of me as much as the good times. If I ignore the bad times, I don't have much of a life left to flash before my eyes. Then I'll just be sitting on my ass waiting for these pricks to come kill me.

The great blank overtaking my mind makes me think of an ocean rising among mountain peaks. The hills vanish first, then the medium-sized mountains. The water keeps rising until there's just a flat surface punctured by only the most prominent memories. Soon there will be nothing but a flat surface, still and featureless as glass. It all depends on how high the tide rises. Maybe a memory or two will poke through. More likely they'll all drown.

It will be interesting to see what that last memory to go will be, what was most prominent.

Of course, if I'm not dead by then, I might as well be. For now, all I have are the few memories that haven't gone under. It doesn't matter if they're good or bad, just that they were huge.

So, as my life flashes before me, I can only recall a few key moments. The earliest one is of the day Mom left. I might as well start there. I always thought of that day as the day I was born. Not physically, of course. I mean the day I became aware that the world is an unpredictable, cold and merciless place. I wouldn't wear the symbol and I wouldn't get the nickname for a few years later, but that was the day I became Zerd.

PETE

USA

2001

I was upstairs in my room drawing when Dad came home. I always recognized him by the sounds of his arrival. First his keys would clank on the dining table, then he'd drop his briefcase. He would find Mom and steal a kiss. They would talk quietly before he trudged upstairs to see me.

Those were the sounds I was desperately listening for, hoping things would get back to normal as soon as possible.

The day before had been maxed-out messed-up. Planes were hijacked and flown into skyscrapers in New York City. Another one hit the Pentagon and another crashed in Pennsylvania. I watched the attacks on a TV set up in my high school auditorium before the principal told us all to go home. When I walked in the front door, Dad and Mom were there. Work had let them go early, too.

They were both sitting on the couch, watching the news. Dad kept rubbing Mom's back as she wailed into her hands and leaned forward onto her knees.

"So many lives," she cried. "Why?"

Dad looked at me but didn't say anything. I went up to my room and broke out my sketchbook. I drew abstracts, just lines and shapes that all somehow ended up looking vaguely like clouds of flame bursting from tall buildings.

Dad made time for me then, even with all that crap going on. I could hear Mom sobbing downstairs while he stood next to me, hand on my shoulder.

"What are you drawing, kid?" he said.

"Just shapes."

"Good. You keep your head up."

"I will."

Mom wailed again. She sounded like a wounded animal. It scared me a little.

"You should go see her," I said.

"Let me know if you need anything, all right?"

"I will, Dad."

The next day, he didn't make his usual sounds when he came home. Instead he called to me.

"Pete?"

"Yeah, Dad, I'm up here."

"Where's your mother? She working late?"

"I don't know. I came straight up after school."

"Did you read this note?"

"What note?"

He didn't answer, and I had a sick feeling that I forgot to do some stupid chore Mom wanted. I heard Dad sit down, then nothing.

I kept drawing, waiting for him to scold me for not pulling my weight.

I loved it when he came up to see me after work. He usually rubbed my head roughly and asked about whatever I was drawing. He had done that every single day since I started school, and never forgot. Even yesterday on September 11th, when Mom was losing it and everyone was freaking out, he came up to see my sketches.

He didn't on September 12th.

He would never do it again.

The day before had been the last day of that ritual, that tradition I loved so much and have missed ever since. I just didn't know it then.

The whole house was still. Something was wrong.

"Dad?"

No answer.

I found him face-down on the kitchen table. He looked like my class did when the jackass teachers punished us for being noisy.

"Dad?" I asked. He shifted, but didn't look up.

A folded slip of paper sat on the table. It seemed so harmless, like something you might write a grocery list on. I picked it up and read.

"To my son, and to my husband, both of whom I love very much." It was Mom's handwriting. "John, I'm sorry. As we learned yesterday, life is too short and ends too soon. I've been thinking about things for a while and there's no other way I can do this unless I make a clean break. Pete, you are a beautiful boy. Don't stop drawing. You have a real talent. Please remember, this isn't your fault. Goodbye to you both. Lots of love."

"That's it?" I asked out loud, my voice whiny. "She didn't even sign it?"

Dad groaned.

"Dad?"

He sat up and rubbed his face, fingers pressing against his eyes under his glasses. He stood up, walked past me like I wasn't there, shuffled into his office and closed the door.

It was a dark autumn evening. I remember feeling cold and angry. I stood there holding the note. My stomach growled like it was asking, "Hey, what about me?"

I nuked two burritos and ate one alone. The house was so damn quiet, I was hearing sounds I never noticed before, lots of creaking, leaves brushing the windows, a stick skipping in the wind across the back porch.

This time of night, Mom usually had the TV on and Dad would be buzzing around, working with her to make dinner together. It was all gone.

I ate across the table from Dad's seat, where his burrito rested untouched, Mom's stupid note sat at her place.

After I finished eating, I knocked on the door of Dad's office but there was no answer. I remember a stab of fear, holding my breath. I thought maybe he was dead, overdosed on sleeping pills, or had shot himself. That's how it always worked in the movies. I pushed the door open slowly.

He was sitting at his desk, head down, snoring softly.

I set the burrito next to him. Strands of steam rose from it.

I watched him sleep for a while before I left.

Up in my room I drew a picture of Mom and scribbled over it, black circles obscuring her fanged and bloody smile.

That was the last time I ever saw her.

* * *

For the next month, what seemed like a year, Dad was on the phone, constantly trying to find Mom.

The September 11 attacks replayed on the mute TV while he yelled and cursed into the phone. The planes flew into the World Trade towers. The buildings smoked and collapsed over and over and over with Dad providing lead vocals.

"I know you know where she is. Can I just talk to her? I just want to fucking talk! Don't give me that shit!"

I hid in my room and put on my headphones, the big kind with the pads around the ears. I didn't need to hear him and I didn't want to relive September 11th. Once was enough. It was fucked up. What more was there to say?

I'll never understand why he kept after Mom so much.

In between calls, he'd pull some crap out of the freezer and I would microwave it. Eventually he stopped even that.

"Can you make yourself dinner?" he'd ask.

"Sure, Dad."

Then he was back on the phone. When the calls ended, the TV volume came on. He was obsessed with those annoying news opinion shows where guys in suits yell at each other. Since the attacks had just happened, that was all they talked about. Dad would start out muttering, raising his voice slowly until by the end of the night he was cursing at the screen.

Sometimes I would watch him from the top of the stairs. It was sort of funny seeing a normally mellow college professor lose his shit.

"Bullcrap! Liar!" he would bark at the screen. "You're such an asshole. Oh, that's just fucking great."

He never noticed me spying on him.

His voice was so full of rage, he got a little scary. Eventually I just stayed in my room, listened to music and drew, living off nuked burritos.

A few weeks later, he showed up in my room's doorway. For a second, my heart leapt. I thought he had come to see what I was drawing. I yanked off my headphones and turned down the heavy metal that was destroying my hearing.

He stared at the floor for a while before looking up.

"We have to talk," he said.

"Okay. About what?"

"I don't think your mother is coming back."

He looked pathetic, his head sagging and shoulders hunched. I had to struggle not to laugh. I just wanted to say, "Duh."

I already knew that from her note, but I was so glad he was talking to me again I made up a question I didn't really care about.

"Do you know why she left?"

"I know as much as you do. I haven't been able to get in touch with her. The few friends we shared, her dumb family, they're not telling me anything."

"What a fucking bitch."

He didn't complain when I called her that, he just smirked like he agreed but didn't want to say so.

"They're shuffling our schedules at work, and with your mom, uh… gone, I'm going to pick up teaching some night classes. Can you handle yourself?"

"Sure."

"I know you can. Come on, let's go get something to eat."

That was the last time we went out for pizza. We placed our orders but didn't talk. There was a television over the bar across the room. He shifted around in the booth and watched it, drinking bottled beer, ignoring me until the food came.

"You sure you'll be okay alone at night?"

"Yeah. I can take care of myself. Nothing is going to happen."

"Good. Good."

"I've been drawing more."

"Excellent."

He used to say, "Excellent. What are you drawing?" Now he just said, "Excellent."

He ordered another beer. Then another. Then another.

The drive home was rough. I probably should have taken the keys. That's what they say to do at school. I should have called a cab or something but he was my father and I didn't have the courage to do it, even when he was staggering toward the driver's side. I couldn't drive yet anyway, so if I took the keys we'd both be stuck and things were messed up enough.

We got home safe. There was always time to die later.

* * *

The first time he was away teaching night school I got edgy. The damn little noises were driving me nuts. Creaks, tapping, drips and whispering breezes were pissing me off, distracting me. I turned up my music even louder so there was nothing but my marker, the paper and the thunder. Sure, a psycho could easily sneak up and stab me in the back, but I would rather get killed than fuck up a drawing.

I always stayed up until Dad got home because I wanted to show I could take care of myself. It was a mistake, though, because that's how I learned he didn't just drink that one time, he was a drunk.

When he got home from teaching night class, he brought the stink of beer with him. He flopped on the couch and flicked on his political yelling shows. Sometimes I would peek downstairs, just to check on him.

Once we were into that routine, he came up to see me only one time. I didn't hear him because of the tunes punishing my eardrums, but I knew he was near when the smell of booze started burning my nose. I took off my earphones.

"You're still up?" he asked, leaning against the door frame.

"I'm always up this late."

"I checked the mail, found this." He held up my report card.

"Oh," I said, but I meant oh shit. I knew my grades were diving and I didn't care, but I should have been smart enough to intercept the mail. He swayed a bit and for a second I thought he was going to tumble backwards over the railing.

"Um. You're not mad, are you?" I asked.

"Hell, no!" He smiled that overly-wide smile drunk people do. "You're passing!"

"I am?"

"Make sure you pass, kid. School is just a conformity farm. Don't be another chicken that gets its head cut off."

"If it's such a conformity farm, why do I have to go?"

He sprayed me when he laughed. "Good question. That's my boy. Go to school, make sure you pass and I won't bitch about your grades. Fair trade?"

We shook on it. His grip was cold and wet. "Fair trade."

"You should read stuff on your own, too. You read, don't you?"

"Sometimes."

"That's all there is to learning. If you can read, you can teach yourself anything. You should try some of my books."

"Your books?"

"I'll get some."

He walked away. I didn't think he was coming back, so I popped on my music and started drawing again. I smelled his return, just before a stack of huge books crashed onto my desk.

They had ridiculously long titles like "The Continual Rise of Imperialism and Subsequent Inevitable Rise of Hegemony in Western Society."

"I don't know, Dad."

"Oh, they'll be difficult, but the great thing about books is there's no time limit. Anyone can finish a book. Just keep reading."

He turned and was gone.

Down in front of the television again, he snored while guys in suits yelled at each other. I flipped through one of the books. I tried to lift it and it practically broke my wrist. The words were so big they hurt my eyes. Life couldn't possibly be that complicated.

I slammed the cover shut and went to bed.

* * *

Being alone isn't so bad when you get used to it. There are certain advantages. You can jerk off where you want, when you want and as much as you want. You can listen to music as loud as you want without headphones unless your jackass neighbor comes over and bitches.

Good thing I wasn't doing both of those at the same time.

The biggest advantage to being alone? You can get stoned as much as you want.

Usually when I smoked pot, my mind would bust out of its cage and leap around like a rowdy dog. One time, though, I scored some weed that was laced with something strong and that rowdy dog got in the space capsule and set a course for the thirteenth dimension.

The trip was fantastic, but my drawings turned out like shit.

"That's just the time-warp interference," I told myself out loud, shouting over the metal playing through my headphones. Normally I got pissed when my art wasn't turning out right, but I was wearing a full mellow jacket. I was exploring, experimenting. I felt like something big was about to reveal itself to me.

After a while, I noticed the smoke was getting thicker. I ignored it. I thought it was just because I was leaning down low, close to the paper, nodding off. I also thought maybe it was because I was feeling everything so deeply. When I get high, colors are deeper and I notice sounds in music I never noticed before, but I also get stupider and clumsier.

That's why I didn't realize my trash can was on fire until the smoke was so thick I couldn't see. I must have knocked the still-burning joint into it.

"Oh, shit! Oh, shit!" I yelled, jumping up, ripping my headphones out of my stereo. The room filled with heavy metal. I had the volume cranked so much, the smoke pulsed to the beat.

I grabbed anything I could and threw it at the fire under my desk. I couldn't get my head together enough to think about what else to do. The flames were huge and burned painfully. Having heightened senses was fun when everything was cool, but when things went to shit, what good is being able to smell every atom of burnt hair?

The flames were roaring, lashing at me like intelligent, malicious whips. At least it seemed like they were thanks to me tripping. I kept backing into the corner of my room, knocking shit all over the place. I thought I saw a demon's face in the fire.

"I don't wanna die!" I kept yelling, trying to climb the wall.

I was terrified. I knew I was alone. Completely alone. Dad wasn't going to help. God wasn't going to help. No one was going to help me. It was me versus the fire. Wrong or right didn't matter. There was only a winner and a loser. My heavy metal provided a soundtrack as the singer screamed the chorus.

"Do or die! You're gonna die! Do or die! Death is near and you're gonna die!"

"Shut the fuck up!" I yelled at the stereo. It didn't listen. It just kept screaming about how death was sure to get me this time, eat my soul and all that.

I had no idea then I would be in a similar situation several years later, meaning now, as I wait for my death here in Iraq. There's no wrong or right here, just a winner and a loser and God doesn't give shit because there is no God.

Back then, cornered by the flames in my bedroom, I didn't think I would live to see the sunrise. The fire had reached some clothes I left tossed on the floor. The bottom of the doorway was spiked with flames rising halfway up. Smoke was filling my room and I was starting to choke. The smoke alarms screamed.

I was aware enough to know I was running out of time. If I didn't get myself under control, I really was going to die. I felt myself detaching, separating from all the noise, the heat, the smoke. I had to act. I looked around the room. Assuming I lived through this, was there anything I wanted to save?

I grabbed my sketch book and tucked it under my arm. Finally having done something useful calmed me down a bit. I counted one, two, three out loud and leapt through the flame, right as this ripping drum solo thundered through my speakers. If only I could have filmed it, it would have been the best action movie sequence ever.

At least the first part would have. As I soared through and over the flames, I hit the hallway floor and almost went over the railing. My ankle twisted painfully, and I fell to my knees with a crunch.

I limped to the nearest phone and dialed for help.

"Fire! Fire! My house is on fucking fire!"

Then I hung up. Smoke was pouring out of my room.

"Shit. Did I just call the cops?" I asked myself.

I staggered outside and stood there, watching orange and yellow flicker inside, the music still pounding away.

"Are you okay?" one of the neighbors yelled as he pulled up in his car. "Oh, my God, is there anyone else in the house?"

"I'm fucking alive!" I screamed.

The moon and stars seemed brighter, more beautiful than I'd ever seen them. "Whoa, cool," I mumbled.

A fire truck rounded the corner, screaming down the street. The flashing lights were made much more exciting thanks to my altered state. One firefighter dude pulled me off the lawn and sat me on the truck's bumper. Time was zooming in and out. Suddenly, a cop was talking to me.

"Do you live here?"

"Yeah."

"Is there anyone else inside?"

"No."

"Are you all right? Are you hurt?"

"No."

"You reek of pot, do you know that?"

"Um, yeah."

"I'm going to ask you to turn around so I can cuff you."

"Okay." I did as I was told. He snapped the cuffs on, wrapped me in a blanket and pushed me into the back of a cruiser. I watched as the fire crew smashed a hose through the front door while blasting it from the outside with a steady stream.

"I really fucked up," I said, leaning my head against the window.

* * *

I woke up to the sound of my Dad yelling at the cop.

"What the hell is he doing in the back of your squad car?"

"Sir, he stinks of marijuana. I could bring him in for that."

"He was just in a fire, of course he's going to smell like smoke."

"Mister Abbott, any one of these men could have been injured or died because of your son's recklessness."

"Recklessness? This was an accident. He didn't do anything on purpose."

"Sir, please-"

"Has he been charged with anything?"

"The investigators will determine if it's arson."

"Arson? Bullshit. More like job security for your investigators. He lives here. Why would he burn the place down?"

"Sir, we're out here saving your property, risking our lives for your benefit. If you continue to verbally assault me, I might let your boy go and haul your ass in instead."

"Go ahead. I'd love it. I'd love to stand before a judge and have you call my honest questions a verbal assault."

Dad was freaking me out. If there was ever a time he would have been justified putting his foot up my ass, this was it, but if he was pissed at the cop, maybe I could deflect some of his anger. I coughed loudly, pretending I was sick.

Dad looked at me, then back to the cop. "Has he been examined? Is he injured?"

"Sir, it's clear your son was smoking pot."

"I don't fucking care about that! Has he been checked for injuries, for smoke inhalation? Anything?"

"No, sir. He's fine."

"According to you? Are you a cop or a doctor?"

"Sir, I refuse to debate this with you."

"Can I see my boy, then?"

The cop unlocked the back door. "Here you go, son," he said, as he released the handcuffs. "I hope you learned your lesson. You sure won't hear it from anyone else."

I hugged Dad tightly, pretending I was terrified. I was definitely sorry. I felt like a jackass.

"Are you all right?" he asked.

"A little shaky, but I'm okay."

"Good. What happened?"

The officer was standing close, listening.

When I whispered, "I was smoking," the cop snickered and spat on the ground. Dad spun around. I thought they were going to rumble right there. That would have been ugly. The cop was monster-huge and Dad just a skinny college prof.

Fortunately, the fire chief showed up.

"You the owner?" he asked Dad.

"Yes."

"You're lucky. The house structure seems pretty much undamaged. We taped off the area. I'd be careful, though. Call your insurance and get that room checked first thing."

The flashing lights winked out as the vehicles drove off one by one. It was around two in the morning by the time the whole mess was over.

Inside, the house smelled like bleach. There were muddy footprints and streaks of ash all over the walls near my room.

We both stared for a while in silence until I said, "Dad, I'm so sorry."

He didn't say anything. He plopped in front of the television and turned on those fucking debate shows like tonight was any other night. I sat on the couch with him, looking up at the black scar that had been my room.

Dad always believed in education, not punishment. He believed it to a fault. The best thing he could have done was beat the crap out of me, but no. He was always the teacher. During a commercial, he muted the TV and spoke, still watching the screen.

"Look, Pete, you're a smart kid, but apparently I can't leave you alone. How about you start coming to my night class? At the best, you'll get a free college education. At the least, you won't burn the house down."

The idea sounded horrible. Why would I want to sit in a classroom at night after I sat in a classroom all day at high school? But I didn't think I had the right to make any complaints. Maybe there was a method to his parenting. He made me feel so guilty, I accepted without resistance.

"Fair trade, Dad."

"Bullshit," he said, turning the TV sound up. "You got the better end of this one."

The debate show came back on, and we were back to silence.

While we were sitting there not talking, I realized something. Dad never used to curse. He only started after Mom left. I don't think it was something she was against. I think it was a standard he held. He felt scholars should be articulate, not crude.

I realize now that was an early sign that he was falling apart.

JAMIL

MOROCCO

2001

Jamil woke up as a sunbeam brushed his face. His gaze drifted over the sports posters on his side of the tiny plaster-walled bedroom. He permitted himself a glance at his father's empty bed before quickly looking away, flipping over to face his calendar.

Ten more days.

Ten more days until his father returned from construction work in Qatar. Ten more days until they sat with his uncle, watching the European football matches, smoking and sipping tea. Soon Jamil would no longer be the only man in the house. He squeezed his eyes shut and imagined those days gone in an instant. When he opened his eyes, only seconds had passed, but he was still smiling.

He crossed yesterday off and re-counted the squares until September twenty-second.

Ten more days.

He rolled out of bed.

* * *

"Not so fast!" his mother scolded as he bolted through their combination kitchen-dining room. He squirmed while she held his face in her hands and she kissed him on both cheeks and the forehead.

"Look at you," she said. "Growing up so quickly. Your father will be proud. He might not even recognize you."

"Mother, please." Jamil broke free and snatched up his football. He balanced it between his shin and the top of his foot.

"Not in the house! I don't see a goal around here."

He kicked the ball up into his hands.

"Be on time for dinner," she commanded.

"I will."

"You had better. I am keeping track of all the things you do. When your father returns he'll receive a full report. If you are late, you will make him mad as well," she said, half-smiling. Jamil knew it wasn't a sincere threat, but it wasn't totally false, either.

"I will be on time, I promise. But if you don't let me go and I'm late for work, Uncle will be the angry one."

His two sisters screamed from their room, fighting over something. His mother turned to scold them. Jamil raced out the front door, bouncing the ball on his knee while he hopped down the three concrete steps to the roughly paved road.

"Salaam!" he said as he made his escape.

He paused to admire the day. The sky was free of clouds, a uniform bold blue. The morning sun had not yet unleashed its full fury, so while the air was hot and dry it was not oppressive. He jogged down the street, past the row homes all made of tan and white brick.

He dropped his ball to the ground, imagining defenders closing in. He slid right, spun left, reared back for a shot and pantomimed booting it home. He raised his arms over his head.

Familiar faces watched his pretend game. The elderly man who always sat on his stoop lifted his arm in a tired wave. Jamil nodded, keeping his eye on the ball.

"Salaam!" Jamil called out.

"Salaam," the old man replied slowly.

Jamil dribbled past the young boy with the growth on his face who was always staring out his window while his mother sat nearby, frowning.

"Go, Jamil!" the boy cheered, his voice gurgling. "Go! Shoot! Goal!"

Jamil waved. The boy's mother unsuccessfully held back a small smile.

Just past the boy was the dog. The creature never failed to startle Jamil, even though he expected it. The dog leapt, barely held by a chain around the neck, yelping hoarsely as the tether caught. Jamil winced and flipped the ball from his toes to his hands. He walked quickly, ball tucked under his arm.

"Don't worry. He's friendly," a man said from the house.

He doesn't look friendly, Jamil thought. What stupid animal would be enraged simply by someone passing by?

He casually crossed the street, forcing the dog to continue choking himself, as he stood on his hind legs, spittle flying from his teeth.

Jamil neared the several intersecting streets that made up the business center and outdoor market. The area was usually packed, but there were few people around today. Maybe he wasn't running late. The thought put a spring in his step.

His good mood was short-lived. More than a full day's work awaited him. He paused at the edge of the crammed parking lot under a sign that read "Automobile Repair" in Arabic, French, and English. He looked over the cars parked bumper-to-bumper in tight interlocking patterns that would require moving several to free the deepest ones. He sighed and entered the garage.

The shop was quiet. His uncle was sitting in his small corner office, resting his forehead on his fists, staring down at his desk. The only other time Jamil had ever seen his uncle in his office and not waist-deep in car parts was the first time he had come to work and they discussed the terms of Jamil's employment.

"Jamil," his uncle had said, closing the door to muffle the sounds of the garage, "Your father and I have agreed on your obligations, but the conditions must remain secret. Your grandfather put us to work from the moment we could walk, but we have devised a gentler plan for you. Be here and ready to work on time every day, but if the load is light, you will be free to play football. Your mother must never know. If she finds out, I will suffer, your father will suffer worse, and you will suffer more, understand?"

The deal had worked for years. With plenty to do today there was no hope of going free, but then why wasn't his uncle busy? Usually the television was on, blaring the news and competing with the roar of engines. Today the TV was off, the garage silent.

"Uncle," Jamil asked quietly, "are you all right?"

His uncle looked up as if he had been startled awake.

"Jamil! I'm sorry. Yes. Yes. I'm all right. I'm just, I'm not feeling well."

Jamil set his ball down.

"Where would you like me to start? Looks like we have plenty to do."

His uncle turned away as a concerned look flashed across his wrinkled face.

"Ah, Jamil. There will always be work, but your youth will one day be gone."

"Why isn't the television on?"

"Huh? Oh. It's all right. The, ah, the satellite dish. A wire came loose. I'll fix it in time for your next football match."

His uncle rubbed his hand across his bald head. Jamil suspected he was lying, but why would he lie about the television?

"Go play while you're still young, nephew. I will handle the work. Just don't tell your mother. She would be so angry with me."

Jamil could not believe his luck, but he kept his face impassive.

"If you insist."

"Look at you," his uncle said, his eyes welling up. "Growing so fast. I love you, Jamil, as if you were my own son."

"I, ah, I love you too," Jamil said nervously. His uncle strode around the desk and embraced Jamil, hugging him tightly, squeezing the breath from him.

"You're a good boy," his uncle said. "Always make sure the people you love know you love them. This morning, did you tell your mother you love her?"

"I, uh... no."

"Then you tell her tonight."

"I will," Jamil stopped hugging, but his uncle squeezed harder. "Uncle?"

His uncle released him and turned away, smiling sadly before plopping down into his chair. "While you're out, pick up a present for your mother. Surprise her with something unusual while your father is away. Promise you will do that for me."

"I promise."

"Good," his uncle looked out the window, "Then you can go. Get out and enjoy this beautiful day. The world can be a cruel place. Enjoy life when you can."

"I will, uncle. Thank you."

As he left the garage, Jamil glanced back. His uncle was rubbing his eyes with his thumb and index finger. Was he brushing away tears? Did he have a headache? Jamil couldn't tell, and he didn't dare stay to find out and risk his uncle changing his mind.

* * *

Jamil stopped running when he reached the empty lot, an impromptu field between buildings where the neighborhood boys met to play pickup football. Usually there were enough players to fill out two full teams of eleven. Today the field was nearly empty. Three boys were kicking a ball around aimlessly.

"Salaam," Jamil said as he approached. "Where is everyone?"

The one nearest to him answered. Jamil knew his face, but not his name. "Their parents told them to stay home because of what's happened."

"What do you mean?"

"In America. Aren't you the one always watching the English football matches on your uncle's television? You should know."

"Know what?"

"You're not a very good liar."

"I don't understand."

"Stop it. You should not make jokes about these things. Mohammed, peace be upon him, would not approve. Let's just play."

Jamil dropped the questioning and began his stretches.

The matches of two versus two were boring. It was obvious who was going to receive a pass. Eventually the game deteriorated into tackling the ball from whoever had it. They played until the sun was high and the shadows of the nearby buildings gone. They leaned against a wall, catching their breath and congratulating each other on a game well-played.

Jamil kicked the ball against the wall, his back to the lot. The other boys chatted about upcoming matches in the Italian league.

They stopped talking abruptly.

The boy Jamil recognized whispered.

"Have you noticed that car has been there a while, those two men watching us?"

Jamil turned. Across the empty space, blocking one of the alleys that led from the lot, a car was parked, its engine running. Two men sat inside.

"It's been there the whole time?"

"Sure. You didn't notice?"

"So?"

"So, maybe they're perverts. I hear some men will pay a lot for young boys with pretty faces. Like yours!"

The others laughed as they shoved back and forth.

"Shut up," Jamil said.

The car was a shining black, its gold and silver highlights sparkling in the sun. Jamil recognized it as a German model. Expensive vehicles like it occasionally came through his uncle's shop. His uncle would whistle as he lifted the hood.

The men were staring at them. Jamil felt himself blush, but he didn't know why.

"Are they police?" he said.

"Who knows? I'm leaving."

"Scared?"

"Very funny."

Jamil glanced back at the car and resumed kicking his ball against the wall. He turned his back to them as a sign of contempt.

He didn't notice when the other two boys left, leaving him alone. Why would they leave? It was a beautiful day to be outside. His luck had taken several strange turns today. His uncle had let him go without work yet there was no one to play football with.

He picked up the ball and headed back toward his uncle's, glad the strange car was not blocking his way. The instant he reached the edge of the lot, the car's engine murmured.

* * *

Jamil kicked the ball as he walked. The car slid alongside of him, the passenger watching through the window. Jamil ignored him.

"You're pretty good," the passenger said.

"Thanks."

"What's your name?"

Jamil kept up his moves.

"You're good. Really good," the man said.

Jamil flicked the ball up into his hands and stopped walking. The car stopped with him. He turned and faced the passenger.

"What do you want?"

"Salaam, my friend, my name is Ahmed, and this," he waved toward the driver, "is my partner, Mohammed."

"So?"

"We're scouts for a pro team and we like your skill," Ahmed said.

Jamil hesitated. "Really? Which team?"

"The East Moroccan Lions."

Jamil laughed. "I've never heard of them."

Ahmed smiled. Jamil noticed his teeth were strikingly perfect, straight and dazzling white like an actor from a toothpaste commercial.

"So, they're minor league," Ahmed said. "But they get paid for playing, and they are looking for new talent. I want to offer you the opportunity to try out. Beats working for someone else, yes?"

Jamil bounced the ball on his knee and walked away. The car kept pace.

"You're almost a man," Ahmed continued. "You'll be working soon. Most boys your age are working now. It's either construction or the office. If you make the team, you have a shot at the pros. A dream has to start somewhere."

"How do I know you're for real?"

Ahmed laughed. "We're sports scouts, not police. We don't carry badges."

Jamil tossed the ball from one hand to another, walking slower.

Ahmed kept talking. "Mohammed here says don't bother, there is no one in this slum good enough, but I said, wait, watch the tall one. I counted you scored five goals."

"Six."

"Six? Mo, did you hear that?"

Mohammed was a large man who seemed to be in a bad mood. He scowled, concentrating on driving.

"Mo is a little upset," Ahmed said. "I won our bet thanks to you."

"I'm glad. Now what do you want?"

"Come meet the coach of the team, show him your moves."

"My mother made me promise to be home."

Mohammed slapped the steering wheel.

"You see?" he bellowed. "He's tall, but not a man. His mother tells him what to do."

Ahmed frowned. He spoke as if talking to the driver, but he looked Jamil in the eye, smiling his bright smile.

"It seems you're right, Mo. We shouldn't have bothered with this little boy."

He slid back into the car.

"Wait," Jamil said, stopping. The car stopped with him.

He studied the men. Would perverts drive such a lavish vehicle? Would they approach him in daylight? Be so clean and kind? Even if they tried something, there were only two of them. He could scream, he could fight. He could leap from the moving car if he had to.

If he turned away, how could he ever expect to go pro? How else was it supposed to happen? A knock at the door? Would they discover his football skills while he was replacing spark plugs in his uncle's shop?

"So," Jamil asked, "you just drive around looking for people playing?"

"Are you saying your neighborhood can't produce good players?"

"He doesn't have the confidence," Mohammed said. The car started rolling again.

"No! Wait!" Jamil reached his hand out, his heart leaping. "It's just, I didn't know this was how it was done."

"Well, what did you expect?"

"An open tryout, I guess."

"Too much trouble," Ahmed said. "Better to let us bring the prime talent to camp and let the coach cut those who don't do well."

"I see."

"We're very selective," Ahmed continued. "We get paid for each one we bring in." He smiled even more brightly after saying that. Even Mohammed grinned a little.

"All right," Jamil said, "I'll go. But I can't stay long."

"Fantastic!"

Ahmed leapt out of the car before it had fully stopped. He opened the back door for Jamil like a chauffeur.

"We won't be long at all."

Jamil hesitated before sliding into the back seat. Ahmed sat in the passenger seat and turned to talk to him. Mohammed stepped on the gas and the car jumped.

"So, who is your favorite pro team?" Ahmed asked.

"I don't have one, but I watch most of the English matches on the satellite dish."

"So, you speak English?"

Jamil replied in English. "I learned it from the television. But I prefer Arabic."

Ahmed spoke English as well, "English speakers do well with the reporters, should your career go that far."

"It will."

Ahmed smiled. "I like this kid, Mo."

Mohammed grunted, driving on.

Jamil tossed the ball from hand to hand as the car merged onto the main highway through the city. He and Ahmed talked about sports while Mohammed drove in silence, occasionally glancing in the rearview mirror. Jamil saw anger or hatred in the man's eyes. He glared back at him, defiant. It must be tough to be a scout, to see young men go on to earn wealth and fame far beyond the ones who discovered him. Or simply drove him around.

"Where are we going?" Jamil asked, watching the skyscrapers fly by. "We just passed downtown."

"We're here," Ahmed said as they turned off into an industrial section, the streets lined with identical nondescript warehouses. Several had windows broken, their metal doors rusted.

They exited the car in an empty and cracked parking lot.

Jamil looked around. "It looks abandoned."

"The city rents these dumps cheap," Ahmed explained. "We move around a lot, so there is no reason for the Lions to lease expensive office space, right?"

"I guess."

Mohammed strode around the front of the car and Jamil was struck by the size of the quiet man. He regretted having glared back at him during the ride.

Ahmed opened the creaking metal door and led them down a hall, Mohammed in the rear. They passed several unfurnished rooms, empty except for buckets, ladders and other tools left behind by a construction crew.

Ahmed continued to a closed door at the end of the hall and touched the doorknob. Jamil stopped. He could hear Mohammed behind him, breathing noisily.

"Let's do something funny," Ahmed said, grinning. "When I open the door, show off your moves for the coach. Make an impression."

Jamil's palms were sweaty. He bounced the ball to his knee before letting it roll down his leg to his foot. He flipped the ball up to his forehead, bouncing it one-two-three.

"Brilliant!" Ahmed cheered quietly. "Keep it up!" He opened the door.

Still bouncing the ball on his head, eyes to the ceiling, Jamil entered the room, took a step, stumbled and lost control. The ball hit the floor. He cursed.

He had expected to see an older man behind a desk. Instead there was only a bench, a bucket and four blank concrete walls. A single light bulb hung from the ceiling.

Someone shoved him from behind. Jamil skidded across the floor, colliding with the bucket. A foul smell filled the air as the liquid inside splashed about.

"Hey!"

He pushed himself up and raced for the door as Ahmed and Mohammed slammed it closed.

A lock clicked.

Jamil kicked the door, hurled himself against it, pounded it with his fists. The metal was cold and unyielding.

"Hey!" he screamed. "Let me out! What are you doing?"

He could hear them whispering, their footsteps fading down the hall.

Jamil pounded his head with his fist.

"I knew it! You bastards! Come back!"

He picked up the wooden bench and used it to ram the door. It was futile, the wood was too soft and too heavy for him to get up enough speed. He kicked the door with all his strength. The sound of the impact thundered in the tiny room, but the door did not show any sign of weakening.

"Let me out!" he screamed until his voice broke.

Panting, he sat down in a corner and studied the room. There was a small hole in the brick of the ceiling, small enough to poke a finger through. Light came through it, disappeared, then reappeared again.

"I see you looking at me!" Jamil yelled. "Let me go!"

He swung the bench against the door. Chunks of rotted wood scattered across the room. He selected the sharpest one and used the metal bucket's edge as a crude whittling tool, improvising a dagger. A foul soup sloshed around in the bucket, smelling of urine and feces.

Someone had been here before.

He looked up to the peephole in the ceiling, waiting for it to go dark again. When it did, he grabbed the bucket and hurled its contents upward. Someone above him yelped.

"Let me out!" he wailed.

He paced the room, forcing his breath to come evenly.

He tore a strip off his shirt and wrapped it around one end of his wooden dagger, making a handle. Clutching the weapon, he sat in a corner and pulled his legs up so he could rest his head on his knees. The sewage he had thrown at the ceiling dripped down slower and slower.

He had to conserve his energy. When they came back, he would need it all. Despite the fear and fury burning his skin from the inside while the cold cement floor making his teeth chatter, he closed his eyes and willed himself to fall asleep, whimpering before nodding off.

* * *

Jamil woke several times, annoyed by the unrelenting light of the single bulb in the ceiling. He considered smashing it but did not. Endless darkness would be much worse.

After several false starts he awoke completely. There were no windows, but the room was warmer. He was greeting a new dawn from inside this cell. He shoved the door, gave it a solid kick and screamed for help. The effort produced no result other than noise.

He pressed his ear to each wall. He thought he heard someone crying, or maybe it was the wind. He slipped his dagger into his belt. Keeping his distance from the drying puddle of urine in the center of the room, he kicked his ball against the wall and thought about his situation.

His captors had to be perverts or gangsters. They intended to sell him as a sex slave or ransom him back to his family. Why else would they take him?

He practiced dropping his hand to the wooden blade and brandishing it quickly. When they returned he would be ready.

* * *

His captors did not return. Kicking the ball entertained him only for so long. He paced, practiced stabbing with his blade, and took a nap. No one came.

"Hey! I'm hungry," Jamil said. "Can you hear me?" He yelled up to the peeking hole in the ceiling. "Hello? Can I get some water?"

He sat down heavily and without warning, burst into tears.

"Mother," he whimpered, "I just want to go home."

He heard a single thump.

He listened. The thump repeated frantically, then stopped again. Jamil punched the wall with his palms until his hands ached. The other thumping intensified. It seemed like a response.

"If you can hear me, knock three times, then stop!" he yelled, but the other sound continued, slower and softer, finally stopping.

He fell to the floor, hanging his head.

Blood pumped stiffly inside his temples, intensifying a headache brought on by thirst. His stomach pulled back, and tightened as if it were shriveling. He closed his eyes.

* * *

When he awoke, he was curled on the floor, cradling his makeshift dagger.

He urinated and defecated in the bucket, tearing loose his shirt and using it to wipe himself. The stench was strong even when he pushed the bucket against the wall and crawled into the opposite corner.

"Hello!" he yelled. "Hello! Can you hear me?"

Jamil gathered his breath and yelled again. His hot breath scratched his dry throat.

"Hey, assholes! I'm thirsty. Whatever you have planned for me, I'm going to die if you don't bring me water!"

No response.

"What do you want?" he screamed, his voice breaking into a hiss. "What do you want?"

Eventually he sat down and gave in to crying again. He wiped the tears off his face and sucked the water from his fingertips.

* * *

He woke up, groaning.

"Water..."

His headache had intensified and was squeezing his skull from all sides, making him squint. He hurled his dagger across the room.

His legs shook as he stood up to stretch. He glanced into the pail that served as his toilet. The lumpy liquid was disgusting, but it was drinkable.

He lifted the pail to his face and tilted it back, the brown sludge creeping toward his cracked lips. He slammed the bucket down, retching.

He fell backward and lay flat. The ceiling spun.

"I'm going to die," he said aloud. His words were barely intelligible.

If they wanted to kill him, why not shoot him? But what if they had been killed by other gangsters and he was forgotten here?

He thought of his mother, nibbling at her fingernails as she watched the door, sitting by the phone. His sisters would be hugging her legs, crying. His uncle smacking himself in the forehead, as tears poured down his face.

"Will you ever forgive me?" he would cry to Jamil's mother. His father would come home to a family without a son.

He still had no idea why. For some reason he didn't understand, not knowing made his headache worse.

* * *

Sleep provided his only relief from thirst and hunger. The pain in his head had changed from a constant pulsing to a squeeze, a crushing. His energy was so diminished all he could do was pace the room a few times, pound the door weakly, try to scream and then sit down again to sleep. Were the days passing quicker or was he sleeping more?

He looked to the waste bucket. One more nap, he told himself. One more and then I'll drink from it.

He forgot his pledge when the voices woke him.

Jamil staggered toward the door, the muscles in his legs too dried out to seize painfully. He pounded the door as hard as he could, barely making a sound. His tongue was swollen inside his mouth, each breath a hiss.

They were speaking English, but with an unusual accent. Not British. American, he guessed.

"...holding cells..."

"…improvised..."

"…a thousand for each..."

"...you'll get your money..."

"...around five of them..."

"...some are in better condition than others..."

"...deprivation … had been here sooner..."

"...doesn't matter … these guys are…"

Something metal rapped on the door, the sound rattled in Jamil's head.

"Jamil?" someone called.

He sat down, leaning against the door, patting his sides frantically. He finally noticed his dagger was on the floor across the cell. He started crawling for it.

"Jamil?"

"Water," he gasped. He felt he could love anyone who brought him a drink, even the men who did this to him. He might even forgive them, he suspected, if they would just rub melting ice on his lips.

"If this is another dead one," an American voice said, "I'm cutting the price. What kind of operation are you running here?"

A voice different from the first yelled to him.

"Jamil, do you understand English?"

"Yes," he gasped in English, adding, "Water. Please." He was still crawling for the dagger. It seemed so far away.

The new voice barked at him.

"We are coming in. Lie down away from the door, face down, your hands and legs spread. Any sudden movements and we will shoot you dead. Understand?"

"Please. Water."

"Just do what I say."

"I didn't do anything," he said, stuttering. His dried tongue flopped about clumsily, barely able to form words. The dagger was still so far.

The voice bellowed, "Do you understand my instructions?"

"Yes."

"Your life will not last more than the next few minutes if you do not do exactly as I have told you."

Jamil closed his eyes. "So tired," he said.

"Jamil?"

He nodded off.

"Jamil!"

"Yes?"

"Are you on the floor, face-down, arms and legs apart?"

"Almost," Jamil said, he forcing the air up his ragged throat. He collapsed from his crawl to his side then rolled, face down.

"We are coming in."

The door flung open, striking the wall with a loud bang. Jamil looked up. A spotlight flared, blinding him. Gun barrels and the shadows of ski masks moved behind the light.

"Water. Please. Water," he groaned.

"Shit. This guy's almost dead," one of the shadows said in English.

A voice with an Arabic accent replied.

"Why waste money buying them food?"

"Because they're no good dead. Now shut up."

Rough hands grabbed Jamil's wrists and twisted them painfully behind his back. A wire bound them. He stared at his football in the corner of the room, the black pentagon panels reflecting the room's single bulb.

"Stand," someone ordered, lifting him by his wrists, wrenching his shoulders. He guessed there were at least three men around him.

"Please," he asked, as they pushed him out the door. "Water."

"Soon."

"My mother," he gasped. "She'll be worried."

Someone behind him chuckled. He walked on, guided by a strong grip above his elbow. The spotlight afterimage finally dissolved, revealing a figure wearing a knit mask walking before him.

"Are you going to kill me?" he whispered.

"You keep talking, we might."

"Water. Please. I haven't had a drink in days."

The man guiding him shook him violently and yelled in his ear.

"Stop talking!"

Jamil prayed in his mind, begging forgiveness from his parents for all his petty infractions. He pleaded to Allah that when these men killed him that it happened quickly.

They passed several empty rooms, all similar to the one he had occupied, all smelling of urine and waste. Only one room still contained its prisoner.

He was hanging by a belt looped through the ceiling light bulb fixture. His neck was stretched, head bent at a sharp angle, face purple, lips open and slack. In his parched stupor, Jamil was less horrified than amazed. For a man so short to have managed the suicide, he must have been extremely determined.

"Damn it. I don't care if we're wearing masks. Put a hood on this guy," someone growled in English.

The sack came down over his head from behind. His vision blacked out but the sight of the man's slowly twisting body remained.

They walked on. Someone was yelling. The sound grew louder, peaked and faded as they went past. This happened several times. Some cursed, some begged. All claimed they were innocent.

"What kind of shithole is this?" the man guiding Jamil asked angrily. "One guy hung, two more dead from dehydration. This fool looks like a skeleton. What the hell?"

"Every harvest loses a few crops."

"The dead guys could have been high value."

"They're all the same to me. One thousand dollars, American."

"Only the living ones, asshole."

They walked on in silence.

"Should we really be discussing this in front of the prisoner?"

"Please. Water," Jamil said in English.

"Hell."

Someone shoved the tip of a plastic bottle in his mouth and poured. Jamil sucked down the water, biting down on the grooves for the plastic lid, so when the bottle was pulled, he was able to drink for an instant more. When the bottle was forcibly yanked out, it banged against his teeth painfully.

The pain was worth it. He never knew water could have a taste, never dreamed it could be so delicious.

"There's been a mistake," he gasped. "I have done nothing wrong. I'm not a criminal. I'm not a terrorist. I've hurt no one."

"Shut up. Watch your step."

They descended a ramp as a cool breeze blew over them. They were outside. Jamil breathed in as deeply as he could, purging the stale air of his cell from his lungs. Even the wind had a taste, a glorious rejuvenating flavor.

A hand pressed on the top of his skull.

"Keep your head down."

He could hear the wheeze of a van engine as he was guided to a bench in the darkness. When he sat down, he felt the thighs of other prisoners press against his.

"Please," he said. "Where are we going?"

"That's it. Gag him," one of the men said. A rag was passed through Jamil's mouth and tied tightly behind his head, pinching his cheeks.

"I warned you not to talk, buddy."

Suddenly he was knocked forward on his face. He yelled against the gag. The captors were shouting and cursing in a mix of Arabic and English.

"We've got a runner!"

"Watch the others!"

Jamil scraped his head on the metal floor of the van, trying to pull loose his hood. Someone fell on him, flopping about, crushing the breath from his chest.

"Tackle him!"

"He's getting-"

The single crack of a gun split the air. Suddenly everyone was quiet. The bodies in the darkness ceased moving. Jamil struggled, trying to draw a breath.

"We could have grabbed him. You didn't have to shoot."

"Shut up and get everyone back in place."

The weight was lifted off Jamil, and air rushed into his lungs. He was slammed onto the bench again, his back pushed against the frame of the vehicle. The van's doors closed with the sound of scraping metal.

Soon the van was bouncing on its way, jostling him against those seated on either side of him.

He listened carefully. Someone in the driver's cab was talking endlessly, giving directions in English and complaining in Arabic. The noise of the engine and tires churning gravel obscured the words.

Jamil flicked his tongue across his lips where some beads of water remained. Each drop released a spark of joy on his tongue, flaring and then burning out in his growing despair.

It was the only pleasure he had experienced in...

How long? A few days? A week? More?

He had no idea.

* * *

Jamil woke up as the van slammed to a stop. The driver cut the engine, its sound replaced by a persistent roar from outside, like a steady, strong wind. The air was unnaturally warm and smelled of petrol. His heart stuttered. Were they at an airport?

He was yanked to his feet and guided through the dark by pulls and shoves.

He thought of the daily jolt of joy when his uncle freed him from the garage at sunset, telling him to watch after his mother and sisters while his father was gone. Jamil would arrive home to the scent of his mother's cooking. The television his uncle had fitted with the satellite dish would be chattering away with soap operas from Spain, his sisters sighing in front of the screen.

His mother would clap her hands and her children would rush to the table. His sisters would gossip about their stories while Jamil and his mother would talk about the work at his uncle's.

What were they doing now? He swallowed hard, imagining his mother calling his uncle, both of them frantically searching for him. Were the police looking for him? Was his father home yet?

That life was gone, replaced by darkness and the boom of a plane's engines.

He resisted moving toward the whooshing sound, but strong arms pushed him up a ramp until the roar muffled. He was inside the plane.

He tripped against stubs in the floor before being pushed face down to lie on a rough blanket over what he guessed was the metal belly of the plane. His gag was removed.

"Where are we?" he yelled out in Arabic.

"A plane," someone yelled back.

"Where are we going?"

"I'm removing the gag in case you vomit."

"Why would I vomit?"

"Have you been on a plane before?"

"No."

"You may get motion sickness."

"But I won't vomit. I haven't eaten in days. I've barely drank anything."

"Keep talking and the gag comes back."

"Where are you taking me?"

"I really shouldn't be talking to you unless you're going to confess. Do you want to relieve a weight from your soul about the people you've hurt? You can tell me."

"I am innocent. I do not know what you believe I have done, but I have never hurt anyone, never stolen. I help my uncle-"

"I warned you."

The gag slid between his teeth, pressing down on his tongue, pinching behind his head. Jamil screamed out his frustration, his voice muffled as his hands and feet were bound to the metal stubs in the floor. He smashed his forehead against the floor and only succeeded in twisting his arms and legs painfully.

Jamil remembered his uncle showing him the satellite dish TV in the auto shop the first time. They both marveled at the thousands of channels, randomly choosing numbers to try. They stumbled across a show where an Arab was cursing the European nations, calling for blood.

"So many channels," his uncle said. "You even get this garbage. Maniacs. Why can't people simply leave their fellow man alone, Jamil?"

His uncle stabbed the remote control at the television. The screen changed to show two naked blonde, blue-eyed women giggling and kissing each other, whispering in a language he couldn't identify.

Jamil looked at his uncle, then back to the TV.

"Don't tell your mother," his uncle said. They watched together for another minute in silence.

His uncle shook his head as if to wake himself and switched the channel again. A map of the world scrolled across the screen, the weather in each major city across the continents appeared at the bottom.

Where on that globe were they taking him now?

A pressure built inside Jamil's ears. The plane lurched. The engine roared even louder. He felt himself lifting, his home falling away beneath him.

He cried himself to sleep.

* * *

Jamil awoke into the blackness of his hood, the sound of the plane's engines still booming. He thrashed against the binds on his ankles and wrists until someone lifted his hood just enough to loosen his gag.

"What's wrong?"

"I have to urinate," he yelled back.

"We can't release you."

"I just need to pee!"

"We're not stopping you."

The gag bit into his cheeks and the hood tightened under his chin. Through his teeth he yelled, "I need to go!"

Something heavy struck him in his lower back. The pain pushed the air from his lungs in a whoosh.

When he could breathe again he yelled, "I'm going to fucking kill you all!"

He relaxed his bladder. Warmth spread out along his pant legs and into the blanket beneath him.

"You're all dead," he whimpered. The warm wetness against his thighs rapidly cooled.

* * *

He was awakened by a loosening feeling in his ears. The plane was descending.

His captors wanted him for something. If they had wanted to kill him, he would be dead already. They didn't want him to see. Did they fear him in some way? Could he use that somehow?

The plane bounced as it hit the ground, tires squeaking, the air thundering as the giant machine slowed. Cold air blew over him when the plane was opened, chilling the damp urine beneath him. He could hear the shuffling noises of the other prisoners being released and pushed away.

Finally it was his turn. The binds holding him to the floor were released, but his ankles and wrists were still bound. Gloved hands lifted him from both sides.

"This guy wet himself," someone said in English.

"What's the count so far?"

"Ten pees, three pukes, one shit."

"Hell yeah, I'm still in the pool."

"What did you have?"

"Twelve piss, five pukes, two shits."

"I don't know, bro. We've still got a lot more to go. I think you're too low."

Jamil staggered into a frigid wind as he was shoved down a ramp, following the clanking of the other prisoners' chains. His teeth chattered against the gag. He was led up cramped stairs and attached to a seat. The sound of a chugging engine and the sharp smell of diesel told him he had been loaded onto a bus.

He was protected from the wind, but still shivering from the cold. He wanted desperately to rub his hands over his arms, but his wrists were bound behind him. He closed his eyes tightly behind the hood, imagining the burning sun of home.

* * *

Whatever happened during the night, his transfer from the bus to the cell he found himself in, Jamil couldn't recall. He had dreamed of snapping jaws, a jackal biting at his throat, spittle flying from yellowed fangs.

He didn't remember walking or being locked up. He didn't remember changing into the orange jumpsuit he now wore or lying down on the plastic-framed cot he found himself on. The hood and the gag were gone, but the grooves the gag made in the skin of his cheeks hadn't filled in yet and still itched.

He vaguely recalled when food had been presented to him. Water in a plastic cup vanished with one gulp. He licked clean the paper plate. It still lay in a metal slot embedded in the concrete wall next to the steel door. He woke slightly rejuvenated to the sound of faint voices talking behind the door, the shadows of movement outside its small, square, wire-reinforced window.

The tray in the metal slot clanged shut, then shot open again. The smell of a warm meal filled the room. Jamil dove across the floor, not caring what the gelatinous shapes were as he stuffed them in his mouth. He drank the plastic cup of cool water, savoring it like an expensive wine. He licked the juices from the plate, leaving thick stripes of sauce and oil around its edges. Then he licked those clean as well.

He stood, surprised to find his legs had regained some of their strength, and examined his cell. The room was featureless except for the cot, the door, the tray and a metal one-piece toilet. Folded toilet paper sheets rested on the floor. Nearly every surface was painted the same pale blue. His only view of the world outside was through the window in the door.

Looking out, he saw cells identical to his extending in all directions. The complex seemed to go on forever. On a walkway above the courtyard, a two man team pushed a cart, slamming meals into the metal trays.

Men wearing black uniforms unadorned with any flags or markings or logos marched the hallways, pistols at their hips, shotguns held across their chests. They strode by his door every several minutes.

When one passed, he knocked on the window. The guard did not respond.

The next time, Jamil pounded on the door, yelling. "Hello! Hey!"

The sound of boots clomped away.

After several failed attempts to get the guards' attention, he tried a different approach.

"I'm innocent!" he yelled. "I didn't do anything."

Still no result. No change in the rhythmic pace.

"I did it! I'm ready to talk!" he called out. Still no response.

He tried both approaches in English and Arabic.

No one acknowledged him.

He sat in the corner of his cell, closed his eyes and imagined positive memories. He recalled watching football with his father. Now recall every detail, he told himself. Savor it.

He tried, but found his mind grasping for details he was unsure of. Was his father's hair brown or black? He thought of the smell of his mother's cooking. Was it spicy or sweet? Already the memories were slipping away.

He whimpered and nodded off.

* * *

After another meal and another gulp of water, someone knocked on his cell door. He was given instructions in Arabic that were becoming familiar.

"Back away from the door and lie face down. Stay still or you will be shot."

He did as he was told and let the men charge in, bind him, gag him and pull a hood over his head. Tight grips on his arms pulled him along. He tried to remember running free, but being yanked along had become the only way he could recall moving about.

He was pushed down into a chair and tied to it, his ankles bound to the legs, a bind slipped under his armpits, across his chest and the back of the chair. His wrists were attached to the floor behind him. The top part of his jumpsuit was pulled off, the Velcro fasteners ripping loose. Goosebumps rippled across his exposed skin.

Someone yanked off his hood, and the first thing he saw was an AK-47 assault rifle. The man holding it was wearing a ski mask, covering his head except his eyes and mouth. He avoided Jamil's eyes before backing away to lean against the concrete wall of the pale blue room. Another man leaned on the wall opposite, also holding an assault rifle, also wearing a ski mask.

Two ceiling light bulb fixtures cast the room in harsh shadows.

Jamil heard a door open behind him and someone walk in. He tried to turn and look, but couldn't twist his neck enough against the strap around his chest. He waited, staring at the armed men before him. They gave away no emotion. The gag fell loosely around Jamil's neck as someone standing behind him released the knot.

He noticed the guards tense a second before the person behind him spoke.

"Jamil."

He was surprised by his observation of the guards' body language. The guard on the right had an itch on his elbow, and when he scratched it, his AK-47 bobbed. The man on the left chewed his tongue nervously. Living with so little stimulation, his deprived senses were picking up subtleties. Starving, they clung to crumbs.

"Jamil," the voice behind him repeated.

"Yes?" he answered.

"Your dossier states you speak both Arabic and English. Smart man. Do you have a preference?"

"Arabic, please."

"Look at the wall in front of you," the man said in Arabic, with only the slightest trace of an accent. Perhaps European? Russian?

Jamil heard a click. His shoulders bunched up. He thought he was going to be shot, but then the empty space across the room between the two guards lit up as a white rectangle.

The rectangle changed to a photograph of a man lying on the sidewalk. More accurately, the meat on the sidewalk had once been a man. The body was mangled. Red, orange and pink gore trailed behind the stretched flesh and torn business suit. The man's white underwear was showing, stretched to accommodate his distorted pelvis. The body reminded him of a small animal run over on the highway.

Another click. The image was replaced by a new photo, just as gory. A body rested on grey pavement. Half its skin was the flaky black of fish grilled far too long, nearly to ash, except for a piece of one leg. A shoe with the lower portion of the leg stood up, as if unaware its body had left it. The cars around the corpse were large. Jamil guessed the photo was from America.

A translucent logo in the lower right corner read in English, "From the Real War website."

Another click and another photograph appeared on the wall. A body rested on concrete steps, the head missing. A greasy stump was in its place, the steps dotted with an enormous splatter of red, pink and white. Jamil felt his stomach tighten, his throat burn. He closed his eyes and looked away.

"What is this?" he asked.

The man behind him answered. "These are pictures of the people from New York City who died jumping from the buildings."

"Why did they jump? What buildings?"

No one answered him.

Jamil continued. "Whatever this is, I had nothing to do with it. Please, I don't understand why I am here. Please stop."

He kept his gaze averted, closing his eyes tightly, but that hid nothing. He could still see the deformed corpses in his mind. He could not remember the color of his father's hair, the scent of his mother's cooking, but he would remember these scenes of slaughter. Tears pushed through his clenched eyelids.

"Look up, Jamil."

Jamil kept his eyes closed.

"Jamil," the voice behind him said firmly, "if you do not look voluntarily, we will open your eyes for you and I assure you it will not be pleasant. Now look."

Jamil slowly turned back to face the images, squinting his eyes. The headless body was still there.

"Don't be a child, Jamil. Open your eyes so I can be certain they are open. If I can't tell, I will assume they are not and I will have your eyelids cut off."

Jamil opened his eyes wide, bulged them out of his head, and turned to face the horrible scene. Nothing could make it go away. Vomit burned in his throat and dribbled over the top of his lower teeth, down his chin. He focused his attention on the lower right corner of the photo. The text "From the Real War website" was written in ghost-letters that floated over a car's rear tire.

"Next," the man behind him said, "I will show you pictures of the people from Afghanistan who died from America's bombs."

Another image. A woman's body was ground into the earth, her pregnant belly slashed open, her arm torn loose, lying nearby.

The scenes flashed by in a shower of blood and pieces of bodies arranged in absurd and random ways that made them obviously real. He kept his eyes bulged out, trying to blot out the carnage, focusing only on the persistent translucent text in the bottom right of all the images: "From the Real War website."

"What do you notice, Mister Jamil?"

"They're dead?"

The unseen speaker chuckled. "You're smarter than that. What am I trying to say, showing you these two sets of photographs? One from the United States and one from Afghanistan?"

"That there's no difference?"

"Exactly. Look at all this death. Look at all these people. You killed Americans, now they are striking back, killing your people."

"I've never killed anyone. I don't know that I've ever met any Americans. And I'm not an Afghan! I'm Moroccan."

"You know what I mean, Jamil. I mean Westerners and Muslims killing each other. Europeans and Arabs."

"I don't! I don't! Please! I've never hurt anyone. I bear no one ill will. I love everyone! Please!"

Jamil stopped when he was smacked in the back of the head. Involuntarily, his breathing became a frightened pant.

"Stop!" the voice behind him said. "Do not waste my time. You will communicate information, not emotion. And you will address me as Mikhail."

Someone laid a hand on Jamil's shoulder. He winced, thinking he was going to be struck again. He tried to look over his shoulder, but Mikhail stood out of his peripheral vision.

"We suspect you are a terrorist," Mikhail said.

Jamil's heart thundered. He could barely breathe. He screamed in response, his voice cracking.

"A terrorist? I've never hurt anyone in my life! Who do you mean by we? Are you the police? Some international agency? I've hurt no one. I don't know what happened in America. Can I speak to someone? Anyone at the Moroccan embassy?"

"Now, Jamil, you say you are innocent, but you understand we would need to make sure that's true, yes? After all this carnage, we wouldn't dare take a chance on releasing those responsible. We wish to avoid such a tragic mistake."

"But why would you think I did something? I'm just a boy, I play football. I help my mother and my uncle. My father works-"

"Mister Jamil!" Mikhail shouted, silencing him like a parent quieting an unruly child. "Everyone says those things. The guilty, the innocent, everyone. Everyone insists they are innocent. You have spoken much, but said nothing."

"There's been some mistake. I don't know how you selected me. Can I speak with an advocate? Someone?"

"I'm afraid that is not how it works. A war has begun. Many people want to defend themselves. You are crying for your freedom. I am the one you need to cry to. You say you are not a terrorist. I am the one you need to convince."

"Check it out, then. Speak to whomever you want."

"I doubt you would like that. Your dossier says you were turned in by two men."

"They were criminals. They kidnapped me. What proof did they have? Why take their word over mine? They were paid to capture me."

"Mister Jamil, I only told you these things because I want you to understand, we are very serious about getting the truth from you."

"I'll tell you anything."

"Even a lie?"

"I have nothing to lie about."

"We shall see," Mikhail said. "Have you ever smuggled weapons?"

"No."

The skin between Jamil's shoulder blades burst with painful heat. He yelped and leaned forward. The reason they had removed his shirt was now clear. He squirmed as the heat pressed into him, but the bindings gave no room. No contortion he could manage offered him mercy. The smell of overcooked meat scraped up his nose.

He screamed.

He had hesitated, not wanting to give them the satisfaction, but the pain was unbearable. He screamed until that too caused him pain. It lessened the burning on his back to transfer the agony to his throat, but he couldn't yell forever, and when he stopped to gather breath, the burning on his back returned, the scalding increased.

Jamil noticed one of the armed guards standing before him shift uncomfortably.

"Help me," Jamil groaned, looking to him. The guard's stony gaze did not respond. When the hot brand finally pulled away, Jamil collapsed forward, gasping, held upright by the bind around his chest. He was sweating as if he had run several miles. Something thicker than sweat dripped down the center of his back.

"I assure you," Mikhail said, after Jamil finished gasping. "If you do not speak to me, that is just the beginning. Be careful before you answer anything I ask. I will know if you are lying and I will know if you are telling the truth. Truth will bring you freedom. Lies will bring you pain. Do you understand?"

Jamil felt the blood in his head pounding, a headache coming on. He held his bound arms by his sides tensely, trying not to flex the flesh on his back.

It didn't matter. The burning pressed against his spine again. "I didn't say anything!" he yelled. The brand pulled away.

"Silence will also bring you pain. You must answer me promptly. Any delay leads me to believe you are crafting a lie. Do you understand?"

"Yes! Yes. I do." Sweat dripped down his face, down the tip of his nose.

"Do you understand?" Mikhail bellowed.

"I said yes!" Jamil answered quickly.

"Good. Good. I see you learn the rules quickly. Now I am going to ask you some questions. Do you know anyone who has ever smuggled bombs or bomb-making material? Did you ever drive them anywhere? Were you ever in their presence as they were discussing these things? Did you ever see a gun sold?"

"No. No. No. I don't even-"

The heat pressed into his back again. Jamil wailed and kicked his legs, vainly trying to find some way to escape the pain. The burning metal pulled from his back, but the heat radiated across his body, up his neck to the top of his scalp, down his spine to between his buttocks. His toes twitched inside the soft shoes they had given him.

"Why?" he croaked. "Why are you doing this to me?"

"We need to be certain, Jamil. We need to be sure that you are not lying."

"I'm not lying."

"How can I know, Jamil? How can I be sure?"

"Tell me! Tell me what I need to do to convince you."

"That is your problem. You want to go free? Convince me of your innocence. You must convince me all on your own. That is all for now."

Jamil let his head droop. Warm thick drops rolled down his spine. The straps on his arms and legs were loosened. His hands were still bound behind his back and he hissed through his teeth as his wounded skin flexed. A hood swept over his head and he was led back to his room. They shoved him into his cell and tossed in his orange top.

He pulled the shirt on gingerly. The roughness scraped across his raw back like skinning his hand on the unyielding metal of a car's frame. The coolness of the fabric was soothing, but it stuck to the wound, pulling painfully with each movement. He yanked the shirt off and stared at the jagged brown mark on its back.

He curled up on the floor next to his cot, lying on his side, crying while Mikhail's command rang in his memory.

"You must convince me all on your own."

PETE

USA

2002

I was nervous and humbled to be attending Dad's lectures. Nervous because I was afraid they would be boring. Humbled because I wanted to argue that I didn't need adult supervision, but it was hard to make that case after almost burning the house down.

I sat in the back of the lecture hall, counting seats. There were twenty rows of fifteen and the place was nearly full. Three hundred people were paying to listen to my Dad talk for hours. The fools.

Just before he started, he looked up at me. Without thinking, I waved like a dork. He turned away like he didn't see.

"Good evening, everyone," he said. "Welcome to Practical Politics and Real World Ethics."

After hearing the name of the course, I whipped out my sketchbook.

"Before we begin," he said, "I have to introduce someone. My son." He pointed. The whole class turned and stared, so I waved again, broadcasting my dorkness.

Most of the class turned back to face Dad, but some hot girls kept peeking at me. "He's cute," one whispered. My cheeks started to burn, so I looked down at my sketchbook, pretending I didn't care.

Dad continued. "I just wanted you to know who the new kid was and who you can give candy to if you want an A."

The class chuckled.

"But seriously, this isn't the White House giving out no-bid contracts." The class laughed at that, whatever it meant. "We're here to learn. Bribing my son will get you nowhere. Now, on to today's topic..."

That's when I stopped listening, but I watched for a little longer. I always thought of Dad as a nerd, but here he was different. He was confident, cocky. He even stood up straighter.

My drawings were turning out like shit. I couldn't concentrate because of the new environment. I finally was inspired to draw a bunch of cavemen (cave-students?) sitting around a fire while Dad told a story. Was that what his ancestors were like? I guess technically they would be both of our ancestors. Whatever.

I listened to Dad a little more. He was going on about Senator Wayne Drake Hanson. His arch-enemy. Dad had bitched about that assclown before, when he came on the TV or the radio, but I never knew how much he wanted to kick the dude's ass until I heard him rave in that lecture.

Dad scribbled huge words on the board, talking passionately while fielding questions. I noticed a full hour had gone by and he hadn't slowed down.

Two more hours to go. I kicked back and closed my eyes.

The sound of the folding wooden half-desks slapping against the metal chair supports woke me up. The students were leaving.

"Cool," I thought. "Time to go home."

The auditorium emptied out except for a small cluster of students who stayed, crowded toward the front, asking questions, throwing in comments and just hanging out.

Dad had fans. Freaky.

I wanted to leave real bad, but I couldn't recall seeing him that excited about something without being pissed off in like forever. So I just dealt. After a while I started getting a little jealous. Hey! Back off, people, I wanted to say, he's my father, not yours.

Finally, Dad started walking up the aisle, still taking questions, the students separating before him like he was their guru.

"All right, professor, we'll see you next time," one of them said when they saw me waiting. They talked excitedly among themselves as they left.

Dad and I were alone.

"How did it go?" he asked me.

"All right."

"Next time you should bring your ear phones. Listen to some music. I know this stuff is boring for you."

"I liked being here," I said. I still feel bad about that lie, but there was no backing out after the way his eyes lit up.

"You did?"

"Uh, yeah. I didn't understand all of it, but it was interesting."

He slapped me on the back. "That's my boy. You'll get it eventually. No one knows everything all at once."

He smiled. A genuine, sober smile. I hadn't seen that since Mom left. I felt bad for lying about liking being here, but it wasn't entirely false. It wasn't the boring lecture I enjoyed, it was the fact that he seemed happy.

* * *

My parents, actually just my dad, raised me to be concerned about those less fortunate than us. I've tried. I appreciate Dad teaching me that, guarding against me becoming just another selfish asshole. If only he had stopped there. But being the intense guy he was, he took it too far.

Here's what I mean. Every night he watched TV, finding more proof that the tough talk about war in Iraq was just cover for a money grab. Then he'd rant about what he'd learned to his class. Then he'd go home and watch more TV and the process would repeat.

Dad knew it all. He said Iraq had nothing to do with September 11, that the buzz about the US invading Iraq was just to steal the oil and establish a military base in the Middle East. He explained it was a giveaway to the mercenaries ("I mean, military contractors," he always sarcastically self-corrected.) He said the conflict would create more terrorists. He made a great case, but then he made the same case over and over.

I agreed with him. I didn't want to go to war just to make the president, the vice president, Senator Hanson and all their rich friends richer. The difference between me and Dad was that I didn't spend every waking second talking about it.

I respected what he did. There's a need for watchdogs that track the bad guys, chase them around and point out everything they do wrong until someone listens. Me, at some point I want to stop fighting and party. There's always going to be assholes and if you spend your whole life going after them, you'll end up doing nothing else. I don't have the endurance to bang that drum over and over.

Dad did. He wanted to fight all the time. He could rattle off the names of senators and the way they voted the same way some guys know sports players and their statistics, the same way some dudes know musicians and all the bands they ever played with. Unfortunately, like lots of people that deep into their interest, Dad never noticed that he was boring the crap out of everyone else with his in-depth knowledge.

I was afraid that if I left his lecture he might take offense or realize I had lied about liking being there, but I reached a point where I just couldn't take it. Night after night, he went on about corrupt politicians. Problem was, I got it the first time. The president, the vice president and Senator Wayne Drake Hanson are criminals. Got it. They should be tried for crimes against humanity. Got it. If found guilty they should be executed like any war criminal. Got it. Got it. Got it!

No one in power was listening. Nothing was going to change. Hanson and his gang were getting away with murder, with starting a war and getting rich off it because of their connections with the mercenary corporations. To a man who loved justice and fairness, criminal scumbags like those dudes drove Dad nuts.

Thing was, he in turn drove those of us close to him nuts by repeating himself and exploding into his rants any chance he got. Maybe that's part of why Mom left.

When I started taking her side, I knew I had to step out no matter how bad it might hurt Dad. I waited until he turned away to write on the board, then quietly got up and walked out, the same polite way his students did.

I liked the empty campus vibe. The rooms were locked, blackness hiding desks behind the windowed doors. The stillness was great inspiration. The only drawback was sometimes I thought of serial killers or demons hiding in the dark, waiting to eat my flesh. That fear made for some interesting sketches.

I went in every unlocked door, exploring even the janitor closets. I found some porn in one utility closet and just for fun, I drew on the chicks, giving them hairy mustaches and hairier cocks. Whoever was using those mags as wank fuel was in for a surprise.

I'm no perv, but I even checked out the women's restrooms. I wasn't breathing heavy or anything. I was just going where I had always been told not to go.

Hell, even if it was some kind of perversion, it was a good one to have. That's how I met two of the best friends I would ever have.

* * *

During one of my ladies' room explorations, I heard high-pitched voices and I thought a couple of girls were coming in. I ducked into a stall and locked it. The voices continued, but never got any closer.

After I chilled, I noticed the voices were coming through the air vent. The girls were in the men's room. I wasn't the only one curious to see how the other half lived!

I snuck out and listened outside the door. There was a lot of giggling inside the men's room. Without the distortion of the vent, it sounded like a guy and girl.

Okay, I said I wasn't a pervert, but I still thought it might be funny to catch these two mid-boink. I like to think I'm a prankster, not a freak. So I pushed the door open quietly and walked in, pretending I was going to take a piss.

My nose perked up automatically, twitching in the air like a dog's nose at a barbecue. They were smoking pot. I heard giggling and shushing. A pair of sneakers and wrinkled pants around ankles showed in the gap between the stall divider and the floor. It might have fooled me if the stoners weren't still shushing each other.

I pushed the stall door open gently. The idiots forgot to lock it. The guy was sitting on the toilet in his tightie-whities, pants down, trying to appear like he was taking a dump. The girl was standing on his thighs, arms spread out, balancing against the walls of the stall, a joint in the corner of her mouth. They both looked at me just before she crashed to the floor, cursing. The guy fell off the toilet, trying to catch her. I backed up, dodging the collapsing mess.

The first thing I noticed before the girl hit the floor was that she was pretty hot. She pushed herself up to her knees while the guy thrashed around, pulling up his pants.

"Oh, shit," she said. The guy groaned and rolled over.

He zipped up and stared at me. "Oh, shit," he said.

They were both stoned. No question.

"It's the prof's son."

"Shit."

"Shit. Shit. Shit."

They hugged each other and stared at me like I was pure evil.

"I need this class, Charles," the girl said. "If I fail, my life is fucked."

"What do you want me to do?" he said. "I'm busted too!"

"I told you we shouldn't smoke during class!"

"Shut up. He's right here, duh. And don't say our names in front of him. Tracy!"

I felt a weird sense of power. They were terrified of me and I could do whatever I wanted. I could run back and tell Dad. I could make them give me money. The possibilities were endless.

After several kinky ideas crossed my mind, I just felt bad for them. I guess that's what separates me from the assholes of the world, like the president and Senator Hanson. Power doesn't make me want to take advantage of people, or steal from them. It makes me want to help them. Dad would be proud.

"It's cool," I said.

They stared at me.

"You're not going to tell?" the girl asked, still on her knees. "Oh, thank you," she said, throwing her arms around my ankles and hugging me.

Bolts of electricity ran up my legs right to my cock.

"Christ," the guy said, standing up. "Why don't you blow him?"

The girl jumped to her feet and punched her friend. "Why don't you, sweetness?"

"He is kinda cute," the guy said, winking at me.

"Um, no thanks," I said, smiling. "Try it and I'll definitely tell my father."

They both spit out a ganja cackle. "I knew you were cool," the guy said, shaking my hand. "I'm Charles. Just Charles. Not Chuck or Chas or anything else."

"Only ever call him Charles," the girl warned.

"And in case you were wondering," Charles went on, "yes, I'm gay. And no, I'm not really going to blow you. You'll have to earn that rare privilege."

"Or pay for it," the girl said. Charles punched her shoulder.

"Ow!" she said. "I'm Tracy." We shook hands.

"Pete."

"We know. When your dad introduced you."

"Well?" Charles asked, picking up the joint and dusting it off.

"Well what?" Tracy said.

They both looked at me.

I thought about how the anti-drug commercials and school assemblies described situations like this. Well, not exactly like this. They never began with a girl and a gay guy in the men's room, trying to hide by pretending the guy was taking a crap, then both of them spilling out and begging for mercy.

But the school powers did warn that a time would come when I would face the temptation of pot and I was supposed to "Just say no."

"I won't tell my dad," I said, "if you share that joint with me."

Okay, maybe I gave in to the power a little.

* * *

So I got stoned and they got stoned some more.

That was how I met Tracy and Charles. Our threesome was solidified there. On that night I learned more about them both than I ever learned about anyone.

I learned (several times because he kept saying it even though it was obvious) that Charles was gay. I also learned that he once blew a security guard to get into a concert.

"I swallowed it and all," he said.

"That must have been a good band," I said, laughing.

"I was so wasted I can't remember what concert it was."

We all burst out laughing.

I learned that Tracy's dad was a hard-ass preacher guy. I learned that she cheated on almost every test she could, even Dad's.

"I feel bad, because your dad," she said, pausing to inhale. She continued in that stuttering, raspy voice when you talk and inhale at the same time. "Your dad is a fucking genius."

Charles cracked up. "No shit, man. I bet your dad is like, the ghost of George Washington reborn, man. Dude knows everything about history. If I were you, I would hire a million bodyguards because when the feds come, they're going to unleash all the bananas." Charles rolled his head back against the stall. He was far gone.

Tracy giggled. "The bananas?"

I found it damn funny too. "How about I hire an army of monkeys and when the feds turn up with the bananas, I'll say go get 'em monkeys and they'll eat all the bananas and hand out coconuts and the SWAT team will be like, what the fuck?"

It sounds stupid now, but when you're stoned, it's the sort of thing you find brilliant.

* * *

Meeting up with Charles and Tracy to smoke in the rarely-used ladies room became my routine during Dad's lectures, but there were times when I stayed for the class. Sometimes he'd say something that caught my attention.

"Let's talk about America's biggest asshole," he said, pausing for drama. I knew this had to be about Senator Hanson.

"I'm referring to the senior senator from Oklahoma," Dad said, his voice just spitting poison, "Senator Wayne Drake Hanson. Also known as Hands-on Hanson to suckers who buy into his hard-working image. Some say it's for the way he cuts through red tape. I say it's because he disregards the rule of law. I suspect his female interns use the nickname for altogether different reasons if you caught that blip in the media. Case was settled out of court and Hush-up Hanson wasn't as catchy."

The class chuckled.

I didn't understand the joke, but I was hooked. Dad was a bookworm, but his tone was straight-up thug. If Hanson walked into the class right then, no doubt Dad would have challenged him to a brawl.

And probably won.

"Hands-On Hanson likes to portray himself as a military man," Dad said. "But really he's a businessman. Has anyone ever heard of the Redfire Corporation?"

Only a few hands went up. I almost raised my hand, too. I'd heard Dad mention it but that was all I knew.

"Not a lot, huh? That's how he likes it. He doesn't want Redfire to be a household name, but it's getting there whether he likes it or not. Hanson was once the CEO of the Redfire Corporation, a mercenary company, I mean a military contractor. That means they lobby the U.S. military to pay them for things the military should do itself. Redfire gets paid ten times as much, then claims that private business is more efficient."

He wrote a big number ten on the chalkboard.

"Companies like Redfire claim to provide all kinds of services, but what do you think they do when they're given a task beyond their core competency as hired guns?"

"Hire another contractor?" a student called out.

"Exactly. Then that contractor hires another and on and on until the responsibility and the money are lost down a chain of obscure connections and legal write-offs. Redfire's business is to be mercenaries, which is a word they never use, because it reveals the truth is that a mercenary is a hit man paid to kill whomever the boss fingers. That's what they are, a private army fighting for the highest bidder. In this case, the United States."

"What happens if someone bids higher?" someone asked.

Dad shrugged. "Great question. No one knows. That's the problem. Government oversight is limited thanks to Redfire's lobbyists and concern for trade secrets." He made those annoying finger quotes as he said the words "trade secrets."

Someone else spoke up: "So it's possible a rich person or another government, or player on the global stage could pay them to attack Americans?" The room buzzed as some students discussed the question and others laughed it off.

Dad paused, opening his mouth to speak, then reconsidered. I could tell he was choosing his words carefully. That was a pretty rare event.

"Americans paid to kill other Americans?" he said. "Definitely possible."

The class got really loud over that. And not in a good way. Dad shouted into the noise, but his words drowned in the angry buzz of students yelling at him and each other. I couldn't tell who was mad at who and I barely understood what Dad was talking about. I just kept my eye on him, leaning forward, both hands fists. If anyone rushed Dad, I would hit them from behind.

The yelling kept going. Dad was trying to regain control. He kept shouting, "Please! Let's discuss this! Like adults! Think logically!" Three students made a big show of packing up their books and storming out. Other students yelled at them to get out, and others clapped for them.

Since I was sitting on the aisle, I was near when one of them caught up with the other two. One dude's face was bright pink, like he was going to explode.

"He's crazy!" Pink-Face said. "He hates this country!"

"I'm dropping this fucking class," the second guy said.

"It's liberal bullshit."

They slammed through the door at the back.

The noise slowly dissipated. "Look," Dad said, "we're getting off topic." I tossed the idea of catching up with Tracy and Charles. I had to bodyguard my dad if necessary.

He walked over to a television stand in the corner of the hall and pushed a button on the ancient VCR.

"Let's move on," he said.

* * *

The video was from one of his political yelling shows. There were two guys behind the desk. One was a clean-cut looking dude with his hair gelled and his face shiny and tan. The other was a large man with white wisps of hair combed over his balding head. Text at the bottom of the screen labeled him as Senator Hanson from Oklahoma. He was stabbing his finger at the desk.

"These are evil people. Terrorists! We need to capture or kill them, in whatever nation houses them. If we're not getting valuable information, why keep them?"

The host leaned forward. "Some might say you want to keep them to see if they eventually talk, but that's not due process."

"This fight is about realities, not eventualities," Hanson said. "Any boxer knows that a missed punch is more dangerous than taking a punch. If we spend time on prisoners that provide us no intel, that hurts us more than if we just let them go."

"Some critics argue this can easily be solved if you allow them to defend themselves through legal means, but you yourself advocated the practice of detention without trial, the elimination of habeas corpus."

"All you have to do is look on that website Real War to see what we're up against. Now I know my critics are going to flip that I'm quoting an unofficial source but I don't care. Go on that site and see what our enemies are. They torture, dismember, behead our troops. Then we'll talk about whether you want them to have rights."

Hanson was practically yelling, but the reporter kept his cool. "I have heard of the Real War site. For our viewers that haven't, it's a website that hosts graphic videos of American soldiers and other prisoners, often journalists, tortured or killed in Afghanistan. Senator Hanson, don't you feel that website is exploiting casualties of war?"

"I consider it journalism. Real War is the only website I know that gives the true, unfiltered picture. We have to chase the terrorists."

"But surely, Senator. Iraq? Now? Before we are done in Afghanistan? Some might say the issue of Iraq being rich in oil is-"

* * *

And so on. Blah blah blah.

The video droned on and then it stopped and my Dad took over the droning and it seemed like the class wasn't going to lynch him after all. One thing did stick in my mind from the video. That innocent people could be imprisoned forever. What if they were picked up by accident?

I closed my eyes and tried to imagine it, but I couldn't. How could I possibly envision being taken away from everything I knew? Sure, I could put it in words, but I couldn't see it, and therefore I couldn't draw it. How do you picture lost years?

What would it be like to simply vanish? To be imprisoned for days, months, years, without knowing if there would be an end?

I'd probably kill myself the first day. Or I'd try to live forever, clinging to the hope that someday I could unleash my revenge on them. Even if I died in the process, even if I killed just one of a thousand enemies, it would be worth it.

* * *

A few weeks after the near riot in the classroom, I felt it was safe to leave Dad alone. I was in the ladies room with Charles and Tracy again.

"I almost forgot," I wheezed as I passed the joint along. I fished in my pocket for the slip of paper. "You guys have a pop quiz next class."

That wasn't the first time I had done that for them. Stealing the answers from Dad's office was becoming a habit.

Charles grinned, taking the paper as Tracy sucked on the joint. It was tough not to stare when she did that, her cheeks caving in, her eyes twinkling. I had fallen for her, but I was trying to play it cool. She smiled at me through the smoke and I found that damn sexy. I looked away as she passed the joint to Charles.

"When the quiz is over," he croaked, inhaling, "we should come up and celebrate our good grades."

"Works for me," Tracy said.

"You know your dad is really awesome," Charles said. "I was hanging out with my people the other day-"

"Were your clothes on?" Tracy asked.

"At first." He smiled sarcastically at her. "Now if I might continue, my friends were going off about Senator Hanson."

"What about him?" I asked.

"The usual. What a hypocrite he is. He's pro-war, says being gay is evil. He pretends to be religious, but completely ignores all the love thy neighbor stuff."

"Sounds like my dad," Tracy said. "Pro-war, anti-gay."

"I'm her best friend," Charles said, poking me with his elbow. "And I've never met her father."

"With good reason," she said. "None of my friends have. You wouldn't like him and he wouldn't like you. Your dad," she pointed at me, "would probably kill him. My dad loves Senator Hanson."

"If only he knew his daughter was smoking pot in the girls' room with the prof's son and a fairy," Charles said, laughing.

"Hey, don't I get a copy?" Tracy said, pointing to the quiz answer key I had given to Charles.

"Um, I only made one copy." I felt like a total moron. I should have given the answers directly to her. I started worrying she would think I had a crush on Charles. Talk about disaster.

"Lighten up, sister," he said, handing her the answers. "Take it. You're the one that needs it."

"Not all of us are gifted like you." They smiled at each other in the exaggerated way they did when they were being sarcastic.

"Here," I said, taking the answers back. "I'll copy it by hand."

The marijuana was snaking its way through my veins, tickling my toes from the inside. I rushed to copy the answers down before I lost the ability to concentrate. I opened my sketchbook on my crossed legs.

"What else is in that pad?" Charles asked. "We've been smoking buddies for months now and you're always carrying that notebook, but we've never seen inside. What's in there? Tracy's dad, naked?"

She punched him.

"Well," I hesitated.

Tracy reached out and touched my knee. My skin twitched. "He's shy," she smiled at me. "How cute."

The pot and Tracy's compliment had loosened me up, so I turned my sketchbook around, letting them page through. They pointed out aspects of the drawings to each other, their mouths open, reciting the stoner's mantra.

"Wow, man. Wow. Cool."

"Each one tells a story," Tracy said. She kept sliding over little by little until she was sitting beside me, rubbing my arm, her fingernails scraping lines of fire on my skin. We were leafing through the book when she suddenly slapped down her hand, preventing the page from turning. "Oh, my God," she yelled. "That's it."

"What?"

"That's the tattoo I want." She pointed to a sketch I had done of a dragon with butterfly wings and the face of a woman. I thought the outline was decent, so I had brightened it with colored pencils. It was all right. Not my best work, but okay.

"See?" she said, "I got my appendix out years ago and I still have the scar." She lifted up her shirt, showing her flat tummy and her belly button where a silver stud shone. I was glad I had the pot swirling in my brain, to mellow me out, or I would have started drooling.

"Right there," she said, dragging her finger across a jagged purple line on her side just above her jeans. "When I wear a swimsuit or a half-shirt, everyone sees the scar."

"That will be sexy," Charles said. I was thinking the same thing, but I couldn't say it without seeming too forward. That's one advantage to being gay: you could talk to girls about how they look. "I was thinking of getting some ink, too," he said. "A pink triangle with a middle finger in it. Right on my ass."

"You're crazy." Tracy laughed, then she added, "We could go together."

"What about you?" they asked me. "Want to come?"

"A tattoo? What would I get?"

"You're an artist. You'll think of something. Come on. We can all lose our virginity together," Charles said.

Tracy agreed. "It will be awesome! You should be there, Pete! You're going to be on my body for the rest of my life."

Charles spat, he laughed so hard. "He wishes!"

Tracy kissed my cheek and continued turning the pages. Fortunately my sketchbook was resting over my lap and hid what I was thinking.

* * *

Dad and I were driving home in the dark after his class, the radio turned, as always, to the opinion call-in shows. Did he ever listen to music?

I took a deep breath. "There's something I've been wanting to ask you, Dad."

"Really? Okay. Ask."

I turned down the volume on the radio. He glanced at my hand but didn't say anything. "Dad, aren't you afraid that someone from the government is going to get you?"

He chuckled. "Get me? You mean kill me? Assassinate me?"

"Well, yeah. Kill you."

He smiled a little. Why would he smile at that?

"I'm not important enough, kid," he said. "A lot of brave men came before me. They were the ones who paid with their lives. Thanks to them, we have free speech. Killing someone is a way of admitting they're right. The powers today realize now that the best way to discredit someone is to ignore them."

"Oh."

"If anything, they'll try to make me look like a crazy old man, which shouldn't be too hard, since that's what I am."

I liked that even with all his smarts and seriousness, he could still sometimes make fun of himself. He turned up the radio and we drove on.

Out of nowhere he said, "Let's go out to eat. Is that okay with you?"

"Sure."

"You can just cut school tomorrow."

I could feel my jaw drop. My dad, the teacher, telling me I could cut? Of course I didn't argue.

He took me to some crappy wooden shack diner I had never seen before. It looked like an abandoned building except for the neon beer signs. The inside was barely lit. Rough guys at the bar glanced at us like they couldn't decide whether to be bored, angry or tired before slowly turning back to their beers. The cushions in our booth were a dark maroon vinyl held together with duct tape, cracking in some places to let stained yellow cushion poke through. The place was a fucking dump.

"Evening, Professor, your usual?" a woman said as she approached our booth. Her hair was curled up in a large blonde-white beehive, her fashion sense about three decades old, Charles would have said. She smiled behind glasses so thick, I don't think she noticed me at first. When she finally did, she stepped back and blinked, surprised. "Oh! Um. Hello."

"Doris, this is my son, Pete. Pete, Doris."

We shook hands.

"Nice to meet you, Pete." She stared at me, blinking a lot.

"I'll take the usual," Dad said.

"You sure?" Doris asked, angling herself so I couldn't see her face.

"Hm. Maybe not," Dad said. "All right, how about two coffees instead?"

I'm not stupid. I don't think Dad ever thought that either. At that point, he just didn't care. This was where he came to drink alone. I wished it was someplace nice, but I was glad he finally let me into his secret world, even if just a little, and even if it did smell like piss.

A television was on over the bar, showing some ancient sitcom. We watched it instead of speaking. No one in the whole place was talking. Everyone just watched the television, they were quiet even when the laugh track reminded them to react. I hated it. Dad and I barely talked anymore and we were letting crap TV fill our time.

That's why I spoke up. "Dad, can I ask you another question?"

"Hm?" he said, turning in the booth. "Sure. Sure, kid. What's up?"

"You might not like it."

"Son, there's nothing wrong with asking. What's on your mind?"

"Do you hate America?"

He looked hurt and immediately I regretted asking, but at least I had his attention. "Do I what?" he said. "Why would you ask that?"

"Well, you're always complaining about this country, that what the military does is wrong, the government is corrupt, big business has taken over. Why don't you leave?"

"Why are you asking this?"

"I heard a couple of your students say it, that's all. I wanted to hear what you would say."

Doris arrived with two steaming mugs of shitty coffee.

"That one with the spoon is for you," she said to Dad. Like I didn't know what was going on.

Dad stirred, looking into his mug while he spoke. "That's a common view, but it's false. I'm not attacking this country. I'm defending it from the criminals who abuse it. I love this country. Part of being a patriot is speaking out."

I understood, but I have to admit I was glad he didn't love me in the same way he loved America. What he said made sense, but if he was insulting me the way he complained about America every day, I would get pissed, even if he called it love.

After that short conversation, he stopped talking. Maybe I offended him. TV commercials and a laugh track filled the silence.

He winced as he drank his coffee. Whatever "the usual" was that Doris had spiked it with was strong stuff.

* * *

That night at the unnamed diner bummed me out. I was smoking pot almost every day, hoping weed could obscure my depression like a fog limiting what I could see.

Dad's lecture nights were the best because that's when I smoked with Charles and Tracy instead of alone. "Our own private clubhouse," Charles called the ladies' bathroom. That wing of the college campus was always empty, so we smoked without fear. We'd joke around, listen to tunes, hang out and talk about anything. Sometimes I would just draw while they talked.

Charles was our time-keeper, but one night, he looked at his watch and laughed. "Damn it. My watch died."

"Shit," Tracy said. "What time is it?"

I pushed open the door. The hallway was black except for the pale yellow emergency lights. Paranoia oozed into my brain, lubed by the pot. Looking down that shadowy hall made me think of an underground dungeon. Charles and Tracy looked out, then we all backed into the ladies' room again.

"The security system must have automatically shut the lights off," Charles said, "We're trapped."

"We better go," Tracy said.

"But we'll set off the alarms."

"There are no alarms."

"How do you know?"

"What the hell do you want to do, sleep over? Let's just run."

I was about to agree with that idea when the door slammed open with a bang and my Dad was standing there, waving away the smoke. We all backed up fast, like he had come to kill us. Tracy flicked the joint into the sink.

"So this is where you've been," he said, stepping inside, folding his arms as he leaned backwards against the closed door. "I've been waiting an hour."

"Um. Sorry," I said.

"And you two," he said, pointing at Tracy and Charles. "You skipped my class?"

"We're sorry," Tracy babbled. "This is the first time we've done this."

"Please," Dad said, "if this is your first time cutting class or smoking pot then I'm a conservative." He had a strange look in his eye. Demented. That's the word. He was having fun with us.

"I'm not mad about the smoking," he said. "It should be your right, just as it is your right to drink alcohol. The government shouldn't legislate your personal life."

"I agree. Sir," Charles said. I wanted to kick him in the nuts just for the way he said it.

"Kiss-ass," Dad laughed. "No, it's not the smoking that offends me. I might even consider a good grade for you two based on your unofficial civil disobedience."

"Really?" Tracy asked.

"No. Not really," he said, deadpan. "What upsets me is the fact that you were skipping my lecture. I work hard on those talks." He rubbed his chin, pausing to make us squirm. "Your punishment will be two-fold. First, I'm going to confiscate that joint."

He pointed to the sink. Tracy looked to me and Charles, unsure, before she picked it up gingerly and held it out in her hand, palm up.

Dad took it and slid the doober under his nose, inhaling like a rich dude smelling a fine Cuban cigar. He exhaled loudly.

"A rich scent," he said. "But the proof is in the pudding, yes? Lighter."

Charles's hand shot out, a flame bursting from his thumb. "Um, professor, sir, what's the second part of our punishment?" he asked.

Dad put his lips to the joint and inhaled deeply, squinting his eyes. I should have known. In his college days, I'll bet he was a pro. Damn hippie.

Tracy and Charles looked at me, their eyes bulging, their slack mouths asking wordless questions. I gave them a tiny shrug. I had no idea what to expect, and I had no idea dad could suck a joint like that. He exhaled a stream of smoke through his nose.

"God damn!" he coughed, as the last of the smoke left his lungs. He turned the joint in his hand and admired it. "Anyone who says the kids of today have no ambition is dead wrong, because this is some good shit. Wrapped well, too."

"Thank you, sir," Charles said. "Ah, what's the second part of our punishment?"

Dad took another drag, this time much more mellow, not trying to shame a vacuum cleaner. Then he straightened his back and cleared his throat.

"The second part? Why, I'm going to give you a bonus lecture to make up for the one you missed. While I smoke, of course. Ahem! All right, students, class is in session. Today's lecture is titled, hm... The United States Government and an Overview of the Illegality of Marijuana and Injustice Thereof. Now-"

"Um," Charles interrupted. "Do we have to take notes?"

Dad spit out a cloud. I thought he was going to puke, he laughed so loud and hard. Smoke puffed from his mouth in time with each gasp. "No. No, you don't have to take notes, but you do have to pay attention. There might be a quiz."

The humor drained from his face and he pointed at us. "Skip another lecture of mine and I'll fail you."

"We won't," we all said in various ways. I didn't know if this rule applied to me, but I didn't want to take a chance. My heart was pounding and I was freaking out. Tracy and Charles kept looking around. They were so scared I wanted to just hurl myself out the window from embarrassment.

We were still all crowded in the corner of the women's bathroom, my Dad leaning against the sinks. At any moment someone else might come in. Then we'd all be fucked.

But he began his lecture anyway.

"Let's begin with a question: Why is pot illegal? Why are you allowed to own firearms that can kill dozens of people in seconds and yet you're not allowed to grow a plant on your own property for your own personal use?"

He took another drag. I could see in his eyes, that one hit home. When he spoke again, his words were slurring.

"The reasons are many-"

Then I lost him. His voice dropped to such a quiet level that I couldn't make out a damn thing he said. He looked like a junkie. He opened his eyes wide and pointed, or punched his palm to emphasize ideas only he could understand. That went on for I-don't-know how long. It felt like an hour.

Finally he looked down at his watch and flicked the roach into an open toilet.

"We should all get the fuck out of here," he said, his words clear.

He turned and walked out.

* * *

Tracy, Charles and I waved goodbye as I ran after Dad, jogging to keep up. Fortunately no alarms went off as we fled the building.

On the way across the parking lot, some students were hanging out, talking. They quieted as we walked past them.

"Good night, students!" Dad yelled, way too loud.

They chuckled nervously. "Um, good night, professor."

One of them whispered, "You smell that?"

Their eyes followed us to the car.

I tried to get in the driver's side, but Dad wouldn't let me.

"But, Dad," I said, "you're um, ah, er..."

"Son, we're both high."

"Should we call a cab?"

"Probably. You should never drive intoxicated." Then he pushed past me and got in the car. I jumped into the passenger side.

As we pulled out on the main road, he said, "If you get pulled over, they'll come down hard on you because you're a kid. I can always pull the depressed professor line, my wife just left me or some shit."

"Dad."

"Son, never hesitate to speak truth to power. Why the delay? Why are you waiting to call me out? Stand up to me, god damn it!"

"Dad, you're drifting!"

He swung the car into the correct lane. "Good thing it's late. Less traffic."

Another car's headlights approached us. Dad overcompensated and moved from the center line into the shoulder. The tires spit rubble.

"Dad!"

We ambled back onto the road.

"Let me drive, Dad."

"No. I've already fucked up my life. If I go to jail it's okay. I want to protect you from the fate of the fuck-up."

We were slowly moving into the oncoming lane. "Dad!"

"It's probably too late," he said as we weaved. "Can't avoid destiny."

Then he looked down, like he couldn't decide whether to cry or laugh. I held the steering wheel steady until he looked up again.

"I'm sorry about your parents," he said. "We gave you the fuck-up gene."

Maybe he was right, but somehow he got us home without killing us or someone else, and believe me, as stoned as he was, that was an accomplishment.

So, he wasn't a total failure. Close, but not total.

JAMIL

UNKNOWN LOCATION

2002

The lights and the tray were the only way Jamil could tell time was passing. The lights, set behind shatter-proof glass in the ceiling of his cell, never went out, but they dimmed to represent night and brightened to mimic the day. After the artificial sunrise, the metal tray would bang open with breakfast.

Sometime after that, he would be ordered to stand in the corner and face the wall while men rushed in. They hooded and bound him before escorting him to a tile-covered room, where they tore off his jumpsuit and sprayed him with a hose that shot a stiff stream of frigid water. He was pushed past several fans as he shivered. Once dry, he received a new orange suit, which he put on quickly so as not to upset the baton-wielding, masked guards. Hooded again, he was taken back to his cell.

A few hours later, the clang of the tray brought him a tall paper cup of water, rectangles of meat and vegetables as well as rice. The food was dry and chewy with only a hint of warmth. That was lunch. Another clang brought the exact same food for dinner. A while after that, the lights dimmed.

That was his daily routine. It went on for weeks, maybe months. The uniform days blended. He considered scratching the wall to mark time, but he didn't want to be constantly reminded how much of his life was being stolen, so he let the days file by uncounted.

He fought the monotony by trying to notice details. He noted that his plastic food tray, his orange suit and nearly everything in the room was marked with an unusual logo like a stylized flame. Sometimes the words "The Redfire Corporation" accompanied the logo in small text, along with "Made in China."

He was almost glad when the men came to take him. Such a break from the routine was a glorious relief in the boredom. Even being questioned by Mikhail wasn't so bad. Only when the searing pain of the hot brand pressed into his back did he wish he was in his cell again.

Over time, even those sessions of pain blended. How many had there been? Were they once a week? Once a fortnight? He had no idea.

Mikhail's words were predictable. The same questions always ended the same torture with the same instructions, spoken over Jamil's gasping insistence that he was innocent.

"Remember, Jamil," Mikhail would say. "You must convince me all on your own."

* * *

Jamil was trembling, sweating over his entire body. His hands were ice cold. Only with extreme effort was he able to clench tight his bladder.

He was standing face-to-face with a lion. Fortunately, a cage separated them, but that did not diminish the size of the beast's massive head, the length of his dirty claws, his huge teeth or the blazing yellow of his pupils. The vertical bars that divided them seemed to Jamil a laughable defense against an animal so clearly built to fulfill its hunger.

"You could fit your whole head in that thing's mouth!" a man nearby said, speaking to his son. The boy was Jamil's age, around ten. He retreated behind his father, gripping the man's pant leg, his lips trembling.

Goosebumps swarmed across Jamil's arms. He stepped closer so all he saw was the beast's face, none of the tiled hall around him, no other zoo visitors, just the lion. He felt like a mythical hero challenging a monster, facing down the embodiment of terror. He looked into the lion's eyes and they locked gazes.

The lion looked away first, jowls twitching as he yawned, showing off thick, vibrating pink muscles and spear tips deep inside his mouth. Jamil gazed into the blackness behind the huge tongue.

The lion pushed himself up to a standing position, muscles rippling under his taut, tan fur. He turned his back to Jamil. The other zoo visitors gasped, stepping back instinctively.

Jamil held his ground.

The animal was living in a cage barely three times his size. He turned and began pacing, claws clicking, paws slapping heavily on the cement floor of the pen, his motion smooth, hypnotic. Down and back, down and back.

Suddenly the lion stopped pacing and faced him. The creature pressed his nose to the bars, opened his mouth and roared. Hot stinking breath blew over Jamil. A baby cried. A woman screamed. Yelps of surprise and fear percolated around him, followed by nervous babbling. Jamil pressed his feet into the floor. Something deep inside his brain scratched at the inside of his skull. "Run!" it commanded. The primal urge electrified his muscles: "Run! Run for your life!" The hair on Jamil's neck rose.

A moment later, his consciousness overrode the panicked command from deep within. The beast was in a cage. Jamil was safe.

Despite the fact he was in no danger, Jamil felt saddened.

Here I am, just a boy, he thought, yet I can boldly stand before this terrible creature because of the cage.

The large cat was pacing again. Jamil continued watching, still mesmerized.

A slouching zoo worker, cigarette dangling from his mouth, opened the cage door at the back. The lion rushed to the opening and lay down. The worker turned his back to fetch a slab of meat. He stepped into the cage, close enough for the lion to bite him, and dropped the meat. He closed the door and locked it before heading to the next cage.

Jamil watched as the lion squatted low and ate. What had they done to this creature to make him so defeated? Why did he not attack the zookeeper? Why was a beast built for ferocity so tame?

Jamil woke as breakfast arrived with a clang.

He clung to the images of his dream, the memory from his youth. The questions he had then still intrigued him.

Surely the lion felt a deep rage that children could stand so close. Wouldn't a day come when the lion refused to be docile? Wouldn't the lion eventually kill the one who fed him and as many of his captors as possible before he was shot?

When would the fear of death succumb to the needs of pride?

* * *

Several days later, Jamil lay in his cot, touching his face, surprised to find it was dry. He was unsure if that was a good or a bad sign. Lately he had been waking up with his face damp from tears released quietly in the night. This morning, there were none. Had he unconsciously accepted his fate?

He vowed not to become docile like the lion. He had to keep his rage alive, to bring back the tears in his sleep.

He rolled off his cot, fell to the floor and started doing push-ups. He did them until he could do no more. Then he continued, pushing beyond his limits until his arms trembled, until his muscles felt hot and he collapsed. He gasped for air, waited until his arms felt rested and tried again.

He continued that cycle all day, breaking only for meals. When the light dimmed, he crawled to his cot, his arms as loose as rubber bands.

The next day, he rose to his feet, closed his eyes and jogged in place. He visualized his neighborhood at home, running to the edge of his memory, then starting over. He ran until he was exhausted, then he caught his breath and started again. He raised his knees high as he had seen the pro football players do to warm up for a match. All day he jogged in the center of his cell, again breaking only for meals.

The next day he boxed his shadow, punching the cement wall hard, harder, then as hard as he could. He shook his knuckles out and continued. The pain made him feel better. He noticed a difference between self-inflicted wounds and those that came from a coward standing behind him, asking questions.

He passed the days this way, keeping in shape with a rotating exercise schedule: push-ups, running, boxing.

Boxing quickly became his favorite.

His knuckles initially left bloody spots on the wall. Now, after what seemed like weeks of punching concrete, his hands were bruised, callused and hardened. He imagined the same happening to his heart.

When the time came, he would be ready. He would be strong enough to snap Mikhail's neck with only his hands, or squeeze shut his throat with his lumpy fingers. All he needed was one chance. And if Mikhail's guard shot him? That would be his fate, but he would take Mikhail with him.

The hardening was not perfect. At random moments, the gravity of his fate would clutch his heart and squeeze. He was a captive, far from home, with no way to return. The knowledge would attack him suddenly and he would fall to the floor crying.

He allowed it, welcoming the return of feeling, for with it came anger.

Nearly all the memories of his past had dissolved. He clung to them as tightly as he could, but without reinforcement from a photograph or a voice, they slipped from his mind. At night he prayed for dreams to bring them back.

Sometimes even that was a curse. Sometimes his memories did return, but they were like matches, flaring once and then dead forever.

It would not be long before all he knew were these pale walls, gory photos, Mikhail's questions and pain.

* * *

His body grew stronger, but his mind was wasting away. Instinctively, he knew the crushing boredom was dangerous. Down that path he would arrive at madness, the docility of the defeated lion and worse.

He continued studying the details of his room, imagining the history behind it. How was the brick manufactured? The bed? The toilet? How was the prison built? By whom? What had to be done first? What problems did they encounter? Where did the supplies come from? He constantly devised questions, imagining answers.

His thinking became an alternative exercise, a mental challenge to enjoy while he rested his body when it was spent by workouts or torture. To avoid the fate of the lion, he would counter his captors' routine with his own.

After Mikhail ended yet another painful talking session with his usual refrain, "You must convince me of your innocence," Jamil quickly gathered his breath and spoke.

"May I have something to read?"

"To read? To entertain you? Are you bored?"

Jamil was silent as the masked men around him chuckled. He waited.

Mikhail spoke. "We can give you a Koran or a Bible. That is all."

"May I have both?"

"Both? What religion are you?"

Jamil said nothing.

"Your religion, Jamil. Answer. Answer now."

"I want to learn about the great religions."

Mikhail hesitated. "Fine, we'll give you both. I don't know about your Muslim world, but in Christianity, we confess our sins. Can you do that for me someday?"

Jamil dared once more. "And may I have something to write with?"

"Write with? You're not on holiday, you know. You can't send letters."

"I need something to mark my favorite passages."

"Is that permitted? Isn't that desecrating of the word of God? Or Allah?"

"I just want to learn."

Mikhail paused a long time. "All I can give you is a soft crayon."

"Thank you, sir, Mikhail. Thank you."

"Remember my kindness and tell me something useful next time. You're not the only one who tires of these meetings."

The next meal came with a Koran, a Bible and a soft crayon, as Mikhail promised. Jamil wept as he gathered up the gifts, clutching them to his chest. He slid his fingers over the paper, turning each page delicately.

Jamil studied the crayon. He concluded it was soft so as to be useless for piercing flesh or scraping at brick, but it was fine for his plan.

He drew the grid of a chessboard on the cardstock inside back cover of the Bible. Using pages ripped from the same book (he dared not damage the Koran) he tore square pieces and drew the symbols of chess tokens on them.

He clenched his fists with excitement at the sight of his own toy. He played a game of chess against himself, smiling and crying simultaneously.

Now his routine was complete. He could keep his body fit and his mind sharp. He also kept his creativity alive, designing puzzles, drawing a word-finder grid over the passages of the Bible every day. After a few days, he would forget where the words were hidden. Then he could work the puzzle as if someone else had created it.

Mikhail and those who brought him here were his captors, but atrophy of mind and muscle was the true danger. Now he was confident he could avoid that fate.

* * *

Though he didn't track the days, by his estimation, he expected to be interrogated today.

He was doing pushups when someone knocked on his door. He rolled to the far wall, awaiting the usual instructions, but the question that followed surprised him.

"Hello, Mister Jamil. Would you like to go for a walk?"

Jamil looked to the tiny window but saw no face, only the back of someone's head covered in a ski mask. He recognized Mikhail's voice.

"A walk?" Jamil asked.

Compared to being bottled up in his cell, a walk would be a glorious adventure, but this was likely a trap, some prelude to agony.

"A walk outside," Mikhail said.

Jamil moved to the door quietly and peeked out the edges of the window. Mikhail's back was to him. He was a little shorter than Jamil, and leaner. Jamil caught the sight of thin hands covered by leather gloves, clasped behind his back.

"Would you like to go?" Mikhail repeated.

Jamil leaned against the door, thinking. This had to be a trick, but did he really have a choice?

"I would," he said.

"Put this on." The metal tray banged open. Inside was a jacket with a thick fur lining. He inspected it carefully. Nothing about it seemed unusual except all the buttons and zippers had been removed. He put it on slowly, trying to imagine what torture was coming.

"Now," Mikhail said. "Against the far wall. Alert me when you are ready."

Jamil moved across the cell and lay face down.

"Ready," he said.

The door crashed open. Jamil did not even attempt to catch a glimpse of Mikhail. The guards were on him in seconds and the familiar hood swept over his head, the plastic wire around his wrists.

He was gripped at both elbows as they walked through several doors that buzzed and hissed as they opened. The air cooled as they progressed. First he was cold, then chilly, then freezing.

Jamil shifted, trying to make the jacket's front close.

"I'm cold. Where are we going?" he asked.

No one answered him. He imagined himself being led to the edge of a pit and then shot in the back of the head. That was a change in the routine he would prefer to avoid.

For now.

"Watch your step," Mikhail said. Jamil felt his feet slide as he walked. They were moving across a slick surface. He guessed it was ice, but he had no idea what ice felt like to walk on. His whole life until now had been spent in a warmer climate. He took small steps to keep his balance.

"We're going to chain you to a wall," Mikhail said.

Someone pulled Jamil's hands back and bound them to a metal ring, pinning him against frigid concrete. He gasped as hard cold penetrated his jacket.

"Are you going to shoot me?" he asked, angry that his voice trembled.

"Do it," Mikhail said.

"Wait!" Jamil screamed.

Before he could say anything more, someone on the opposite side of the wall grabbed the top of his hood and yanked it upwards. The blackness was replaced with blinding white. Jamil squinted, his eyes taking long to adjust. He looked away from the brightness at the ground. The dirt was dry and cracked, covered with patches of frost. His breath turned white before vanishing.

He looked up slowly, his jaw dropping.

He had seen these vistas in pictures, on television, but seeing it directly before him was entirely different. He was dumbstruck at the awesome beauty.

As far as he could see were snow-capped mountains. Further down, their sides were covered with green. The sky was a deep blue, fading to purple at the horizon. Nothing indicated that these silent peaks had ever been touched by man.

He stared for a long time, alone with the majestic scene except for a man standing at his side, wearing a thick coat and a ski mask, his rifle pointed at Jamil's side.

Jamil noticed the far away mountain snow glistened like tiny colorful prisms on the pure white.

Mikhail broke his meditation.

"Isn't my country beautiful?" he asked.

Jamil wondered how something as huge as a mountain could radiate such silence. He wished he had witnessed such beauty voluntarily, but having seen it at all touched him with a small spark of happiness deep inside.

"Beautiful, yes," he said. His habit of looking for details activated. At first glance, the green on the mountainsides seemed uniform, but it wasn't. There were clusters of pink and yellow flowers scattered about.

"It's incredible," Jamil said. "Wonderful!"

"I am not showing you this to amuse you. I am showing you this so you will not ever entertain any notions of escape."

Mikhail paused to let the gravity of his words sink in. Jamil was unmoved. He knew he would never get past the guards anyway. If this was meant to crush his hope, it did little. Mikhail couldn't crush something that wasn't there.

"Men much harder than you or I have died in those mountains, and they had years of preparation, training and equipment. You have no such resources. You must know there is no hope of escape."

Jamil studied the mountain tops, the black rock under the white snow. He wondered if snow was smooth or if it scratched. He wondered so much. Exactly what was snow? Frozen rain? Was it then like small pebbles or was it grainy like sand?

"Jamil!" Mikhail had been talking.

"Yes?"

"I said there is only one hope of leaving here. Do you know what it is?"

"If I convince you of my innocence," Jamil said, barely paying attention to his own words.

"That, or if you admit what you've done. Whatever it is, say it, no matter how small you think it is. You are here until I am convinced you are not a problem."

Jamil stared at the mountains.

"Jamil?"

Jamil watched a single bird fly below him. How high they must be to look down on a bird! What must it be like to fly? To be so free you can go anywhere you can see?

"Jamil!" Mikhail barked.

"What?"

"Do not adopt a tone with me. I asked if you received your books? Your crayon?"

Mikhail's interruptions were annoying. Before Jamil could stop himself, he snapped.

"I did. I'm thinking of writing my confession."

From behind the wall, someone smacked him in the back of the head.

"You think this is funny?" Mikhail said. "Maybe I'll take those gifts back or take away your light or refuse to bring you water, yes?"

Jamil smirked. With Mikhail angry, he had more time to stare at the beautiful view. How far away were the mountains? Did people actually attempt to climb them?

"Jamil. Do you think this is funny?" Mikhail asked.

"No."

"Move him."

The hood was pulled over his head. Jamil held back a whimper.

Their steps crunched across the dry dirt, the tone of their footfalls changing as they entered an enclosed area. Jamil was pushed down to a frigid concrete floor and made to lie on his back. His hands were chained to a ring in the floor above his head, and his feet to a ring below him. He rocked from side to side to alleviate the chill on his buttocks and shoulders.

"Hello?" he called from inside his hood.

He jolted as sound blared into the chamber. It was a pop song, the high-pitched tones typical of mediocre discotheque music. Though he understood English, he couldn't make out what the singer was saying.

A synthetic keyboard beeped out the melody. *Plink-plink-plink-plink-plink-plink!* Over and over.

The song finished. It was loud, but it wasn't a bad tune. The first time.

The song played again with only an instant of silence between the first run and the next. Jamil tried to stand up, fighting against his bindings.

The song played again, its repetitive melody running over and over. *Plink-plink-plink-plink-plink-plink!*

It played again. Then again. Again. Again.

He soon had every bit of it memorized. The high-pitched *plink* tone felt like a tiny hammering inside his skull. He tried to visualize the mountains, but that new memory was consistently obliterated by the repeating sound: *plink-plink-plink-plink-plink-plink!*

They played the song several more times with no gap of silence in between.

He began to hear the pauses between the sounds. There were words behind the English singing, someone was speaking in Arabic very slowly, or so he thought. It sounded like—*plink-plink-plink-plink-plink-plink!*—no, he couldn't make it out—*plink-plink-plink-plink-plink-plink!* something they were–

No.

Yes.

Every time he thought he heard it, it was gone again, then *plink-plink-plink-plink-plink-plink!*

He wanted to fall asleep, but the song was far too loud. The floor too cold.

"Make it stop!" he screamed. "Turn it off!"

Plink-plink-plink-plink-plink-plink!

He twisted on the floor, until his muscles stretched and burned. The vibrations shook his bones, the recurring melody plucked at his sanity.

"Stop it!"

After several more repetitions, the music stopped. Despite the cold, he was sweating. The echoing send of footsteps came near.

"Do you want to talk, Mister Jamil?" Mikhail asked from above him. *Plink-plink-plink-plink-plink-plink!* was all Jamil could hear.

"Jamil!"

Jamil groaned.

Mikhail's footsteps receded. The music began again.

Plink-plink-plink-plink-plink-plink!

He couldn't cover his ears. Again the song finished. Again it began. Again. Again. Again. *Plink-plink-plink-plink-plink-plink!*

Jamil lifted his head and banged his skull on the floor hard, trying to knock himself unconscious. The pain made him dizzy, made the *plink!* sound worse.

"Jamil?" Mikhail asked after the song ended once more.

"Please. Make it stop!" Jamil yelled.

"What have you to tell me?"

Jamil spoke quickly. "I must convince you. I know. I must find a way. I will. I will! I promise! I'll convince you! For now make it stop. Please!" The melody rattled in his head. *Plink-plink-plink-plink-plink-plink!*

"I will. For now."

Jamil staggered back to his cell, the song still bouncing around his skull. He smashed his palms against his ears, but the *plink!* would not stop. *Plink-plink-plink-plink-plink-plink!* Every noise he heard was close enough in tone to some aspect of the tune to restart the whole song in his mind. The melody always brought with it the whispering Arabic voice that he could not quite understand.

PETE

USA

2003

When you consider how dumb most people are, it's hard to understand complaining that someone thinks too much. Most people don't use their brains at all, so you might expect to be glad when someone actually uses theirs, and you might forgive someone who uses it a lot. Problem is, thinking can be pushed too far, and my dad was proof. I definitely got my impulsive streak from Mom.

Ugh. I hate to say I'm like her in any way.

When the Iraq War started in early 2003, I thought it was fucked up. I considered it my patriotic duty to party harder than ever because people across the world were dying for oil and money. That's all the thought I gave the whole topic.

Dad was the opposite. He was a political junkie before the Iraq War (or as he sometimes called it, the second Iraq War, since there apparently was another one going on when I was a pup.) My point is, Dad was already deeply into world news and political shit, but when the invasion started, he became even more intense about that stuff, which I didn't think was possible.

He watched TV all night, flipping through the news channels and the shows with guys arguing, with people calling in. He recorded them and re-watched them while taking notes. When he bought a second VCR to make his own tapes for class, I knew I was in trouble. He became a monk and the TV was his god.

He accidentally encouraged me to go to school, just to get away from the noise. On his days off, he'd start on the couch watching news, and when I came home, he'd be in the same place, surrounded by opened Chinese food delivery containers. Then we'd be off to his night class where he would talk about the war.

Driving home, he put war news on the radio.

Tracy and Charles hadn't taken Dad's class that semester. We kept in touch, but I had no one to escape the lectures with.

I should have been relieved when Dad told me I didn't have to go to his class anymore. I had no life, so I kept going anyway, just to get out of the house and because even though all he did during class was talk about the war, it was the only time he talked.

Plus, I wanted to keep an eye on him. He was obsessed. No. He was nuts. Insane. He spent every class raving about the crimes of the president, the vice president and Senator Wayne Drake "Hands-on" Hanson. Dad was losing it, and I wasn't surprised when he self-destructed.

* * *

Dad sucked with technology, so I had to help him with the slide projector. He only had two pictures, but he still couldn't manage it.

His lecture was about his standard freak-out that the army was staying in Iraq. What started as an invasion had become an occupation. There was no exit plan because there was never any plan to exit. Over and over he repeated those phrases.

The first photo was of several rows of coffins, lined up neatly in a hangar, each draped with the American flag. The caskets stretched into the distance, out of sight, like when two mirrors face each other. Looking at it made me sick. That many coffins could hold everyone I knew several times over.

"Did you know it's illegal to photograph a dead soldier's casket?" Dad asked his class. "Take a good look at this picture. Your government doesn't want you to see the price of war."

He paused to let that sink in.

"But dead Iraqis?" he said. "Take as many pictures as you want."

On his signal, I flipped to the next slide. A woman dressed in black was wailing over several bodies lying in the street, their faces the bluish-green color of the dead.

A girl nearby leapt up and ran from the hall, hand over her mouth, her eyes wide.

"Notice there are no weapons near the bodies," Dad said. "The victims are elderly and or female. In other words, civilians. This is your tax dollars at work, people. You are paying the U.S. military and the mercenaries they employ to kill innocents."

A violent bang echoed through the auditorium as a student jumped up yelling. "Are you serious? Are you saying our troops did this?"

"This is what war does," Dad said calmly.

"You're calling our troops criminals!" The guy was shaking, his face burning red.

Dad was so chill he could have just said 'fuck you.' Instead he shrugged. "War is a crime. That's what this is."

"How do you know the U.S. did it and not the terrorists?" someone called out.

Dad turned toward the voice and yelled in that direction. "Remember how horrible 9/11 was? Our country is causing a 9/11 in Iraq every single day. Every! Single! Day! Now you tell me who the terrorists are."

The whole class was buzzing.

"This is bullshit!" another student yelled back. He grabbed his pack and left. Several others followed him out. Some people clapped. Some laughed.

I watched Dad's reaction. He just folded his arms. If I had offered him two shits for free he would have declined. He didn't flinch. I should have guessed what was coming next. Looking back, I think he knew it too but just didn't care. I have to wonder if he didn't even do it on purpose.

* * *

It all went down the very next class.

It was a shame because I had spent an hour ahead of time showing Dad how to use the college VCR. It was different than the ones we had at home, a newer model with a DVD player, too. That really stumped him. I'll never understand how someone so smart could suck so bad with technology. I would've preferred to teach a cat how to ride a bike.

When class began, he fired up a clip of some news show profiling Senator Hanson. Hanson strolled among soldiers, shaking their hands. The voiceover said, "Enrollment in the military is at an all-time low, threatening to reduce troop strength to unsafe levels. Hanson showed up as this platoon was ready to ship out to Iraq. There's a reason they call him Hands-on Hanson."

The screen switched to a reporter interviewing Hanson in his office.

"There have been several warnings about not having enough troops," the reporter said. "What's your take on that?"

"I've drafted a bill for the Non-Combat Squad Support program."

Dad pushed pause. "For those who don't know," he said, "that mouthful is more commonly known as the Cons-to-Soldiers bill." After way too much time, he found the play button and restarted the video.

The reporter leaned forward. "Critics say that's creating a class of slave labor. Exploiting people doing time."

Hanson smirked. "The same critics whine about jail overcrowding. I'm killing two birds with one stone. We've got too many prisoners and we need help in Iraq. My program helps those who have no history of violence and requires they pass a psych exam. America is about opportunity. Let's give them an opportunity to give back to the society they damaged."

It's weird thinking about that interview now. At the time, I barely paid attention, but that video was the speck in the sky that grew and grew and finally crashed into my world.

Dad stopped the video.

"On and on it goes," he said. "More ass-kissing from the reporter. Hanson doesn't mention that the con-soldiers actually work for contractors, not the U.S. Government. So the contractor gets paid by your taxes to provide a home for the convicts, and at the same time receives money for the work those convicts do. Two incomes for the price of one. Two birds with one stone, just like the good senator said."

I almost lost it right there.

I got it, Dad! I wanted to scream. We've all got it! Senator Hanson is an evil man. He's crooked, criminal, all that. Can't we just watch a movie? Have a father-son talk? Play catch? Something? Anything? I got it! He's a dick! Check! Now let's go do something else. Talk about anything else!

Instead, I pulled out my sketchbook while he raved on. I was sitting toward the back, so I noticed when the three suits sat down in the last row. They were whispering, but kind of loud because they were arguing. When I looked back, one caught my eye and gave me a forced smile.

I drew a quick self-portrait, giving myself rabbit ears while I listened.

"Like this? Here?"

"We could take him to our office."

"This is how it has to be."

"What if he sees us?"

"Of course he's going to see us. It's what he wants anyway. To play the martyr."

"But all those years."

"It has to be done. We've decided, the board's decided and we're here."

"We can still back out."

"No. We can't. We've had enough complaints."

"Enough?"

"We've had significant complaints. We have to do this. The war changes things. He's only going to get worse. Best to care for it now."

"He isn't going to take it lightly."

"Stop worrying. It will all be over soon."

Maybe Dad had some supernatural awareness as a teacher, a sense that told him about the entire classroom. That's the only way I can explain how he noticed the suits in the crowded auditorium so quickly. He dropped his arms to his sides, stopped talking and stared at the back of the hall. A few students turned to follow his gaze.

"Shit," one of the suits mumbled.

Dad turned his back to the class and looked up at the ceiling. He stood that way quietly, not long, but long enough for everyone to notice something was wrong.

Then he turned around and made his final stand.

"I apologize," he said. "I got distracted. I thought this moment might come. I suppose it's no surprise. In essence, war is a celebration of cowardice."

The classroom buzzed. No one seemed to know what he was talking about. I only knew because I was near the suits. My heart was pounding. What was he going to do?

"Let me begin with a history of Iraq, this nation about to be destroyed in your name," he said. "Starting from 5,000 B.C. That means, 5,000 years before the cult known as Christianity began."

Then he was off, talking about how much of our civilization was derived from ancient Iraq, or at least that area. From there he spoke on every topic imaginable: culture, law, society, architecture, agriculture. It was like he was unloading everything he ever learned.

He barely took a breath. It was sort of interesting, but I was watching the clock. We were a few minutes past nine, when he usually ended the class, but he just kept going. A student got up and dropped into the seat next to me.

"What is your dad doing?"

"I think those dudes behind us are here to fire him."

The guy turned around. "Holy shit," he said. "That's the dean. What do we do?"

"I don't know."

Dad was still talking.

"He's stalling," the unknown student said. "How long can he go?"

We both looked at each other seriously.

"I'm going to tell people."

Dude got up, sat next to some other students and whispered. They turned around to check out the suits and then split up and moved around the class. Word was spreading, and Dad just kept on talking. Iraq this, Iraq that. Civilization blah, blah, blah.

It was 9:15. I yawned and leaned my head back. I didn't mean to, but I nodded off. When I woke up again, my neck was stiff and my eyes foggy. The clock was at 11:30.

Dad was still talking.

Only around twenty students remained. The suits were still behind me. Their bickering was getting louder.

"This is ridiculous."

"How long is he going to keep this up?"

"You think he knows?"

"Of course he knows. That's why he's not stopping."

"Can we wait him out?"

"We promised it would be taken care of today, so that's what we're going to do."

"In another half-hour it will be tomorrow."

"All right. Let me end this."

One of them stood up. Dad acknowledged him.

"Oh, hello, Dean. I'm honored you finally decided to visit my class. It's been years. Do you have a question?"

"When is this lecture going to end, John?"

"That's Professor Abbott, Dean," he said. His students clapped and hooted. "What's the problem?"

"It's getting late. Your allotted class time is over."

"There's no hurry."

"There is. The security alarms will be activating. We need to vacate the building."

"Nonsense. I've been here late before."

"John. Please."

Dad smiled sadly.

"Remember, class," he said, "you only know a democracy is working if your views are being challenged. It's been an honor. Good night."

At a quarter to midnight, Dad ended his filibuster. The remaining students leapt to their feet and applauded. They surrounded him, buzzing with excitement, thanking him, asking questions. The suits stood at the edge of the small crowd, major pissed-off. I waited nearby. One by one, each student filed out until it was just me, Dad and the suits.

"We need to talk with your professor in private," the Dean said to me.

"He's not a student. He's my son," Dad said, folding his arms and leaning against the wall.

"You're bringing your son to your class?" The Dean was the only one talking. The other two stared at their feet.

"Say what you have to say," Dad said, packing his briefcase.

"We've had some complaints."

"Go on."

"Some students claim that your lecture is very one-sided."

"That's happened every year since I've been here. What was it this time? Too liberal?"

"Not liberal. Radical. You may be coming on too strong because of... recent developments."

"You mean my wife leaving?"

"That's not what I mean, John."

"Oh. The war. We all have to shut up now? Isn't it times like these when we educators need to stand together? When did war become something we had to protect?"

"You were always the idealist, John."

"Still am. What are the terms?"

"Terms?"

"Of my removal. Come on, I'm sick of talking to you. Tell me."

The Dean sighed. "You're relieved of this class. You'll be eligible for substitution during the week-"

"Forget it."

"John, none of us wanted it to come to this."

"Then why didn't you fight?"

"We are fighting. For those who don't fight us."

Dad pushed through the three of them.

"We need you to sign the paperwork."

"Mail it to me," he yelled back, walking away.

I hustled after him, slamming through the exit.

We drove home in complete silence. He didn't even turn the radio on. I thought he was going to scream at any moment, but he didn't, just kept staring ahead, the lights flashing against his glasses.

He stopped the car at the curb but didn't cut the engine.

"You can take care of yourself?" he asked without looking at me.

"Sure."

"All right. I have to go blow off some steam. Alone."

"Where are you going?"

"I'll be home later."

I found him asleep on the couch the next morning, lying crooked, half on the floor. He had wet himself, too. Nice. He stunk of beer and smoke and piss, but I was glad he at least made it home alive.

The television was playing some stupid infomercial. I flicked it off and lifted his legs onto the couch so he wouldn't wake up with kinks in his back.

He had reached a point where he finally decided to be one hundred percent himself, not holding back anything, even if it ruined him. Maybe he even knew it would ruin him and he didn't care. He just wanted to go out on his terms.

I can relate.

* * *

A few weeks after Dad got fired I met Charles and Tracy at Tattoo Steve's. Tracy greeted me with a big hug.

"I'm sorry about what happened with your dad," she said. "A bunch of us have a petition going to bring him back."

"That's great," I said, barely able to talk. The hug she had given me left an afterimage on my flesh. I could still feel the press of her arms around my shoulders, her breasts against my collarbone.

"Make sure you tell him," she said.

"I will." If I ever see him, I thought. Dad was staying out later each night, drinking and who knows what else, before coming home to yell at the TV and pass out on the couch.

"Is he doing all right?"

"As good as he can."

"We need to hang out more," she said. "I haven't seen you in a while."

"Uh, yeah," I said, trying to sound interested but not too desperate.

"I'm glad you made it. You drew the picture, you should see where it goes."

I'd never been in a tattoo shop before, but something about the place instantly felt right.

There were pictures all over the wall. Needles buzzed like insects on a summer night, relentlessly drawing drops of blood. There were two torn couches covered with stains in the lobby. The crash of old-style rock thundered over the buzzing. It was the kind of music Dad liked, where you can understand the words.

Charles was smoking with a couple of girls in the corner. He waved. The girls were dressed in black, had piercings all over their faces and were covered in tattoos. They looked at me like I was a piece of crap.

Despite the cranky goth chicks, I liked the vibe of the shop. It was part hangout, part gallery. Some of the art was on the walls, but most of it walked around. A lot of the drawings were really bad, weak, the lines unnatural and out of proportion. The gore-art, skeletons and demons and all that, was the worst. Guys who drew that stuff tended to suck at art.

"You can do better than this," Tracy said, slipping her arm into mine as we checked out the wall.

"Look. I'm going to get it right here." She lifted up her shirt and slid her fingertip over the scar just above her jeans. My heart sped up.

"Looks great," I said.

"I can't wait! It's going to be so sexy."

I laughed like a dork. The few girls I knew from high school were either hot or friendly. They were never both, like Tracy. I felt like an idiot around her. All I wanted to do was throw her down and have sex with her right there. If girls knew that we guys thought like that, they would probably all head for another planet.

"All right, who's Tracy?" a booming voice asked.

The room seemed to shrink as a huge bulk moved into its center. He looked more like a bouncer than an artist. His green eyes scanned the lobby. His shirt was black with the sleeves torn off to make room for his muscular arms, tattooed from shoulder to fingertips. His thick, grey ponytail gave him the appearance of a mythical hero. A cigarette smoldered in one hand. Every visible part of his flesh up to his face was covered with artwork, like he had rolled along the walls and the pictures stuck to him.

Tracy leapt forward. "Me!"

Big Guy looked her up and down. I wasn't sure I liked the look in his eye, but I kept it to myself. My survival instinct knew he was the Alpha Male and I was not to mess with him, no matter what.

He stuffed the cigarette in his mouth and shook Tracy's hand with gentlemanly respect. I hate to admit it, but his appearance had tricked me into thinking he was incapable of manners. I had yet to learn that the inked are just as kind or cruel as blanks.

"Nice to meet you," the Alpha Male said to Tracy, cigarette bobbing between his lips. "I'm Tattoo Steve. What are you looking to get?"

* * *

Charles, Tracy and I followed Steve to a room covered in posters of motorcycles, each being polished by a sweaty girl wearing a bikini. Maybe women do know what men are thinking. We sure don't hide it. Did Tracy know what was on my mind? And if she did and was still around, did that mean she wasn't opposed?

Steve handed her a clipboard.

"This contract is to cover my big fat ass," he said. "It says you're eighteen or older and you know what you're doing." We all took a seat. Steve plopped onto a stool that creaked every time he moved.

Tracy lifted her shirt again, showing her mid-section. She wasn't bony or rigid like the goth sisters in the lobby, she had a little flesh on her tummy. Very sexy.

"Appendectomy scar?" Steve asked, tapping his cigarette into the top of a skull-shaped ashtray.

"I hate it," she said.

"We cover those up all the time. So, what art do you want?"

She handed him my sketch.

Tattoo Steve checked it out. It had been a while since I'd seen it, the dragon with the lady's face and the butterfly wings. The smoke from his cigarette drifted across his acne-covered face. A couple scars on his cheek looked like they had been made by a knife.

"Pretty cool," he said. "Where did you get this? An album cover?"

Tracy smiled wide. Charles pointed at me. Tattoo Steve turned and looked into my eyes. "You did this?"

"Yeah," I said, trying to sound cool.

"It's an original?"

"Yep."

"Fucking nice, man. Real nice."

He touched the drawing with his dirty fingernails, running his hairy fingers over it, stroking it. He looked back at me, then back at the drawing.

"Let me show you how to ink someone. If you like it, later we can talk. If not, no harm. You want to learn?"

"I guess," I said. I wasn't really interested. I just liked the idea of getting closer to Tracy.

"He'd be great, I bet," Charles added.

"He might be," Steve said. "But I have to ask the lady. Do you trust this guy?"

"Of course," she said, smiling.

"All right, then. Watch and learn, kid. Before we get started, we take the 'before' picture." He pulled out a digital camera and nodded at Tracy. "Stand and lift your shirt up." She did. "More," he said. She lifted her shirt a little more. "More," he said, smiling.

"Um, no," she snapped.

"Can't blame a guy for trying," Steve said, laughing as he took the picture.

"Next," he said, "we draw the outline image on some of this magic trace paper. Then we wet it and roll it on so we can see how it looks before we commit to anything." He handed me the drawing and a sheet of paper.

"Go do it."

That quickly, my apprenticeship began.

After Tracy signed the contract, I followed Steve through every step. First I copied my drawing onto the paper, then we wet it. We pressed the drawing onto Tracy's belly as she sat in the dentist-style padded chair. She squirmed as we rubbed the lines in.

"It tickles," she said.

She was giggling, staring at the ceiling. Steve winked at me and gestured, inviting me to rub the picture more. I did. Tracy wiggled.

"Some people draw the flash right on with the needle, but I think that's bullshit," Steve said. "A tattoo is a serious thing. You have to get it right. Get some fucking humility and lay down the outline first. This way, the person getting inked is sure to be happy. It's about them, not you."

Tracy rolled on her side and looked in the mirror. The outline of the dragon flexed with her movement.

"It's not in color, but we'll add that later," Steve said. "How's it look for now?"

"It looks awesome," she said, rolling on her back. Steve stomped a pedal to make the chair recline. He spoke quickly as he fished out plastic-wrapped needles and little paint pots, explaining what he was doing. In minutes he was leaning over Tracy, his face near her hip, raking the buzzing needle over her flesh, tracking tiny dots of blood and lines of color. With his other hand, he wiped away the excess ink quickly. He was constantly moving. Draw a line, wipe. Draw a line, wipe.

"You're not afraid of blood, are you, miss?" Steve asked as he kept going.

"Nope."

"You've got to give to get. Can't expect to look cool and not pay for it."

After the outline was complete, Steve looked at Tracy but flicked his thumb at me.

"Miss, do you trust this guy?" he asked.

She looked at me, smiling. "I do."

Charles rolled his eyes.

Tattoo Steve offered me the needle. "Your turn, then."

The needle vibrated in my hand, almost popping loose. Steve yelled over the buzz as I moved toward her flesh.

"Don't stab her but don't back off. You've got to set the ink right. Besides, chicks like it rough."

"Oh, yeah, we do," Charles said and everyone laughed.

"Wait," Steve said. "Let me show you."

He wrapped his giant fist around mine. Together we pressed down. I felt the needle pierce Tracy's skin, not too deep, but definitely in. It felt right.

Steve let me go for a few lines, then took the needle back. When it left my hand, my fingers tingled. I missed the buzzing energy and couldn't wait to feel that insistent power again.

* * *

When Steve finished, he took another picture and showed us the before and after in his digital camera's window. In the before, Tracy was holding her shirt up, her scar showing, in the after, she was in the same pose, but instead of a scar, a colorful dragon with a woman's face and butterfly wings graced her belly. She was smiling broadly. I was too. My art was now a part of her. I would be with her forever.

"I'll never have to see that scar again," she said, laughing. She turned around, modeling the ink. "My dad will be so pissed if he ever finds out."

Steve was cleaning up. "Don't send him bitching to me. Everyone here signs the release first."

"I love it," Tracy said, still looking in the mirror.

Steve turned to me. "See, kid? This job isn't just drawing. It's rewarding. Look at that smile on your girlfriend's face."

Girlfriend? I didn't correct him.

She didn't either.

"Do me next," Charles said.

"You should all get them," Steve said. "Seal the friendship with blood."

"Are you really going to?" Tracy asked Charles.

"Can I get something on my ass?"

Tattoo Steve laughed. "Sure. That's actually a pretty easy place to tattoo. It's even, lots of padding. If you have a lot of hair, I'll have to shave it."

Charles looked at him with mock offense. "Please. There's no hair on my ass. Right here at the top of my cheek. I want a pink triangle with a middle finger in it."

"No problem."

"I don't know if I want to witness this," Tracy said, standing.

"Oh, come on," Charles said.

"I just need some air," she said. "I'll be back."

I jumped up behind Tracy. "I'll go with you."

"Fuck!" Steve said. "You're going to leave me with this cute boy's hot ass?"

While Charles was getting his butt inked, Tracy and I walked around the strip mall near Tattoo Steve's. She had rolled up and knotted her shirt so her dragon could be seen. We sat at a rotting picnic table near the dumpsters. I pulled out my sketchbook and started flipping through it.

"What are you going to get?" she asked me.

"I can't decide."

"Draw something new. Whatever comes to mind."

I started with a curved line. I drew some fangs on it and angry, snake-like eyes. I added some claws. I didn't know what the hell I was drawing. I just went with it.

* * *

"Oh, God, that felt good," Charles said, laughing.

We spent several minutes admiring the pink triangle with the middle finger in it riding on top of his right butt cheek.

Finally Steve slapped his hands on his thighs. "Next?"

I handed him my sketch. He turned the page and looked at it from all angles. "Cool, but what the fuck is it?"

Charles looked away from the mirror. "Looks like a crazy pissed off lizard."

"I think it's cute," Tracy said.

"He's supposed to be like me. I think," I said.

"It does look like a lizard," Steve said. He wrote underneath the picture: L-I-Z-E-R-D and held it at arm's length. "Lizard. I can put the word in a banner underneath if you want. That will be cool."

Charles, Tracy and I all looked at each other and grinned.

"Um, I think you messed up," Charles said.

"What?" Steve asked, his voice angry. "Messed up your tattoo?"

"Oh, no," Charles said quickly. "I was looking at it wrong. Don't mind me. I'm feeling faint. I think I lost too much blood."

Tracy smiled at me. I didn't say anything. So the guy couldn't spell, so what? I took a seat and pulled up my sleeve.

"Add the banner," I said.

Steve traced the image and laid the outline onto my shoulder with the wet paper. It looked awesome. The misspelling of "lizard" made it unique. I liked it.

He tapped a button and the needle buzzed. "Mind if I call you Lizard? You look like a lizard. I mean you look like a guy who would be nicknamed Lizard, you know? Skinny, but sneaky. A survivor, too. Is it okay if I call you that?"

The needle stung as he pressed it into my shoulder.

"No problem," I said.

* * *

Later we were smoking a massive joint in Charles' basement when Tracy spat out, "Let's take a picture!"

Charles set his camera on a shelf and activated the delay timer. I rolled up my sleeve, Tracy lifted her shirt, and he pulled down his pants to moon the camera. There we were: three friends, three new tattoos, three new symbols. A dragon-butterfly, a middle finger inside a pink triangle, and a crazy lizard.

After the picture we sat on the sofa again.

"I thought Steve was going to kill me when I said he messed up," Charles said, laughing. "I was about to say you spelled lizard wrong, but then I was like, whoa!"

"Good thing," Tracy said. "He would have kicked our asses."

"Oh, he's just a big bear. Not my type, but I'm not afraid of him. Not too much."

Tracy poked me. "I can't believe you let him put a spelling mistake on you."

I looked at my shoulder. "I guess I'm no ordinary lizard."

"We have to shorten that," Charles said. "Lizard is too much. How about just Z?"

"What's up, Z?" Tracy said, striking a pose that I think was meant to be like a gang-bangin' gangsta. It was embarrassing. She looked like her spine was deformed.

"I like Zerd," I said.

"Too close to nerd," Charles added.

"Yeah, just like him." Tracy laughed, punching me in the arm where the tattoo was just starting to heal. It hurt like being slapped on sunburn. I yelped.

"Oh, my God, I'm so sorry," she said, laughing. She tilted her head and smiled, like a five-year-old trying to beg forgiveness by looking cute.

It worked. Completely.

"That's okay," I said, smiling.

"You two make me sick," Charles said.

We both gave him the finger. He gave us it back with both hands, one for each of us. Then he turned and used the spare one on his ass. We all found that damn funny.

* * *

I remember Steve showing me my own chair. It sat in the middle of my work area, a small cubicle easily visible from his workspace. The chair was an older version of his, the padding torn, the metal base rusting. It wasn't glamorous but I was psyched.

"I don't go for the you-be-my-bitch and do-stupid-errands apprentice shit," he said. "There's no point in a gifted artist doing stuff anyone can do."

Customers were given a ten percent discount since I was a rookie. Steve watched over me to make sure I didn't mess them up. He was a great teacher.

I remember him saying, "Once the ink gets in your blood you'll be addicted. I bet you're covered soon."

He was right. I would ink walk-ins and the smaller, less detailed one-color stuff, but slowly word spread. It was the only place I've ever felt like I wasn't a total fuck-up. I was earning money, doing something I enjoyed, working around cool people and grateful customers.

It was a fun place, too, part-hangout for Steve's local buddies and part-hotel for his friends drifting by. People came and went, sharing stories and sometimes drugs as they passed through. Most of them, I forget their names.

Lots of people got inked to remember a person or pet they loved. The sad smile on their faces afterwards squeezed my heart so hard I often had to fight back tears. This big dude once rubbed his eyes red as he sat there looking at the picture of a husky I'd just inked on him. He finally gurgled, "I'm the living memorial for you now, buddy."

I liked the idea. Why not make my body tell my own story? That's where I got the tattoo of the hanging woman. Carved into the tree she hung from were the words, "Good luck, Son! Love, Mother."

It was a fitting tribute to Mom but after that I went back to inking myself with whatever looked cool without any reason. Some things I wanted to forget, and what kind of freak would want to know my story anyway?

* * *

While working the tattoo place, I was up to three friends, the most I would ever have: Steve, Tracy and Charles.

Charles was my social connection. He was always getting invited to parties and he brought me and Tracy along as his entourage. He had such an easy manner, everyone liked him. He wasn't so fruity that guys avoided him and he wasn't interested in having sex with girls, so they liked him too.

He would start the party by immediately lighting up a cigarette, or if we had it, a joint. Tracy and I would chill by ourselves and get drunk or stoned and talk. Charles would check in with us every so often and discuss the guys who were pretending to be straight that he thought he could score with.

We went to countless parties, but one sticks out, a low-key event where the lights were off and we watched a dumb horror movie while passing around a bong.

Sometimes pot just gave me a headache. Most of the time, it made me think everything was hilarious. Every once in a while, I felt exactly what the hippies were talking about, that I was connected to the universe and we were all part of one people, one tribe, one love.

I was stoned in that hippie sense, enjoying my place in the universe when suddenly Tracy said, "I love you, too."

I looked around, believing it was her who spoke, but in my baked stupor, not quite sure. "I didn't say anything," I said.

"I know you didn't," she laughed, leaning into me. "But I can read your mind."

"Oh, yeah? Well, what am I thinking now?"

"You're thinking that I can't read your mind," she cracked up.

"You think so?"

"Am I right?"

"About what? Reading my mind or do I love you?"

She slipped her hand around the back of my head and mashed our faces together in a kiss. Her warm tongue flicked inside my mouth and I welcomed it.

She stood up without a word and lifted me from the couch by my hand, leading me outside. A few guys were on the porch snorting coke. They watched us suspiciously as Tracy pulled me into the woods behind the house. We crashed through the growth until the porch was a distant light in the darkness. I could barely see.

"I hope there's no poison ivy around here," I said.

"There isn't," Tracy whispered. "The goddess will protect those who honor her with love."

"Um… Okay."

"You've got a beautiful soul, Zerd."

"I do?"

She tore off my shirt and ran her finger over the lines of my ink. When her nails passed over the drawings, the lines burned like new. I pulled off her shirt clumsily. I wanted her so badly but I didn't know what the hell I was doing. She laughed warmly.

"You're new to this, aren't you?"

"A little."

"A lot," she smiled.

"Here," I said. I took her hand and pressed it against the back of mine so her fingers could operate my fingers. "Guide my hand."

She grinned, the corners of her eyes curving upward devilishly. She slid both our hands down her belly, under her jeans to curve underneath her pelvis, and into her warm, wet flesh. Together we pressed our fingers inside her. She moaned, her fingertips rolling against mine, tracing a circle, stroking up and down, helping me press across the nub of flesh. Finally she shuddered and groaned, collapsing onto me, clutching with her free hand so she wouldn't fall. I kissed her neck as she stood there shaking, twitching.

Then she dropped to her knees and began tearing at my zipper.

"Fuck me," she commanded. "Now. Make love to me."

My cock snapped out of my pants and she grabbed it and began to suck. I stared up to the darkened sky, feeling like I could fly up to touch the moon. When she stopped it felt like pain. She was taking off her pants.

She pulled me down on top of her, grabbed my penis and shoved it inside her. She pulled on my ass, making my cock glide inside her as deeply as I could go. She pushed me back until I was almost out again, then pulled me in.

"Like that," she said.

The animal part of my brain took over from there. I was following my instincts. I pumped her harder and harder as she clawed my back, banged her fists against my shoulders, wrapped her legs around my waist.

When I came, I lost complete control of my body, the strength vanished from my arms and I blacked out, collapsing on top of her.

I stayed inside her, kissing her while we both laughed. Finally I rolled off and out of her to lie on my back. She rolled on her side and stroked my chest, again tracing the drawings on my skin with her fingernail. I stroked her hair as a cool night wind blew over both of us, softly rattling tree branches in the dark.

I know when I first started recalling what I could about my life, I said I would remember the good and bad times because they make up the whole of my history. When I think about that night, lying in the breeze in the near blackness with the most wonderful woman in the world, I have to reconsider. Why am I bothering to relive any part of my life other than that moment?

JAMIL

UNKNOWN LOCATION

2003

First pain, now sound.

The beatings had stopped, but the freezing container and its inane pop songs were Jamil's new regimen of agony. In an effort to cling to his sanity, he tried to comprehend the whispering Arabic voice, but he never could make out the words.

Back in his cell, he rubbed the cold from his body as the song echoed in his head. He pressed his palms against his temples, banging the sides of his skull. He threw himself on the floor and started doing pushups. Extreme exercise sometimes banished the tune.

As he collapsed, gasping for air, he looked under his cot where streaks of paint ran down. The latex had dripped and formed a tiny pool barely the width of two fingers where the wall met the floor. It was a detail he had noted countless times.

The glob was peeling from the floor as the days dragged on. Jamil rolled under his cot and began picking at the lump.

"Sloppy work is unacceptable," his uncle once said. He tried to remember where, when or why, but couldn't. All he could recall was the phrase. What did his uncle look like? He searched through the darkness of his memory, unable to visualize any details. He scratched at the paint bead in frustration.

The lights dimmed, signifying bed time.

Jamil kept tearing loose chunks of dried paint the size of his pinky fingernail. He fell into the same obsessive trance that overtook him when picking at a scab.

Suddenly a smudge of light appeared on the floor. Beneath the paint, the brick was aligned poorly and he could see into another room. The light winked off for a second, then returned. His heart leapt with such excitement he was ashamed of himself. Is this what I am reduced to? He wondered. Was this that much of a thrill?

With the paint cleared away, Jamil could hear footsteps. Then he was certain he heard music. Someone was whistling! The torture song from the container assaulted his mind again, but Jamil was too excited to care. He was grateful for the unfamiliar melody, relishing something new for his mind to toy with.

He pressed his cheek closer to the hole, so he could see the light from the corner of his eye and catch any sounds on the edge of his ear.

Jamil listened to the melody. Once he grasped it, he whistled it back. For a moment they were whistling together. The other person's whistling stopped. Jamil stopped also.

The stranger whistled five distinct notes.

Jamil echoed it as best he could.

A bolt of terror shot through him. What if this was a guard station? Or Mikhail's office?

The pacing footsteps stopped. The light from the hole darkened, then brightened again. He heard the creak of someone sitting on a cot.

Across the darkness, an eye appeared. Someone was looking back at him! Jamil lifted his lips to the hole.

"Salaam," he whispered. He waited. The tune from the container bounced around in his head, competing with his throbbing heart. He held his breath.

"Salaam," he heard, whispered back.

He burst into tears, yelling in Arabic, "Salaam! How are you? Good day to you!"

"Sh!" the other voice commanded. "Quiet!"

"Yes," Jamil said. "Hello. What is your name?"

For a long time there was no reply.

"Please," Jamil said, barely able to breathe. "Your name?"

"My name?" the voice whispered back.

"Yes! What is your name?" Jamil could barely control the volume of his voice. His heart skipped with joy. Someone to speak with! Someone who did not command him! He wiped tears from his eyes as the song they had tortured him with dissolved, its melody fading away.

"My name?" the stranger whispered. "What is your name?"

Jamil hesitated. "Ah. You don't have to tell me your real name."

"Call me Prasad. You should make up a name as well."

"Call me Mohammed. Mo for short." Jamil hated using the name of one of his kidnappers, but he could think of no name more common.

"Mo. How are you?"

"I am all right."

Jamil never knew conversation could bring so much pleasure.

"There are many things I want to ask you, Prasad," he whispered. "What is this place? Where are we? How can we get out?"

"We can't. They believe we are terrorists."

"But I haven't done anything. I've never killed anyone in my life."

"Neither have I, but it does not matter. They want their paychecks."

"Has Mikhail interrogated you also?"

Prasad snorted. "Mikhail? No. My tormentor is a man named Carlson. I have never seen his face. He stands behind me like a coward. Likely, he is the same man."

"How can we convince him we are innocent?"

"Mo, if I knew that, I would not be here. They do not want to believe us."

"How did they capture you?"

"You ask a lot of questions, Mo."

"Because I don't know what's happening. I just want to go home."

"Be careful when you ask questions and who you give answers to."

Jamil thought about that, but if Prasad was an informant, would he have alerted him? Another comment from his uncle came to him: "Thieves disguise themselves by warning you about thieves."

Jamil felt his raw enthusiasm giving way to itchy paranoia. "At least tell me one thing, Prasad. What happened in America? It must have been a year ago. Maybe two? What do they blame us for? What started this?"

"You don't know? Do not joke of it."

"I'm not joking. I know there was an attack. Many people in America died, but I know nothing more."

"If you are telling the truth, you are likely the only person on the planet who does not know."

"Tell me, please."

"In America, planes were hijacked and crashed into skyscrapers. Their president, son of a dog that he is, swore they would find the culprits, that they would launch a crusade. Naturally, we Muslims were sensitive to that word. The Americans offered rewards for terrorists. Innocents like us were turned in by jackals who simply wanted to collect the bounty."

"They ruined our lives just for money?"

"And why else? The Americans are hungry to catch who arranged the attack. Failing that, they are eager to punish someone as proof they are in pursuit. We are caught in a great wave, Mo, swept along by the merciless current of history. Can you tell I was a writer?" Prasad laughed.

Jamil thought about this. "How will I know anything you say is true?"

"You won't. The only truth you know is what's before you."

"You are right, Prasad. You are a wise man."

"How do you even know I'm a man?"

They shared an uneasy laugh.

"Mo," Prasad said, "I am sorry, but I am very tired. I must go to sleep."

"Wait! Wait. Can we talk again?"

"Tomorrow. When the lights dim. If you keep your voice down."

"I will," Jamil whispered. "I promise. Please come back. You will, won't you?"

"I will. Tomorrow night. For now, take your rest."

"Good night, Prasad."

"Good night, Mo."

Jamil ran his finger across the crack where the wall met the floor. He watched the tiny smudge of light return while he listened for the gentle creak of Prasad reclining on his cot.

Jamil couldn't sleep. He paced the room in the near darkness, skipping sometimes, laughing and clapping quietly.

* * *

Jamil knew he should be concerned that they were not taking him to the freezing container. Whatever they were planning would cause him pain, but for an instant, he didn't care. He was simply glad he wouldn't have to hear the song again.

He was led to the familiar interrogation room and bound to a chair, facing the blank wall and two masked armed guards. Mikhail spoke from behind him. "Jamil, you are wasting my time, so I need to increase the intensity of our meetings."

Jamil replied quickly. "I am innocent. I have done nothing. There is no evidence against me." He had spoken that same phrase so many times he was almost as tired of hearing it as he was the accursed song.

"Then why are you here? If you are innocent, why were you brought to me?"

A man appeared to Jamil's side. Like all his captors, his face was covered with a black ski mask. Wearing rubber gloves, he flicked a needle, spraying clear drops. Jamil recoiled as best he could while bound.

"Hold still," Mikhail advised from behind him. "If you move, the needle may break in your arm."

"What is it?"

"Something to help you relax."

Jamil held still and looked away, feeling the pinch in his flesh. The masked doctor held a pen light up to Jamil's eyes.

When the light moved away, it left a trail in the air. Jamil felt sleepy, delirious. He slumped in the chair, leaning to the side so much he felt as though he would fall, but somehow the chair didn't tip. At the same time, he felt weightless, as if he were a floating balloon tied down.

"So, Jamil," Mikhail said, "how are you feeling?"

Jamil opened and closed his mouth several times, trying to speak, but no words came out.

"Are you comfortable?"

Someone was tapping his shoulder.

"Mister Jamil, are you in there?"

Jamil stared at the wall. Someone was calling him.

"Jamil?" A gloveless hand waved in front of his eyes. Was it Mikhail's hand? If it was, that was the first time he had ever seen any part of Mikhail that wasn't covered.

"Can you hear me?"

Why bother answering? They'll just torture me, Jamil thought. A ripple of warmth rolled down to his toes.

"Jamil!" Mikhail barked.

A part of him did want to answer, but he couldn't gather the drive to do it. He just kept staring forward.

Mikhail smacked him across the back of the skull. Jamil's head rolled to the side. He felt a pounding in his scalp, as blood rushed to where he was hit. The throbbing felt like someone was massaging his head with a gentle rhythm.

"Do you want to go home?" Mikhail asked.

His body betrayed him. At the word 'home' he straightened up, a misbehaving schoolboy righting his posture.

"Yesssss," Jamil said, involuntarily drawing out the word.

"About your uncle. You said he was a mechanic. Did he ever discuss wiring vehicles to explode?"

"No. Garage. Repair," Jamil said, sounding unfamiliar to himself. "Change tires. Change oil."

"Did your uncle ever mention secret jobs? Ones that only he could work on?"

"No. We did. Everything. Together."

"Did he ever show you how to sabotage automobiles? Say, disable the brakes?"

"Nooooo."

"Did he have a Koran in his office?"

"Yesssss."

"Did he have one in his home?"

"What? One whaaaaa?"

"A Koran. The Muslim holy book. Did he have one in his home?"

"I think sooooo."

"Did he ever quote the Koran? Say that Allah wanted you to kill Westerners?"

"Nooooo. Be good. Person. He. Said there. Nothing more. Life simple."

"Did men ever show up with a delivery that he would not let you see?"

"Nooooo."

Jamil tilted his head. He noticed the sound of his skin on the orange outfit, the rustle of the shifting guards before him. His sense of time was slowed but his sense of hearing was sharper.

Someone whispered, "I'll give him some more. It's not working."

Mikhail's reply was testy. "If you give him more he'll fall asleep."

"Then what do you want me to do?"

"Do they want results, or fabrications? We have to proceed gently."

"They won't want to hear that."

"He's gone. Untie him," Mikhail said.

Jamil passed out.

* * *

Jamil was pushed into his cell and the hood yanked from his head. He stood in the middle of the tiny room, swaying and giggling, tears pouring down his cheeks. The walls wavered like ripples on a pond.

He stood that way until the lights dimmed. Carefully, he lowered himself to the floor. With much effort and grunting, he slid underneath his cot, placing his lips to the hole where the wall met the floor.

"Mister Prasad?" he said. "Oh, Mister Prasad? Are you there?"

"Yes, I'm here, but you agreed to be quiet. Stop yelling."

"I'm sorry. They gave me some drugs. I am very confused."

"Drink all of the liquid they give you. That will flush out the poison."

"Are you a doctor?" Jamil laughed.

"I told you, I am a writer. That's all you need to know."

"What did you write?"

"Mo, let's talk about something else. Stop acting like a child."

"But I am a child. Only sixteen. I think. When I came here. Hard to track time. How old are you?"

"You're a boy? And they kidnapped you? They torture you like a man?"

Jamil started to reply, but he was too slow. He giggled.

"Death to them," Prasad hissed. "Torturing children. The savages."

"Let's play chess," Jamil slurred.

"Now where would I get a chess set?"

"I made one. Asked for books. They gave me. Bible and Koran. And a crayon. I tore pages out. Out of the Bible. Made a chess set."

Prasad chuckled.

"Am I clever?" Jamil grinned.

"You did not do the same with the Koran, did you?"

"Of course not."

"Smart boy," Prasad said. "The Koran is a book of love and peace. The Bible advocates violence. It is disgusting. No wonder Westerners are so cruel. You may be the first person in history to make something positive from that vile book."

"I want to play chess. You ask, too."

"If I do that, they'll know we've talked. It will make them suspicious."

"You're a writer. Ask for pad and pen."

Prasad was slow to reply. "You are a smart boy, Mohammed. Mo?"

Jamil was asleep, snoring loudly.

* * *

Mikhail didn't send for him the next day, so Jamil entertained himself by playing several games of chess as both sides. In between, he jogged to sweat the lingering drugs from his body. His motor skills returned, but a headache stayed with him all day.

When the lights darkened, he crawled under his cot.

"You are brilliant," Prasad said. "Your plan worked!"

"Did you enjoy destroying the Bible?"

"I would have, but I only requested a pad and the crayon. Besides, I am obviously not a Christian because I am compassionate," he laughed bitterly.

"Did you make your board?"

"You are so eager to lose?"

For hours they whispered moves to each other, complimenting and taunting one another. Prasad won several games to Jamil's two, but

Jamil didn't care. It was thrilling to interact with another person in a friendly way.

They played until the lights brightened.

"How do we preserve the game?" Prasad whispered.

"I press mine inside my Bible. The real art is opening the book while leaving the pieces in place." Jamil said. "I will also have the board. So don't try to cheat!"

"I will do the same with my pad. You are shrewd, Mohammed."

Each night, if the day's torture had not worn one of them down, they played chess. Prasad continued to deflect any questions about his personal life. If it was his turn he would say, "Don't distract me." If Jamil asked something during his move, Prasad would say, "Just take your turn."

Jamil gave up asking. He didn't care anyway. He was glad he had someone to speak to. He found himself smiling. He hadn't casually smiled in as long as he could remember. When it happened, he closed his eyes and savored the feeling.

* * *

"Come on," Jamil whispered impatiently, staring up at the fluorescent lights behind the reinforced plastic. He was waiting for them to dim. The moment they did, he rolled off his cot and slid under it in one fluid movement. He gently opened his Bible and noted the chess board situation.

He coughed into the small crevice. A signal: are you there?

Prasad coughed back: I am here.

"Good evening, Mister Prasad."

"Good evening, Mister Mohammed."

"Are you ready to continue our game?" Jamil asked.

"In a moment. I have a question for you. Sometimes during the day, I hear sounds, an irregular thumping, do you know what that is?"

"That's me. I'm punching the wall."

"Punching the wall?"

"I practice boxing. I hit the wall to toughen up my fists, so should I ever get the chance to strike our captors, they will be sure to feel it." He punched the wall. "Is that what you hear?"

"Yes. Interesting. You must be strong."

"It's exercise, that's all," Jamil said, blushing from the compliment. "How do you pass the hours?"

"How do I pass the days and years?" Prasad said. "I think. I think of the books I used to read. I think of my children."

Jamil held his breath. Prasad had never before revealed so much.

"It's a balance," Prasad continued. "You must remember enough to keep your spirit strong, but you don't want to despair from missing them."

"How do you keep the memories? I can't remember much anymore unless it comes to me in a dream. And then it never returns."

"I'm a thinker. I suppose it comes naturally to me, but do not be so sad to forget. Wars carry on for centuries because people remember what was done to them, always living in the past. If they could just all forget one night, the world might be better. If we could forget the day before, our confinement here would not be so bad."

Jamil thought about this. "But it is said that if one forgets the past, he will surely repeat it. So how do you only forget that which causes you pain, but not that which causes you to avoid mistakes you've already made?"

Prasad laughed. "Well said, young man! Intelligence and athletic ability are a rare combination. What other talents do you have?"

Jamil hesitated. Why was Prasad suddenly interested in him? Was it wise to tell him more or was he being paranoid?

"The noise of my boxing," Jamil said. "Does it bother you?"

Prasad laughed. "Don't mind me. I am much happier knowing it is you boxing rather than some poor fellow getting his head smashed against the wall. Like they did to me early on."

Jamil thought of Prasad as an elderly man. He envisioned thugs ramming his tiny body against the wall. He raised his voice. "Someday, Prasad, I am going to kill them. I will clench my fists around their throats. Mikhail will not be so smug when I am cutting off his breath."

Jamil surprised himself, speaking that way. Prasad didn't respond for a long time.

"Prasad?" he asked. "Prasad? Are you still there?"

Prasad's voice quivered. "Curse them for what they have done to you," he said. "To fill an innocent boy with such anger." He was quiet a long time. "What was the man's name? The one who interrogates you?"

"Mikhail."

"We are a boy and a teacher," Prasad went on. "They have no reason to fear us, but they must pretend that they do. Otherwise, those who pay them would not feel they were interrogating terrorists. So much our captors do is for show."

"They ask us to convince them of our innocence, while they are constantly convincing themselves of our guilt," Jamil said.

"Well said again, my boy."

"Can you teach me?"

"Teach you?"

"You said you were a teacher."

"Well, I-"

"And before that, you said you were a writer."

Prasad was silent a long time. "I am both. I write textbooks."

"Then I could learn something. What are your textbooks about? What subject?"

"Discussion is the best method of teaching. Let's stick with that. Your turn."

Jamil frowned at the terse end to the conversation. He looked down on his makeshift chessboard and contemplated his next move.

* * *

Jamil never asked Prasad to teach him again. Night after night all they did was play chess and exchange small talk until it seemed that was all they had ever done.

"Checkmate," Jamil said.

"Excellent move, Mo!" Prasad cried. "You've won again. You are getting better. How many wins does that make for you?"

"I don't keep track. You told me not to track things. It makes you obsessed with the past. I think that was a wise decision."

Prasad didn't reply.

"Prasad?"

"You sound so much like my son," he said, his voice stuttering as if he were resisting the urge to cry.

Jamil frowned, resetting the chessboard, unsure how to reply.

"You play chess like him, too, " Prasad continued. "He is aggressive while I focus on defense. A lesson for life. Offense wins, defense merely holds."

"But you win more than I, that much I know."

"You are humble, too," Prasad choked. "Like him."

Jamil did not know what to say.

"He would be twenty this week."

"How do you know how old he would be if you don't track the days?"

Prasad didn't answer.

"You told me it was sometimes wise to forget things, so I assumed you didn't count. I always thought that would cause me pain each time I looked at the growing total. Are you counting them?"

"Oh, I am just guessing."

Jamil paused, certain Prasad was lying. "How old was he when you last saw him?"

"I last saw him at school. He was being honored for high marks. He was a candidate for a scholarship. His mother…and I…"

Prasad let out a tiny wail that choked off.

"Prasad, are you all right?"

When Prasad spoke again, his voice gurgled through tears. "His mother and sisters were so beautiful, so proud. We cheered when they called his name. That's my boy, I yelled. My boy! Stay true to your heart, I told him. Never lie and things will be all right. Work hard and everything will work out. What a fool I was."

Prasad was raising his voice. "What they have done to you, Mo, is what they have done to my son. To all men's sons. The Koran teaches that as one sins against any, one sins against all."

Jamil was crying. He wanted to comfort his friend with an embrace. He pounded the wall with his fist. "What they have done to you, Prasad, is the same as if they had done it to my father or my uncle. All fathers and uncles." Jamil felt his chest tighten. He imagined his father returning to Morocco, learning his son had vanished. Would he cry like Prasad?

"I can't continue, Mo," Prasad said. "I'm sorry." His thin sobbing penetrated the wall.

"It's all right, Prasad. I will stay here. I won't say a word. Just know I'm here."

"Thank you," Prasad stammered. Jamil closed his Bible on the chessboard and slid back onto his cot. Even away from the thin hole in the wall, he could hear Prasad choking and wailing.

"You must convince me all on your own," Mikhail's repeated command rang across Jamil's memory.

Listen to my friend cry, Jamil screamed inside his head. How can that sound not persuade you? Can you ignore the suffering of this gentle man?

Jamil closed his eyes as tightly as he could, but the tears burst through. He banged his fists at his sides, punching down on the cot until he fell asleep.

ZERD

USA

2004

Home totally changed after Dad got fired.

When Mom was around, evenings were noisy fun. After she left, the house was depressing, quiet and stale.

I hung out at the tattoo shop as much as I could. I think Steve grew to like me because I would do any shit job without bitching. Collect the trash? Sweep the floor? Clean the toilets? No problem.

No matter how late I came home, Dad would be sitting in the dark watching his news and opinion shows. We barely spoke.

I knew him in only one of two ways: asleep drunk or awake silent.

That's why I jumped out of my seat the night he screamed.

"Dad?" I called out. My heart was pounding. Instantly, I had a vicious headache.

He was yelling, "What the holy fuck!"

Smash! Something glass broke.

"You total asshole! Bastard! Prick!"

Crash! It sounded like furniture was tipped over.

"Crazy criminal murderer predator son of a whore!"

He sounded like he was fighting for his life. I grabbed the closest thing to a weapon I could find, which happened to be a screwdriver. I charged to the top of the stairs, ready to rumble.

Down in the living room, Dad was hurling stuff at the wall. The TV cabinet was covered with broken glass, beer, shattered plant pots and dirt. His lounge chair was on its side.

The blue glow from the television made him look sickly thin. He hadn't shaved in days. With just his boxers on he looked like a mental patient off his meds.

"Dad, what's wrong?" I said.

By then he was spitting animal noises. He had totally lost his shit.

"Dad!" I yelled. "What the fuck?"

He looked up. I couldn't see his eyes through the TV's reflection on his glasses. He pointed at me with a shaking finger.

"Son, come here."

I hesitated.

"Now," he said. "Your survival depends on it."

I descended the steps, but kept a firm grip on my screwdriver. My hand was shaking. Downstairs, I stayed out of his reach.

"What day is it?" he asked.

"What?"

"I said what fucking day is it?" he yelled, still staring at the television. The screen was paused, showing people in tuxedos at a dinner.

"I don't know!" I yelled back.

He dove into the stack of newspapers he kept near the couch, pulled a front page out and shook it before me.

"March twenty-four. Two thousand-four," he said. "The day America was officially taken over. The day the president had his 'let them eat cake' moment."

There's very few things I remember, so it's a big deal I can recall March 24, 2004.

"Watch this," he said. He pushed play.

The president was speaking in a ballroom decorated with lots of crystal and thick golden drapes. He smirked at a picture of himself peeking under a desk. He said to the crowd, "Those weapons of mass destruction must be here somewhere, maybe under here." The crowd laughed.

Dad stopped the video and screamed at the ceiling like he was in an operatic tragedy or something.

"Oh, my fucking God!"

I had heard him angry before, but never like this. Not even when he was calling around trying to find out where Mom went.

"What a dick," I said, giving him the response he wanted. I hoped.

"That man," Dad said, holding a trembling fist at the screen, "sent kids your age to die. He told them they were looking for weapons of mass destruction, but that turned out to be a lie. Now he makes a joke of it! A fucking joke! Children died so his criminal family could make money and he makes a joke!"

I had heard it all before, just not at that volume. "Can I go back to bed now?" I asked.

"No."

He grabbed my shoulders with both hands and looked me in the eye. He spoke loudly, like a preacher healing someone, blasting me with the scent of booze.

"Son," he said, "I would rather you did anything but join the military. No matter what you have to do to survive, do it. Be a bank robber. A thief. Do whatever you have to but never ever join the armed forces, ever! You're just a disposable pawn to them. Your life means nothing to those animals."

"Okay, Dad, I won't."

"I want you to swear. I would rather that you dealt the hardest drugs imaginable, got arrested and spent your life in jail than you ever joined the military. War is far more destructive than drugs. Do you hear me?"

"Okay. Okay."

"You hear me? Never! Never ever join the military. Say it!"

"I heard you. I'll never join the military."

"Promise."

"I promise."

"Promise what?"

"Dad. Come on."

"Promise me!"

"I promise I will never join the military. I will deal drugs instead. I will steal. I will go to jail. Whatever it takes to survive I will do, except join the armed forces. Can I go to bed now?"

He relaxed his hold.

He turned back to the TV. "No son of mine is going to feed the military-industrial complex."

Oh, Dad. If both of us only knew then how things would turn out. I like to think we would have laughed at our helplessness to resist the family curse of being a fuck-up.

He plopped back on the couch, energy spent, the living room a ruin all around him. I started to clean up.

"Leave it," he said.

"Fine."

I stomped back to my bedroom. Only then did I realize I was still gripping the screwdriver. When I let it go, my fingers ached and my palm was indented with grooves from the handle.

* * *

I don't know why I was still attending high school back then. I hated it and no one was making me go. Plus, there was this asshole who shoved me whenever he saw me.

"Hey, freak, got enough tattoos?" he'd ask, laughing.

I guess I wanted to get some kind of revenge before I took off. His name was Brent but I only knew that because it was written on his football jacket, which he always wore, even in summer. The guy was a living cliché.

During a slow night at the tattoo shop, I mentioned school to Steve while he was inking up another biker guy made of leather, denim, hair and muscle like him.

"You're still going to school? Why? You've got a job here," Steve said, laughing. "Get a G.E.D. and be done with it. Any fucktard can pass it. Hell, I did."

"I want to go out with style," I said. "There's this one asshole, and I want to slash his tires or something before I go."

"Shoot him," the biker said.

"I want to piss him off."

"Call him an asshole, then shoot him."

Steve leaned back, cigarette dangling from his mouth.

"Oh, shit," the biker said, "Preacher Steve's got something to say."

"My Dad was a professor," I said. "I'm used to boring lectures."

Steve flipped us both the finger while pretending to scratch his cheek.

"It's obvious," he said. "You need to fight this guy. Then you can leave school. If you lose, you're gone. If you win, you're gone. You don't get in trouble, you don't get embarrassed. You win either way."

I was concerned that his comment made sense to me.

"I'd prefer to win," I said.

"Sure," Steve said, "but remember, most people don't realize fighting hurts. Even the winner walks away hurting. If he wins right he's not going to be hurt as much as the other guy, but he's still going to feel pain. You have to expect that."

"Got it."

"You've got an advantage, though. You're an ink-fiend, pain is an old friend."

"True."

"The second thing you have to do is stay calm."

"Calm? When I'm fighting?" I laughed.

"I say he freaks out," the biker said.

"No. That's bullshit. Gotta stay calm. Check this out."

He made two fists and showed us the tops of them. Learning to ink from him, I always noticed the writing on his left hand when he held the needle. Words curled from the first knuckle of his index finger across the webbing leading to his thumb. They read "Expect pain." I always thought it was a joke for the people he was inking. I never noticed the scripted letters in the same style on his right hand in the same place. They read "Stay calm."

He stood up in a boxing stance and glanced down at his fists. "No matter how drunk I get, the rules for winning a fight are always right in front of me."

I mimicked his stance. Reading left to right, expect pain, stay calm. It sounded good to me.

* * *

I wanted to try out Steve's advice. Like he said, if I won, no problem. If I lost, I'd never go back to school anyway. Most of all I wanted to pummel someone. Pent-up rage over Mom leaving and Dad losing it needed to be vented, and who better to send it all to than a complete asshole?

Brent found me, as usual. I swear he followed me around.

"Hey, freak! Get any tattoos?" he asked while his friends snickered behind him.

This time I spoke up. "Dude, why are you so gay for me?"

His friends thought that was funny. Brent's face turned red. "After school!"

"Now you're asking me on a date."

He shoved me into the lockers. A lock smashed into my hip. I could feel the bruise forming.

I shoved him back. "Right now."

"No, man, the teachers are around."

"Fucking pussy," I said. I swung at him and caught him in the jaw.

"Fuck you. And your mother!" He swung at me so fairy-like I wondered if maybe he really was a closeted gay.

"You can fuck my mother all you want," I told him. He looked confused at that response. So I belted him again, and again, and then, all the rage came out. I jumped on him, knocked him down and pounded away, left right left right, on his head. He threw his hands over his face and I just punched right on top of them.

"Fight! Fight! Fight!" everyone started chanting. A circle formed around us.

Steve was right. My fists hurt like hell. The "expect pain" part was on the money. Being ready for it helped. The "stay calm" part? That I didn't do so well. I kept punching until Brent was crying behind his busted fingers.

"Sto-o-o-p! P-uh-uh-leese!"

At some point, the teachers pushed through the circle around us, and pulled me off. They helped poor bloody Brent sit up. He was crying, just bawling, wailing out loud like a baby in the mall. My hands were covered with his blood and mine.

The teachers grabbed me, one on each arm and led me away. I didn't struggle. As we turned down the halls, heading for the principal's office, they relaxed their grips. When we passed a door to the outside, I snapped my arms loose and bolted.

"Come back!" they yelled.

That was the end of my high school career.

* * *

I felt pretty good about my explosive exit from high school until I saw I was banged-up in the reflection of the tattoo shop's door. I crept inside, trying not to ring the bell tied to the handle.

Steve was tattooing yet another biker. The guy's girlfriend sat on a stool, paging through one of the flash books.

I tried to sneak by, but for some reason that never works. Steve sat up and wiped the sweat from his forehead. "What the fuck?"

I stepped back. "I got in a fight."

The guy in the chair looked up, observing me in the full-length mirror before him. He nodded his approval.

"Blood makes the best ink," the biker said. "And the other guy?"

"Last I saw him, he was on the floor crying."

He raised his fist. "Fuckin' A."

Steve leaned into his work again. "All right, tough guy. You can tell us later. She needs a tattoo." He flicked his hand toward the biker's girlfriend.

She followed me to my space silently. "Sorry, I ran into some trouble," I said as I was getting ready. She didn't say anything, just looked at me like I was shit. Every part of my body was aching. I tried to redraw the ankh she wanted onto tracing paper, but my fingers were swollen and I couldn't grab the pencil.

I wrapped some masking tape around it and tried again, but it looked awful.

The bitch slapped her thighs. "I'll wait."

"I'm fine," I said. "I just… shit!" I dropped the pencil and it rolled off my desk.

She stood up and left.

I sat there shaking my fat fingers, trying to pick up the damn pencil. Even with the tape around it, I couldn't. Funny thing about me. I always find the fuck-up angle. I had just scored a victory, kicking the crap out of some douche and quitting school all in the same exciting day.

Now things were getting back to normal, which for me meant back to stupid.

I knew what was coming so I waited for it to come to me. After some tense whispering, Steve came around the barrier between our workspaces.

"What the fuck?"

"My hands are swollen from punching the shit out of that guy. I can't draw."

"You dumbass. She's been waiting an hour. If you can't do your job, go home. And I'm not paying you."

The biker customer yelled from the other chair.

"Steve, leave the kid alone. Get in here. Both of you."

I followed Steve. I had no idea what was going to happen. I was thinking, if this guy talks to Steve like that he's going to make it worse on me. Hell, he might make things rough on himself.

We stood in Steve's cramped cubicle. The big customer leaned forward in the chair, a skull with a crown of snakes half-drawn on his shoulder.

"So the kid got in a fight," he said to Steve. "She can get ink anytime. She was going to deliver the package after, but if you're just sending him home, maybe I'll have the kid do it. I don't like her going there."

Steve slowly shook his head no.

"Come on," the guy said. "You were just talking about how much you like the kid, now you're giving him shit."

Steve was talking about how much he liked me? That was cool, but he still looked angry. "Don't talk to me about my business," he said to his friend, "or I'll tattoo 'I'm a homo' on your ass."

The big customer guy looked to me. "Well, kid? Want to earn some bucks and make up for ruining Steve's entire pathetic life?" He winked. "I need a package delivered. Take it where I tell you and the guy there will give you some money. Bring the money back here. Simple."

"You asshole," Steve said to the big guy.

"The name's Butch," he said.

We shook hands. I ground my teeth when he squeezed my fingers so I wouldn't cry out.

Butch's girlfriend reached in her purse and pulled out the package, a plastic shopping bag wrapped around a small box. The bag was rubber-banded tightly to form a small brick about as big as my swollen hand.

* * *

That's how I became a drug courier.

"Take the package to that address," Butch said. "Pick up the money and come back. It's the easiest cash you'll ever make." I barely listened. I was repeating the address in my head since he wouldn't let me write it down.

I hid the bag in my trunk, under all the tools and crap. I drove a couple miles, pulled into the back of a mall parking lot and popped the hood so it would look like I was adding some oil. I dug around in the trunk and opened the plastic bag.

I almost choked.

Inside was a plastic case containing tiny clear bags of white powder, some joints, and several crystals. A buffet of drugs. If I got caught with all that, I would be in serious trouble and probably do some serious jail time. I quickly re-sealed the bag and hid it under my stuff again.

I thought about swiping some drugs for myself. If I took a tiny bit from that huge collection, Butch's pals would never notice. That would save Charles, Tracy and me some money. Maybe I could even sell some. I was at least smart enough not to do it the first time. I had to establish trust before planning a big score.

The drop-off was in a crappy part of town getting on towards the city. Paint was peeling off the houses, cars were torn up in people's front yards, and the porches sagged. Graffiti was everywhere and small clusters of dudes hung out on the corners, watching me as I drove past. No one wanted to be there, but they were still ready to shoot me if I stepped on their turf.

The house I was looking for seemed abandoned. First, I made sure no one was walking by on my side of the street. No one seemed to have followed me. I'd never done this before, but everything seemed clear. My heart was racing. Then I popped the trunk from inside the car, leapt out, grabbed the bundle, slammed the trunk closed and took the stairs to the door two at a time.

The cement steps were seriously cracked. Weeds brushed my shins. The wooden porch was speckled black with mold, the planks bowed and peeling.

I knocked on the door. Almost immediately, it opened a crack, a security chain taut across the gap.

"Who are you?" the slice-of-face asked, its eyes hidden behind sunglasses.

"Butch told me to bring you this." I held the package in front of me.

"Why didn't he send his whore?"

"She's getting a tattoo. I work at the shop."

"What happened to your face?"

"I got in a fight."

"All right, shut up. I don't want your life story."

He let me in.

I stepped into a dark wooden hall covered with dust. Dude was junkie-thin with long hair, pale and bony, wearing only jeans. He was a hippie with more emphasis on drugs and less on peace and love. He stunk, too. I could guess how messed up and red his eyes were behind the shades.

It was evening but still bright outside. Inside, all the curtains were pulled and the windows closed. Smells from the other rooms worked their way past the hippie's body odor. Bleach, artificial lemon and the scent of something burning stung my nostrils.

Whatever they were making was hard-core. Books about growing mushrooms were stacked on the floor and in an open cabinet were several tools for getting drugs into a body: needles, screens, spoons, matches and more. All the options reminded me of art class.

The guy didn't even look at me. He snatched the package, set the cash on a low table and disappeared behind a bed sheet tacked up in a doorway. Beyond I could hear TV cartoons, the volume low.

"Um, is this for me?" I asked out loud. Someone in the other room laughed.

A woman's voice whispered. "Who is that asshole?"

"Some prick Butch sent."

"What about the whore?"

"I guess he's done with her."

"How the fuck does Butch know this new guy is all right?"

"Hell if I know."

"Why didn't he come himself?"

"He's scared shitless about violating his parole."

"What a pussy."

I took the money and left, leaving the door open just enough so that it might blow open and scare the piss out of them. I sprinted down to my car and drove back as fast as I could, slamming the brakes at every red light. My pulse pounded in my swollen fingers the whole way back.

* * *

Back at Steve's shop, Butch counted the wad of money. He peeled off a hundred and handed it to me.

"See, kid? Easy money." He punched Steve in the arm. "More than this asshole will pay you."

The goth girl was admiring her new ankh tramp-stamp in the mirror. Steve must have picked up my slack. When I came in she frowned. Skank.

They left quickly as Butch added, "Let's make this a regular thing."

"Fine with me," I said.

Steve grunted. We were alone. He flipped the sign in the window to show the shop was closed.

"Look," he said, "I know you're not stupid, so I realize I don't have to tell you to keep your mouth shut about this."

"No, you don't."

"Well, I'm telling you anyway. Keep your mouth shut."

"You got it."

"Butch is an old friend, so I let him and his girl do their thing while they're here, but I don't trust the guy."

I didn't say I didn't care as long as the money kept coming. Butch was right, it was the easiest cash I ever made. So I changed the subject.

"Sorry I got myself fucked up."

"Go home and put your hands in ice. If you don't, tomorrow you'll be sore as a whore at the Fuck Me Free store."

"Right home," I said. "No detours."

I felt bad about lying. I was actually going to pick up Tracy. I was still seeing her a couple nights a week. We'd drive around, find a secluded spot to smoke and fuck. It was a ritual I wasn't about to pass up, no matter how much my body ached.

* * *

One night, for no reason I can remember, I woke up. I just had a bad feeling that wouldn't go away. Something was wrong. I crept to Dad's bedroom and peeked in. He wasn't there, but that wasn't surprising. He usually fell asleep on the couch, but he wasn't there either.

The television was still on, coating the walls with flickering silver. I couldn't find him and both our cars were still in the driveway.

I turned to search the house again when through the window, I saw him sitting on the lawn, moon-bathing in nothing but his boxers.

"Dad!" I called out in a half-yell, half-whisper. "Dad! What the hell?"

His was facing away from me. He was rocking back and forth, knees up to his chin. He seemed to be whispering something. I crept up behind him, listening. When I got close, I could hear what he was saying.

"I'm going to kill them. I'm going to kill them. I'm going to kill them."

He kept saying it. His words slurred, but from the rage in his voice I knew he wasn't completely drunk.

I sat down next to him, the stiff, frosted grass poking my butt.

"Kill who?" I asked, as if we'd been talking all night.

"The president," he said casually. "And the vice president. Senator Hanson. All the bastards behind the Iraq War. Then I'll be done."

"Dad, come inside. It's freezing and you're almost naked."

"No, son, I'm going to do it."

"Dad."

"It's my duty as a patriotic American. Families are being destroyed. Children murdered. The most precious thing people have is their kids, but they're being sent to die so the president and his criminal friends like Senator Hanson can make money."

That's when he reached between his legs and pulled out the gun. An arc of moonlight raced down the barrel. I never even knew he owned one. With his political leanings, I always assumed he was against them.

"Dad!" The words just flew out of me. "Oh, my God, Dad. Put the gun down."

"But if I kill them, fewer people will die."

"Uh, you're probably right, but you said in your class that someone will always take their place."

I wasn't sure he was listening. He was admiring his gun.

"Dad, please."

"Can you imagine it?" he said. "Do you think some poor slob in Iraq gives a shit about freedom and democracy when he's holding the remains of his child? So he reacts naturally. Like we all would. And then we call those people terrorists."

"That's why I don't want you to do this. They'll take you away from me."

I guess I said the right thing by accident. He bowed his head, defeated. I saw him a little more clearly in that weird moment. In the most indirect way possible, he had admitted he loved me. Somewhere in his crazy mind, he did care more for me than the agenda he gave all his time to.

He put the gun down in the grass out of my reach. We sat there together for a long time, our tiny family, Dad, me and his gun.

"Let's go inside," I finally said. "You can always kill the president later."

He went in without another word.

I sat staring at the moon, alone with the gun and the night.

* * *

I lost count of how many times I ferried drugs between Steve's and the house. I would ink all day, grab the goods from Butch, make a delivery at night. Slipped into the back of my pants was Dad's gun. I had no idea how to use it, but the metal freezing my ass crack gave me confidence to visit the creepy hippie and his shit neighborhood. I was raking in the bucks according to my usual standards and life was good.

I don't make the rules for this pre-death, life-flash-review thing. If I did, I wouldn't remember what came next at all. I guess it goes back to prominence. When the water rises, only the highest peaks remain, it doesn't matter what's joyous or painful, just what was huge.

So, let's relive it quickly. Once was one time too many.

Steve and I were closing when a car pulled up to the shop, brakes squealing. Their lights were on high beam, filling the front of the store. I was in the back mopping.

"We're closed!" Steve yelled.

The headlights went out and I thought the problem was over. Then I heard a crash.

"What the fuck?" Steve yelled.

"Where is it?" an unfamiliar a voice bellowed back.

"Where's what?"

"The shit you shaved off the top."

"What the fuck are you talking about?"

Steve was yelling extra loud, I think as a way of warning me. I dialed the cops and set the phone down, off the hook. I didn't want to make any noise.

"I know you took some, motherfucker."

I slipped the gun out of my belt.

I heard a sickening smack, metal on meat.

"No one fucking hits me!" Steve roared.

"Give me the shit you stole! Now!"

"I don't know what you're talking about."

"Butch said the courier was here. Is there anyone else here?"

"No. It's just me."

"Then you're the one who's got to pay."

Gunshots are loud. Really fucking loud, but they don't sound nearly as bad as the body of your best friend hitting the floor.

"Go! Go!" the killer screamed, his voice trailing into the night. Tires squealed and the shop was quiet.

I tiptoed out to the front of the store.

Steve's massive body was curled up on the floor, his chest rising and falling mechanically.

I pressed a towel against the holes in his body, but it was soaked in seconds. I found another towel. Same thing. Blood started to ooze from his mouth. His eyelids fluttered. I sat down on the worn rug and held his hand. His body twitched.

"I love you, man. I really love you," I said, through a wet fog.

I lifted his hand up and kissed it. He was still warm. My lips smeared off some of his blood, revealing the tattoo at the top of his fist: Expect pain.

I felt a surge inside me, a massive strength building. It electrified my muscles and for an instant, I felt ten times stronger than I ever felt. I breathed in, caught my breath. It was exhilarating, terrifying. I never felt anything like it before. Then it was suddenly and silently gone.

I swear it was Steve passing through me as he left. I put my head on his still chest and a wail just came out of my mouth. I didn't put any thought or effort behind it, it came out all on its own and just kept going.

The flashing lights of the ambulance and the cops speared the front window. They charged into the shop, but I knew they were too late.

Being the fuck-up I am, it was all my fault.

After Butch started trusting me, I took a joint here and there. He never said anything. Then I started taking some coke. Charles loved that shit. Then I took some crystal and sold it at parties. The gun man, that fucking murderer, was right. Someone had been skimming off the top. Me. But they killed Steve for it.

I'm such an asshole.

There's something positive to be said for dying. I'll never again experience the memory of holding my dead friend's limp and bloody hand. I won't ever relive that surge of energy as his life dispersed into the universe. I won't ever again see the face of my best friend spattered with his own blood.

Thank every fucking god for that.

* * *

Dad made it all worse, of course. We argued about my lawyer. If I had won that argument, I might not be where I am now. If I hadn't been trying to make some extra money, Steve might still be alive. Reminds me of a crappy tattoo I once did on some guy's leg that said, 'If is half of life.'

"A public defender?" I said. "Dad, come on." That's how it started.

"Son," he said, "the system is corrupt. It favors those who buy private lawyers. I'm not letting one cent of mine go to supporting our two societies system."

"Make an exception just this once. I don't want to go to jail. I've heard that relying on a public defender is like playing Russian Roulette."

"You won't go to jail. It's your first offense, you'll go to Juvenile."

"How do you know?"

"That's how it works."

I lost it. "Don't tell me how shit works! You haven't even realized I've been paying the fucking bills!"

Dad looked down at his feet. I hadn't told him to save his pride, but I had been paying his way for a while. He was such a drunken mess, I'd come home one day and the electricity and the heat were off. I called the utility company and found out we were way behind. It was easier to just start paying it myself then listen to Dad's bullshit. In my anger, I sprung all of that against him as a weapon, and I didn't hold back.

"I've been dealing drugs to pay your way and now my friend is dead. For once I need your help and you're giving me shit! I've been supporting us both. Alone. Taking care of my own father, a guy with huge college degrees, like he's a fucking baby. And you never noticed."

He was too tired to fight back. He didn't even look up.

"I'll get what I can," he said.

"Forget it. Just go away. No. You know what, I can't get you to go away, so fine, I'll take the public defender. Let them send me away to juvey. That works for me because you won't be there."

I'd like to say I was sorry, but it was something that needed to be said.

I soon realized how empty my life was without the tattoo shop.

With the place closed, I sat at home and inked myself all day. Every part of my body that I could reach I covered with angry demons, bloody skulls, zombies holding their smiling heads in their hands, kittens devouring sharks, evil mushrooms, anything. When a tattoo artist gets depressed, look out.

Rest in Peace, Steve. That tattoo used to be right here on my left forearm. I cried so much when I inked myself with it, I felt dehydrated by the time I was done.

How can I escape shit like that? There's no way to clear the past, to bring Steve back and start over. Suicide wouldn't help. So I decided to stay alive and feel the pain because I knew I deserved it.

JAMIL

UNKNOWN LOCATION

2004

Jamil was bound to the chair, Mikhail addressing him from behind.

"Do you think garbage collectors enjoy their work, Jamil? I am like this. I do not enjoy what I do, but I fill a need, yes?"

"So," Jamil said, "you see me as garbage."

Mikhail clicked his tongue.

"Respect," he said. "I would think you understood by now. You waste my time these years, so I am forced to hurt you."

The masked men closed in on Jamil, tearing off his brittle uniform's orange shirt. He shivered as a cold gel was rubbed into his back, and something pressed against him. Without warning, electricity shot through his body, burning him. He ground his teeth, trying to ward off the agony.

"Let me die," he prayed. "Allah, please kill me."

The room was filled with an angry buzz while his body convulsed involuntarily, muscles contracting and cramping painfully. He urinated as his nervous system overloaded.

He was blacking out.

Jamil let go. He gave up. He stopped trying to control his muscles. He stopped caring about the pain. He cast aside his fear of death. He released all desire to stay in his assaulted body. His flesh and bone, punished to the point of destruction, had lost its hold on him.

He felt a pulling, a straining across his entire body, a seizure that tightened and did not pulse, but held. He expected to burn all over from muscles gone tight, but instead he felt less, felt no muscles at all. No skin. Instead of the torture climaxing at a pinnacle of agony, where it could increase no more, it was gone, completely, in an instant and with no warning or signal. He felt as if his taut muscles, his raw skin had never been there at all. He had felt only a faint pull then nothing. He could only liken it to removing a shirt, or getting his hair cut. Or perhaps working at his uncle's garage, twisting a stuck oil filter, his wrist straining, burning, and then, a gliding feeling as the threads found grease.

He had somehow, in some way, separated.

He was floating upward. A feeling of terror shot through his being, but it had nothing to cling to and passed away. He was looking down on a skinny brown body lashed to a chair. The body twitched violently all over, its every muscle unnaturally savaged by an uneven rhythm of seizures. Two wires leading from an automobile battery were attached to its skin via clamps.

Jamil realized in an instant he was looking down on himself.

Thin trails of smoke climbed from where the clamps met his skin toward his viewpoint on the ceiling. The buzzing sound was gone. All sounds were gone. Outside his body, sight was all that remained. There was no feeling, no sound, no smell. A passing sadness gave way to uncaring serenity. The flesh below was no longer his, so there was no need to burden himself with care for it.

His attention was drawn to a tall, thin, balding man sitting in the corner, legs crossed, tapping ashes from a cigarette into an ashtray with his left hand, his right thumb working a cell phone's key pad.

Mikhail.

For the first time in the years since he had known him, Jamil saw his tormentor without a mask. He willed himself lower and looked closely into the man's face as if they were nose to nose. Mikhail's cold blue eyes did not lift from the cell phone or acknowledge Jamil's presence in any way. Mikhail took another heavy drag from his cigarette, the skin of his pockmarked face stretched tightly over sharp cheekbones.

Jamil lost interest and began to float upward. As he looked about the room, it was clear no one there felt hatred toward him. The men operating the electric terminals did not smile. Mikhail seemed bored. This was simply a job to them all, as Mikhail had said, like collecting garbage.

Jamil also did not feel anger, despite what they were doing to the body. His body, he reminded himself. But was it any longer? Wasn't it under Mikhail's control?

Jamil turned his awareness away and willed himself up through the ceiling.

Suddenly he was outside, above the jagged mountains clawing the blue, cloudless sky. The sun blazed with Allah's majesty.

He had escaped!

"If this is death, then let me die," he prayed. "Great Allah, all-merciful, I am ready. Please, take me away from the physical world, away from the suffering."

His admiration of the white-capped mountains pulled him toward them.

"I am ready, great Allah," Jamil thought. "I want to die."

He struggled to push forward, to accelerate toward the mountains, but found himself descending. The gray of the building surrounded him again. As he passed through the roof, he could see the electrical device operators looking to Mikhail. Mikhail was standing, waving a delicate hand towards them, signaling them to leave.

Jamil fell toward his unconscious body, his ravaged back pink with blisters, some ruptured and seeping yellow pus. His skin had turned purple-blue from bruising.

"No!" he tried to scream, but he had no mouth. He tried to resist, but he had no arms to push away.

Suddenly he was back in his flesh. The sum of the torture hit him all at once with such force he had trouble drawing breath. He cried, more from sadness than from pain.

"So, Jamil," Mikhail said, "do you want to tell me anything?"

Jamil sobbed aloud, thinking only of the mountains, the clear sky, the beauty taken from him again.

Mikhail clucked his tongue.

"You can end this, Jamil. All you have to do is talk."

* * *

Jamil stared at the tiny chessboard hidden in his Bible, considering his next move. The lights dimmed. He slowly slid under his cot, muscles still tender from the electrocution.

He coughed, wincing as his back stretched against the raw sores.

Prasad did not cough in response.

Jamil tried again and waited without success. Finally he whispered. "Prasad? Prasad? Mister Prasad? It is time to continue our game."

No answer.

Jamil whistled aimlessly.

Prasad did not echo the whistle.

"Mister Prasad?"

He listened, hearing nothing but his heartbeat. Maybe they had taken Prasad for questioning.

He looked through the hole. The light was low, but he thought he saw a shadow move across the floor. He hadn't imagined it.

Had he?

He called as loud as he dared.

"Prasad!"

No response. The shadow he thought he saw did not move.

He frowned and stared at the chessboard, waiting.

* * *

The metal tray clanged open. Jamil startled awake. He had fallen asleep under his cot. He slid away from the wall, gasping as he his healing electrical burns cracked open again.

He peeked out the cell door window, his heart racing. Two guards were dispensing breakfast from a rolling cart, followed by a third holding a shotgun across his chest. All three wore ski-masks and chatted in a language Jamil had never heard.

Such was their routine.

Jamil jogged in place with his eyes closed. Against Prasad's advice, he had started counting. Three nights had now passed with no response from his friend.

What was the motion he had glimpsed that first night? Was it his hopeful imagination? Had they moved Prasad? If that was the case, why did the new person in the cell not respond at all? Even if to tell him to be quiet? Maybe the new occupant was deaf?

What if they had killed Prasad?

No, Jamil thought, don't even consider it.

His sore body and worry made him stiff. He slid under the cot again, breaking his and Prasad's rule: do not attempt to communicate unless the lights are dim. This was worth the risk, Jamil thought. He coughed.

Someone coughed in reply.

"Prasad!" Jamil squealed. His eyes welled with tears.

"Quiet! It's daytime. We shouldn't be talking."

"Where have you been? It's so good to hear your voice."

"Wait until evening. When the lights are down."

"Just a few words." Jamil's wrists hurt. He didn't realize until he felt them aching that he was pressing against the wall, trying to push through. "You sound different."

"We will talk tonight."

"But I have something wonderful to tell you. I saw the outside! The mountain range! It was beautiful, incredible, and I saw it. I floated outside my body!"

"Enough nonsense. Silence!"

"Prasad! Please, my friend."

"Make me ask again and I won't talk to you at all."

Jamil's lower lip quivered. He waited under his cot for a long time before pushing himself out to continue jogging. Prasad was back, he kept reminding himself, alive and ready to talk. That was reason to be joyful.

Jamil almost wished Mikhail would come for him. That would make the day pass faster. Waiting to speak with his beloved friend caused him pain beyond any torture Mikhail could inflict.

* * *

The instant the lights dimmed, Jamil was under his cot, coughing.

"I'm here," Prasad snapped. "Enough."

"I'm sorry. It's just that I've been worried about you."

"I've been with them," Prasad said. "I feel ill."

"Is it the drugs? Your advice worked well for me. Make sure to drink all the water they provide."

"Nothing will make me feel right again," Prasad grumbled.

"You said your thinking kept you going. Cling to that. Don't lose your will."

Prasad sighed several times, sounding more exhausted with each breath. "You are a beautiful boy, Mohammed, an honor to your family and your father. I am sure he would understand. One day I believe you will also."

"Understand what?"

"Have you ever wondered about the people they think we are? Why such men strap bombs to themselves? Kill themselves to kill others?"

"Why are you talking about this?"

"You said we could talk about anything. Have you ever wondered about them?"

"No. I always thought they were crazed."

"Ah. That is what their enemies want you to think. But they are not crazed with insanity. They are crazed with rage. They are not born with a desire to explode themselves or to kill others. Madmen convince them to do it, and they are easily convinced because they have been beaten into something sub-human."

"I don't understand why-"

"A terrorist is not wrong alone," Prasad went on. "Those who have left him with only wrong options are his partners. A man has a choice. He can be walked on, or he can harm others. I know you will likely-" Jamil couldn't make out the words. Prasad was coughing. "Only Allah can judge. Forgive me."

"Forgive you? Forgive you what?"

Prasad did not answer.

"Prasad, are you? Are you one of those... terrorists? Have you killed innocents?"

Prasad wailed. Jamil continued.

"These men make me want to kill them, too, Prasad. I cannot judge you or your actions, only Allah can do that. You are still my friend."

Prasad said nothing. He kept making a strange choking noise.

"No matter what you have done," Jamil said, "we are brothers. Please, Prasad. Speak to me."

Jamil stared at the crack in the wall. "Prasad?" he said. "You're frightening me."

Prasad whispered. "Forgive me, boy."

Jamil jolted as Mikhail's voice called from the hallway.

"Mister Jamil! We know what you are doing!"

The door slammed open. Several guards crashed into the room, guns drawn. Jamil was yanked out from under the cot and hurled against the wall. They bound his hands behind his back and dropped a hood over his head.

He was marched from his room, slammed roughly into the interrogation chair and bound to it. Someone removed the hood.

Once more Jamil was staring at the blank wall, two masked soldiers before him. Another two dragged a long tub of water in front of him. He looked down into the dark basin. A plank of wood was attached to the chair's back.

"So, you fantasize about killing me?" Mikhail asked.

Jamil said nothing.

"Let me test your honesty. Do you hate me?"

Prasad's words made sense now, but Jamil closed his mind to the revelation. He didn't want to acknowledge it, so he lived in the moment, fearing the water and what pain it might bring.

Feet shuffled behind him. The chair tilted. Hanging by the ropes around the chair's back, he plunged into the basin. Cool water gushed up his nose and down his throat, cutting off his breath. He bucked, but couldn't rise into the air. His lungs tightened painfully. He vomited underwater.

The ropes around his upper chest pulled taut. He rose, spitting and drooling.

"You fantasized about killing me, yes?" Mikhail asked him. "Did you not?"

Jamil hesitated.

"Again," Mikhail ordered.

"Wait!" Jamil yelled, but he was already splashing into the dark pool. His protest exploded in an eruption of bubbles. He held his breath until blood pounded behind his eyes.

Finally having no choice, he inhaled the water, coughing and gagging.

As he was lifted he cried out through his hacking.

"I did! I did!"

"You did what?"

"I fantasized about killing you," he said, coughing. "Please, no more."

"Good," Mikhail sighed. "Some truth. Now, in order for this meeting to be productive, I must know all you know."

"I have told you everything."

"Have you really?" The chair started to tip forward.

"Yes. Yes!" Jamil squealed. The chair rocked back. Water sloshed from him onto the concrete floor.

"I know that's not true. How do you think I learned of your desire to kill me?"

Jamil stared at the floor.

"You must answer quickly or it's in the water. Again."

"No! Please!"

Jamil fell forward, splashing into dark pain.

It occurred to him he might be able to kill himself. He inhaled, taking in the water, fighting the pain. He coughed, the skin of his throat shredding from the battle between his mind's commands and his muscles' reflex.

He was lifted again, spitting.

"How do I know?" Mikhail asked. "How do I know you want to kill me?"

"Prasad," Jamil stuttered between coughs. "He told you."

"Prasad? Ah, yes. That is what he told you to call him."

Jamil hung his head.

Mikhail laughed. "So far from his real name. If you only knew. What else?"

"He said he was a teacher. Had a family."

"I mean about you, Jamil. What else about you?"

"I live in Morocco. I've never killed anyone. I play football. Ask the questions, I've told you everything, I'll tell you again."

"How did you find Prasad?"

"There was a hole in the wall. I peeled off some paint, that's all."

"You don't have any sharp tools in your cell?"

"No."

Jamil retched, coughing up bile and water while Mikhail whispered to someone before speaking again.

"Let's go back to your father."

"He is a construction worker. He was out of the country."

"Where?"

"Qatar."

"Did you see his travel papers? A work visa?"

"No."

"Then you are really not sure."

Jamil paused. "No, but he told everyone he was going to Doha."

"Did he go on long trips before?"

"A few times, when I was younger. I remember little."

"Did he keep weapons? Explosive materials?"

"No, never. None that I know of."

"So, you cannot say he did not."

"No." Jamil sobbed as he spit out the words. "No, I can't." His head was aching. He shook the water loose from his head and stared at the ceiling, crying. "I cannot say anything for sure."

Mikhail let him cry for a long time, his sobs echoing thinly in the small room. The guards shifted their stances.

"Look into the black water before you, Jamil. Remember it. You will visit it again if you defy me."

They untied him, replaced his hood and walked him back to his cell. He cried aloud the whole way.

* * *

Jamil stood shivering under the dim light, spinning slowly to face the four walls that had been his life the last few years.

He jumped when the metal slot banged open. A small towel was in the tray. It was far too small to dry his whole body and therefore too small to hang himself. The Redfire logo was embroidered into the fabric. He rubbed the towel over his eyes, crying into it as he sank down to sit on his cot.

He slid to the floor. The hole where he spoke to Prasad was covered over with caulk. Jamil picked at it, but couldn't budge the dried adhesive.

"It's all right, Prasad," he said out loud. "Speak to me. Please. I just need to talk."

He scratched at the ragged caulk, scraping his fingertips.

"Prasad, if you want my forgiveness, you must talk to me."

Jamil waited. The caulk didn't give. It was dried solid as stone.

"You made a deal with them, didn't you?"

No sound emerged from the sealed hole.

Jamil yelled, his voice a shrill crescendo. "You needed something to tell, so you told them lies about me. Not only have you damned me, you have taken away my only friend! Enjoy your freedom! Enjoy your family! You have paid for it with my blood!"

Jamil leapt up, knocking his cot across the cell. He kicked the wall, pounding his fists on the cement with such force that he broke through his long-standing calluses, his knuckles painting a cloud of bloody dots. The bones in his fingers shuddered with every impact. He hurled his entire body against the wall and screamed.

"Hear that, Prasad? That's the sound of torture. You torturing me!" He smashed his head against the brick. The pain was so strong that, for an instant, it obscured the rage.

"This world is full of traitors, liars, thieves, murderers!" he screamed.

He hurled himself against the wall again, ramming his head against the concrete. He touched his scalp. His fingertips came away bloody. The room spun, a red splotch on the wall growing. He staggered backward and fell.

* * *

Jamil woke in a hospital room that seemed to be full of smoke. Slowly, he realized the milky white was the haze of his vision. Devices nearby chirped and beeped.

Goosebumps broke out on his skin as a click sounded and an icy chemical slid into his blood via a needle in his wrist. A minute later, a great calm descended on him.

He tried to raise himself, but his wrists caught with a clanking noise. Handcuffs held him to rails along the sides of the bed. He fell back. His scalp felt sticky and cool, open.

His rolled his head lazily from side to side, dazedly examining the recovery room. An armed guard standing at the door looked at him then quickly turned away.

"Look what they have done to me," Jamil mumbled just before he blacked out.

* * *

Jamil woke and faded that way several times. When he was taken back to his cell, half-dragged, half-staggering, his head was shaved and staples ran across his scalp, forming a bloody crown. He collapsed on his cot.

Now he understood how the lion had been defeated. What made him think he could survive what such a powerful beast could not? He stared at the ceiling, barely blinking. Even that seemed like an effort.

* * *

Jamil no longer exercised. His routine had lost its rhythm. He paced the cell and stared at the walls, as idle as if he were waiting for a bus.

He felt himself pulled along, hopeless to control anything. At random times, thinking of nothing, he would laugh hysterically. Other moments just as unremarkable, he would burst into tears. Sometimes he ate his meal and was still starving. Other times he had no interest in food. For several days he was tired, sleeping constantly. That would be followed by periods of manic behavior, when he paged through the Koran and the Bible unable to concentrate long enough to read more than a few words.

He was descending into madness and he knew it. He didn't try to resist.

* * *

"How dare you?" Mikhail asked, once Jamil was back in the interrogation room.

Jamil said nothing.

"How dare you try to kill yourself? Your life is mine, Jamil. Understand?"

Jamil made a mental note of how agitated Mikhail sounded. Should he ever desire to irritate Mikhail, he could attempt suicide again. The thought skipped away. For no reason he knew of, he suddenly felt giddy.

"I am ready for my pain, sir," he giggled.

"You think this is funny?" Mikhail growled.

"All I said was I was ready."

"Your tone is insolent. I do not like it."

"Of course." He held his laughter poorly, like a misbehaving schoolboy.

"I had hoped to talk, Jamil, but since you desire pain, I will provide."

"I do not desire pain. I desire death."

"Do not push me, Jamil. I can take you to the edge of death."

Suddenly, Jamil's mood swung to complete seriousness. "Do not push me, Mikhail. If you bring me close, I will finish the journey."

The masked men slid a low wooden platform before him. Jamil was pushed forward face down, his arms and legs spread out, bound to a hook bolted into each corner of the table. His shirt was torn off his chest.

He heard a whistling sound and a second later a stripe of fire slapped across his back on his right. He yelled, startled. Before he could draw his breath, a lash struck from the other side. He looked over his right shoulder, then the left. Two masked men were standing at his sides holding large leather straps.

Mikhail counted off, "Left, right, one, two." With each word, the whipping straps landed on Jamil's back in an alternating pattern.

The pain was vicious and thick as they fell into a rhythm, striking him one at a time. A blazing X burned across his back. Each time he tried to inhale, a leather strap came down and squeezed the oxygen from his chest.

Jamil ground his teeth, screaming through them. He strained against his bindings.

Mikhail had fallen for his trick.

With every part of his being, Jamil pushed. He urinated and his bowels loosened. Sludge trickled down his crotch. He pushed from inside his mind, riding the force of the pain as it crushed him from above.

He imagined himself flying outward, propelled by the impact of the whips.

His consciousness shot free.

It worked! He would have yelped if he had a voice.

He was floating above the scene again.

Mikhail conducted the men with his hand. The men beating the frail body between them had removed their shirts but not their masks. They struck the thin boy's back with such immense force, the skin did not stop rippling as the next blow arrived. A purple X formed across the boy's back.

First the man on the right raised high and swung down. Then the man on the left did the same while the man on the right readied himself. Their movements were so coordinated, it was almost appealing, like watching dancers.

Mikhail's mobile phone rested on a small table near him as he sat down and took notes. Jamil forced himself to descend. A form rested on Mikhail's clipboard, the text in English. An unfamiliar logo was in the upper right, underneath it was written "A limited partner of The Redfire Corporation."

"Top Secret" was stenciled across the page.

The top of the form read "Subject." Mikhail's blocky handwriting filled the nearby blank. "Jamil."

Jamil kept scanning.

"Year of acquisition: 2001."

"Today's date: 5 October 2004."

He was stunned. Only three years? It seemed so much longer.

At the bottom of the form was an empty box marked "Progress." Mikhail had written, "Subject weak. Mentally unstable. Still no intel. Suggest not as valuable as collectors expressed. Continuing as ordered until further notice."

The words could have filled Jamil with hope, but he knew not to entertain that most dangerous emotion. The feeling of floating was too fantastic for him to waste time with concerns of the physical world.

Was this what doing drugs felt like? Was this light sensation why people in his neighborhood became addicted to hash or opium? He had only ever been drunk before, but it was a heavy feeling, a sensation of being trapped in flesh, not liberated from it.

Jamil emerged from the roof as he had before, to gaze out on the snowy mountain range. Maybe he could pull so far from his body that he could break loose and never return. He reached out to touch the mountains, looking down into the canyon below where a river sparkled silver between the white peaks.

So beautiful, he thought. Goodbye, Mikhail!

Jamil had never gone swimming in his life, but he had seen races on the satellite television during the Olympics. He imagined himself moving his arms like a swimmer, pulling himself through the air with huge strokes. Maybe he could ascend into the sky, to the stars! So many places to go-

No!

The scene below him jerked as his awareness was yanked backward.

No. Please no.

The snow-capped mountains retreated.

No! I want to die! Please! Let me go!

He was being pulled back toward the compound.

All I want is to be free!

He passed through the roof, through the ceiling.

* * *

Jamil gasped. His bruised ribs and lungs ached every time they flexed, trying to draw breath.

"Jamil!" Mikhail was yelling. "I am talking to you!"

Jamil lay on the table. The whipping had stopped and the smell of blood filled the air.

"Hello, Jamil. Are you in there?"

Jamil couldn't talk. His mouth opened and closed.

"Yes," Jamil tried to say, but it came out as a breathless grunt. He felt his blood trickle down his sides, greasing the bench beneath him.

"I cannot understand you," Mikhail said.

Jamil laid his head down and closed his eyes tightly. He sobbed, wincing with each tiny movement.

"Every man breaks, Jamil. If you do not cooperate, I must keep at this."

Jamil's mouth flopped open, spilling saliva.

"I… want… to… die…" he gasped.

"Take him back to his cell," Mikhail said.

Jamil blacked out.

ZERD

USA

2005

Steve was right.

It hurts to think of him even now, even after so many years gone, but it hurt a lot more to think of him on that first day in Juvenile Jail, or Jail Junior, or juvey as most called it. Steve's dead, I kept saying to myself, get used to it. Like a tattoo, sometimes you have to keep scraping until it takes.

Among the thousands of discussions he and I had with customers, once we'd ended up talking about how unfair the legal system is.

Dad would have agreed with his views but the difference was Steve accepted that sometimes you should play by the unfair rules. Not Dad. Even after our argument, he pitched in some money and I still couldn't afford a decent lawyer. So I accepted a court-appointed one and some hand-me-down justice.

I wasn't that upset. Suppose I had escaped going to this halfway slammer for problem teens and retards. What the hell would I do? Working in another ink shack was my only decent option, and that would have been a too-soon reminder of Steve.

So I can't say I was excited, but I needed the break from ordinary life. I was bummed about Steve, bummed about losing touch with Tracy, and bummed that I hadn't heard from Charles in a long time. He was traveling Europe, getting a degree in library science. The rare postcard he sent told me more about parties than any schoolwork.

* * *

I understood I belonged in juvey because I was transporting drugs, but I didn't feel like I belonged. The place was full of idiots. Most of the guys were the worst kind of morons: violent, illiterate, unwilling to learn, and they thought they knew everything.

Fighting was all they cared about. There was at least one a day. If there wasn't one, toward the evening, two (or more) idiots would start one to break the boredom.

The dopes I was surrounded by made me angry at Dad. I kept thinking, "These are the common people my father is ruining himself to speak out for."

Sure there are good common people, but shit. After a few days in juvey, I'd be surprised if even Dad didn't change his opinions a little.

Besides normal stuff like eating and sleeping and break time hanging around outside, juvey involved sitting in a room learning elementary school stuff, and what they called "Basic Living" where we learned things like you should take a shower and brush your teeth daily.

I drew the whole time and never got a grade less than a B. Then it was back to break time outside. They let us out into a giant fenced in pen with a weightlifting area and two basketball courts. Unarmed rent-a-cops patrolled the perimeter. Smoking was permitted. Break time seemed to be most of what we did. I think it was easiest for the teachers and guards, so they gave us plenty of it

I kept to myself and walked around the inside of the fence, thinking of what trade I'd like to take on. For those of us who weren't semi-retarded, they offered construction and road work training. Road work looked harder, but I thought it might be cool because then I could go anywhere in the country.

That's what I was thinking when I met Brainiac.

"Hey."

A short kid with thick glasses was standing in front of me, eyes magnified by bug-eye lenses.

I kept walking.

Someone stepped on my foot and pinched the back of my left arm. I tried to swing my right fist around, but I was held so tightly I couldn't turn. I twisted my neck and looked into the smiling, gap-toothed face of an enormous ogre, easily a foot taller than me and fat as an elephant's hairy ass.

"Get the fuck off me," I snarled. My left hand was going numb, he was pinching so hard to stop the blood.

"He wants to talk," the ogre said, tilting his head toward the kid with glasses.

"All right," I said. "Let me go."

He did. I stepped to the twerp with the glasses, the ogre literally breathing down my neck.

"Nice ink," the little guy said.

"Yeah."

"You do those tats yourself?"

"Who are you, my social worker?"

The ogre smacked the back of my head. I wanted to hit him back, but the dude was huge and there was no life in his eyes. He had that look people have when they're stoned, but not the fun kind, the "I'm brain dead" kind.

The short kid was still talking. "You're new. I wanted to introduce myself. I'm Brainiac. Part brain and part maniac."

"Really? I hadn't figured that out."

The big guy hit me in the back of the head again. A rent-a-cop guard strolled by, not taking any notice. I watched him walk away.

"Don't bother to look for help," Brainiac said. "Especially not to the pigs. We have an arrangement."

"So?"

The ogre hit me again.

"Fuck!" I yelled. "Can you tell him to stop doing that?"

"What makes you think I control him?"

"I thought you guys were lovers."

Brainiac held up his hand, sparing me from another slap.

"Beast is my friend, not my slave. He's unhappy because you're not showing me the proper respect."

"Okay. I'll show respect."

"Beast, please," Brainiac said. Beast took a step back. His hot breath left my neck.

"So," Brainiac asked, "what's your name?"

"Zerd."

"That your real name?"

"No."

"How do you spell it?"

"Z. E. R. D."

"Nerd with a z." A malicious rumble sounded behind me. Beast was chuckling.

"Can I go now?" I turned and asked Beast. He smacked me again.

Brainiac clucked his tongue. "Address me, Zerd. That's respect. Your cheeks are burning red. You must be getting angry, so take time to phrase your questions properly."

"Can I go now, Brainiac? Sir?"

"Not yet. I want to explain the rules to you, since you're a newb."

"Okay. Brainiac. Sir."

"I'm curious about that tattoo of the hand reaching up from the grave giving the world the finger. That one on your arm. The tombstone reads P.S.F.U. Does that stand for anything?"

"It's the guy's final statement to the world, P.S. Fuck You."

"I thought it meant Patron Saint of Fuck Ups."

He snorted a nerd's laugh.

I stared at him.

"Right," he said, clearing his throat. "So far, my assessment is as follows: intelligence, above average, owing to your verbal responses;

strength, below average, owing to your quick submission to Beast; self-esteem, below average, owing to the desire to modify your own skin." He paused a moment. "What do you think?"

I stared at him, wondering if this asshole was for real.

"No response?" he continued. "Like I said, above-average intelligence. You'd be surprised how many times Beast has to smack some guys before they understand how things are going to be. Speaking of, I'll start with a few simple rules. When Beast summons you, come immediately. When I ask you a question, you answer. Clear?"

"Sure."

"Good. Now I know you're probably thinking I'm some kind of jerk, but I encourage you to work with me. Together we can make this dull place fun."

"Right."

"There is a certain X-factor about you," he continued. "You don't strike me as the average loser this place collects."

"Sure. I'm an above average loser. Brainiac, sir."

"Clever. I find you funny."

"Thanks. Brainiac. Sir."

"You may go now, Zerd."

I took off. I didn't look back until I knew I was clear of Beast's huge paws. My head hurt and my neck felt kinked from being knocked around.

The two of them moved to the bleachers near the basketball court. Brainiac sat on the top row alone, reading a book, while Beast stood on the ground behind him, arms folded, eyes scanning like a bodyguard.

About a dozen guys crowded onto the other set of bleachers, leaving Brainiac several rows all to himself.

* * *

To fight boredom at juvey, I started smoking. Boring normal cigarettes were all I could get. Eventually there was nothing else I wanted to do during break besides smoke, walk and think about nothing. Months passed where that was all I did.

I kept my distance from Brainiac and Beast, and everyone, until I met Rory.

"Hey, white boy with the tattoos!" someone called out.

A large black kid approached me. He was smiling, but I tensed anyway.

"Expect pain," I thought to myself. "Stay calm."

"Relax," he said, extending his hand. "My name's Rory." We shook. I had seen him before, but only because I had seen every guy in the place a hundred times. "Call me Eighty-Three. Defensive line, right?"

"Eighty-Three. Rory. Nice to meet you. I'm Zerd. What's up?"

"Brainiac is holding a meeting at the basketball court in ten minutes."

"What's it about?"

"You know that freak doesn't tell nobody nothing. Thinks we're his computer bits or some shit. You have somewhere else to be?"

"How come you're his messenger? What about Beast?"

"I don't know. This took more brains than Beast has, right?" he smiled again.

I liked his attitude, and I was bored.

"What the hell, I said. I'll be there."

* * *

Guys hung out by the basketball courts all the time, waiting to play or watching the game, so we shouldn't have appeared suspicious, but we were. For once, Brainiac and Beast were permitting others to sit on their bleachers instead of everyone crowded on one while they had the other all to themselves. Even now, with permission, no one dared sit on Brainiac's top row.

A game was in progress. Brainiac looked over our heads, pretending he was interested. With him and Beast, there were eight of us, including myself and Rory. The rent-a-cops went walking around the outside of the fence, not giving a shit as usual.

"All right," Brainiac said. "You were selected from the rabble because you are slightly smarter than average. There are no morons on this job. And before you ask 'what job?' I'll tell you. I want to plan an escape."

Everyone chuckled a bit. Brainiac shifted like he was annoyed and we all got quiet. Despite his size, he had a commanding aura. We just did what he said like we were hypnotized. Of course, the fact that Beast growled a little helped.

"I'm going to say something," Brainiac went on, "but I don't want you to turn and look. Understand?"

Everyone nodded.

"The gate facing the parking lot is getting weak," he said. Then he immediately squealed, "I said don't look, asshole!"

Beast marched around the bleachers and smacked a tall, thin kid with bad acne in the back of the head. As he lumbered back to his post, Brainiac frowned in disgust.

"How do I know the gate is weak?" he asked.

No one said anything.

"I know because I've been dripping some acid on those big fat metal hinges every day. They're dissolving little by little as we speak. Once the gate is loose enough we can bust out. It's slow going, so I need your help dripping the acid on. Who's in?"

No one moved.

"You bitches like it here? I thought you had balls. Maybe I was wrong. A shame because now that I've told you my plan, Beast will have to kick each one of your asses to make sure you don't talk."

I couldn't believe this kid. He brought us all here, asked for our help and then threatened us if we said no. Dad would have said it was like the Vietnam War draft. Over the course of a five-hour talk.

The thin, bad-acne kid was the first to agree. "I'm down."

"I'm in," I said next. Why not?

One by one the group agreed.

"Good," Brainiac said. "I knew you guys were smart."

"So," Bad Acne said, "where do we get this acid shit?"

Beast waddled around the bleachers and smacked him again and returned to Brainiac's side.

"Ow! Sorry. I mean, Brainiac sir, where do we get this acid shit?"

"I know what you're thinking," Brainiac said, laying his hand gently on Beast's shoulder, calming his pet. "It's acid as in battery acid, not hippie acid. Don't put a drop of it on your tongue unless you want to burn yourself. To answer your question, you get it from me."

Bad Acne kept talking. "Mister Brainiac, sir, where did you get it?"

"From the medical lab."

"How did you get in there?"

Beast turned slowly.

Bad Acne got the message. "Brainiac, sir. How did you get into the medical lab?"

"I have my ways."

Why was that dumbass asking so many questions? I'll tell you why. Just like Dad taught. He was a plant. The whole thing played out like those videos he showed in class, where the press fed the president easy questions so he could say what he wanted the way he wanted. His buddies lob him softballs and he knocks them out of the park while everyone cheers. Something about this whole thing was jacked up, but I didn't care too much. I was curious to play it out and see what happened.

Beast held his palm out. He was holding six vials with eye-dropper rubber caps. He handed one to each of us.

"You each get a vial," Brainiac said. "We'll take turns going up to the fence and putting a drop on the hinge. If I did it alone, the pigs would get suspicious. If we each go once a day they'll never notice. I've calculated that it will take a little more than a month to damage the metal to the point where we could smash through."

Everyone was quiet, listening.

"When the gate is weak enough, we'll wait until noon and go."

"Why noon, Mister Brainiac?" Bad Acne the Plant asked.

"Because that's when the train comes. We'll race across the parking lot, across the field, hop the train and it will carry us out of here. Then we're free."

We were all looking at the vials we received.

"Hey, retards!" Brainiac yelled. "Pay attention! I'm talking." We each stuffed the vials in our pockets.

Rory raised his hand. "Mister Brainiac, sir?"

"Yes, Eighty-Three, what is your question?"

"Mister Brainiac, sir. Your highness, I was wondering, does our team have a name?"

Beast stepped up to Rory. Rory looked him in the eye. "What up, meatloaf? I respected massa."

"Easy, Beast," Brainiac said, touching Beast's elbow. "It's okay."

Brainiac smiled his creepy psycho smile. "Well, Rory. I've done all the important thinking here. I'll leave that bullshit job up to you. What name would you like?"

"I was thinking of Brainiac's Bozo Brigade."

Everyone laughed.

"As you wish," Brainiac said. "Meeting adjourned." Everyone stood around until Brainiac squeaked, "That means go!"

We all took off while Beast cracked his knuckles.

* * *

Every day outside, each person in Brainiac's Bozo Brigade took a moment to stand at the fence and drop some acid, ha ha.

The first time I pinched a few drops on the hinge, the metal smoked and boiled like water. The hissing bubbles were trippy to look at. I guess I must have gotten careless, because around the third time I did it, I got busted.

"Hey! What are you doing?"

One of the rent-a-cops had snuck up on me. He was a young guy about my age, hair cut short, taking the job way too seriously. I think he even annoyed the older pigs with his attitude.

"I'm just standing here," I said.

"What's in your hand? Show me."

"It's for my allergies. They're eye drops." I held out the vial, palm up.

"It is kind of dry out." He rubbed his eyes. "Shit, now you're making my eyes itch. Give me those drops."

"These are all I have."

"Hand them over."

"No. These are special drops, they're for my allergies."

"Bullshit. Give 'em to me." He was quick and snatched them before I could pull away. He unscrewed the cap and leaned his head back. I was going to have to tackle him. I hesitated.

"What's going on here?" a voice said. The guard leaned forward blinking, the drops unused. I swallowed hard. I could not let that dude use those drops in his eye.

Brainiac stood nearby, hands on his hips. "I thought I just witnessed an officer stealing from an inmate."

"These are mine," the piglet said.

"I don't think so."

Brainiac and Beast stared at the rent-a-cop kid. He stared back. I was stuck in the middle. My hands were trembling. Dude was an asshole, but I couldn't let him go blind." Fuck you," the piglet said dropping the closed vial in the grass. He kicked dirt over it and walked away.

I grabbed the vial and brushed it off while Brainiac lectured me.

"I had to call in a lot of favors to get that juice, Zerd. Fuck up like that again and Beast will put those drops in your eyes. You'll cry blood like a make-up lab rabbit. But you don't have any idea what I'm talking about, do you?"

"Brainiac, sir, it won't happen again."

"I know. Now go away."

Beast grinned stupidly as I walked off.

* * *

One month later, just as Brainiac had predicted, the fence was wobbling.

Breakout day was closing in and Rory and I and the rest of the guys were going nuts with the waiting. No one dared consider defying Brainiac and getting their own crew together and busting loose without his permission. The last time I dripped acid on the hinge, the metal was corroded so bad it looked like chewed hamburger.

Finally Brainiac called his Bozo Brigade together and gave the word: tomorrow at noon. We were to all rush the fence, push it over and take off. After crossing the field, we would jump the daily train, which would rocket us out of there. He didn't say anything about keeping it secret. The news was spreading outside the brigade and, surprisingly, Brainiac didn't complain.

It seemed like everyone knew. They repeated it to friends and enemies. They knew success of the breakout depended on a lot of us hitting the fence at once with enough force to snap the weakened hinges. You could tell everyone was hyped because there were no fights all that night and during morning break. I think that was the only day that ever happened in all my time at juvey.

I thought about what I was going to do when I got out. My first goal was to rush to Tracy's house and fuck her for ten days straight before I worried about my next move.

The thought made me smile, but suddenly a cloud blocked the sun, interrupting my mental picture. Beast was standing over me.

"All right," I said. "Let's go see him."

Brainiac was looking out beyond the fence, away from the weakened gate, apart from everyone, alone with Beast as usual.

"You called?" I said. "Brainiac, sir," I added quickly.

"Yes. Zerd. I want to speak with you. Alone."

Beast moved away from us, facing the recess yard with his arms folded, his back to us. It was just me and the psycho in the corner office.

"I wanted to warn you," Brainiac said. "The pigs know about our plan."

"What?"

"They've got extras hiding beyond that shed at the edge of the parking lot. Look."

I did. A small building that held lawnmowers and crap separated the parking lot from the field and the railroad tracks. I noticed a guard slip behind it. He didn't come back out.

"See that?" Brainiac said. "They've been doing that all day. Lots of them. They're going to ambush anyone who runs."

A million questions were running through my mind. "Are you sure they know?"

"I'm certain. I told them."

"What?" I squealed, the word just shooting out of me.

Brainiac doubled over, giggling.

"You sound like a little bitch," he gasped, pointing at me with one hand, holding his belly with the other. Right then, I totally understood why Dad hated those who lust for power.

"You're wondering why," he continued, still chuckling. "Why sabotage my own plan? Why do you think, Zerd?"

"Because you're an asshole?" I stole a look over my shoulder at Beast. His back was still to us.

Brainiac smiled. Instead of crunching his eyes up like a normal person, they grew wide, demented. His thick glasses magnified the effect.

"I warned Beast you might get angry but not to do anything. Lucky you. If he heard you say that, he'd strangle you."

I looked away to the crowd. Everyone was slapping each other on the back, shaking hands, laughing. No one was playing basketball. No one was lifting weights. No one was fighting. Everyone was conserving their energy for the escape, coming together for a common purpose. It was almost beautiful in a one-world-hippie-song kind of way. Brainiac had made it happen, and now he was going to wreck it.

"Why, Zerd?" Brainiac asked. "The same reason I'm here at all. I'm bored. I want to see what happens. I calculate there's a ten percent probability that any of you get to the train. And that's being generous. I rounded up my statistical figures."

I looked around at the peaceful scene. Carnage was coming and I was the only one sane enough to do anything about it. My mind was racing but coming up short. I had to stall.

"But you're telling me," I said. "Why?"

"Bravo. I knew you were going to ask that," he said, smiling. "You're of slightly more interest to me than the other lab rats. You're a wild card, Zerd. You possess a certain mystique, but I think I have you figured out. In addition to enjoying the chaos that's about to come, I want to see how you in particular react."

"I'm fucking honored."

"You really should take it as a compliment. You're an interesting specimen, but I don't think you have the guts to go for it now."

The guy was scaring me. Someone who knifes you in a fight is scary, but Brainiac, he's the kind of guy that knifes you, dissects you, then feeds you to your family. While smiling.

Beast and Brainiac had an odd relationship if you only looked at their outward appearance, but they were of the same stock: insane, violent and cruel. They just used different means to be that way.

"See, Zerd," he said. "All that ink. What are you hiding? What are you compensating for? You must feel as though your identity is insufficient. I just said you won't go for it, but just by me saying that, I know you will. You think you're a badass, but you're not. Your ink proves it. You're all surface."

"You realize when they get caught, it's going to add to their term."

"Oh, I think it will be worse than that. For a coordinated escape like this, they'll be off to real jail."

"If not they'll come after you."

"Beast would love the exercise. No. They won't come for me. There's really only two possible outcomes. You get caught, you go to jail. Adult jail. You escape, you're gone. Either way, I don't see you again."

"You can't be sure."

"No. I can't. The future is all about probabilities but I've got them all covered. Anyone who stays here won't do shit. That jerkoff who almost stole your drops, you think I scared him with my voice? With Beast? Of course not. He knows to leave me alone."

I didn't know what to say.

"You want to ask how. I'll tell you. A certain person in a high-level position here has some interesting pictures of children on his computer. If those were released to the public, which I could make happen with one phone call, well, that would be very damaging to the state funding this fine institution receives."

"Bullshit."

"Oh, Zerd. Look at me. Do you think anyone would hesitate to beat my ass if I wasn't a master of leverage?"

"You're a real fucking asshole."

"I'm that, too. Isn't it fun?" The prick would not stop smiling.

I was stuck. If I hit him, Beast would kill me or the pigs would grab me and I'd miss out on the escape. I could possibly rally the guys against him, but if Brainiac really had someone in his pocket, and it seemed he did, no revolution would matter. But what if I was just buying his bullshit, falling for his story? Scaring myself? Was he psyching me out?

Brainiac was smarter than me, and Beast was stronger. Together they were unstoppable. How the hell could I win in a world of people more powerful than myself?

That's when I thought of Dad. All those sermons he gave about the poor answered that question. When the poor fight the power, how do they prevail?

Persistence. Unity. Tenacity. Sacrifice. A little luck.

None of which I had.

Brainiac was still talking. "Right now, Zerd, your mind is flailing, you're thinking about going for it. You're wondering if you can unite the others against me and Beast."

It was like he was reading my mind.

"There's no escape from my perception," he said. "Every action tells so much about you. I think someday I'd like to be a profiler. Someone who tracks criminals by understanding the clues to a person's motives. I'd be good at that, don't you think? If I got bored, I could always lead my fellow detectives on a wild goose chase."

"Sounds great."

"Don't be bitter, Zerd. I am curious to see your response so I can recalibrate my assessment of you. Accurate appraisals are necessary to determine meaningful probabilities. I'm not always-"

I stepped toward him. "I'm going to recalibrate your tiny dick."

He yawned, and didn't flinch. "No, you're not."

"You don't care about any of these guys you're setting up?"

"Does a spider give a shit about a fly? There's a reason I made sure all the smart guys were in on this. It diminishes my genius if there's all these semi-intelligent dudes around. It's all relative. Suppose everyone was as inked up as you are. How different would you be?"

"So you'll be King of the Retards."

"King is what matters."

"Fuck you."

I walked away. I heard (and felt) footsteps chasing me, then Brainiac called out.

"Let him go, Beast."

The footsteps stopped. Brainiac yelled one more time.

"I'll be watching you, Zerd."

* * *

That night, I couldn't sleep. As the sun rose, I realized that whatever was going to happen was out of my control. When the sun set I would either be with Tracy or sitting in a real jail cell. I went through the day's motions, determined to survive.

Every hour crawled until we were minutes before noon, then seconds.

A crowd clustered near the weakened gate, slapping each other on the back and laughing. The clock began its noon chimes.

"Twelve, eleven, ten, nine, eight."

We all started counting in our heads, but eventually we were counting out loud, the whole yard filled with guys counting like New Year's Eve. The guards whipped their heads in all directions, trying to make sense of it.

"Seven. Six. Five. Four."

The crowd was hooting and yelling.

"Three! Two! One!"

The last chime sounded.

A beat passed in silence.

"Now!"

With a roar, a huge mass of juvenile delinquents hurled themselves against the main gate. It flexed for a moment before it snapped, exactly as Brainiac said, the acid-burned hinge popping loose.

An alarm howled. Everyone started running, pushing out and under the gate, twisting it open, its upper hinge still connected.

I stepped back and grabbed Rory, stopping him.

"Wait," I yelled as the group rushed past us, whooping and screaming.

"Wait? Are you nuts? Come on, man." He pulled on my arm.

"It's a trap."

"A what?"

"Brainiac. He tipped off the pigs."

"I'll take my chances," he said, trying to break free.

I grabbed him with both hands. "You go now, you're busted."

His eyes were wide, wild. "What the fuck, man!"

Guys were hurtling past us. The upper hinge gave out. The gate broke loose and fell over, catching some pigs underneath. The juvies stomped on them on their way into the parking lot.

"Follow behind them. They'll set off any traps before we do. Okay? Just wait."

Rory calmed a bit, his struggling weakening. "You better be fucking right about this." The alarm blasted our eardrums.

Guys were fanning out. Some went to the parking lot, trying to steal a car. A police van screamed out of nowhere and blocked the exit. A group ran toward the field, past the storage building. Several cops leapt out from behind the shed, tackling them. Some of the runners decided to turn back, but they were caught by the herd of pigs pouring from the admin buildings.

"Oh, shit," Rory said. "You were right. Fucking Brainiac."

I let him go, but now he stayed by my side. The escapees were confused by the sudden ambush. Some turned back into the yard, some jumped on the cops in a full-on brawl. Some fell to the ground, face forward, covering their heads, anticipating the beating that inevitably came.

"Okay," I said, "they're all tangled up. Let's go."

"Fuckin' A."

We were off.

* * *

Running through that clusterfuck was like running through a war zone. Fists were flying, batons swinging, dudes grappling everywhere. A painful mist of pepper spray floated in the air, mixing with the dust kicked up by the rumble.

Rory and I floored it, running between inmates and guards. We didn't help anyone, shoving friend and foe to the ground as necessary, every man for himself. We stayed clear of the shed where the mass of the fight was going on.

A few pigs noticed us. The rest were too busy kicking ass or getting their asses kicked.

"Stop! Come back!" a couple pigs yelled as they turned from the fray and followed us. We were the only ones who had made it past the shed. Brainiac's plan was working almost perfectly. No one was getting out.

"We got friends," Rory gasped as we sprinted across the field toward the train tracks.

I looked over my shoulder. One guy was a donut cop, his belly way over his belt, winded already. I wasn't worried about him. I was worried about the crew-cut jackass that almost burned his eyes out with my acid dropper. He was closing fast.

Ahead of us, the train whistle cried.

"Oh, shit!" Rory shouted.

"I hear it."

"We're not going to make it!"

"Like fuck we aren't," I said but I could see Rory was right. It wasn't that we weren't going to meet the train, it's that the pigs were gaining on us too fast. Even the fat one kept pumping along, all the crap he had on his belt and his gut bouncing in sync. By ourselves, we could hop the train, but the pigs were going to grab us first.

I never ran as fast as I ran that day. I pictured myself like a cartoon character, instead of propelling myself across the ground, my legs were kicking, spinning the earth beneath me, bringing the train closer.

"Zerd! Z!" Rory called.

I ignored him.

"Z! I'm done!"

I looked over my shoulder. He was staggering, out of breath. The guards were behind him, closing.

I turned, jogging backwards.

"Fuck it, Rory! Come on! Rest later!"

He leaned over, coughing, spitting. "I'm a defensive end, not a wide receiver!"

"Shut up and run!" I yelled. The fat guy was almost to him, the psycho was coming my way. Rory glanced back, then forward to me. I saw his broad shoulders rise and fall as he took a deep breath.

He waved goodbye.

"Good luck, Z!" he shouted. "You get to that end zone!"

"Rory!" I screamed, but he had stopped and turned.

He dropped into a football linesman's three-point stance as the guard ran towards him. When the pig was a few steps away, Rory lunged forward, his shoulder low. He hit the guard in the mid-section so hard the guy's hat popped off and flew straight up. Rory crushed him to the ground and got back up. The guard didn't move. Rory's legs pumped up and down like he was running in place and he took down another pig that had joined the chase. Two more swarmed over him.

166

Fuckin' A to Eighty-Three.

"Shit!" I hissed as I gasped for air. I turned and bolted. I had to make it. I wasn't just running for myself, I was running for Rory, too. For his sacrifice I had to make it. I fucking had to. And to shove it in Brainiac's psycho-nerd face. That made me want to make it most of all.

"Stop!" the red-faced psycho yelled. He had gotten past my defender.

I could turn and fight, but I had only one goal: the train.

It was huge, fast, loud. From far away the whistle was peaceful, the chugging a gentle rhythm. Up close it was nothing but a shrieking terrifying roar, a monster that would kill anything in its path. I stumbled as I hit the gravel around the tracks, nearly flying forward under the metal wheels. At the speed they were going they might as well have been rotating blades.

I ran alongside it.

Now what?

The cop hit the gravel, coming for me. I kept running parallel with the train, glancing back, then searching for some kind of hand-hold.

A boxcar with a ladder swept past the pig. I reached out my left hand as it came to me and clamped, lifting. Suddenly I was flying. I grabbed on with both hands. After propelling myself with my own effort for so long, it felt fantastic to speed along without effort.

The rent-a-cop poured on a burst of speed and grabbed my leg. I bent one arm around a rung and kicked with all my might. My heel caught him with a square shot in the middle of his face. His nose exploded red down his chin. He bounced off the speeding train and tumbled into the gravel face down.

Oh, shit.

I didn't have time to see if he moved again. The train rounded a bend and his prone body was gone.

I had escaped. I gathered my breath as juvey flew into the distance behind me. I screamed, hoping Brainiac could hear.

"Recalibrate that, motherfucker!"

* * *

I jumped off the train when I had flown along for what I guessed was a half hour. I wanted to bail before it stopped or got too far from home. All I could see was forest, so that seemed a good place to ditch.

I waited for a grassy area and jumped, running as I landed to soften the impact, allowing myself to tumble.

I wiped out but was unhurt except for some scrapes. I crashed into the forest and leaned against a tree, resting. The train roared into the distance until I was alone with the quiet. After being in a skanky group home for so long, the air smelled so fresh it almost had a taste. I just sat there and breathed.

I closed my eyes and slept, waking into the dark.

* * *

I pushed through branches, heading toward lights in the distance until I emerged in front of some no-name mini-mart. They had a pay phone and, fortunately, I had been there once before with Charles and Tracy, during a pre-smoke snack run. I found some change behind the place, bummed a little off people walking out and with my pooled cash, called Tracy, hoping I wouldn't get her voicemail.

"Hello?" she answered, her voice like music.

"Hey, it's me."

"Zerd?"

"Yeah."

"I didn't know they let you call this late."

"They don't."

"What do you mean?"

"I need you to pick me up. Alone."

"You're out?"

"Remember that place where Charles got mad at the cashier?"

"Oh, my God, Z. I can't believe it."

"Can you get a car and meet me? I'm at that place where we picked up munchies. We bought sodas, but Charles was flipping out because he wanted iced tea and they were out. Do you remember that place?"

"Oh, shit. I think so. Charles spazzed out in lots of places."

"I'll be across the street in the woods. Bring some food and water if you can."

"Z. You're crazy. It's why I love you."

"Thanks. I should go." I really appreciated her saying she loved me, but I couldn't bring myself to say it back, even though I felt it. What a jackass I am. I hung up and bolted across the road, dove into the forest and waited.

* * *

From my hiding place in the bushes, I watched as a car made a U-turn, headlights slashing through the trees. It rolled along the shoulder across from the mini-mart then rolled to a stop, its engine running. The store across the road was quiet. The car looked like Tracy's, but I wasn't taking any chances. She got out of it and stood in front. I recognized her hips swaying in the headlights.

"Zerd?" she half-whispered, half-called out. "Z?"

I looked up and back down the road. No other cars were coming.

"Are you alone?" I called out.

"Z. Is that you?"

"Are you alone?"

"Yes. You're scaring me. Where are you?"

I stepped out. She charged over and jumped me, wrapping her legs around me so I had no choice but to hold her up, my hands sliding under her ass. Her butt flexed beneath tight jeans as she reared up to kiss down on me.

"Oh, my God, you feel so good," I said. She kissed me hard and slid to the ground, tearing at my pants.

"Oh, shit," she said. She ran back to her car, and shut off the lights. Then she came bolting back to me.

"First things first," she said as she yanked down my zipper and pulled me into her car's back seat.

* * *

After we fucked, she drove me around. I held a small picnic cooler she had filled in my lap. She had made me a peanut butter sandwich and brought some water and potato chips. I thought I was going to come again the homemade food was so good.

"So, what happened?" she asked.

"What happened?" I said, spitting bits of food out. "Sorry." I swallowed before talking again. "A bunch of us rushed the exit. I think I'm the only one who got out."

I told her the whole adventure, about Brainiac and Beast, Rory and all the others. She even cried a little over Rory's sacrifice. That really bummed me out. Dude was probably in deep shit for leveling those pigs.

We drove on in silence until she asked the question I was dreading.

"What are you going to do now?"

* * *

The next morning I woke up in her closet under a pile of clothes. Her scent was all over me. I don't mean deodorant or perfume, but her natural smell. Even without the artificial scents, she smelled awesome. I was in love. At least, I think I was. That's got to be a part of love, right? When you enjoy someone's body odor?

Through the wall I could hear her talking to her mother and father as all three got ready for work. Tracy had some office job and was getting dressed. She looked so different, so bland. The angular drab outfit covered up the curves of her hot body in a way that pissed me off.

"You be good," she whispered to me through a crack in the closet.

"I will. I'll just watch TV or something."

"Fine. I left out some postcards that Charles wrote me from Europe. I wonder what he would say about this situation."

"Probably something about waiting for me to come out of the closet."

She laughed, her hair falling over her face. She tucked it behind her ear like I imagine she did at the office.

"I'm usually done around five," she said, "but I'll sneak back at lunch time. Dad's already gone, but don't come out until after ten when my mom leaves."

She kissed me on the forehead and closed me in. I sat in darkness with only the sound of her mother singing to herself keeping me awake. I felt like a pervert.

What was I going to do? I couldn't stay here forever. The cops would be chasing me. I had to think of something.

All the excitement had tired me out. The dark and the warm smell of Tracy knocked me out. When I woke up, the house was quiet. Tracy's clock read eleven a.m.

* * *

I pushed my way out of the closet slowly. All these years we knew each other and I had never been to her place for any length of time, and she hadn't been to mine. We were both ashamed of our fathers.

I wandered around. The house was huge and clean, like a museum compared to mine and Dad's dumpy bachelor pad. Everything was trimmed in gold, or made of glass, angels and crosses everywhere. At least three Bibles were lying around. There were several photos of Tracy, her mother and father in shiny frames, engraved with phrases like "May God watch over our family."

The pictures made me ill. She didn't look like the Tracy I knew. Her home life and her life with me were too different. She would have to choose one someday and I was confident she would not choose me.

She looked so different, so unlike my wild chick. My girlfriend, I guess. I wonder if her parents even knew she'd been inked.

I flopped on the soft couch. When I moved around, a fruity smell emerged from the sparkly white cushions.

Daytime TV makes my brain hurt. It's mostly soaps and women crying about how mean men are. I ended up channel surfing to one of Dad's news shows. It reminded me of home. The only thing missing was the smell of alcohol.

So who is on the screen, but Dad's old enemy, Senator Hanson.

The text at the bottom of the screen read: "Cons to Soldiers. A good idea?"

I changed the channel quickly. That was a little too much like home. Fortunately, I found something worth watching: a talk show host was trying to determine which of six guys was the father of a tranny's kid.

* * *

All the time I was watching TV I was itching. It finally occurred to me that I hadn't cleaned off in a couple days. Since I was on my own, there were so many details to think about. Where could I get a change of clothes? Where would I stay tomorrow? How was I going to get food? I hated the idea of taking a shower and getting back into the same sweaty clothes, but I had no choice.

I wish I had done it sooner. Tracy's family had a shower like a spa. The tub was huge, the water jet hot and powerful. I stood there forever, letting the stream massage the back of my head.

When I opened the steamy door, a towel was held out for me.

"You got out for lunch?" I yelled over the vent fan. "Why don't you get naked and come in here? When I'm done with you, you're going to need a cleaning."

Tracy didn't say anything.

I took the towel and rubbed the water off my face and out of my eyes. Then I looked around the corner.

Two cops stood there in the steam, smirking. Tracy's dad was standing in the hall behind them, frowning.

Shit.

JAMIL

UNKNOWN LOCATION

2005

Jamil felt ill. He hadn't been the same since returning to his cell from the infirmary. He spent days sitting on the floor, staring at the lump of caulk that cut him off from Prasad.

He had stopped exercising. He was certain that he was not going to leave here alive. They were going to kill him or he was going to kill himself. Sometimes he would half-heartedly drop to the floor to do pushups, but he would lose count before he reached ten and lie there until it was time for bed.

Mostly he was exhausted. Were sedatives in his food? He couldn't be sure. He started to see value in dropping all resistance. There was no torment when he let the days blend and flow past. There was no sense of wasted years that way, just a sense of being.

When they came for him he was almost glad. He offered no stiffness as they roughly bound his hands and covered his head. He let them manipulate him like he was their plaything.

That was all he was anyway.

* * *

He leaned forward, nodding off.

"Jamil! Do you hear me?" Mikhail yelled in his ear.

Jamil was slumped to the side. Only the bindings of the chair held him upright.

Mikhail's voice pierced his skull from behind. "Jamil. I am tired of your antics. The more you refuse me information, the more, how shall I say, creative I must become."

Jamil said nothing. He had learned that much.

"Your friend, the one you called Prasad, told us there are a great many things you might be able to enlighten me about. Still you do not share. Will you offer them voluntarily?"

Jamil thought about trying to push himself from his body again, but couldn't muster the desire necessary. His eyelids fluttered.

Mikhail was abrupt. "Your silence limits my choices. I must be absolutely certain you have told us everything. Proceed."

The guards slid a low wooden bench before Jamil. He was released from the chair and his clothes sliced off with a small knife, the guard's deft cuts never damaging skin. Jamil shivered as a chill rippled across his naked body. They bent him down across the bench and, using metal cuffs, attached his hands to a metal ring under the bench's legs below his chin. His legs were pulled forward, and his ankles cuffed to the same ring so his buttocks poked out behind the far end of the bench. Lastly, a metal strip was placed about his neck, holding his head in place, preventing him from rearing up.

In seconds he had gone from clothed and seated to naked and folded on a platform just inches above the floor, his buttocks sticking up in the air.

Jamil's head, lower than the rest of his body, felt heavy as the blood rushed to it. He started to panic and that gave him a perverse hope. He was not completely destroyed if he could still fear. Then again, if he still had remnants of a will, his death might take longer.

"I don't know anything," Jamil said. "I left my mother and went to my uncle's garage. He told me to go play football. So I did. Then two men-"

"Tell me something new, Jamil. Prasad said you had much to offer."

"I don't. Prasad lied about me to free himself."

"If he did then he was most convincing, something I have advised you to be many times. When are you going to learn, Jamil? You must convince me."

"He was a teacher, a writer. He was skilled at telling stories."

Mikhail did not reply.

Jamil smelled something unusual, like antiseptic. Someone rubbed a slippery gel between his buttocks, poking a fingertip into his anus then pulling out quickly. Jamil lunged, but succeeded only in rattling his metal bindings and straining against the collar.

"Did you like that?" Mikhail asked.

Jamil said nothing. Even naked in this cold room, he was breaking into a sweat.

He heard the door open behind him followed by a clicking noise, then the sound of someone breathing rapidly. Jamil looked over his shoulder and saw a large dog. A black and brown German shepherd snarled and drooled, leaping forward. He stood on his hind legs for a moment, restrained only by his leash.

Jamil's heart fluttered.

"Don't let him bite me," he squealed, his voice cracking.

"He will not bite you," Mikhail said, laughing. "He is friendly. Perhaps too friendly."

The masked handler walked the dog around Jamil. Jamil turned his head away from the smell of the beast's damp fur. The dog kept leaping up toward Jamil, straining his collar, slobber flying off his tongue.

"He likes you, Jamil. He wants to know you better."

Fur brushed against Jamil's side as they let the dog rub against him.

"He likes to fuck any hole there is."

The handler guided the dog behind Jamil.

"No! No! No!" Jamil screamed.

He stretched his neck to look behind him. The dog's sniffing snout was wedging between his butt cheeks. The handler pulled up on the leash, so the dog could rest his paws on Jamil's back. The scratching claws raked his lower back as the dog mounted him.

"Please! Make him stop!"

Mikhail kneeled down next to Jamil and whispered in his ear. "Tell me everything or this dog will fuck you in the ass."

Jamil flashed outside from his body, then back in again. He heard himself crying, "No! No! Please! No!"

"You will never be a man again."

"No! No! No!"

"Your whole life, you will remember the day that you had sex with a dog. Unless you tell me something, right now, Jamil. Right this very second. Now. Talk to me."

Jamil was still yelling. The "No! No! No!" erupting from his lips was mechanical, unconscious. His heart pounded in his ears, sweat poured out of him.

"Tell me something, Jamil," Mikhail yelled over the pleas. "Don't make him do this. I can make him go away, but you have to talk!"

The dog inched forward, hot fur brushing Jamil's head, the twitching muscles pressing closer. Jamil bucked against the chains, cutting his wrists, pinching his neck. Something small and firm, warm and wet, poked between the edges of his buttocks.

Suddenly the room was filled with a rotten food smell.

"Fuck, the dude shit himself," someone said in English.

"No! No! No!" Jamil screamed.

He had lost all control. He was wailing, straining against the binds, cutting off the circulation to his wrists. Drops of the dog's saliva tapped him on his back moving up his spine. Jamil was weeping, moaning, and crying hysterically. This couldn't be happening. This had to be a nightmare.

"I want to die!" he screamed, his voice peaking, cracking. "Kill me! Kill me now! I beg you!"

His entire backside was warmed by the fur on the dog's bare abdomen as the creature pressed against him. A twitching worm vibrated against the tender skin of his anus, pressing forward.

"Dog's popping that cherry!" the English commentary went on.

"Jesus fucking Christ."

"More like Rover fucking Jerry Jihad."

They are laughing, Jamil thought. This horrible, cruel thing they were doing to him and they were laughing. This was not a world worth living in.

"Kill me!" Jamil yelled, he banged his chin on the bench, rattling his teeth, his skin rupturing.

"Shit. He's losing it."

"Tell me something, Jamil!" Mikhail boomed over the chaos, "Anything!"

"Noooooo!" Jamil yelled, the sound growing louder and louder. He gasped for air and continued.

He tried to force himself from his body, but there was no pain to trigger it, no physical agony to dislodge him from the flesh. Even removed from his body, he would have to come back to it, and violated by a dog, he wouldn't want to.

"No! No!" he squealed. "Please, no! Kill me! Just kill me!"

The pinched scent of urine filled the room.

"Now he's pissed himself. Damn!" The men laughed. "Ram it home, Rover."

Jamil felt something wet and stiff push apart his anus. He let loose a primal scream, more high-pitched than he thought any human could.

Just as he did, the dog yelped. Fur brushed against Jamil's back as the animal was wrenched away violently. Someone cursed in an unfamiliar language.

The room fell silent except for the whimpering of the dog and Jamil's frenzied gasping. Blood oozed from his chin, urine slid down the incline and pooled around his belly and diarrhea dripped onto the floor with a wet slap. Jamil was crying, openly and outwardly.

"He's broken," someone whispered.

"No shit," someone replied.

The room remained uncomfortably quiet except for the tones of a cell phone being dialed. The only noise Jamil wanted to hear was a gun cocking so he would soon be dead.

"Kill me," he whispered.

"It's me," Mikhail said sharply. "I'm ending this. We took it as far as we could. We broke him completely and he gave us nothing. Absolutely nothing! Tell your fucking collectors to be more selective!"

Jamil jolted as the cell phone exploded on the far wall. A door opened and slammed. Men yelled behind it. The clack of claws faded into the distance. The door banged open and closed again.

Jamil was wailing like a child, each gasp racking his body. The men were gone. The dog was gone. He was alone, strapped down, his tears, blood, shit, piss and snot draining from him. He sobbed and whimpered, not bothering to resist. They had beaten him, destroyed him.

He understood now why the lion did not lash out.

He understood completely.

* * *

The lights dimmed, the lights brightened.

The food tray clanged open, the food tray clanged shut.

Jamil barely moved.

He thought of nothing. He lay on his cot, staring at the ceiling, rising only when his body commanded him to relieve himself. Sometimes he ignored the call and his room began to smell.

The time between the lights brightening and dimming flashed with the speed of blinking. The guards no longer brought him before Mikhail.

When they forced him to shower, he offered no resistance. He didn't eat. He spent every waking moment wishing to die.

He knew time was passing, but had no idea how much.

* * *

The cell door opened suddenly and without warning, without the usual preceding commands and threats.

Jamil turned his head to look over with sleepy apathy. A thin man stood in the open doorway, wearing a ski mask, his bright blue eyes striking against the black fabric.

"Jamil."

It was Mikhail's voice.

Jamil didn't respond. He turned his attention back to the ceiling.

"Jamil. Please look at me."

Mikhail entered the room, followed by a single guard. No weapons were drawn.

"Jamil," Mikhail said again. Jamil gazed at him limply. Mikhail stood over him, then crouched, sliding his hands under Jamil's legs. He gently pulled to twist Jamil on the cot so he was sitting up.

Jamil stared into the bright blue eyes, swaying as he sat. Mikhail kneeled before him to meet him face to face.

Mikhail reached up. Jamil flinched.

The guard standing behind Mikhail grabbed Mikhail's wrist, stopping him. Mikhail snapped his hand loose and pulled at the bottom of his ski mask, lifting it over his head to expose his small, round, gentle face. His white hair was thinning on top, his face pockmarked. He frowned as he cupped Jamil's chin in his hands, like his mother once did. Or did she?

"You see, Jamil?" Mikhail said. "We cover our faces to prevent retribution from terrorists, but I believe you now. You are no murderer. Now, please wake up. We're going to let you go, but you need to eat, to care for yourself."

Jamil stared at him. The man before him had kind eyes, his tone seemed sincere, but his appearance meant nothing. It had to be a trick.

Mikhail frowned. "Jamil, there is a war going on, and people do terrible things in war. Sometimes the innocent get caught in the middle. When a bomber pushes a button, he believes he is doing so to kill evil men. But sometimes good men are killed as well. Sometimes women, even children. Sometimes a soldier shoots a child by accident and regrets it the rest of his life. If it makes you feel any better, I will see your face and cry in my sleep for the rest of my days. I hate those who started this war, but I hope you understand I was just doing my job, as any soldier would."

Jamil thought of saying something, but he just couldn't muster the drive to do it. The words turned to vapor in his mind.

Mikhail continued, his eyes watering. "Sometimes commanders make mistakes and entire regiments are killed. Errors are as inevitable in war as they are in any activity. You are not alone in your trials. I am harmed just as permanently as you are. I simply wanted to say I am sorry for what happened to you."

Jamil stared through him. Mikhail shook his shoulders.

"Jamil. You must wake up."

Jamil didn't move.

Mikhail sighed. "I am sorry," he said as he stood and strode to the door, carrying his mask. He was at the doorway when Jamil spoke.

"You have blue eyes," Jamil said.

Mikhail turned. "Yes."

"Your face is scarred, and you are balding on top."

"Yes, it's true. This job has made me age before my-"

Jamil cackled.

Mikhail frowned. "Why does that matter? What does that mean?"

Jamil kept laughing, holding his belly, ignoring the question.

Mikhail pulled on his ski mask. He and the guard left without another word, closing the door gently behind them.

"That means it was real. It wasn't a dream," Jamil whispered intensely. His throat burned, but he couldn't stop the maniacal laughter bursting from him.

"I knew!" he screamed. "I knew! I knew!"

The bolt in the metal door banged shut.

Jamil laughed and laughed until the lights dimmed and he passed out.

* * *

Jamil was again catatonic days later when there was another knock on his cell door. He was ordered prone in the familiar way.

"Jamil! Lie face down against the far wall or we will shoot you."

Jamil considered the opportunity. He could rush them or grab one of their guns and shoot himself. He could shoot as many of them as possible until he was dead. But he was too tired for all that. He rolled off his cot and curled up against the wall.

The door crashed open. Strong hands grabbed him, rubbing and patting as they searched for weapons.

"Do what you want," he said. "I am dead."

* * *

He awoke to a rumbling sound, a vibration that shook his whole body. The radiation of bright light glowed through the hood on his head. He was sweating.

As best he could guess in the semi-darkness, he was in a van. The air was blazing hot. He didn't bother to ask where they were going. There would only be more lies, more commands to stay silent. The warmth and bouncing lulled him to sleep. Each time he woke, nothing had changed. Their journey seemed incredibly long.

When the vehicle stopped, he was dragged out into the heat, the binds cut from his wrists.

"We have many guns pointed at you," someone said. "You may relieve yourself."

Jamil fumbled at his pants, for the Velcro fly and was surprised to find he was wearing slacks. How long had it been since he wore genuine pants?

He unzipped and urinated.

After that, the hood was loosened so his mouth was exposed. A bottle of water was pressed roughly to his lips. Someone fed him rice and meat with a spoon with simple commands: "Open your mouth. Chew. Swallow. Again."

Then they were back in the van. He leaned his head against the frame and slept. They made two more stops to relieve themselves and eat and drink. Jamil did not ask a single question and he did not entertain hope. He simply went along as he was told.

* * *

He woke up as he was being lifted and shoved. He stumbled and fell face-first onto what felt like concrete. A fist ground between his shoulder blades and pinned him to the dusty, hard surface. He could hear the sound of people nearby. The heavy cylinder of a gun pressed painfully into the back of his head.

He closed his eyes calmly. "I'm going to die, Inshallah," he thought. He opened his heart to accept peace, eager for oblivion, hoping there was no afterlife.

Someone whispered in his ear in Arabic. "Lie here and count to five hundred before you get up. If you rise any sooner, you'll be shot."

Jamil didn't answer.

"But if you lie still and count to five hundred, you are free."

Jamil didn't answer. It was some trick, certainly. The obnoxious pressure of the gun lifted from his skull. Dust and heat sprayed over him as he heard what sounded like the vehicle driving off.

With his hood on, he couldn't see, but could hear sounds of a street nearby, people talking, cars driving slowly. Was he home? Did it matter? A breeze blew over him.

He faded in and out of sleep.

Someone was shaking him, searching his pockets. Jamil let them. He had nothing to take. When he moved, the bandit yelped and ran off. Jamil pulled off his hood. The light made everything black and white and he saw only the shadow of the robber skitter around a corner and was gone.

Jamil looked around. He was seated in a narrow alley between two tall buildings, the sky a faint blue line above. The walkway opened onto larger streets filled with sunlight, crowded with people, merchant carts and cars rolling by. He stood up. He stretched his arms and looked down at his clothes. He was wearing a simple button-up shirt, plain shoes and slacks made for a man his height, but weighing much more.

He spun around. He was alone. The cramped alleyway around him seemed vast. He started to walk toward the street, one pace, two, three, four. He hesitated, expecting to hit a wall, even though the space before him was empty. He took another step, then another. No one stopped him or took notice. He didn't hit a wall.

He ran toward the street.

He felt like he was flying. The feeling to power himself forward, unconstrained seemed to lift him. He charged down the alley, wind rushing past his ears, sprinting toward the sunlight before him like a plane speeding toward takeoff. He leapt out, jumping as high and as far as he could, into the street, into the sun.

A car's horn blared as it swerved and barely missed him.

Jamil stepped back carefully and laughed. He leaned against a wall, squeezing his forehead, weeping softly. He slid down the wall to sit, still hysterical. He knew he must look completely insane and felt that he probably was.

* * *

No one took notice of him for very long. People strolled and cars cruised in both directions at a quick pace, heading to their business somewhere else in this unfamiliar city. Some women wore burqas, some wore Western clothes. A vendor selling snacks pushed a cart past. Jamil approached him. "Excuse me, sir, could you tell me where I am?"

The man frowned and quickly hurried away.

Jamil strolled up to a stopped cab. The driver had the window down, his arm resting outside the car as he smoked.

"I'm sorry, sir," Jamil said in Arabic. "Can you tell me where I am?"

The driver took a drag, looked at him, then smirked. "Too much fun last night?"

Jamil smiled and shrugged, playing along.

"You're in Baghdad."

"Baghdad? Iraq?"

"Is there another?"

"Can you tell me where a phone is?"

"Try the market." He waved his hand in the direction his cab was facing.

Jamil strolled down the street, flexing his hands, stretching his legs. He tried not to giggle. The sensation was exhilarating, terrifying and enjoyable all at once. Simply walking had never before brought him such ecstasy.

* * *

He entered a small, dark and dusty grocery store. He wandered the three aisles, marveling at the selection of fruits, spiced rice packets and many flavors of sodas. The choices were overwhelming. How could anybody pick just one?

The shopkeeper was a rotund man who eyed him suspiciously. "What do you want, boy?"

"May I use your phone?"

"Anyone may use it, provided they pay first."

"I don't have money."

"Well, go get some, then give it to me, and then you can use the phone."

"But I have nothing. I was recently kidnapped. I'm trying to get home."

The shopkeeper chuckled. "Kidnapped? Were you, now? Well, now that you are free again, you can just run home."

"But I'm from Morocco, I need to call home."

"Morocco? Really?"

"Yes, and I-"

"Leave my store, thief, or I'll call the police. Maybe I'll even call the Americans, and you'll see what they do to you."

"What are Americans doing in Iraq?"

"Out!"

Jamil wandered the streets, not paying attention to where he was going. Some blocks were crowded with people hurrying in all directions. Others were empty, populated only by suspicious faces peeking out of windows reinforced with wood. Still other blocks were nothing but crumbled buildings and bullet-pocked walls.

Enormous combat jeeps rumbled by. The American flag was stenciled on the side, the windows bristling with gun barrels. Americans were in Baghdad. But why?

"Incoming, three o'clock!" someone yelled in English.

Jamil had strolled to the edge of a parking lot. In the center of it sat one of the combat vehicles, six soldiers crouched around it, their guns pointed toward him. Jamil slowly raised his hands. Five of the soldiers lowered their guns.

"Chill out, it's just a kid."

"Fuck that, even the kids are killers."

"Stand down, jackass," the soldier nearest to Jamil said. He was huge and muscular, with dark African skin. So much equipment hung from him he looked like a machine. He pushed the gun barrel of his fellow soldier toward the ground.

"Come here, kid," the large man said. "Slowly."

"I just need some money," Jamil said in English, keeping his hands up.

"Hey, you speak good English," the soldier said. He held his chin for a moment before speaking again. "Tell you what, buddy. I'll give you some money, but you have to do something for me."

"What is it?"

"You need to tell everyone in this neighborhood that we're not bothering anyone, we're just finishing our tour, okay? If we don't get any trouble from them, we won't come into their homes. Spread the word."

"I will."

The giant reached into his pocket and pulled out some bills. "Now I'll give you some cash. You bring back some cold sodas, and I'll give you more. All right?"

"Make sure the sodas are sealed," one of the other soldiers said.

Without looking back to his companions, the soldier continued. "Nothing that's already open, all right, kid? If the cans are open, no money."

The large man handed him some green bills. American dollars.

* * *

Jamil bolted from the lot and after much wandering through a maze of market stalls selling dry goods, he finally found his way back to the store. He selected a variety of sodas, stored on a shelf in front of a battery-operated fan used to cool them. Jamil grabbed as many as he could carry and set them on the counter, grinning proudly. He placed a five-dollar American bill next to them.

"And where did you find this?" the store owner asked, squinting at the bill.

"I'm supposed to tell you that the soldiers in the lot aren't bothering anyone."

The store owner chuckled as he packed the cans into a paper bag. "Someone tells me that at least once a week. Maybe when the bodies stop piling up, I'll believe it. Still, I should not complain. Those bastards bring me a lot of business."

Jamil took the sodas back to the Americans. Each can was passed among the group and inspected. The large black man tossed one to him. "Here, kid. Keep one. And spread the word. We're not fucking with them, so they shouldn't fuck with us."

* * *

Even with money, surviving seemed sure to require much effort. His basic needs had been provided to him for so long, he wasn't sure what to do. He needed to find food and water and a place to sleep, but how? He knew he'd better think of something quickly, the sun was just passing its high point.

There was something even more important he had to do first.

Asking directions, he found his way to a bus depot and stood before the payphone bank, pausing a long time before inserting his money, following the directions for calling Morocco. He couldn't mentally remember the number he wanted, but his fingers did.

The phone rang after a series of clicks. He held the handset over the switch in the cradle, ready to hang up, but then pulled back. He did this twice while waiting.

Finally a man answered. "Salaam."

He immediately recognized the voice as his uncle's. Jamil said nothing.

"Hello?" his uncle said louder. "Who is calling?"

Jamil imagined him yelling into the phone, trying to be heard over the noise of the auto shop. He was surely pressing the receiver against his ear hard, looking out into the garage where the cars were being worked on by his team. Jamil could hear the sound of tools clanking.

"I can't hear you," his uncle said. "Call back."

Jamil was still. He said nothing. His uncle did not hang up. Jamil pushed the phone toward its cradle, then quickly pressed it against his ear again.

"Jamil? If that is you, make a sound. We will come to you, wherever you are. Whatever it costs."

Jamil slammed down the phone. He leaned his head against it for a long time, squeezing his eyes closed.

He put more money into the phone and made another call, again letting the memory of moving his fingers do the dialing.

"Salaam," a woman answered. Tears poured down Jamil's face. He bit his fist so he would not make a noise.

He could hear his sisters arguing in the background, the television blaring as couples professed their love for each other in Spanish. His heart lightened painfully, seeming to expand against a sharp crust around it. Jamil had missed the noisy chaos of home. The clamor was a delight compared to the stony silence of his cell.

"I can't hear you," his mother said.

A whimper escaped Jamil's mouth.

"Hello?" his mother asked. "Girls! Be quiet! Shut that off!" The shrillness of his mother's voice pierced the girls' natural resistance. The television quieted.

"Who is this?" his mother asked.

Jamil was shaking as tears streamed down his cheeks in rivulets thick enough to drop onto the floor. He turned his back to people walking through the depot staring at him, concerned.

"Jamil, if this is you, say something. Anything. Make a sound."

He clenched the mouthpiece tighter so his knuckles hurt.

"I hear that you have not hung up," she said. Even across this much time and distance, she could see through her son's deception the way only a mother could.

"Say where you are and we will move mountains to bring you home."

"Is it him?" one of his sisters asked.

"Quiet!"

Jamil slammed the handset down and leaned his head against the phone and wept, unable to explain to himself what he had just done.

* * *

Outside, the daylight was dimming. The sidewalk crowds were clearing except for groups of young men, their voices rowdy, often angry. Jamil walked in an approximate spiral, always turning left until he found what he was looking for: a block demolished by bombing. He climbed over the rubble, crawling deeper into the ruin of a home. In the final light of the day he found an abandoned bed.

The mattress smelled and was covered with pulverized brick, but sleeping on it felt like he was lying on cotton a meter thick. The cool night wind blew over him as he gazed upward through the damaged roof at the stars. The dark sky was so beautiful he almost smiled.

* * *

Warmth woke him.

Dust floated in the sunbeams that lanced his ruined shelter. He was hungry and thirsty. His first idea was to find a store and steal something, but if he were caught, they would take him to a jail, back to a cell, or worse.

No, he thought, I will die first. No one will ever take me alive.

Never, ever again.

Exploring the streets, he found his way back to a neighborhood alive with activity, free of the shot-up homes. Everywhere there was motion: people rode bicycles, cleaned their market stands, purchased food, drove or walked by. Everyone was heading somewhere. Occasionally, a vehicle carrying solders rumbled past, leaving in its wake people emerging from behind something solid.

Jamil was searching for the lot with the American soldiers, looking to earn more money. Instead he found a rubble-strewn field where boys were kicking a ball around. Large chunks of brick defined the field boundaries of the improvised arena. The goal borders were formed by a tire, an empty rocket shell, and engine parts.

He joined in without asking for permission, without even declaring whose team he was on. He was thrilled to play football again, but his height no longer provided him the advantage it once did. His muscles and his reflexes had atrophied. He could think of the moves he should make, but when he actually made them, he was clumsy or slow and the ball was stripped from him easily.

He strained harder and harder, sweating, cursing, elbowing his opponents. The game continued without anyone scoring. He was dribbling the ball along when suddenly the other players seemed to vanish before him. He had an open shot! Without hesitation he took it. The ball sailed free, over the goal line and kept going.

Goal!

He raised his arms in victory, but no one was celebrating with him. Most of the boys were quickly making their way down side streets. Some of them leaned against a building, resting in the shade.

Jamil looked around, confused. He picked up the ball and ran to the few boys who had stayed.

"What's going on?"

"That car," one of them said, lifting his chin toward where a road passed the field. "It comes around when we play. They're always looking for young boys."

Jamil clenched his fist. The shining black car's darkened windows were closed. It rolled up to the corner of the lot, radiating wealth and authority. Most cars Jamil had seen here in Baghdad were military vehicles or dented and dusty civilian autos. This polished vehicle stood out, hub caps glistening silver.

The tinted back window rolled down. A man leaned his head out. He looked like a movie star. His beard was manicured, his hair gelled into a wave. His skin was bronze, almost glowing, to complement his reflective sunglasses. He looked to the boys lounging in the shade.

"Who is that?" Jamil asked.

"That's Mister K."

"He doesn't have a full name?"

"That's what everyone calls him."

"What's he doing here?"

"I told you. He offers the boys jobs. Pays them money."

"So, why did so many run?"

"Because sometimes the boys who work for him never come back."

"What happens to them?"

"No one knows. Some say that he sells them to visitors from Saudi Arabia. Others think he sells them to the Americans for their organs."

"You're a fool. You believe anything," a second boy said, shoving the one who had been talking with Jamil. Jamil stared at the car; the back of his neck felt burning hot.

"I may have nothing," the first boy said, "but no money will make me take it in the ass."

"You all right?" the second boy asked Jamil. "You look sick. Or angry."

"Hm? I'm fine. I'm hungry, that's all."

"Then go see Mister K."

* * *

Mister K leaned out of the car, his pastel blue shirt unbuttoned at the top, a clutch of chest hair curling out. He called across the lot, speaking Arabic.

"Hello and good day, brave young men! I need help with some errands. Come work for me and I'll pay you well."

Jamil noticed Mister K's teeth. Their perfect whiteness matched Ahmed's, the man who had kidnapped him. Jamil shrunk back, but his stomach growled, protested.

"Come on," Mister K called out as the boys looked away. "It's just some simple errands. I'll pay you. With money you can do anything. Buy some food. Feed your family. Maybe you even pay a girl to be nice to you for a while."

Jamil scanned the area, plotting several escape routes.

"Don't tell me you strong young men are going to play games while your mothers and sisters sell their bodies. Have you no honor?"

The car rolled across the lot slowly. More boys crept away.

"This isn't a safe neighborhood," Mister K called after them. "It's only a matter of time before you're killed. You can get out with money. Do you want some or not?"

Jamil strode to the side of Mister K's car, staying out of arm's reach. Mister K sat back inside. The driver watched Jamil in his mirror.

"Here's one with a sense of pride," Mister K said. "You seem too old to be among these homeless children. You seem like a man."

"I'm tall," Jamil answered in Arabic.

Through the open window, Mister K looked him up and down. "All right, get in."

"No," Jamil said. "I'm not a fool. Meet me down that alley, we'll talk in private as long as you like but I'm not getting in your car."

"There are plenty of other boys watching us. We would not try anything before so many witnesses. You are safe. Come. Get in."

"Do you want a stupid boy working for you? One that's not even smart enough to avoid getting in a stranger's car?"

Mister K frowned. "You've got some balls, kid."

189

"That's why you want me to work for you."

"All right. Down that alley, but you try anything unusual, you will end up hurt."

"I offer you the same advice."

Mister K smirked and leaned back.

Jamil walked down the dead end and waited. The car turned around and rolled down the street backwards. Jamil stood near the back window again and wiped his sweaty palms on his pants.

The boys restarted their game, stealing timid glances down the alley.

Jamil checked his escape. If Mister K tried to grab him, he would run to the end of the street, staying close to the buildings, then make a sharp right and dive into the rubble beyond. The car could never follow him over the large chunks of concrete. Satisfied, he spoke to Mister K through the back window.

"So, what do I have to do?"

"I am a traveling businessman," Mister K said. "My colleague has forgotten his pack. I need you to bring it to him."

"Why can't you bring it yourself?"

"I have a business meeting to go to, for which I am already very late."

"What business are you in?"

"That's none of your concern."

"I want to know what I'm getting into."

"You make a delivery, that's all."

Jamil squinted. "All right."

"We have a deal?"

"For now."

The door opposite Jamil opened. Mister K slid across the seat and exited the vehicle. He walked to the back of the car and gently knocked on the trunk. The driver released it from inside the car. Four identical black backpacks were lying in the storage bed, each stuffed to their capacity, their zippers pulled taut and sealed by padlock.

Mister K lifted out one of the thick canvas packs.

"I've added the lock to make sure no one runs off with the contents," he said.

"What's in it?"

Mister K turned to him, eyes still hidden by reflective sunglasses. Jamil saw his own reflection: a dirty, sweaty, homeless kid dressed in ill-fitting clothes.

"You are a courier, boy," Mister K scolded, pointing in Jamil's face. "You never ask what is in the package. Respect the customer's privacy, yes? You deliver it and collect your fee. If you look inside, my friend will know and he'll tell me. Then you won't get paid."

"Where should I take it?"

"Walk back out to the field, turn left. Make a quick right at the main street and follow that. Past the old monument that was torn down, there is a club the Americans frequent. You cannot miss it. Go inside and drop this off at the end of the bar. When you do, you pull this cord." Mister K showed him a wire tied to a key. "When my friend calls and I know he's received the package, come back here to get paid."

"Why do I have to pull the cord?"

Mister K didn't answer. He just handed him the backpack.

"How will your friend know where to pick it up?" Jamil asked as he took the pack. It was far heavier than it appeared. A tiny logo was embossed on the shoulder strap, a symbol he had seen every day for the past few years: the insignia of the Redfire Corporation.

"That symbol," he said. "Is that Chinese? American?"

"I told you to stop asking questions!"

Jamil didn't move.

Mister K sighed. "All right, I will satisfy your curiosity. The pack is made in China. The symbol is American."

"But it is not the American flag."

"No. It represents an American company that sends soldiers to fight for America."

"America has two armies?"

"So many questions! Yes. Two different armies. One is paid more than the other."

"I don't understand."

"What is there to understand? They are American. Just hate them both. Now go. Drop the bag off at the club, pull the cord, then come back here. And no more questions!"

* * *

Jamil approached the club, the pack's weight rubbing painfully into the small of his back. Sweat pooled where the tough canvas met his shirt.

The building stood out among the ruins around him. It was new, shining with glass, polished marble, and lighted signs inside the tinted windows. It was obviously alien to the neighborhood.

Someone grabbed his shoulder and barked in his ear in Arabic.

"May I help you?"

The Iraqi doorman was wearing a white buttoned shirt and black slacks, his face handsomely tan and shaved smooth. He looked at Jamil with disgust.

"I'm looking for a friend," Jamil said.

"Oh, really?"

"To give him a message."

"Is that so? What's your friend's name?"

"Mohammed."

The doorman frowned.

"He forgot his bag," Jamil said. "That's all. I'm returning it to him."

The doorman stared at him, quietly thinking.

"Please," Jamil said, "I was paid by his business partner to bring it, that's all."

"All right," the doorman said. "You seem harmless. Can I trust you not to make trouble?"

"Of course," Jamil said.

"Well, you can't stay if you don't buy any drinks. Don't let me see you here in five minutes. Do what you must and get out, your clothes are filthy."

Jamil pushed though the crowd.

The café was packed. Despite the blazing heat outside, the inside was cool and dark. Women in tight, revealing clothing smoked and laughed, surrounded by men in military uniforms or suits. Waiters rushed in and out of the back room as Western music played. The scene reminded him of his sisters' television romance stories. The simple bass beat of dance music boomed through the tiny space.

The stool at the end of the bar was empty. He sat there and put the package down gently. He knew what was going to happen, he just didn't know when.

He reached down, held his breath and closed his eyes. He yanked the key. The cord came loose. He slipped the key in his pocket and walked out of the club as quickly as he could without being obvious. He was certain someone had seen him. There were so many people around, how could they not? There had to be cameras.

"Don't come back," the doorman said as he left.

Jamil lifted his foot to descend the steps to the street when a hot wind pushed against his back, throwing him forward. He tumbled, protecting his head with his arms. Dust blew around him in an instant before the sound of an explosion pushed his ears to the limit, causing the roar to disappear into silence, followed by a high-pitched squeal.

He was on his hands and knees at the base of the stairs, coughing, struggling to stand. Someone tumbled against him, clutching his forearm, looking dazedly at the stump where his hand had once been. His face was burned black, his eyes speckled red.

"You," the doorman gasped before falling forward. Blood spurted from his wrist, shooting up the stairs in time with the pumping of his heart.

Jamil staggered to his feet and ran.

* * *

He was still dusting himself off as he arrived at the field where he had met Mister K. The car sat alone in the middle of the lot, darkened windows rolled up, the engine on. None of the boys were around.

Jamil approached cautiously, scanning for side streets, places to run, just in case. The car's tinted back window slid down and Mister K smiled at him. "My friend tells me the package arrived. He thanks you."

He tossed an envelope out the window. Jamil caught it and slid it in his pocket.

The window closed and the car roared off.

* * *

Minutes later, Jamil was shoving food into his mouth at an outdoor falafel cart. A radio was on in the background, its scratchy sound barely understandable.

"…another explosion. Six dead now, more to surely follow. Dozens wounded."

Jamil stopped eating for a moment. He stared at the food in his hands. He sipped the cool mango and ice drink sitting before him.

"More bloodshed," the cart owner muttered. "It's never going to end."

Jamil resumed eating. The radio news report continued, in its frantic clipped tones, but his stomach fell silent.

* * *

Jamil returned to the ruined home he had claimed. Other street boys were sleeping among the debris, but they were out in the open, where anyone could see them. Fools, Jamil thought. He knew the difficulty in getting to his hideaway would deter anyone inclined to molest him in the night. He pushed through the destruction, crawling across rubble and squeezing between fallen walls, scraping his knees and elbows, still raw from his tumble at the café where the explosion had hurled him across the concrete.

He sat on the bed. The sun was setting. He wasn't hungry or thirsty and he felt physically content. He leaned his head back and closed his eyes.

He thought of the people he had killed today. He didn't know any of them. He had nothing against them, and yet, he was surprised that he felt so little concern. He only did it to survive. Wasn't that like something Mikhail had said?

He looked up through the ragged partial roof to the night sky. Allah was not there. No one was there.

"I could have been them or they could have been me," he said aloud to himself.

* * *

In the same way he had interrupted the game the day before, Mister K's glistening black car rolled to the edge of the lot and stopped, the engine idling. Boys scattered while Jamil approached the car confidently.

The back window slid down. Mister K grinned from inside. "Here to earn more money, my young friend?"

"I am."

"Shall we talk here or in your office?" he chuckled.

"My office," Jamil said, neither laughing along nor smiling.

"Down the dead end alley again?"

"Of course."

Jamil followed the car as it backed down the alley. The few remaining boys stared and whispered.

Down the alley, Mister K leapt out of the car. "You keep up the good work, I might make you a regular partner. I have so many deliveries to make, and boys your age are rarely as reliable as you. They take the packages and run away, or they do something foolish and... What I'm saying is I'm always needing new help."

"So, you'll pay me more than last time?" Jamil asked.

Inside the darkness of the car, the driver chuckled. Mister K hesitated before slamming his door shut. At the back of the car he playfully slapped Jamil on the cheek. "There's something about you, kid. I like you."

The trunk popped loose. The hatch held four packs, all identical to the ones from yesterday. Each was the same size, stuffed to capacity, the zippers padlocked. All were marked with the Redfire logo, and a key dangled from a cord. Mister K removed a pack and set it on the ground gingerly.

Jamil shivered as he imagined what might happen if the car hit one of the many potholes in the ragged Baghdad streets.

"Can you believe it?" Mister K said as he lightly closed the trunk. He gently slapped himself in the forehead. "I missed my friend again. He is traveling and forgot his luggage. Can you get this to him on bus number 49?"

"Your friend is awfully forgetful."

Mister K frowned.

"It's not a question," Jamil said.

"Your mouth might be your end, boy. Remember to pull the cord."

* * *

The bus terminal was crowded.

A line of bags and suitcases sat on the curb as a porter loaded them into the compartment underneath bus 49. When he turned to push in an especially large bag, Jamil yanked the key on his package loose, stuffing it and the cord in his pocket. He set the pack down near the pile.

The porter turned quickly and rose up, fist raised, lunging toward Jamil. "Get away from here, kid," he barked. "Don't let me catch you stealing anything."

Jamil jogged off. Ducking behind the corner of a building, he watched as the porter loaded the bags, including the one he had left. The porter closed and latched the storage door, waved to the driver and stepped back.

At the bus door, a man embraced three people, another man, a young girl and a woman. The three boarded bus 49 and the man waved from the curb as the girl smiled at him from the window. Her little hand pressed against the glass. The man stepped forward and laid his hand flat on the glass against hers. She giggled.

Jamil turned and ran. He sprinted as hard as he could, turning corners quickly, fingers plugging his ears. The boom was still frighteningly loud. Buildings nearby him shook dust loose.

He stopped running.

Later he stuffed his face with food, concentrating on the flavor, pushing from his mind the memory of the little girl with her hand on the glass.

* * *

The following day, Mister K did not show at the lot. Jamil was pleased.

During a breather from the pick-up football game, he approached one boy standing apart, quietly watching the action.

"Salaam," Jamil began.

"Salaam," the boy said, not turning to face him.

"Want to earn some money?"

The boy still didn't look at him. "Go away, pervert. I'm not sucking it for anything."

Jamil laughed. "Not like that. I run a delivery service for businessmen. All you have to do is take a package and leave it at a location."

The younger boy finally turned.

"That's all? And you'll pay me money?"

"That's it. Then you can buy anything you want."

"How much do you pay?"

* * *

"I'll take them all," Jamil said.

Mister K held the trunk lid up. "All four?"

"Sure. Save yourself some time. Give them to me, pay me for each and you can do what you like the rest of the day. Attend to other business ventures."

Mister K hesitated, rubbing his chin. The driver inside the car called out. "It would save us having to cruise these shitty neighborhoods and deal with the little bandits."

Jamil noted Mister K's uncertainty and spoke to it, using the same reassuring tone his uncle did when negotiating with customers. "It's a great deal for you. I blend in with the boys who know the streets. I've proven I'm reliable. One stop and you're done."

"I like the idea," the driver said. "They don't care who does it."

"Shut up," Mister K snapped, stepping away from the car and pressing the trunk down but not closed.

"You realize these packages are very important."

"I do."

"There will be terrible consequences for you if something goes wrong."

"My work already speaks for itself. If I make a mistake, you don't pay me. That is my personal guarantee." He emphasized the promise with a solemn nod, as his uncle had always done.

Mister K looked away, considering. He lifted the trunk lid and took out the four packs, using two hands as always, gentle with each.

"All right, boy. I'll try your idea, but I will be monitoring your progress. If there are any problems, you will suffer dearly."

"There won't be any trouble."

"Let's shake on it."

They shook hands.

"I don't even know your name."

"My name is Jamil." They embraced with a polite kiss on either cheek.

"Listen then, Jamil. Nothing gets written down. You must memorize the four addresses I give you."

"Not a problem, sir. I assure you all will be well."

Mister K paid him and described the destinations of all four packages.

"This will be good for both of us," Jamil said.

"Make sure you buy yourself some clothes. If you're going to be my middle man, you need to command respect."

"Can you provide me with extra money to do that?"

"Buy yourself some clothes." Mister K said. He got into the car and drove off.

* * *

Jamil led four boys from the lot to the abandoned doorway where he had hidden the packages. The boys stared at the bulky packs.

"So, what's in them?" one boy asked.

Jamil spoke firmly. "You never ask that question. We are a courier business. We deliver, but we do not invade the privacy of our customers. Assume what is in them is very fragile."

"So, we can't ask why we have to pull the cord?" another boy asked.

"No," Jamil said tersely.

"If you have to ask, you're stupid," another boy said. They chuckled, shoving back and forth.

"Enough," Jamil said. The boys quieted and were still. "I will pay you some now, and more when I confirm you've done the job. Now listen carefully and remember your goal. You cannot write it down. Yours goes to the bus stop, on bus thirteen."

"Yours goes to that new restaurant where the Americans eat."

"Yours goes to the post office."

"Yours goes under the bridge."

"Where did you get these?" one of the boys asked.

"Do you want to make money or do you want to ask questions?"

"Sorry."

Jamil showed them the bills, but kept them out of reach. "Can I really trust you?"

"Yes. Yes. Please. I'm hungry. We're all hungry."

"All right, then. Deliver your packs and meet me back here tonight. If you do this properly, you'll have enough money to buy food and some left over."

Later that night, the boys returned to the lot, one by one. Jamil paid each of them a fraction of what Mister K had given him and kept the rest for himself. The boys didn't mind. When he handed over the money, each one expressed only gratitude and begged for more work in the future.

All four walked away smiling.

* * *

The next day, Jamil waited by the lot as the boys kicked a ball around. He was dressed in a suit he had purchased at a used clothes stand. The familiar glistening car rolled up. Mister K leapt out before the vehicle had fully stopped and kissed Jamil on both cheeks.

"Salaam, Jamil! I hardly recognized you in your new clothes! My boss was very pleased. Thanks be to Allah for you coming into my life.

I will have more packages soon. I will bring as many as I can. We're going to be rich! May I call you my partner?"

Jamil smiled humbly, bowing slightly.

"Of course, Mister K. I consider us more than partners. We are friends."

ZERD

USA

2006

I suspect a lot of guys wonder the same thing I was wondering as I sat in my jail cell: How did I get here?

It all happened so fast. One day I was tattooing people and the next thing I knew, I was locked in a cage surrounded by psychos.

Jail sucked.

When I reviewed my fate I wondered what would have changed if that rent-a-cop I kicked as I busted out of juvey hadn't fallen and hit his head on some random piece of concrete. What if he hadn't gone into a coma for three days? I never meant to hurt the guy, I just wanted him to let go of my leg.

My life philosophy had been distilled down to "Fuck it."

Fate was going to take me where it wanted. If I tried to fight it, things got stupid, so I resolved not to resist anymore. I took the public defender without a fight, I let Tracy cry on my shoulder, I welcomed my family's destiny as fuck-ups, and I headed off to the slammer.

* * *

The guys in prison were crazy, violent, addicts, abused or all of those. They would tell their stories during "Workshop" and they were the most brutal tales I ever heard. The crap some people went through made my stupid life seem like a party.

"Workshop" was a round-table meeting where we talked about our feelings, our lives and why we were in jail. It was funny to see our social worker, barely out of college, this pretty little thing with long straight blonde hair and bright blue eyes surrounded by us hairy inked-up muscle-bound (or just fat) thugs. She tried but was obviously out of place. She wanted to teach us all respect, so she was extremely polite, which meant she spent most of her time fending off the guys' come-ons.

"Hey, Miss Joanne, what are you doing tonight?"

"Now, Kevin, let's stay on the topic."

"Don't bother with him, I'll show you a good time, girl. I'm classy."

"Dusty, I'm sure you are."

"Yo, I got culture. Be wit' me. Talk about poems and shit."

"Randall, I'm glad to hear you're reading. Now back to our discussion. Can you tell me why you think what you did was wrong?"

"Because I got caught."

Charles used to say that college was high school and high school was elementary school and real life was no different: authority, bullies, idiots and assholes. I never understood why he was going for a master's degree since he had that attitude, but he called it right as usual.

Miss Joanne never gave up, though, I'll give her that. She seemed sincere about trying to help. I admired that she listened and had a killer memory. She knew all the stupid things we said from week to week. During our one-on-one sessions, I would give her enough answers to make her stop asking questions but not enough that she knew anything meaningful about me.

So I thought.

* * *

"You're quite the artist," Miss Joanne said at the start of one of our one-on-one counseling sessions.

"I try."

"Do you need any supplies?"

"For what?"

"Art. Paints, canvas, markers? Don't you want to keep tattooing? Or at least draw in a sketch book?"

"How could I do tattooing? This is jail."

"It's actually safer that way. Guys will mark themselves any way they can, using heated pins or paperclips. Anything. It's better that it's done with safe equipment by a pro. Plus, I want to help you with your vocation. When you get out of here, you need to have a future. There's nothing wrong with giving people tattoos. How about it?"

I was speechless for a moment. I thought I was supposed to be as unhappy and bored as possible in jail. Miss Joanne saw the big house as something more, a place to turn people around, to keep them from sinking completely. "You really think they'd let me ink people?"

"Under supervision, of course," she said. "As long as everything is safe and sterile, it will be a good thing for you. It can't hurt for me to ask."

I was a loser in this stupid place and a complete stranger to her. I had nothing to offer here she was, trying to build me a future. Maybe that was what it felt like to have a mom. Or a dad that cared.

"Are you in there?" she asked.

"Yeah. Sorry. Daydreaming."

"I'll look into this. Understand there will probably be some limitations, but everything depends on your behavior. If you want to help me, just stay out of trouble. Don't get too hopeful, but don't count me out."

* * *

A week later, I was staring at some supplies. I couldn't believe it. They weren't the best tools, like Steve had, and I was only allowed to use black ink, but it was something. In jail, it was a whole lot. I started to tear up as Miss Joanne laid out the conditions: I had to be supervised by at least two guards and all appointments had to be scheduled ahead of time. All images had to be approved by her. I must have thanked her a hundred times.

During outside break, like magic, this guy I didn't know stopped me.

"Hey, tattoo man," he said.

"Yeah?" I asked like I was pissed off. That was my long-range defense: act pissed off and willing to fight.

"Miss Joanne said you're looking for customers."

I immediately relaxed. "What do you want?"

"A panther right here." He pointed to the top of his forearm.

* * *

I couldn't remember how long it had been since I had inked someone. When I told Miss Joanne I already had my first client, she got it all set up and gave the okay to the art. She watched along with two guards and the warden's assistant. I was nervous to have an audience, but once the machine buzzed in my fingers, and the smell of burning ink and cooked blood reached my nose, I felt like I was home, even in that place.

There wasn't a dude in the complex that first guy didn't show his ink to. Even if it was see-your-breath freezing outside, he kept his left sleeve rolled up. It made me feel good too, knowing I had a satisfied customer raving about my work.

Then the requests came pouring in. Guys came asking for all kinds of ink. Dragons, skulls, motorcycles, naked babes, and panthers. The Latin guys loved that panther image. It was the same damn thing each time, but I didn't care. I was just glad to be inking again.

* * *

Miss Joanne was pleased with herself, too. "Miguel has spoken highly of you."

Dudes who didn't even speak English were coming to me and asking for ink by pointing to their friends and then themselves. Another panther. After the fifth one, I was cleaning up and getting ready to do another when Miss Joanne turned to the guards.

"Can I speak privately with Pete?" she asked them.

"We'll be across the room." They moved to the far wall.

"What's up?" I asked, laying out my stuff on the small table in the visitor's room.

"You know what's going on, don't you?"

"What do you mean?"

"The panther. It's a symbol for one of the Latino gangs."

So, this was how it all fell apart.

"Shit," I said, "I should have known something I liked wouldn't last. Does that mean today is cancelled? I have one more."

"Hold on a second. I didn't say anything. I'm looking the other way. For now."

"You are? For me? But you could-"

"I could get in trouble. I know. But I don't want you to lose something you love. If I'm questioned, I'll defend it from the health angle. They're going to mark themselves. Best that it's disease-free. I didn't want to tell you, but in case we have to cancel it, well, I wanted you to know why. "

Dad would have liked Miss Joanne. Maybe he was right about the natural goodness of the little guy. Or girl.

"Zerd?"

I was crying, just a little. I could barely look at her. "Thank you."

She patted my hand. I almost flinched. It had been forever that I'd felt a gentle touch.

"I'm just doing my job," she said.

* * *

I kept inking, panthers included. Miss Joanne didn't show up all the time anymore. Either she trusted me or wanted to be able to say she didn't know fully what was going on, in case they gave her shit about the panthers. Every day could be my last, but then, that's how life always is. Just most of the time we don't think about it.

So, one day I was cleaning up when one of the guards spoke up.

"Hey, can you ink us?"

"Um."

"It's okay. We'll cover for you."

"I'll be late for check-in."

"I said we'll cover for you."

I was tired and I would have to skip dinner time, but if I did this for them, they might be able to help Miss Joanne somehow. I didn't really have a choice, but I acted like I did to get on their good side.

"No problem. What do you want?"

He whipped out this shitty cartoon of a pig smashing a guy's head with a baton. Stupid, but I didn't care. It was better than drawing ankh tramp stamps on nasty goth chicks. Well, maybe it was a tie. I prefer the more complex art of a mean pig to the simple symbol of the ankh, but I'd prefer a woman's body close to my face than overweight dudes who were legally allowed to taser me in the balls.

* * *

"Just like old times," I said across the table, "except I'm in jail."

Tracy and Charles had surprised me with a visit. They were both obviously terrified, their eyes darting in all directions. Charles looked different. His hair was cut extra-short and he had a tiny moustache and a goatee.

"Man, you've turned up the gay, haven't you?" I asked, trying to joke with him.

He smiled uncomfortably.

"Hey," I said, "I'm still the same. It's good to see you guys. Don't be nervous."

"We can't help it," Tracy said.

We sat in silence. She wouldn't meet my eyes. Charles talked a little between drags from his cigarette.

"How are you, Zerd? You okay?"

"It sucks in here, but they let me ink. That's something. It keeps me busy."

Charles put his hand on Tracy's shoulder. She still wouldn't look up.

"I'm so glad to see you two," I said, "but you're bumming me out."

"We came here with some news," Charles said, grinning painfully.

"What news?"

Charles grimaced again, then lifted Tracy's head by her chin. She was crying.

"I'm pregnant," she said.

My first reaction was appropriately stupid. "What? No you're not."

"I am, Zerd. Pete."

"No you aren't."

"I am."

"Seriously?"

"Seriously." They both said at once.

"And I'm-"

"You're the father," she said.

"How do you know?"

"You've been the only one. I've been busy with school and work and..." She started sobbing. Charles rubbed her back as she hunched over. "And I guess I love you."

"Um, what do we do?" I asked. "What do you want to do?" Again I missed a chance to say "I love you" back.

"I think I'm going to have the baby."

"Have the baby?"

"Sure. Why not?"

"Why not?" I could barely talk straight. "What am I going to do? I'll be a father. I never. I don't. I never thought. I'm in jail."

"Hey," she said, reaching her hand across the table, sharp fingertips in my palm. "You're shaking."

I expected the cop watching over us to say something. We technically weren't supposed to touch, but he looked away.

"No shit I'm shaking. I'm freaking out. Me? A father?"

"I think you'll make a great dad."

"But my dad's a jerk."

Tracy smiled bravely through her tears. "My dad's an asshole and my mom does what he says without a thought. We'll be great parents because we won't want to be like our own. We know exactly what not to do. A bad example sometimes teaches better than a good example."

"Huh?"

"That's from my dad's stupid church sermons, but I thought it was smart."

I could feel my shaking slow down. Her touch was soothing.

"You're freaking," Charles said to me. "That's a good sign."

"It is?"

"It means you care. You want to do the right thing."

Good old Charles. The dude was just magic.

I don't remember much else that we said other than she would call me soon. I went back to my cell in a daze. Me? A father? I barely even remembered having sex with her. It seemed a lifetime ago. Was it really that easy to create another human being? Was it right when we were both stoned and the only thing I was thinking about was getting my rocks off? Was that any way to bring an innocent child into the world?

I didn't sleep at all that night.

I alternated between complete panic and a strange, light feeling that I finally recognized as joy. I was going to be a father. Why should I fear it? Maybe this was a way to turn my talent for fucking up into a positive. I should have used a condom, but since I didn't, we were going to make another human life, and that was pretty cool.

The grey walls glowed orange as the sunlight hit the building, filling me with hope. Maybe this wasn't so bad. Maybe this was the direction I needed. Maybe I could do all the fuck-ups for the kid, and save him or her from problems. With my natural magnetism for stupidity, there would be none left for the kid to endure. He or she was going to have the best life ever.

Steve once said any asshole can be a father, it takes a real asshole to be a Dad.

I was already overqualified.

* * *

For a time, I was in denial. Not denial about being a father, but denial that somehow I would avoid fucking things up. I was high on the idea of being a dad once I got used to it. For almost a full month, I believed things would get better and my life would turn around.

My ink job had been going so smoothly, Miss Joanne said she trusted me and I didn't have to run the artwork by her first anymore.

At least once a week, a dude speaking Spanish would come up to me and point to his forearm. Another panther. Very rarely did I get something different, but occasionally I did, like a tribute to a girlfriend, a child or a murdered friend. I even did a couple dragons and that was cool, because those suckers are hard, all those scales have to be done right.

Suddenly, guys were shaking my hand and nodding at me in a way that wasn't threatening or followed by a blown kiss. Word was getting out that Zerd was an all right guy. Not only did this add up to more customers, but the guards started talking to me more, and that was surely some good karma to cash in on someday.

So, how could I turn all this good fortune to shit? Listen and learn from the expert.

I was walking around the yard, getting some fresh air (or what passed for it in a jail courtyard) when the Panthers (Los Pantheros as they would say) surrounded me. It was a subtle thing. They kept walking as if they were just together, and suddenly I was in the middle of a crowd with nowhere to go. One guy walked alongside me, his shoulder pressed against mine.

"Ay, puto. What the fuck you think you're doing?" he said, and he sounded pissed off.

"What are you talking about?"

"The tattoos, man. We noticed you inked up the Dragons."

"The who?"

"The Dragons, puto. White Power shit. Mierda blanca, sí?"

"What are the dragons?"

"Who, man. Who. Don't play stupid. They're our fucking blood enemies, puto. We don't want you inking them. You're our provider," he showed me his tattoo. "Los Pantheros. Remember?"

"I just do the ink, I'm not-"

"Shut the fuck up, man. I don't want any of your neutrality bullshit."

"But I'm not with anyone. I'm not in any gang."

"We're okay if you ink pigs and independents, but if the person has an affiliation, especially with the Dragons, you tell them to fuck off."

"I don't-"

Someone shoved me from behind. The guys surrounding me laughed and chattered in Spanish.

"I mean it," their leader said. "You ink anyone else and you'll be considered an enemy. Worse, a traitor. Panthers shed blood for you, man. That's serious."

"I didn't agree to this shit ahead of time."

He laughed. "So?"

"So, what do I get since I'm part of your gang but not really a part of it?"

"You get that we don't kick your ass."

He whistled and the group slowly dispersed until I was walking alone again.

Now I was pissed. Couldn't a dragon just be a fucking dragon? Or a panther just be a panther? Did it have to have deeper meaning?

Of course it did. Everything had a deeper meaning. My profession was all about symbols. Hell, more than half the ink I wore was a symbol for something else. Even the dudes who said they got tattoos just to get them, the act of getting inked meant something.

I looked at my tat with P.S.F.U. on the gravestone. Was it, "Postscript, Fuck You?" Or was it like Brainiac said, "Patron Saint of Fuck Ups?"

Shit, I know the answer to that one.

* * *

It shouldn't be too hard to imagine how things went when one of the Dragons came around. I vaguely remembered him like I sort of remembered anyone I had inked, but I didn't know his name. He was a huge muscular white guy with long blond-red hair that merged with his beard. A thousand years ago, he would have been a Viking. At least that was the look he was going for.

"I was wondering if you could put a swastika here," he asked. "Right near this dragon you did for me."

"I don't know, man," I said. Damn. I should have had a lie ready.

"You don't know? Why?"

"I don't know. Um, I'm not feeling it."

"Not feeling it?"

"Yeah, plus, you know, that symbol won't get approved."

"Fuck that. Pigs owe me, they'll let it happen. Same with that social worker chick. She wants me bad. She'll let it go. So, what's your problem?"

"I don't know, I'm not doing tattoos lately. I'm busy."

"You're full of shit. I know what's up. Are the Panthers threatening you?"

"What?"

"Don't lie to me. There's no secrets in here. Tell you what. Ink me up and the Dragons will provide you protection. If you don't, I can't guarantee your safety. Fuck the Panthers. They're pussies. Literally. Panthers are cats and cats are pussies. Get it?"

"Yeah, I got it."

"Besides, you're on our side. The white side. We've got to stick together or we'll be in the minority soon. Shit, we already are the minority, surrounded by leeches and cockroaches."

"I'm not on anyone's side."

"So, you want to play this neutral act, but you don't want to tattoo us? That sounds like you're with them. The quickest way to get run over is to stand in the middle of the road, son."

"The Panthers get pissed when I ink other gangs. Can you see it from my view?"

"I am, retard. I see a bunch of pussies threatening you and a gang of real men from your own race offering to stand up for you. You going to ink me or what?"

"Let me think about it."

"Don't think too hard. Or too long. Things could get rough. I might have to complain to Miss Joanne, or maybe even her boss."

"Fuck. All right. I'll do it. Leave Miss Joanne out of it. Don't say shit. I'll do it."

* * *

The whole situation was stupid. Soon enough the Panthers or the Dragons would come after me for inking the other. It seemed like something from grade school: you're not in my club, so I hate you. Only the average grade-schooler wasn't a muscle-bound psychopath.

I could tell Miss Joanne that I didn't want to ink anymore. That option sucked because I loved inking people and I hated being beaten by thugs with infant minds.

The word "infant" set me off.

My kid was going to have to face this stupid world. What if he came home and said some bullies were bothering him? Would I say, just give up like your pop? Hell no! I'd teach like my father taught me. Stand up to those pricks. Fuck 'em. If the kid saw me shrink before a herd of jerk-offs, what kind of example would that be?

I leapt up from my cot and stood at the cell door, watching morning arrive through the tiny roof window. I was really juiced about the kid. I wasn't getting any sleep, but I was suddenly so excited I wasn't tired.

The kid wasn't even born yet and the little peanut was already inspiring me with courage. I wanted to keep inking people, so that's what I'd do. If the Panthers tried to kick my ass, I wouldn't ink any more of them. Then they couldn't add anyone to their stupid gang. I'd treat the Dragons the same way.

I'm neutral in the war of idiots, so take your fight somewhere else, motherfuckers.

I would have to stop using language like that around the kid, too.

* * *

The next day I explained it all and set it up with Miss Joanne. She frowned about the swastika but said she would look the other way for my benefit. I never really got to put my new resolve to the test, because soon after, everything fell apart.

"Yo, Z. You got a call," one of the guards barked at me during outdoor break.

"Hey," Tracy said when I picked up the phone.

"Hey, babe, what's going on?"

"Just had to call you."

"You sound ill. Is that the morning sickness?"

"I'm... out of it. Woozy."

"You'll be okay, you've got to take care of yourself for the little one. Drink some orange juice or something."

"That won't help. Nothing will help."

"Hey, come on. Be positive. Our kid's going to be raised around tough and brave people. You'll be all right."

She was quiet for a long time.

"Charles told me to just go ahead and say it."

"Say it? Say what?"

"What I have to tell you." Her speech was slurred. Was she drinking? No. She wouldn't do that. Not while pregnant. I might not have known everything about her, but I didn't think she'd do something that low. That wasn't like her.

"Tracy? You there?"

"I..." She breathed in. "There's no more baby."

When she said that, a red mist dropped over the whole world.

"What? What did you say?"

"The baby. It's gone."

I could feel my mind pulling away. Zerd was clear for take-off.

"It?" I said, my voice squeaking.

"I had to."

"Had to what?"

"My dad said the baby was conceived out of wedlock, it was immoral, so I had to get rid of it."

What she was saying was sinking in, but not fully. I was resisting it, holding off my inevitable explosion.

"Don't call my child a fucking it," I said.

"It doesn't matter anymore."

"Yes, it fucking does. You. You. Fuck."

I banged my head against the metal box around the phone.

"Zerd?"

I couldn't speak.

"I'm sorry," she whispered, crying.

I leaned my forehead against the wall and closed my eyes. The pain across my skull felt right. I was crying.

"I was just thinking about being a father."

She started to say something else, but I wasn't listening. All the emotion was starting to come out of me in words.

"I thought your dad was a religious nut," I said. "I thought he was against abortion."

"He is, but we're not married. He said we had to weigh the two evils and go with the lesser."

"He thinks abortion is murder and he calls that a lesser evil than us not being married? Don't I get a say in this?"

"I'm sorry. He said I had to. If I wanted to live here, I had to."

"We could have moved in together. We could have run away."

She was choking as she said, "But you're in jail. I'm working and in school. How could I run away? I don't know what I was thinking, Zerd. I'm sorry. You sound so upset."

"Tell your dad to get fucked."

She got quiet, so I kept going.

"You don't understand shit. You have no fucking idea. You go fuck your dad and you can abort your inbred brothers and sisters, you fucking whore."

I wish that hadn't been the last thing I ever said to her, but it was.

I slammed the phone down. Then I started kicking it. Then I started punching it. Then I tore it out of the wall.

I fought the guards when they grabbed me, just so someone would beat the shit out of me.

* * *

Miss Joanne handed me a glossy pamphlet. Across the front was a picture of a guy wearing his prison blues, smiling and lifting a box. The title on the brochure read "About your future."

That folded slip of paper led to me being in this messed up situation. Of course, I never could have known it, and after Tracy's abortion, I'm not sure I would have cared even if I did know.

"I don't know if you follow politics," Miss Joanne said.

"I try not to."

"I'm only mentioning it because this has been in the news lately. Senator Hanson and some other high level politicians have sponsored a bill to help incarcerated people gain job skills. Inmates on good behavior support the overtaxed military. They call it the Con-to-Soldiers law. I hate that term 'con' but that's what most people call it. And they don't become soldiers, they're more like janitors. I'm required by the new law to make you aware of the opportunity."

"Oh, my God. My dad would shit a golden nugget."

"Not interested?"

"Actually, that makes me more interested."

"It's something to think about. You could make money and learn a trade, or at least get some work experience. After the board review, if you do a good job, you could possibly reduce your time by up to six months."

"I don't want to get shot."

"You won't be in combat. They aren't interested in giving weapons to those with the stigma of, um, having a history. You have to pass a physical and psychological screening, so it's not guaranteed, even if you're interested. They mostly want help while the armed forces focus on, you know. Their mission."

"Killing," I said for her.

She frowned. "Yes. Killing."

I thought about the promise I made to Dad. "I promise I will never join the military." Between the gang crap and losing Tracy, my life had gone to shit. I could escape almost all of it if I just took off. The only thing that would come with me was my skill at fucking up and the guilt over getting Steve killed.

This was as close to a fresh start as I would ever get.

"Miss Joanne. I'd definitely like to do this," I said, looking through the pamphlet. Cons of mixed races were lifting boxes while soldiers of mixed races stood behind them, watching. I didn't think for a second it would be like that idealistic staged photo, but there was one thing it could give me: an exit.

The only drawback was it couldn't take me to the moon. Had Senator Hanson written up a bill like that, I would have jumped on the first rocket off this planet. Cons in space, hell yeah.

"Later today we'll be watching an orientation video," Miss Joanne said. "Would you like to attend?"

"Definitely."

* * *

Twelve of us sat in a classroom, a TV at the front.

A deep voice spoke to us over the shifting logos of the Redfire Corporation. "The Redfire Corporation proudly offers the diverse services needed to meet the challenges presented by rapidly changing technology and the expanding needs of an ever-growing population. We are the foremost provider of development and security for the infrastructure of mature and emerging economies..."

Dude went on for a while. "Blah, blah, blah" was all I heard.

The screen showed a bunch of African children running toward a truck painted with the Redfire logo. Each kid walked away smiling, eating a candy bar, while their parents shouldered a sack of rice.

"As an employee or volunteer for Redfire, you will be joining the global leader in building and rebuilding our world. Redfire. Leading the way. To the future."

Dad would have barfed. I chuckled to myself.

* * *

Miss Joanne set up my psych test.

I waited outside a med ward alone with a cop. Someone inside kept shouting like a kid playing cops and robbers.

"Pow! Pow!" his voice boomed. "Blam! Ka-blam! Rat-at-tata-tat!"

"What the hell is going on in there?" I asked the pig.

He shrugged. The guy came out. He was one of the oafs I had inked from the white power gang, the Dragons. He raised his head to me.

"That was fun!"

"Shut up," the cop said. "Keep moving."

It was my turn. The room was empty except for a doctor, another cop, a slide projector and a screen. Another reminder of Dad.

The doctor was wearing a white lab coat with the Redfire Corporation logo embroidered on the pocket.

"Hello, Peter. Peter Abbott. I'm Doctor Webster."

"Hey."

"We need to get the legal speak out of the way. I'm going to administer a test sponsored by the Redfire Corporation, approved by…" He kept talking. I pretended I was listening.

"Have you understood the terms I've laid out?"

"Yes," I said. "Yes, sir," I added, trying to be military. The cop smirked. Dick.

Doc Webster handed me a dark two-by-four as long as my arm. I took it.

"What's this?"

"What's it look like?"

"It looks like a two-by-four that was painted brown."

"It's supposed to be a fake gun," he snapped. "A rifle."

I looked at it. A trigger had been roughly drawn on the side. "I thought we wouldn't be handling guns?"

"You'll be around them. Now can I do my job?"

I inspected it closely. The paint was scraped away in some areas, showing bright blue underneath. If I squinted and had several bong hits it might look like some kind of weapon.

Click.

The doc threw a switch. On the screen the projector showed a picture of a car parked in a parking lot.

I stared at it. "Has the test started?" I asked.

"It has."

"Um. Okay."

I waited for him to ask me a question, or something to change on the screen. A very long minute passed silently.

Click.

A new slide was shown, a picture of a camel in the desert.

I looked down at the fake rifle. What was I supposed to do? I looked at the cop, be he was wearing a full-on poker-face. Another long minute and then...

Click.

A picture of a woman wearing a burqa.

I looked around the room. I had to be missing something. I could hear the clock ticking. Watch me fail this damn thing, I thought.

Click.

A picture of a man wearing a turban, shooting a rifle in the air.

I looked at the doctor. He met my gaze and raised his eyebrows, as if to ask, "Are you sure?"

I shrugged at him and he shrugged back at me. He made some notes on his clipboard and flicked on the lights.

I handed him the rifle-stick. "How did I do?"

"Better than most. You got them all right except one."

* * *

A few days later one of the pigs came by while I was reading on my bunk. "Hey, Zerd. Your father's here to see you."

I thought about it, then I went back to my book. "I don't want to see him."

"You sure? Don't you even want to say hi?"

"Nope."

"It will break up your day."

"Fuck it."

"Come on. You'll regret it. You know how many guys in here wish they had a father to come visit them? How many wish they even knew their father?"

"They can have mine."

"Don't make me go out there and tell a guy his own son doesn't want to see him."

"Then don't."

"Asshole."

I didn't care what Dad had to say. I just wanted to go.

JAMIL

IRAQ

2006

"Jamil, my partner! My son!"

Mister K bellowed as he stepped from his car. Behind Jamil boys were playing football in the rubble-strewn lot.

"Look at you," Mister K said. "Wearing a suit! So clean and sharp, my young friend, you have grown so much so fast."

"I have been saving money," Jamil said, trying not to pull at his suit where it scratched against his neck.

"Consider moving to another neighborhood as well. This place is crawling with street children. Little thieves, all of them."

"I have a place I stay."

"But where?"

Jamil didn't answer.

"Ah, yes," Mister K said. "I taught you not to ask questions, and you only expect the same of me. A smart boy you are. But please don't hold it against me that I'm concerned for your well-being. Some places may seem safe, but are not. I only ask to make sure you are not in danger. That is all I care about. It is not a crime to be concerned with those we love and respect. And it is not foolish for you to seek the advice of your elders."

Jamil bit his tongue to prevent himself from saying how insulted he was. Mister K didn't ask questions, but may as well have been. It seemed a tactic borrowed from parents trying to coax a secret from a child. I am not so dumb to fall for that, Jamil wanted to say, but he stayed silent. Or should he lie? Give Mister K the wrong information and let him think he was stupid anyway?

He had already decided never to tell Mister K of the demolished house he had been squatting in or the United Nations shelter where he showered and shaved. The less Mister K knew, the better.

"I am ready for more deliveries," Jamil said.

"Always in such a hurry," Mister K scolded. "Always all business and no conversation. Ah, have it your way. Today there is only one special package. You and I must deliver it together."

"And the pay?"

"Oh, this job pays very well, we simply need the most reliable people to do it. Meet me here tonight."

* * *

Jamil stood alone in the empty lot, moonlight accenting the angles of the ruined buildings, casting sharp shadows everywhere. He rubbed his hands together for warmth.

A car rolled up nearby. Jamil rested his hand on the jagged concrete slab he could use for cover, just in case. The car stopped. From behind the blinding lights, a familiar voice called out.

"Get in the car," Mister K said.

Jamil hesitated.

"Jamil. It's me. Is something wrong?"

"No," Jamil snapped. He pulled open the passenger door. Mister K was driving, and he was alone. Jamil confirmed the back seat was empty before settling in to the thickly padded leather seat. He did not put on his seatbelt.

"Relax, my friend. You're sure you're all right?"

"I'm fine. Let's begin."

Mister K stepped on the accelerator. The car leapt forward with a whisper.

Jamil looked behind him again. The back seat was still empty. Memories of his kidnapping flashed across his mind, contrasting sharply with the car's physical comforts. He felt like he was floating, like the damaged city outside was something that he could see but never touch or be touched by.

Mister K spoke as he drove, dodging the debris and potholes in the darkened streets.

"My friend who supplies the bags tells me, bring only your best. So, of course, I bring you."

Jamil wiped his sweating palms on his pants. He pulled at the collar of his suit.

They stopped at the end of a line of cars. Traffic had bunched at a checkpoint where American soldiers, each one armored and carrying a rifle, milled about behind a concrete barrier.

"You have to approach these points slowly or they will shoot," Mister K said. "Americans are cowardly and that makes them jumpy."

The queue moved forward slowly. They waited for several minutes in silence.

"You are so quiet, Jamil."

"I have nothing to say."

"For once, I am glad of that. Let me do the talking here."

They came closer to the barrier one car length at a time, as each vehicle was let through. Soldiers strolled past their car, looking in and under it several times. Jamil gripped the door handle.

Finally it was their turn at the front of the line.

"Good day to you fellows," Mister K said in English as he rolled down the window. Soldiers surrounded the car, waving electronic wands over it. Green and yellow lights blinked on the devices.

"What's your business down this road, sir?" the soldier asked.

"I'm here to visit a nice restaurant."

"Which one would that be?"

"The American Oasis."

"And who is this riding with you?"

"My nephew."

The soldier looked through the driver window at Jamil. Jamil nodded at him.

"He doesn't speak English," Mister K explained. Jamil did not correct him.

"All right, move along."

The soldier waved them forward.

Driving on, Mister K continued speaking in Arabic. "Some say that the Americans coming to our country is a bad thing. But change is inevitable. If it wasn't the Americans, it would have been the Chinese, the Russians, or the Europeans. If you learn to adapt, then no matter who is in power, you will find opportunity."

Jamil watched as a lighted neighborhood swept by. The roads were cleaned. There were no demolished buildings, no young boys wandering about, no garbage in the street. Beyond the barrier was the ruin of Baghdad. Inside seemed like the wealthy subdivisions in Morocco. He jolted, spinning his head as they passed a sign with the familiar logo of the Redfire Corporation.

"Quiet is good," Mister K said. "But as business partners we can be social."

Jamil didn't respond. Mister K sighed heavily.

They pulled into a crowded and well-lit parking lot. Formally dressed Americans and Iraqis were coming and going from a busy restaurant. A huge pink neon sign over the front read in English "The American Oasis." Colorful birds were painted around the sign, perched inside the letters.

Mister K shut the car off and turned to Jamil. "You are a smart boy, but I need to warn you. Say nothing. You will see many things, including women in Western clothing. Do not stare at them. Follow me closely and keep your mouth shut."

"I understand."

"The mute boy finally talks." Mister K smiled. Jamil did not.

The perimeter was patrolled by soldiers with their assault rifles pointed down. Giant cement cylinders were spaced about the entire building, a defense against suicide vehicles. Men and women leaned on the barriers, smoking and chatting. Inside, the restaurant was buzzing with music and tipsy conversations.

Each table, both indoors and outside on a fenced-in porch, was full. The colors of fresh fruit, meat, breads and olives bounced past on silver platters carried by the Iraqi staff. Jamil's stomach growled.

The bar was pounding with music. Women were all around him, all of them wearing Western clothing, which to Jamil meant wearing very little. He was glad Mister K had reminded him not to stare, because that was all he could think to do.

On the way into the dark, smoke-filled lounge, Mister K acknowledged many of the men he passed like they were old friends. They bellowed friendly greetings, shook hands, clapped each other on the back, hugged. They did not kiss on the cheeks as Jamil expected men to do. The other men glanced at him warily, but looked away when Mister K intervened.

"He's with me. A nephew. No English."

Mister K guided Jamil to one of the tables. It was a polished wooden disc, high off the ground so they could drink while standing.

"What would you like, Mister K?" a woman asked in Arabic. Her hair was so blonde it appeared white. She looked at Jamil, her bright blue eyes stunning him with their alien beauty. He remembered Mikhail begging for forgiveness.

Jamil looked down at the table.

"Two lemonades, please," Mister K said in English.

"Of course."

Mister K switched back to Arabic. "Such beautiful women, yes?"

Jamil resisted the urge to glance around. "Yes."

"Unfortunately, we will only be here a moment."

The woman with the white hair returned with two thin tall glasses of lemonade on a silver tray. Jamil stared at the tube of glass and the small paper umbrella at the top.

Mister K chuckled. "It's a decoration. And you can look around. Just don't stare."

Jamil turned, scanning the room. A man sat on a low couch, a woman under each arm. Three women stood at a table like his. They were drinking and talking into mobile phones. One of them met his eyes and nudged another. They both looked up and giggled. Jamil looked away quickly.

"You dropped this, sir," someone said in Arabic. Jamil turned around in time to see Mister K pocketing a slip of paper and a waiter disappearing into the crowd. Jamil never saw his face.

Mister K finished his lemonade in one gulp. He slapped an American bill down on the table.

"We leave now."

* * *

Exiting the neighborhood was much easier than entering. Mister K simply waved to the soldier in the booth and a second later, the concrete barrier blocking them sank into the earth with a grinding noise. After they drove over it, it rose again. Several kilometers along the dark highway through the desert, where the only things visible were stars and distant city lights, Mister K stopped, pulled out the note and his cell phone.

"See this?" he said, showing Jamil the phone. A crude map filled its screen. "We are the green dot. Our contact is the red dot. We are to meet at these numbers." He showed Jamil the typewritten numbers on the slip and entered them. The phone beeped.

"Coordinates received," it spoke. "Drive west fifteen kilometers."

"Amazing, isn't it?" Mister K grinned. "You hold it."

The phone continued to talk, providing updates on their progress and directions which Mister K followed. Jamil watched as the dots moved closer along the digital map.

"Incredible," he said.

The phone guided them further into darkness. The only way Jamil could be sure they were moving was by watching the road itself, its cracks and dashed lines zooming by underneath them.

They drove for an hour in silence. Jamil found the darkness calming. He appreciated its simplicity. The phone's map was blank except for a single line representing the highway. He didn't speak until the dot signifying their contact began to move.

"We're getting close," Jamil said.

"I need to show you more gadgets," Mister K said. "They get you to talk."

"Your turn is coming up, ahead on the left."

"Turn left to destination," the phone echoed.

Mister K slowed and turned onto a paved road cracked into enormous chunks, sand pushing up through the rifts. They bounced over the jagged blacktop.

"Are the dots coming closer together?" Mister K asked.

"Yes."

They crested a dune and descended its other side so they could no longer see the highway they had come from. At the bottom of the small valley a van was waiting, the engine running, lights on. Mister K stopped his car several yards away, but did not shut off the engine. The driver in the van flashed his headlights three times. Mister K did the same. The van shuddered and stopped. A huge, muscular white man stepped out, dressed in military camouflage.

"Do exactly as I say," Mister K said in Arabic. "And move slowly. This is a very serious and dangerous man."

Mister K exited the car.

"Hello, Tom!" he called out in English, as he walked toward the large man with Jamil following. "How are you?"

"Fine, Mister K. You've brought an assistant?"

"I have."

Tom reached out his hand. Jamil shook it. The huge man's grip hurt his fingers.

"Nice to meet you," Tom said.

"Our friend doesn't speak English," Mister K said. Jamil did not correct him. He then turned to Jamil and spoke Arabic. "He says nice to meet you. Now, bow your head and smile."

Jamil did.

"Let's do this," Tom said. "I'll drive. Have your boy get in the back."

Jamil understood, but he made sure he did not move toward the vehicle until Mister K commanded him in Arabic.

* * *

The back of the van was packed solid. A tarp covered several crates labeled as containing toilet paper. In the middle of the crates sat a large backpack, similar to the bombs Jamil had been distributing. This pack was slightly different in that it gave off a faint foul smell, and no Redfire logo identified it. Jamil pushed it aside to make room. It made a small clanking noise as though it contained a metal canister.

"Shit!" Tom yelled in English. "Tell him not to touch that!"

"Don't touch that!" Mister K said in Arabic.

Jamil lifted his hands palms-up before cautiously crowding into the van, sitting on the metal wheel well.

Tom and Mister K spoke in English.

"Fuck," Tom said. "He'll get us killed."

"He's a good boy. He didn't know."

"Damn it, K, I'm trusting you."

"I have never given you reason to doubt me."

"Right."

Tom started the van and drove back to the main highway. Jamil stared out the tinted back door windows into the darkness.

"So, where did you find him?" Tom asked.

"He's a homeless kid, but reliable," Mister K answered. "Doesn't know anything, doesn't speak English. Does what he's told. Perfect."

"A homeless kid? In those clothes? A suit?"

"I lent it to him. Better than grimy street clothes for this."

"Does he know what we're doing?"

"I told him we were dropping off a package. No big deal."

"If we get caught, just point to him. I'll vouch for you. We'll say he stowed away."

"No problem."

"Plus, if the thing goes off too early, better him than us."

"It won't fire immediately?"

"It's timed or else we'd need a new starving Iraqi each time. We've got a few of these tasks to do. If your boy here performs well, we might use him again. Assuming, of course, the chemical doesn't get him."

They drove into the night.

Jamil pressed himself against the van's metal body, staring at the pack, wincing every time it bounced or rocked, no matter how slightly. The crates packed in around it held it steady, but Jamil slid his feet around it to provide extra support.

He nodded off, but woke when the uniform blackness outside was broken by harsh light among the dunes. They had arrived at a small city made of tents and plastic portable buildings. Floodlights outlined circles around the perimeter fence.

They passed a sign bearing the images of the American flag and a logo familiar to Jamil. Text at the top of the sign read: "Camp Tokyo Zulu. Redfire Corporation."

"We're here," Tom said. "Tell your boy to get under the tarp and to stay still or the guards will shoot him."

"Keep your head down," Mister K said in Arabic. "Hide and stay still or we will all be shot."

Jamil did as he was told, crouching among the crates, pressing against the pack, the metal canister inside chilling his skin. He held the tarp over his head, leaving room for fresh air free of the pack's odd smell.

"In case you're ever driving," Tom said to Mister K, "remember you need to be careful at these checkpoints. Don't stop too far back and definitely don't go too fast."

"I know the rules. Is this the place? Won't there be guards here? Cameras?"

"Of course. We want to be seen. We want to go in, dick around publicly and then take off. The kid has the tough part."

The van jolted to a stop. Jamil's stomach fluttered, his breath came in stutters. Whatever was going to happen, whatever they wanted him to do with the pack, he could always run, just run for his life. The muscular American said he would live, the weapon inside was timed, but he always mentioned something could go wrong.

"What's your business here?" an unfamiliar voice asked in English.

"Fucking your mom," Tom said.

"What the- Tom Rimsky!"

"It's me, retard."

"Fuck off. It's dark. I didn't recognize you. What are you doing here so late?"

"Making the rounds, checking in. The usual shit."

"Most of the crew is asleep."

"I'll wake them up."

"Jackass. Who's your friend?"

"A translator."

"Nice to meet you," Mister K said in English.

The third voice paused. "All right, head on through."

"Yeah, dickhead," Rimsky said. "Like I need your permission."

They drove forward slowly.

"I want to park here until they forget about us," Rimsky said. They waited in silence for several minutes. Jamil could smell them smoking.

"Okay," Tom said, "now translate for me. Tell the kid to stick his head out."

"Poke your head out and listen," Mister K said in Arabic. Jamil did.

"We're going for a walk," Tom said. "You carry the pack to that low white building straight ahead, bring it inside and pull the cord. There might be a small noise when you do. After that, come back to the van and cover yourself up again. Don't let anyone see you, but if they do, don't panic, keep walking. Just don't run."

Mister K translated into Arabic. Jamil pretended to listen as though he was hearing the instructions for the first time.

Rimsky and Mister K exited the van and walked toward one of the huts, talking out loud, their voices fading.

Jamil waited in the silence.

He unlatched the van's back doors and gently dragged the pack with him, stepping backwards onto the sand. He pressed the doors closed but made sure they didn't latch.

Somewhere in the dark a dog barked sharply. Jamil froze, then saw the creature in the light of a nearby building. Mister K and Rimsky were taunting the beast and chatting with a soldier. They disappeared inside.

The target building was only a few steps away, its door ajar. Jamil entered and closed the door behind him. He stood in the dark silence among several rows of metal shelves stocked with boxes and cans.

He set the pack on a bottom shelf near some small kerosene tanks and pulled down the canvas bag like peeling a fruit. The canister inside was indistinguishable from the others nearby except for the cord sticking out of its top.

He grabbed the cord, his heart pounding as he started to count, wrapping the cord around his fingers. Then he noticed a ball of twine.

He stopped his countdown and tied the twine to the cord and walked across the room to the door. He inhaled deeply, held his breath and pulled.

The cord popped loose with a hiss. A yellowish puff shot out and glided down the sides of the canister. The gas expanded slowly across the floor, like a living thing, a snake, hunting. As it grew, it disappeared.

Jamil dropped the twine and darted out the door, leaving it open behind him before jogging the few steps back to the van.

Back under the tarp, he allowed himself to exhale. The quiet was broken only by the sound of his breathing. He realized his whole body was shaking. He closed his eyes, squeezing them tightly to ward off the tremors. Voices were near, calling to each other, coming closer.

Should he run? Should he surrender?

He burrowed out from under the canvas and grabbed the back door handle, just as the familiar voice of Mister K reached him. He ducked back into hiding.

Mister K and Rimsky got in the van, slamming the doors shut.

"Is your window closed?" Rimsky asked Mister K.

"Yes."

"Okay, we can talk. Is he back there?"

"Are you back there?" Mister K asked in Arabic.

"I'm here," Jamil replied, also using Arabic.

Mister K switched back to English. "We're good."

"Ask him if anyone saw him."

"Did anyone see you?"

"No."

"Did he pull the cord?"

"Did you pull the cord?"

"Yes."

"Good," Rimsky said. "Tell him to stay hidden."

"Stay under there," Mister K said in Arabic.

Jamil curled up on his side and rested his head on his hand to cushion it against the metal floor. He listened as best he could to the English conversation between the other two men.

"You think the kid did all right?" Rimsky said.

"I have no doubt. He is very reliable."

"Good help is hard to find."

"You found me, didn't you?"

"I did, but you're expensive."

"Please, Tom. No more haggling. Especially after what I just worked for you."

"The kid did it, not you."

"Let us leave aside the business and celebrate a job well done."

"We'll see. If he didn't pull that cord, we've got a problem."

"He did. Don't worry."

"We'll find out soon enough."

* * *

The van stopped. Jamil snapped out of a light sleep. Mister K and Rimsky were talking.

"See you tomorrow at the regular place?" Mister K asked.

"The American Oasis, as always," Tom Rimsky said.

"Jamil, get in my car," Mister K said in Arabic.

Jamil crawled out of the van and walked back to the car without a word. Using the remote, Mister K unlocked it. Jamil sat in the passenger seat and watched as the two other men sat in the van talking. Mister K eventually returned to the car.

"That fucking bastard," he spat.

"You don't like him," Jamil said.

"I don't trust him and he doesn't trust me. He's always going on about how much I charge. Does he want quality work? Then he needs to pay for it."

They drove in silence back into Baghdad.

* * *

An hour later at the lot that served as their rendezvous, Mister K counted out several bills and handed them to Jamil. He looked around the dark streets. Shadows darted between the ruins.

"You should get a nice place, Jamil," Mister K said. "This neighborhood isn't safe."

"I will. Soon."

"Good night, then. Good job tonight."

Jamil walked away.

* * *

Jamil's brand new suit made his armpits and shoulders itch. As he neared his destination, the fabric's stiffness was eased by his cold sweat. He stood across the street and watched The American Oasis restaurant.

Once, after work, he and his uncle had watched a Japanese action movie on the satellite television. An assassin had studied a fortress from a distance, noting the location of the watchmen. Then he killed them all, carefully, methodically, one by one, until none were left.

Watching from this vantage reminded Jamil of that hero. He wished his life was so simple. Why he should so clearly remember that fictional scene and not real memories was a mystery to him. His mind was like the ruins in which he lived, some pieces of the structure were unharmed while others were pulverized. There was no sense as to what survived and what did not. A cataclysm did not leave logical patterns in its wake.

Jamil spied his target easily. On the patio where umbrellas shielded tables from the harsh sun, Mister K was smiling brightly and sharing a drink with the muscular man named Tom Rimsky.

The fair-haired American was wearing a tight short-sleeved polo shirt. On the breast pocket was the familiar Redfire logo, a flame embroidered in red. Jamil stood outside the elevated patio, staring through the gate. Neither Rimsky nor Mister K noticed him yet, even though he was just a few meters from them. Nearby, a line of bullet-proof black SUVs dispensed men in suits and ladies in tight skirts and high heels.

"Hey! Come in or leave." A bulky Iraqi barked at him in English. The man was wearing a tuxedo and a pistol in his hip-holster.

"I am looking for my friend," Jamil said.

The man looked him over. Jamil quickly snatched some money from his pocket and held his hand out.

"Sorry for your trouble," the Iraqi said in Arabic as he pocketed the money with a smooth motion. He placed his hand on Jamil's back and escorted him toward the entrance.

"I apologize, my friend. Let me show you to your table." He half-followed, half-pushed Jamil while walking behind him.

Jamil realized he had no idea what he was going to do and now had no way to back out.

He had been here before with Mister K, but the pub was no less alien. Everywhere women caught his eye, flirting mercilessly. The men were well-dressed and almost as manicured as the women. Iraqi waiters darted in all directions, crashing through the doors to the kitchen, yelling their orders in Arabic. The scene was like the celebrity photos in the fashion magazines his sisters fought over.

The bouncer guided him through the bar and into the restaurant.

"Where is your friend, sir?"

"The patio," Jamil said, walking out into the heat. The bouncer followed.

They maneuvered around the tables, ducking the many umbrellas.

Jamil no longer felt his heart flutter. He felt calm.

Either I succeed or seal my death here, he thought. He stopped at the table's edge.

"The work's not the issue, it's the cost," Rimsky was saying to Mister K. "More water," he added, shaking his glass so the ice cubes inside rattled. He had mistaken Jamil for a waiter.

Mister K looked up and his jaw dropped. He quickly rubbed his hand over his mouth to hide his shock. Jamil grabbed Mister K's hand and shook vigorously.

"Good to see you," Jamil said in Arabic. Mister K's grip was limp.

The bouncer pushed a chair underneath Jamil, forcing him to sit.

"Glad to be of service, my friend. Please come again," he said before heading back outside.

Jamil reached for Rimsky's hand. Rimsky pulled back and stared at him, his eyes hidden behind reflective sunglasses.

Jamil withdrew his hand and spoke quickly in English. "Everything went so well the other night, I thought I would stop by to discuss future arrangements."

Rimsky leaned back, folded his arms and frowned.

"Nice to see you again, Mister Tom Rimsky. You do remember me?" Jamil said.

"I didn't know you spoke English."

Mister K forced a smile as he spoke to Jamil in Arabic. "It is good to see you, my friend, but we were conducting business."

"English is fine, Mister K. Tom. And talking business is why I'm here."

Rimsky snorted. "Cut the shit, kid. What's this all about?"

Jamil clasped his hands together. "As I said. I want to talk with you. The man that I have been working for all this time. The one I've really been working for."

Mister K leaned forward. "I think we should discuss something else."

"No. I don't think so," Jamil said. "We are businessmen. We should help our customer save money. You want to save money, don't you, Tom?"

Rimsky raised his eyebrows.

Jamil took a deep breath before he spoke. "Whatever you are paying Mister K, I will accept half of it and I will provide the same results. I have already been doing everything but collecting the packs already."

Rimsky frowned and tapped his fingers on the table. He shifted in his seat.

"All right. I get it. So, Mister K, that's your secret to how you get so much done, huh? Working the middle?"

"Tom, there are so many, ah, packages you want me to deliver, of course, I would separate them."

"Separate them?" Jamil said. "More like drop them off."

"Tom," Mister K said, "you can't be taking this seriously."

"I'm just taking it all in," Rimsky said, folding his arms.

Mister K turned to Jamil, glaring at him as he spoke to Rimsky. "Jamil is an enthusiastic young man, but he has no sense of protocol. Or loyalty, obviously."

"Really?" Jamil countered. "We both know I do all the work." Jamil turned directly to face Rimsky. "So, Tom, would you like to do business with me, or keep over-paying this unnecessary fool?"

Rimsky threw his head back and laughed. "I love it! A hostile takeover!" He looked to Mister K. "Are you going to just sit there and take this like a pussy?"

Mister K spoke in Arabic through clenched teeth. "This is very foolish, Jamil. Leave now and you may see tomorrow."

Jamil countered in English. "How rude. You don't speak Arabic, do you, Tom?"

Rimsky shrugged. "Never said anything about it."

"We are all friends here," Jamil said. "Mister K, please speak so our friend and partner can understand."

Mister K pounded his fist on the table. The glass and silverware jumped. "I told him he is a fool."

Jamil returned his gaze. "Yet I am the same one that you send to deliver your packages. I even delivered the special one last night."

Rimsky laughed. "Boys! Boys! Enough. I love a good fight, but I only need one contact and I don't care who it is, as long as the job gets done."

"Then I will call the manager and have this child removed," Mister K said.

"Slow down a minute, K. This kid has balls. He obviously knows what's going on. That means you were confident enough in him to sub-contract with him. That shit might work for my bosses, but we all know sub-contracting is just keeping some money and finding someone to do it for less. So, get to it. Begin the bidding war."

Jamil spoke first. "You have my offer. Same work for half of what he's charging. That is probably what he pays me already."

"Tom, this is absurd," Mister K pleaded. "Your work requires delicacy. It would be foolish to work with a street urchin."

Jamil chuckled. "Street urchins run this whole program. You give me the bags and I distribute them to homeless boys. You are just a middle man."

Tom laughed again. "I'm really enjoying this. Keep going." He made a circular motion with his finger. "In America we would probably call this something like generational restructuring."

"But this is Iraq," Mister K stammered. "This is not America."

"Not yet," Rimsky smiled.

"This is ridiculous!" Mister K stood up, knocking his chair over. The people at nearby tables grew quiet, heads turning to watch the spectacle. "You would even consider working with this arrogant child?" Mister K righted his chair and sat down again, his face burning purple.

Rimsky leaned forward, sinister mirth gone from his voice. "What's one of my rules, Kahled?"

Mister K bowed his head. "Do not draw attention."

"Exactly. But you just did. And this young guy baited you into it. I should thank him for exposing you. In fact, I will. He's my new partner. Now get out."

"Tom, we have-"

"Get out before I have the staff throw you out."

"Not like this, Tom," Mister K said. "We have trust, we have history."

"Hell, now you sound like the bitches I fucked in high school."

"And the savings, Tom? Will you keep them? Suppose your bosses learn this?"

Rimsky stood up and barked, drawing the attention of the other patrons again. "Don't threaten me, asshole. You don't know who my bosses are because I'm not stupid enough to let you find out. Else then you might replace me. Idiot. This kid is cheaper, and he does good work. He gets the job. It's just business. Now go."

Mister K grabbed Jamil's arm. "You will die, boy," he snarled in Arabic. He released his grip and walked away, the eyes of the crowd following him. Jamil brushed off his suit, his heart racing.

He and Tom were alone.

A waiter rushed to their table. He bowed, speaking quickly in English. "Gentlemen, do you require anything? Is everything okay?"

"We're good," Rimsky said. "No trouble."

To Jamil he said, "Go ahead, order what you like."

"A water. Water, please."

"Just water?" Rimsky asked. "Come on, live a little. I'm buying."

"A lemonade, please." The waiter hustled away.

"Wow, now that's living," Rimsky snorted. "Now, are you going to introduce yourself formally?"

"Jamil."

"Tom Rimsky." They shook hands across the table. "Nice to meet you. Again. You did well on that other job. The night one. Everything worked perfectly."

"I'm pleased."

"And I'm eager to begin our new partnership."

"Of course," Jamil said calmly. "I have only one immediate concern. Mister K. I'll need a handgun."

"You walk these streets and you don't have a gun?"

Jamil said nothing.

"I'll see what I can do. Don't worry about Mister K, though. I have a feeling he'll be taking an early retirement. I'm sure you understand."

Jamil was not sure he understood at all. A straight answer had been impossible to come by in years. So much was answered indirectly, with innuendo. As with Mikhail, each word seemed to have a hidden meaning.

"Are you scared of Mister K?" Tom asked. "This business requires a bit of nerve. Don't make me regret my decision. I'm good at assessing people and I think you'll do fine, but occasionally I'm wrong."

"Oh, no," Jamil said, "I'm not frightened, just realistic and aware. Consider it evidence you made a wise decision."

"I hope so. You won't last long if you disappoint me."

Obviously, Jamil almost said, but he simply waited.

Rimsky cocked his head slightly as if he were considering something.

Jamil's drink arrived. He took a quick sip. The lemon acid mixed with bile in his mouth. He had been that close to throwing up from nerves. He gargled with the drink, swishing it around to wash the graininess from his mouth, and give him precious seconds to focus his thoughts.

Rimsky finally spoke. "All right. We want this coming month to be especially productive. We may have some VIPs on the way and that could be cause for even more activity."

Jamil nodded and took a gulp of his drink. Productive, Rimsky said, but he meant destructive. Jamil had learned English on his own, but now he felt like he was learning a whole new language so he could speak aloud in code.

"Yes," Jamil nodded.

"We will have a lot of shipments for you." Shipments, the secret word for bombs.

"A lot of missing backpacks," Jamil said.

"Right. Now let's get started. Give me a description of your car."

"I don't have one."

"No car? How did you get here?"

"I took the bus with the Iraqi workers."

"No car? Christ," Rimsky laughed. "You have a cell phone?"

"No."

"Where do you live?"

"In the ruins of a home destroyed by bombs."

"Damn, you've got nothing except balls."

"And brains."

Tom lifted his beer, toasting Jamil. "A good combination, but even Mister K started with his own car." Tom sipped the beer and wiped his mouth with the back of his wrist. "Remind me again why I got rid of him."

"My cheaper price will pay for my start-up costs. I'm not afraid to go into sections of Baghdad that those with a Western appearance avoid. I speak Arabic and I come from the desperate boys we need. They trust me. They fled from Mister K, as he looked suspicious, out of place. Over time he had fewer and fewer to help. I'll have an endless supply. They look up to me."

"Okay, okay," Rimsky said, holding up his hand. "Enough with the pitch. I'm re-sold. Plus, turnover in this business... It's a good thing. Keeps people sharp. Market competition is what my country's all about. So, the kids ran from Mister K? I expected as much. He didn't know I was aware of his other activities."

"I had heard the rumors."

"They were true. He took boys. Not just for the work I had. He sold them for other kinds of services."

Jamil did not want to think about what that was code for.

"That stuff's a big time liability. Damn fool. I need someone with a low profile. You happened along at the right time, Jamil, my friend."

"Glad to hear it."

Tom continued. "Shit, since September 11th it's been a damned free-for-all."

"It is understandable," Jamil was learning to say words but say nothing, to use phrases that took up time and allowed others to release information. Was the urge to converse and prevent silence so strong? It seemed so.

"It's been crazy," Rimsky said. "Uncle Sam was so determined to get someone, we did nothing else. Just bag and brag. A lot of people who had nothing to do with anything ended up disappearing, but that's business. That's war. Same thing."

Jamil nodded, trying not to appear too intent. "Go on."

"Nothing else to say on that."

"But there's much you could tell," Jamil said.

"No shit. The stories I could share would make your skin crawl. For now, let's get to business. You start today."

* * *

Jamil smiled broadly as he pulled his shiny new car into the lot. The boys scattered, taking their ball with them. He stepped out, wearing his new suit and sunglasses.

"Hey, guys," he yelled. "Where are you going? It's me. Jamil!"

The boys all came running up to the car, laughing, greeting him with a kiss on each cheek, mock-bowing before him. He stood among the small crowd of mostly-younger homeless boys, basking in their stunned looks.

"Don't touch the car," he said. "I've got work for the fastest runners, so if you want some money, line up to race. The winners get some easy work and easier money."

The boys lined up. Jamil yelled out, "Ready. Set. Go!"

They ran across the lot and back. Jamil invited the fastest three into his car. He drove off as his passengers waved and yelled to the boys restarting their football match.

"Can you keep a secret?" Jamil asked.

"Yes," they all answered eagerly.

After a short joyride, he took them to a secluded part of the ruined neighborhood. He warned against questions, told them to stay quiet, gave them each an address and a pack, then let them go.

Exactly as Mister K had done for him.

* * *

Jamil rested on the bed of his hotel room, surprised he wasn't shaking, but unable to fall asleep. The encounter with Mister K and Tom Rimsky had gone so smoothly, he knew he had surmised correctly that Rimsky was already looking for a reason to dump his old partner. Success didn't make Jamil any less tense.

He ran his hands over the soft, lightly-scented sheets. This single room, not even counting the bathroom, was larger than his entire house he remembered in Morocco. Did he have a home anymore?

Using the remote, he flipped through the television stations. A news channel showed an American senator bellowing and gesturing forcefully, punctuating his statements with raised fist. Arabic subtitles flashed underneath.

"For years people have claimed that there were no weapons of mass destruction. They've been saying the USA attacked Iraq for nothing. They say we should pull out! They're saying all this, even after the chemical attack on camp Tokyo-Zulu. Proof of unconventional weapons! No one is talking about that! We cannot back down from this war!"

Jamil changed the channel, found a football game and watched it.

He toyed with the cell phone Tom had given him. After the game he called home.

"Salaam. Who is it?" his mother answered.

He listened and almost smiled to himself. In the background he could hear the television, its sappy music playing. His sisters sighed happily, a familiar noise they made when someone on their romance shows proposed marriage, which seemed to be every day. Did anything ever change there?

"Who is this?" his mother said through the static. "Talk to me. If you have my son, please, we'll pay anything."

Jamil closed his eyes, listening to the sounds so far away.

"Jamil, if this is you, remember you can always come home. No matter what has happened, no matter what you've done or what they have done to you, we love you and always will."

Jamil kept the phone to his ear, rose from the bed and stared out the window. It was reinforced with metal wire, a protection against explosive shock waves. The window was a larger version of the one from his cell.

"Whoever this is," his mother said, "please just say something."

A grey cloud burst from behind buildings a kilometer away. A second later, the building vibrated gently.

"Did you say something?" his mother asked.

Jamil slapped the phone shut. He closed the curtain and turned away from the window so he could no longer see the thin column of smoke rising from the city.

ZERD

IRAQ

2007

Hot.

That's the first thing I thought when I got to Iraq. The plane was cooler because of the air-conditioned cabin, but I could still feel the sun pressing in.

The second thing I thought was, okay, when do I get the hell out of here?

The flight in was quiet. Our small plane was carrying about twenty of us cons hoping to improve our fate, thanks to Senator Hanson's Cons-to-Soldiers bill. I think everyone was reconsidering their decision as we flew over bombed and blackened ruins before diving into a sickening corkscrew landing to avoid gunfire from the ground.

Welcome to your new home. Vomit.

We walked across a sticky tarmac under pounding dry heat, passing huge construction equipment and several tanks. In the shade of a hangar we stood in line for a long time while each of us stepped behind a curtain for a quick physical.

That was my first meeting with Doctor Love, his actual name, as I learned from the tag on his white lab coat. He seemed like an all-right guy, except for the fact that he was going to touch my balls.

So, there they are, my remaining memories of arriving in Iraq: it's damn hot, when do I get out, and some dude is touching my balls. Nice. Six more months to go.

Maybe because of his job as nad-juggler, Doctor Love had a quirky sense of humor.

"I'm Doctor Love," he said, extending his hand, "of the United States military."

"Pete Abbott." I shook his hand.

"Do you realize you just got the ball sweat of a bunch of other guys on your fingers?" he asked, deadpan.

I cracked up. He smirked. "Okay, enough laughs. Drop 'em." While I was unzipping my pants, he was pulling on rubber gloves.

"I already had a physical before I came here," I told him.

"I know. You got approval from Redfire. I'm with the U.S. military. This is to make sure they did it right."

"Why fly us out here if there's a chance we'll fail? Isn't that wasteful?"

Doctor Love laughed. "There's no such thing as waste to a contractor, just billable expenses."

"So, why don't you just quit and work for Redfire?"

He threw his hands in the air, hopeless. "All right, you caught me. I like grabbing balls. Okay? Guilty. Now shut up and drop 'em."

I did.

"Shit, all these tattoos are making me dizzy," he said. "Where's your dick in all this mess?" He laughed as he pressed in the area around my package. "Oh, there's the little guy."

I coughed.

"You're good," he said. "Now get out."

After my sack passed inspection, I was directed to a bland classroom. Folding chairs were set in rows and a white dry-erase board hung on the wall. A large window looked out on the hangar. One by one, post-scrotal fondling, we cons took our seats.

Once the room was filled, a short dude in desert camouflage stomped to the front of the class, looking at us like bird crap on his brand new car. I guess he was our drill sergeant. He started barking and didn't let up.

Leaving out the dozens of times he emphasized his statements with fuckin' this and fuckin' that, our welcome went like this:

"You are not a United States soldier. That is an honor you currently do not share. You are a temporary employee of the Redfire Corporation. You will be assigned your team and your tasks. You will not have choices. If you step out of line, you will be shipped back to the states and to continue your time in a cell. Any questions? The correct answer is no."

No one moved except a blubbery guy in the front row. He raised a pudgy hand.

"What is it, son?" Sarge screamed. "I said no questions!"

The fat guy shook in his seat. "Will we see combat?"

"Do you want to see some?"

"No, sir. I don't want to die."

"What did I say about you being soldiers?"

"You said we were not soldiers."

"You'll be providing support, cleaning toilets, doing the laundry and seeing to the housework of real men. You will be given adequate defensive hardware, a gas mask and the like, in the case of a chemical attack. Screw up and your ass and the rest of your worthless body will be shipped back home to serve out your time. Any further questions? The correct answer is no."

No one moved.

"Good. When I call you, raise your hand. We're splitting into squads of four."

* * *

He called a name, pointed to a different corner of the room, breaking the group up. When he called my name, he pointed me to a corner where an angry-looking, wiry guy stood. The thin guy smiled at me, but it wasn't a friendly smile. He was clearly a wise-ass. He shook my hand.

"What's going on, Graffiti-man?"

"Call me Zerd."

"You can't pick your own nickname."

"So, you make the rules?"

He shrugged. "They're the only ones I follow."

The next guy was called to our group. He was a bit overweight, his hair graying on the sides. "How's it going, Tubbs?" the wiry guy said.

"My name's Daniel."

"I'm going to call you Tubbs."

"Nice to meet you Daniel," I said. "I'm Zerd."

"Zerd?"

"Yeah, Zerd."

"Zerd. Huh. All right. All right," Tubbs or Daniel chuckled. "Did he pick that name for you?" He pointed to the thin, wiry guy.

I laughed. "No. It's my nickname. Long story."

"Zerd it is, then."

Names were called and everyone was split up into groups of four. The chubby guy who had asked the question at the end of our introduction was the last one sitting and our group had only three. Obviously we were going to get him. Still, he sat there, waiting.

"Just like gym class, right?" Sarge said.

"Aw, gosh," the blubbery guy whined.

Everyone laughed.

"Asshole," the skinny spaz in my group said, coughing into his hand. Everyone laughed again.

"Squad Five, son."

The fat guy got up and waddled over to our team.

"How's it going, Grits?" the wiry guy said. He was really getting on my nerves. He was constantly fidgeting, humming and singing to himself. It was impossible to relax around him.

"Grits?" the chubby guy said.

"That's your nickname."

"But I'm not from the South," he said in his dopey voice.

"Doesn't matter. You're Grits now."

"Well, gosh. What are your nicknames?"

"This big fellow here is Tubbs. The guy with the tattoos is... Graffiti-man, or what did you say your name was again?"

"Zerd."

"Zerd. I might choose that over Graffiti-man. It's easier to say. Zerd with a Z as in Zee-row. Like the average I.Q. of everyone here. Z as in zebra. Like us. We've got two, how y'all say it? People of color. Myself and Tubbs. And two slices of white bread, Z and Grits. We'll count you as white, Z, even though you're tie-dyed."

"Nice to meet you all," Grits said, shaking hands all around. "What's your nickname?" he asked the wiry guy. I hadn't thought to ask. I just wanted him to stop talking.

"Me? Call me Sly."

"I thought you couldn't choose your own nickname," I said.

"Serves you right for tryin' to think. You in the army now, son."

So there we were, Squad Five. Sly, the wiry, talkative, annoying guy; Tubbs, the chunky old guy; Grits, the really fat pasty dude; and me.

"All right, clowns," Sarge said. "One more thing before I feed you to your squad leaders. No matter what hell you think you came from, it was a playground compared to Iraq. This is a dangerous place. Camp Tokyo-Zulu was recently hit by a chemical weapon. Twenty men dead. Several more are coughing up their own blood."

Everyone was quiet, absorbing the news as five big guys headed across the hangar toward us. They were all wearing white polo shirts with the Redfire Corporation logo on the breast pocket, camouflage pants and tan combat boots. One of them wore his camo cap backwards, a big, hugely muscular dude who carried himself like the king of the jungle. His build immediately reminded me of steroid-addicted gym hounds. His eyes were hidden by mirrored shades and he was chewing an enormous gob of something. The only thing missing was the neon sign over his head flashing "Major Douche."

So of course he ended up being my squad leader.

"My name's Rimsky," he said. "Tom Rimsky." He shook each of our hands and guided us to the mess hall. "You four stick together and help yourself to a meal. I'll be back soon," he said, and left.

"I can't be the only one that's thinking we got ourselves a genuine dickhead for a boss," Sly said.

We all laughed. Maybe having him around was going to be a good thing.

* * *

The cafeteria was crowded with soldiers and con-soldiers and other guys like Rimsky, buff dudes wearing Redfire polo shirts a few sizes too small.

Sly did most of the talking over our meal. He explained he was half black and half Latino and to prove it, he babbled in a language that sounded like Spanish. I was picking at my food when Grits asked me a question.

"So, Z, what were you in for?"

"Drug dealing. What about you?"

"I don't want to talk about it."

"Then why did you bring it up?"

Grits quickly looked down and avoided making eye contact.

"So, Z," Sly asked, "why all the ink? Those tats mean anything?"

"Some do. Some don't. This one gave me my nickname. Lizard. Zerd. Z."

"Where are you from, Sly?" Grits asked.

"Shut the hell up," Sly said, malice in his voice.

"Okay." Grits went back to staring at his food.

"I'm just kidding, my white brother," Sly said, poking Grits in the side.

"Quit it!" Grits squealed.

"This is quite a bunch," Tubbs mumbled, shaking his head.

"No shit," Sly and I said at the same time.

We ate in silence while Sly chattered on in English and Spanish, keeping the conversation about nothing, going on all by himself. Suddenly he slapped the table and raised his paper cup of warm water, the only thing we had to drink. "A toast to The Four Fucked-Up Losers!"

"To the Four Fucked-Up Losers," Tubbs said, raising his cup.

"To the Four Fucked-Up Losers," I said, raising mine.

"To my new friends, the Four Losers," Grits said.

We all stared at him.

"Momma used to beat me when I cursed," he said.

"I rest my case," Sly said. "Drink up!"

We all drank.

* * *

We walked across the hot sand through rows of tents, following Rimsky. Our boots slid in the sand, keeping up with him was tough. I almost had to jog. Guys cleaning weapons glanced up and stared, their faces various combinations of annoyance and contempt. We obviously weren't welcome.

In the middle of the tent maze Rimsky turned sharply and poked his head inside a flap. "Honey, I'm home," he said, holding back the fabric to let us in. "And I brought the kids."

The tent was a poor shield from the sun's light and heat, but it was something.

Three guys were sitting on their cots, pulling apart guns, brushing sand from the barrels and lubricating the moving parts. They barely looked up.

"Con-soldiers in the house," Rimsky said. "Guys, meet our support group."

Grits got himself caught on the tent's heavy-duty zipper. Rimsky pulled his shirt loose, ripping it. "You're letting the sand in, idiot."

"Sorry."

While Grits was untangling himself, I looked around the tent at all the hardware. Miss Joanne had said we wouldn't be around weapons. That was, as Steve once said, "as wrong as my dick is long." There were guns, grenades and bullets everywhere. Everything you needed to kill lots and lots of people really fast was stored in this place, in full view and easily accessible by us con-soldiers.

"Good thing we took that bullshit psych test," Sly snickered.

Rimsky pointed around the tent, introducing us.

To the short, angry-looking guy with the mustache he said, "This is Spitz." Spitz kept cleaning his gun and didn't respond, didn't even look up.

He pointed to a tall black guy. "That's Carter." Carter nodded.

Then he pointed to a medium-height guy with thick, slicked back black hair. "And Belladonna."

"Hey, guys. Nice to meet you," Belladonna said, smiling. "How about a roll call?" It was freaky that he seemed to care about us at all. He stood up and shook our hands.

247

Grits started to open his mouth when Rimsky said, "Shit, I can barely remember their names. This skinny guy is…"

"Sly," Sly finished for him.

"The guy with the ink?" Belladonna asked.

"Zerd."

"How about this chunky black dude?"

"They're calling me Tubbs, sir."

"What about the fat white kid who let in the sand?"

"I'm sorry about that, officer. My name is-"

"Call him Grits," Sly said.

"So, are they a group or do we each get to pick a bitch?" Carter asked, smiling.

"Fuck you very much," Sly said, smiling back.

"Ooh, Sly's got a mouth on him," Carter said, falsetto.

"What did you say?" Rimsky asked, standing nose-to-nose with Sly.

Sly said nothing for a moment, then smiled wide. "I said I'm just glad to be here, sir. A proud American lucky to be working for the Dream Team."

"That's what I thought," Rimsky said. "Remember, you're here to clean up after real soldiers, got it?"

"I thought you were a contractor, not a real soldier." Sly said.

"You want to go back home right now, smart ass?"

"No, sir!" Sly yelled as loud as he could, ridiculously snapping to attention.

"That idiot is going to get us killed," Tubbs whispered to me.

"Or sent back," I said. Still, I couldn't help but admire Sly's fearlessness. At least he kept things from being boring.

* * *

It only took the next two days to learn everything there was to know about our new jobs for the coming six months: sweep these buildings, mop in here, clean these toilets, load these trucks, unload these others. Basically, we were janitors for the Redfire Corporation encampment. After our tour, for me at least, my time would be complete. Six months in Iraq equaled one year of jail time. If I was good.

Thank you, Senator Hanson. Sorry, Dad.

The camp complex was a bunch of pre-fab buildings inside a tall perimeter fence topped with concertina wire. The fence encircled both Redfire's camp and the U.S. military's, but the two were clearly separate, which was fine by me because the U.S. base looked like a slum compared to our place. Just like Dad said, the contractors were living in luxury, compliments of the U.S. taxpayer, while the regular military made do. It sucked for them, but I was on the good side for once, so I wasn't too concerned. Nothing I could do about it anyway.

Our cots were bunched in a corner of our tent, where we collapsed every day as the sun set. Usually I was asleep right away, drained from the heat and work and boredom.

We slept in the same tent as the squad we were supporting, who we were calling the Dream Team, another nickname courtesy of Sly. All eight of us used the same portable bathroom and the same portable shower unit. Of course they got first run on the shower, which left us only cold water. Each morning we awoke to the sounds of the national anthem played through the camp's loudspeakers.

Once we showered and dressed in our standard-issue work overalls, the Dream Team prepared their weapons while we Four Losers grabbed our mops and brooms.

Rimsky addressed us as we prepared to part ways, his assault rifle slung over his shoulder. He'd give us orders and threats like this: "We're going out to waste some bad guys. When we come back, I want everything spotless and free of sand. If it isn't, you're going back stateside for a fresh jailhouse butt-fucking."

The Dream Team would then head out, laughing. All except the short guy, Spitz. He didn't laugh or talk. He just looked pissed off. All the time.

Sometimes, right before they took off, the stocky one, Belladonna, would call them together with a low "Hey, amigos." Rimsky would roll his eyes and remove his helmet. They all put their heads together and bowed as Belladonna led a prayer.

"Lord, we ask for your protection as we prepare to be the might of your righteous arm." He said something in Spanish and then "Amen."

"Amen," the others repeated. Except for Spitz.

"Let's move out," Rimsky said.

Then they were gone and we were left alone with all their spare weapons. Exactly as Miss Joanne said we wouldn't be.

Every day was pretty much the same, just like that.

Sly often wished them well. "I hope you get a pipe bomb up your ass," he'd growl once they were gone, giving their side of the tent the finger.

Tubbs didn't appreciate Sly's attitude. "You're going to get your dumb ass shot. Those crazy white boys and their tokens don't care about you."

"They're not here, so what's the problem? Besides, I can't help it."

"Start helping it. Just shut up and do your time."

"Whatever, Tubbs. Oh, and congratulations on your promotion."

"Promotion?"

"Yeah, to fuckin' ruler of my world."

"Shut up." Tubbs would try to stay mad, but he always ended up laughing. Sly was like that. He made you laugh, because otherwise you'd want to kick his ass.

* * *

I certainly didn't expect the con-soldier gig to be exciting, but I didn't expect it to be so mundane, either. I guess janitorial skills were part of Hands-on Hanson's plan. When we returned to the USA and maybe someday became ex-cons, we could assume our rightful place in society cleaning up other people's shit. Meantime, Redfire got to look like a good corporate citizen while getting cheap labor, making a profit off our work and scoring a tax write-off all at once.

Crap, I sound like my dad.

There was a constant stream of supply trucks rolling in and out of the camp. The drivers and their soldier escorts would stand in the shade and drink ice water while we unloaded boxes and piled them up somewhere else. The inside of the truck was like an oven, and soon, our shirts were off. Of course, Sly always had to comment.

"Damn, they're some of the finest tits I've seen in at least a year," he said, his hands on his hips while admiring a blushing Grits.

"Knock it off," Grits said, his voice squeaking in a way that made us all laugh.

We were covered with sweat. Tubbs and Grits moved very slow, their huge bellies spilling over the front of their pants.

"Looks like you forgot to take your shirt off," Sly said to me, laughing. It was a lame joke the first time, but it got much worse because he said it every day, and he always laughed. No one else did. I ignored him.

Someone once said war is a lot of boredom punctuated by moments of terror, or something like that. I could relate to the boredom part. I was practically hoping for some moments of terror to break the monotony.

Instead, I got annoyance. The highlight of my day was when the Dream Team returned, and for the few hours before we went to sleep, Sly would antagonize them. Or one of them (except the silent Spitz) would antagonize us. After a while, I began to wonder if I could fall asleep without some kind of verbal battle in progress.

Here's an example of the chatter that functioned as my Iraq lullaby:

"Hey, Grits," Carter asked, "they ever rape you when you were in prison?"

"No," Grits said, "but I saw it happen once. It was not good."

"You saw it happen?" Rimsky said. "And you kept watching?"

"Did you start jacking off to the free gay porn?" Belladonna asked.

"You guys are too much," Grits chuckled nervously.

"I'm serious, G," Carter said. "They ever butt-rape you? You look like the kind of guy they might go for with your man-boobs. If some ass-fucker wrapped his mitts around you, with a little imagination, you'd feel just like a fat chick."

"Oh, gosh. Now quit it."

The Dream Team chimed in, all of them cackling, except, of course, Spitz, who just kept polishing his weapons. "Come on, Grits! You know you got it in the ass. How was it? Are you a squealer? Do you shit easier now?"

"Come on, guys. Gosh."

"I'll bet you loved it. I'll bet you fuckin' loved it."

Tubbs pulled his pillow over his head. No one could make the Dream Team stop taunting Grits, so we just had to ignore it until it went away.

Of course, Sly would yell back at them, cursing in Spanish. Belladonna spoke Spanish too and they would go on for hours, the tone of their voices bubbling with insults understood only by each other.

The situation was totally stupid, but I didn't care. I was using the time to step away from my old life.

That's how we fell asleep each night, Sly and Belladonna cursing each other in Spanish until an unfamiliar voice yelled out, "Shut the fuck up!" It always took me a second to realize it had to be Spitz. This was the only thing he had to say, apparently.

Then all would be quiet for a while and it would start up again slowly, Belladonna and Sly cursing each other with Spanish whispers, until they were laughing at their own insults and shouting again. Then Spitz would silence them with a shout.

Our tent was a miniature version of the whole war. We tried to sleep while ignoring the voices from the dark cursing us in a language we couldn't understand.

* * *

So the Redfire Dream Team was Spitz, Carter, Belladonna and Rimsky, their leader. The Four Losers were myself, Grits, Tubbs and Sly.

Belladonna was the only Dream Team member who didn't treat us like shit. He and Sly had built a reluctant bridge. On Sundays, the Dream Team would lie around and read the newspaper. We Four Losers never got a day off. That was built into Hanson's program. I can hear him now: "They don't get a day off in jail, why should they when they're working for our country?"

Belladonna was one of those people who would constantly share aloud what he read in the paper. "Look at this, Rimsky, it says that Real War website shows some dude getting acid poured on his stomach and genitals. Aw, man, that's cold."

"I'm telling you," Rimsky said, "we're in the land of the savages, the Wild West meets the Middle East. We're cowboys surrounded by Indians, the civilized surrounded by the barbarians. And I'm not talking about the help." They laughed.

Tubbs and I ignored them, cleaning the tent, doing all the mindless chores we were assigned. Fortunately, Grits and Sly had gone out for a quick supply run. Sly would rarely let an insult pass without a smartass comeback, and that always led to an argument, so things tended to go smoother when he wasn't around.

When he and Grits got back, Carter leapt up from his cot. "Work, white boys! Work!" he yelled in my ear. He would do that occasionally, harass only me and Grits.

"It's payback time," he said. "What your granddaddy did to my granddaddy is coming back to you. The sins of the father shall be visited upon the son. So it says in the Bible or some shit."

"Hey," Belladonna said, "don't use 'shit' and 'Bible' in the same sentence."

"Why not?" Carter said. "You just did."

"I did? Aw, fuck. Damn it, Carter, it's your fault if I go to hell."

"Scrub, white boys, scrub!"

I showed no emotion and eventually Carter got bored. Grits laughed uncomfortably or tried to make conversation. That never worked. Carter only yelled louder.

Sometimes when the Dream Team was riding our asses, Sly would jump in and annoy them. I think it was his way of sticking up for us, or maybe he just couldn't stop himself like he said. Either way, he only made things worse.

"Hey, Dream Team," he said, "how do you know you're only killing bad guys?"

Carter laughed. "If they're wearing rags on their heads, they're bad guys." He punched Spitz in the shoulder, "Right, Spitz?"

Spitz didn't reply.

"So, you see a ten year old boy wearing a turban," Sly said. "You shoot him?"

Rimsky interrupted. "Isn't there a toilet somewhere you should be scrubbing? A bed pan that needs cleaning?"

"I just want to know how you decide who the bad guys are. Where I grew up, little kids got shot all the time. Y'all have turned Iraq into one big-ass ghetto."

"Shut the fuck up," Carter said.

"Answer my question. Do you guys ever kill civilians?"

When Sly used the word "civilian," the tent practically inflated with silent tension from the Dream Team.

Sly had balls. You had to give him that. He was always pushing his luck to the edge of a cliff. Only problem was, his luck was tied to the rest of us losers.

Belladonna turned red. He leapt to his feet and immediately started yelling at Sly in Spanish. Sly took it for a moment, grinning before firing back. Belladonna's eyes widened as his fury intensified. Soon they were nose to nose, their mouths bubbling with the bouncing sounds of angry Spanish.

"Jesus Christ, it's like Cinco de Mayo in here," Rimsky said. "Sit the fuck down." He shoved Sly, causing him to stagger backwards and fall onto his cot, collapsing it. Wincing, Sly held his lower back and was slow to get up. None of us moved to help him.

In the quiet, Rimsky dressed himself in his Redfire polo shirt and shorts while Carter and Belladonna went back to reading the newspaper. Spitz, creepy dude that he was, ignored us all, sharpening his knives in the corner. Carter looked at Rimsky as he admired himself in the mirror, flexing his muscles.

"Where you going, boss?" Carter asked.

"Working on the N.Y.F.B. project." Rimsky answered as he left the tent.

"What's the N.Y.F.B. project?" Grits asked.

"None of Your Fucking Business," Belladonna said.

"Hey, Uncle Tom and Uncle Puto," Sly said, gasping as he stood up. "How do you deal with that dickhead?"

Carter answered. "That crazy white boy is the kind you want on your side. Them white boys on your team ain't worth shit."

Fortunately, at that point, it was time to take a trash bag out to the dumpster. The heat sucked, but I was glad to be away from the tension. I saw Rimsky get in a hard-top jeep alone and drive off. He went off on his own frequently, which was a good thing. When he wasn't around, the asshole tendencies of the Dream Team were greatly reduced.

Back in the tent, Belladonna was showing off his newspaper again.

"Holy shit. I think I know what Rimsky's N.Y.F.B. project is." He stood up and started reading out loud, "Senator Wayne Drake Hanson will be visiting Iraq. The trip is meant as a morale boost to a weary fighting force facing extended tours." He lowered the paper and added his own comment: "Your average G.I. is such a pussy, man!"

Then he went back to reading. "Critics have called the timing of the trip, to occur in a few months, 'highly suspicious' as the visit coincides with a congressional committee's investigation, looking into potential misconduct regarding the hiring and use of war contractors in Iraq."

"Oh, shit, that's you guys," Sly said. "You might be out of a job."

"Shut up," Belladonna said.

He kept reading. "A spokesman for Hanson's office said the Senator will cooperate fully with any investigation but that, quote, 'The needs of those offering up the greatest sacrifice come first.'"

Sly smiled broadly. "Maybe I'll get to be his shoulder ornament."

"His what?" Belladonna asked.

"His shoulder ornament. His over-the-shoulder black. Every time a white man makes a speech, he makes sure a black man sits behind him and to the side. Adds color, you know?"

"Bullshit," Belladonna said. "No senator is coming near us."

"He is Hands-on Hanson, right?" Sly said. "Got to promote his success with the Cons-to-Soldiers. He'll be here for his photo-op. If not us than some other cons. And a black dude will be his shoulder ornament. You watch."

"You're crazy," Carter added.

Grits stared into space, eyes wide, his voice dreamy. "You really think he'll visit with us? If my folks could see that, maybe they wouldn't think I messed up my life. They'd be so proud."

Sly leapt across the room and put his arm around Grits. "My chubby white friend, I know when that big important man sees you, he's going to say, now there's a prime example of Grade-A American flesh. I need to shake that fine young man's hand."

"You think?" Grits asked.

Everyone except him burst out laughing.

JAMIL

IRAQ

2007

Seated in the shade of the table's umbrella, Jamil sipped his lemonade. He was wearing sunglasses, so he felt safe letting his eyes follow the women in the crowd at The American Oasis. The ladies and men too, everyone here, was chatting and smiling, oblivious to the civil war going on just a few miles away in all directions.

Tom Rimsky sat across from Jamil, also wearing shades that obscured his eyes. Both of them were hiding from each other. Rimsky was tinkering with his cell phone, as always. He set it down and blew out his cheeks to show he was bored.

"You know, you're kind of boring. You rarely talk, do you?" Rimsky asked.

"No," Jamil said.

"Strictly business, huh?"

"Strictly business."

"We've met here a bunch of times over the last, what is it, almost a year now? We've distributed tons of packages, and all you do is talk business, eat in silence and leave."

"You are paying me for competence, not companionship, yes?"

"That's true, but a little conversation wouldn't hurt. You know, shoot the breeze. Exchange information. Network."

"You told me not to ask questions."

"About our business partnership. We can still have a conversation."

"Okay. Let's converse. Name the topic."

"Shit, that's natural," Rimsky said, shaking his head. "Forget it. Look, things are getting delicate. I'm going to need your help on a couple jobs. Personally. I want you to care for them yourself. No street kids, all right?"

"No problem."

"Remember when we first met? When you dropped off that special package? Right before Mister K retired?"

"Yes, Tokyo-Zulu," Jamil said, recalling the night he armed the chemical weapon. "I remember."

"We need to do it again. Same delivery, different place. Just you and I."

"Another night job should be easy."

"This one is during the day. You will pose as my translator. Then I'll have another standard job that needs to occur immediately after. Then we're done."

"Done? Our business concluded?"

"No. No. I didn't mean it like that. I meant after the one similar to Tokyo-Zulu, I have another important one, but it's the normal delivery. Get it? I want you to handle both personally back-to-back. Quickly, too. Both within a week of each other. One-two punch. Boom. Bababoom."

"Both?"

"Yes. They're very important. I only trust you, so you have to be the one."

Jamil hesitated. "All right. When will we go on the first one?"

"Right the fuck now."

* * *

Rimsky pulled the black SUV up to the entrance barrier of the fenced-in encampment. The guard looked up from his booth. Rimsky flipped him the middle finger. The guard smiled and called out, "Yeah, yeah. Take it easy, Rimsky!"

The barrier sunk into the sand and they drove over it.

Jamil looked into the side mirror at the pack in the back seat. It bounced with a clanking noise as they drove over the hard-packed sand.

Rimsky drove into the camp, passing a billboard with the American flag on the left and the Redfire logo on the right. Jamil clenched his fist at the sight of the stylized flames. Rimsky took the road to the right.

"Are you ready?" he asked.

"But this is an American base," Jamil said.

"I said, are you ready?"

"I am. We are leaving the package with Americans."

Rimsky kept driving, not looking at his passenger. Jamil looked out into the compound, the sunlight dim through the tinted windows. It seemed most of the soldiers were out on missions. The grounds were almost completely deserted.

"You're a clever guy, Jamil," Rimsky said as he drove on, slower now, "I know what you're doing. You're making statements that aren't questions, hoping I will give you information."

"I was just-"

"So, you finally decide to make conversation, and you try to trick me into revealing classified info. Stuff I'd rather keep secret."

"Tom, I-"

"Don't even think of questions, Jamil. Take your curiosity and put it away. We do what we do and we get paid. We don't ask why. Ever."

"Yes."

"Just follow orders. That's what I do. It makes life simpler."

"Of course. I am sorry if you-"

"Forget about it. Just focus on the task."

Rimsky parked the car next to a long low building with few windows in it. A stencil on the side read simply "Storage."

"Now I'm going to get out and walk away," Rimsky said. "Wait a few minutes, make sure no one sees you, and put the bag in that building in front of us. Unzip it so you can get to the canister, then pull the cord loose as before. You remember when you used to do these?"

"I do."

"Good man. See you soon."

Rimsky jumped out of the van and walked over to the prefabricated building holding the latrine. Jamil stepped out of the SUV and stretched as if he was waiting. He opened the rear door and delicately lifted the canvas pack. He backed into the storage shed door and stepped into the darkness. The spring hinges closed the door behind him.

He set the pack down with a gentle clank and unzipped the top, revealing the canister and a cord wrapped around a key on one end, disappearing into the tank's nozzle on the other. He gently slid the canister among similar ones labeled "compressed air."

Jamil looked around and found some twine. He tied the line to the key and walked across the storage area.

Suddenly he heard voices nearby. He crouched down, his chest tightening.

Had Rimsky set him up?

The voices were not angry or commanding, they were simply talking. Through the windows, he could see men milling around, peeking in. Jamil looked about frantically for a place to hide, but he was in the empty space, the shelves stacked against the walls.

He stayed low. The men outside were carrying mops and wearing denim overalls. The tops of their outfits dropped around their waists, showing their bare, sweaty upper bodies.

"Is this it?" one of them said.

A man opened the door and stood before Jamil.

He was painted all over. Strange creatures, skulls, flames and designs of every imaginable color were tattooed all over his thin, muscular chest. He looked at Jamil. Jamil stared back at him.

"Oh," the man said. "Hello."

Before Jamil could say anything more, the door was slammed shut.

"What the hell are you fucktards doing?" Jamil recognized Rimsky's voice.

"We're looking for the building we're supposed to clean up," the painted man responded.

"Well, it's not this one."

"You told us it was the one labeled storage."

"On the west side of camp, this is the east side."

"How the hell are we supposed to know that?"

"By not being dumbasses," Rimsky barked. "Now, go."

The men's voices faded. Jamil heard the door to the SUV open and close. He had no time. He ran to the canister and, holding his breath, grabbed the arming cord key and pulled. The canister hissed, spitting out a puff of yellow as before. Jamil ran outside and leapt into the SUV, finally exhaling. Rimsky gunned the engine.

"Did they see you?" he asked.

"No," Jamil said.

"Good."

They drove out of the camp in silence. Jamil touched his face, and examined his fingertips. He saw no chemical residue.

* * *

Once they had driven outside the base and were on the highway back to Baghdad, Rimsky spoke.

"Good work, Jamil. The second job is going to come up quickly. It's another one that requires precision. Do you know what a V.I.P. is?"

"I have heard this phrase. Very Important Person."

"Right. This job is critical, so no working with local kids. I know you like to help them out, give them some work, or use them because no one's going to miss one if something goes wrong, but I want you to do this one, because it requires finesse."

"Another special package."

"I told you to knock that shit off," Rimsky said, slapping the steering wheel. "I'll tell you what you need to know, but not more. Okay?"

"All right."

"Right. There is a V.I.P. coming through soon and I want him near to the explosion, but unharmed. Do you understand? This one must be placed perfectly. Close, but not too close. That's why I need you."

Jamil bit his tongue. He desperately wanted to ask several questions.

"It will be done," he said.

"Good. For a second I thought you were going to try to weasel out some info. You're learning, bro. The timing is important here. When the V.I.P. is ready, we'll have to move quickly, so always have your phone on you."

"I always do."

"Be ready to go at any second. We won't get much notice on this one."

* * *

Back at his hotel, Jamil took a shower, harshly scrubbing his hands and face, anywhere the chemical cloud may have touched. He lay on his bed and turned on the television, searching for the football games that were never hard to find, except for today. Instead, every channel was showing the same news report. The information at the bottom of the screen read "American Senator 'Hands-On' Hanson to visit Iraq."

A tall, chubby man was standing at a podium, holding a press conference. His wispy, white hair flopped about in the wind as he stood on a runway wearing fatigues, flanked by soldiers.

"The chemical attack on the Tokyo-Zulu compound last year shows the type of enemy we're dealing with," Hanson yelled. "Anyone who says there were no weapons of mass destruction in Iraq should be ashamed. The reasons for the necessity of this war have been proven correct."

"Senator," a reporter yelled out, "how can you be sure Tokyo-Zulu was hit by a chemical attack?"

"The alarm went off, first of all. Those who were able to get to their safety gear did not have any symptoms. Those who did not experienced a painful cough, then internal bleeding and finally cancer. It's a painful way to die. Our enemies have chemical weapons and they will use them, even against civilian support staff."

"But that was just one attack, and it occurred almost a year ago."

"Just one attack? I'm not going to dignify that with a response."

"Senator Hanson," a different reporter spoke, "the Tokyo-Zulu compound was operated primarily by the Redfire Corporation, correct?"

"That's correct, and irrelevant. An American is an American as far as I'm concerned. Military, contractor, or civilian."

"What about the timing, Senator? You may be called to explain how contracts were awarded. You may have to answer to the congressional oversight committee."

"I will cooperate fully with any official investigation, but that doesn't mean my job gets put on hold."

"Don't you think-"

Hanson turned away from the follow-up questions and fell in with the soldiers boarding the plane.

A British newsreader in the studio appeared on the screen. "And that was the United States senator from Oklahoma, Wayne Drake 'Hands-on' Hanson. Always good for some fireworks, that one. Hanson is off to Iraq on what he describes as 'a morale-boosting mission' that critics decry as a cynical move intended to dodge investigation into his contractor-selection bidding process. Senator Hanson most assuredly didn't win any fans from the press corps with his tone, but he's got friends in the rank and f-"

Jamil shut off the television and thought of home. He picked up his cell phone, punched a few numbers and then stopped.

He cancelled the call, lay back and stared at the ceiling.

* * *

Jamil stepped from his car as the boys playing football in the lot waved to him. He waved back, leaned against the driver's door and loosened the collar of his suit, turning his head to follow the players stampeding past. He didn't try to join in.

"Any jobs for us today, Jamil?" a boy yelled out.

"None today," Jamil said back. "I'll let you know."

A boy with a severe limp made his way around the field and stood by Jamil so closely, Jamil pressed his hand against his chest, feeling for the heaviness of the gun beneath his jacket. The boy pivoted on his weaker leg and it was then Jamil noticed it was a prosthetic. Standing between Jamil and the pitch, as upright as he could, the boy saluted.

"Hello. Good sir," he said slowly in English. "You are the Mister Jamil?"

"I speak Arabic," Jamil said.

"Excellent," the boy replied in Arabic. He dropped his salute, revealing a bright pink scar across his dark-skinned forehead. "My name is Omar and I am at your service. I hear you offer work for boys as couriers."

"Sometimes."

Omar spoke rigidly, measuring every word. "I have been waiting here for you all day. My father was killed by the Iranians years ago. My older brother and my uncle were killed by the Americans and now I must earn money to support myself, my mother, and my younger sisters. When I heard you had work, I was pleased. I am very reliable. You will give thanks to great Allah when I work for you."

"If your family suffers so much, you could go to the United Nations compound. They provide basic aid."

"I would not accept it. I must earn it. I am, I mean, we are not charity. So, when can I start?"

"The boys I hire must be able to carry their packages and move quickly. I am sorry, Omar, but-"

"Please, Mister Jamil. Other boys may move faster, but none are as trustworthy as I. The other boys will run when there is trouble, but I will not because I cannot. My family needs money. As of now, I beg, but this is not befitting a man. Please."

Jamil removed his sunglasses and studied the boy. Omar moved his lips as if he were saying a prayer to himself. He shifted to stay balanced.

"Please," Omar said, his eyes watery with tears, "help me support my mother and my sisters."

Jamil looked away. A thought flashed across his mind. The boy's pleading reminded him of his own sisters, begging their mother for more time with the television before bed.

Jamil sighed. "All right. I'll find something for you."

"Thank you!" Omar threw his tiny arms around Jamil and squeezed, leaving faint lines of grime along his suit. Jamil resisted immediately brushing them off.

"I will need your assistance soon, Omar. You won't go alone, but I'll pay you."

"Thank you, Mister Jamil. Peace, joy and courage to you."

"To you as well."

"I will be the best worker you have ever had, Mister Jamil. I will."

"I am sure you will. Now, here's an advance." Jamil slipped him an American ten dollar bill. The boy's face glowed as if Jamil had restored his leg.

"Bless you, Mister Jamil."

"Now, go care for your mother and your sisters."

"Who? Oh. Oh, yes. I will. And I will return, sir. I am ready to work!"

Jamil watched him hobble away. Omar sat opposite the field, talking with the boys on break before they plunged onto the pitch once more.

* * *

"So, who are you calling in Morocco?" Rimsky asked.

Jamil hesitated, pretending he was distracted. He looked about The American Oasis, thinking frantically. He wanted to ask "How do you know?" but that was a question and therefore not permitted.

"You said the phone was mine to use as I like."

Rimsky frowned and cracked his knuckles. "Answer me. Who are you calling?"

"My family. I check up on them."

"Really? I didn't know you were from Morocco. I didn't even know you had a family. Maybe if you were more social, I would. Yeah, so your phone bill showed Morocco, Morocco, Morocco, usually less than a minute, almost every day for the past year. You've been doing that since I gave you the phone."

"I didn't think there was any harm."

"If I noticed, someone else might. We're always being watched. That's why I deal with you and only you. It's better for everyone in the chain if contact is minimal between each level. I really shouldn't have to tell you that."

"But if you only know contacts above and below, you can't be sure who gave the original order, or what that order was."

"Eager to change the subject?"

"Well, I-"

"Or are you fishing for information again even though I told you not to?"

Jamil said nothing.

"Who cares about the original order?" Rimsky said. "This is about making money. All you have to do is find someone willing to do the job cheaper. Hell, my country outsources everything. Sneakers, cars, customer service, capturing terrorists, you name it. The only thing we seem to do anymore is pay other people to do things."

"But then you lose control over the work."

"So you can always say someone else fucked up."

"But why-"

"Let's get back to your phone calls."

"You told me to talk. This is what I want to talk about."

"Oh, now you're a social butterfly. Fine. Go ahead."

"You said your country pays people to capture terrorists, but you would not know how they got them. How would you know they were actually guilty?"

"You wouldn't," Tom said. "But why would you care? Nobody complains as long as everyone gets paid."

Jamil ground his teeth.

"Now can we talk about what I want to talk about?" Rimsky asked.

Jamil was glad he was wearing sunglasses. Otherwise, Rimsky might notice the rage in his eyes.

"This next job is sensitive," Rimsky said. "Handle it personally. The timing must be precise but even more important is the location. I want you to get close, but not too close. The target is not to be eliminated. Figure about twenty feet. In your language, around seven meters."

Target. Eliminated. Code for murdering a person.

Rimsky kept talking, but his previous words were still rattling in Jamil's mind, making his skin burn.

Why would you care? As long as everyone gets paid.

"Jamil!" Rimsky barked. "Pay attention. This is crucial."

"Civic center," Jamil said. "Close but not too close."

"You don't seem like you're listening."

"I am." Jamil absently looked down at his hand, willing his boiling blood inside to cool down. "Continue."

"In a few minutes when you get back to your car," Rimsky said, "the bag will be in your trunk. It's like the others, but you have a lot more time after you pull the cord."

"Right. More time."

"You'll be in a crowd waiting to hear the V.I.P. speak at the civic center. I don't want you running and drawing attention. Ten minutes is plenty of time to get clear."

"No problem. Seven meters away. Pull the cord and leave. Don't run."

"Shit, Jamil, you sound like a robot. Mister K may have been robbing me blind, but at least he was human."

Jamil wrapped his left hand around his lemonade. He gripped his fork with his right. The motion kept him from leaping across the table and wrapping his fingers around Rimsky's neck.

"Maybe I should appreciate your sincerity," Rimsky said. "You're just weird, that's all. But what do I care if you spend all your time in your hotel room?"

"How do you know that?" Jamil asked, before he could catch himself.

Tom rose from his chair. "You should get out more."

"I will try, Tom."

"It doesn't matter. Just do this job right." Rimsky threw a bill on the table and left.

When Jamil finally set down his fork, he noticed he had been gripping it so tightly, dark purple grooves had formed in his palm.

ZERD

IRAQ

2007

The day my end began started like any other day.

We Four Losers were done work but the Dream Team was late, finally returning around sunset, covered in sweat and grime. Instead of bragging about how much ass they kicked, they were quiet. Their mission, whatever it was, obviously hadn't gone well. They threw their equipment down and slammed their storage cabinets closed. They were just looking for an excuse to take out their anger on us.

So, of course, Sly provided.

"Hey, Rimsky," he called across the tent, "you got a girl? A fuck-buddy? Other than your momma?"

"There's always your momma," Rimsky countered, pushing buttons on his cell phone, not bothering to look up.

"I was thinking," Sly continued. "If you had a regular bitch, maybe you wouldn't want to kill Arabs. I figure all that rage you got is probably due to sexual frustration."

"Shut up," Carter snorted.

Rimsky was unusually subdued, still thumbing his phone. "That's why God invented hookers. Hell, Iraqi whores are the best. They're starving, their children and families are starving, so they work extra hard to ensure customer satisfaction, if you know what I mean."

Carter and Belladonna smirked and fist-bumped.

"So, they're like crack hos?" Sly asked.

"Yeah, whatever," Rimsky said. "Now shut the fuck up."

"How do you expense that to Redfire?"

"What?"

"Shut your dumb-ass mouth!" Carter yelled.

Tubbs and I made eye contact. He shook his head.

Sly kept on going. "You've got to itemize what you charge the American taxpayer. So, how do you note you paid some Iraqi ho? Entertainment costs? No, I got it. You probably call it supporting local businesses. All those holy roller pro-war politicians would shit a brick if they knew their tax money was financing Iraqi pimps."

"Shut the fuck up, man," Carter snapped.

"Give a rest, huh, Sly?" Tubbs whispered.

"But Tubbs," Sly said, "my white brother here said he pays for hos. And the U.S. taxpayer pays him. Shoot Rimsky, you ain't even got the courtesy to take it out of your own paycheck."

Rimsky snapped his cell phone shut and unstrapped his combat knife. "Shut the fuck up or I'll have you sent back to the slammer where some fat retards will gang rape you in the ass, all right?"

"Enough of this shit," Carter said. He strode across the tent and stood in front of Sly, looking down on him. Sly stepped up to him so their noses were practically touching. Carter was at least a head taller and much more muscular. They stared into each other's eyes. I imagined a referee standing between them, shouting ignored instructions before a boxing match.

"Don't do it, son," Tubbs mumbled.

"You sound quiet now, boy," Carter said. "You wanna back that shit up?"

"I ain't gonna touch you, house nigga. You'd report my ass."

Carter sniffed the air. "I smell chicken shit."

"We both know you'd get stretched."

Carter spread his arms out wide. "Crowd's waiting, chump."

Before I knew what I was doing, I was at Sly's side. "Carter, back off. He's just fucking with you."

In an instant Belladonna was face-to-face with me. "You wanna go, motherfucker? You wanna?" I stared into his eyes.

Fuck it, I thought, let this happen.

Rimsky clapped his hands. "Hell yeah. We got a rumble! Come on, Spitz and you two fat-ass con-soldiers, get over here."

Spitz stopped cleaning his weapon. He took his shirt off, folded it neatly on his cot and toed the line, beckoning to Grits, who just stood in the corner, violently shaking his head no. Tubbs sat down on a cot and stared at his feet.

The argument dissolved into an all-out screaming match, just me and Sly versus the Dream Team, everyone cursing at once. I wished I could get out of the whole thing, but I wasn't about to let Sly stand there alone. If one punch was thrown, the entire tent was going to explode. I hated the idea of going back to jail, but I didn't care right then.

Stay calm, I told myself. Expect pain.

Suddenly, an alarm screamed.

For a second, everyone kept yelling, their faces tense, mouths forming words lost in the wail.

The alarm stopped screaming and dropped into a low whoop-whoop-whoop.

We all spun around, looking for guidance. Rimsky yelled, "Chemical attack!"

The Dream Team rushed to their lockers and began pulling on gas masks and squeezing themselves into baggy rubber suits. "Nuc-Bio-

Chem Res" was stenciled across the front. The body-length outfits had gloves and booties so large a man could completely fit inside even with all their normal gear still on.

"Oh, Jesus! What do we do?" Grits cried.

"Get your body condoms, boys!" Rimsky yelled.

"Where?" I asked.

"Put on your gasmasks, idiots!" Carter yelled back.

I made my way over to the lockers where the Dream Team was dressing, but I couldn't get past the four of them.

"Hand us some masks!" I yelled over the alarm.

They ignored me until I shoved my way through.

"Watch it!" Belladonna said. "There's none left."

I flung open the lockers. They were empty. The siren continued to whoop.

I ran for the tent's flap.

"Don't go out there! It's not safe!" Rimsky yelled through his gas mask.

"We need masks! Where's ours?" I screamed. Through the transparent sections of our tent, the so-called windows, I could see that even the sun, the always-present, always-burning sun, was blotted out, muted to a fuzzy circle behind a yellowish fog.

In seconds, the Dream Team was fully suited in their rubber protection outfits. Grits, Sly, Tubbs and I were tearing the place apart, overturning cots, shoving aside piles of weapons, throwing open storage lockers and crates, looking for protection. We tore the place apart but found nothing.

"Let's try another tent," I yelled. "Come on!"

The Dream Team moved to block our way out. "Everyone stays inside," Rimsky yelled. "It decreases exposure."

"Crazy white boy!" Sly yelled. "We're going to die!"

"Didn't they give you a hazmat kit?"

"They didn't give us shit!"

"You stand a better chance in the tent, then."

"Cover your mouth and nose," Belladonna yelled, demonstrating with his hand in front of his mask.

"Let us out!" I yelled. A forest of arms kept pushing me back. Sly helped me try to push through, but it was two against four again.

"Nobody leaves the fucking tent!" Rimsky kept yelling.

Sly grabbed the first weapon-like thing he could find, a block of wood. I did the same, snatching a metal bar. All four of the Dream

Team raised the pistols they were wearing on their belts. The ominous sound of releasing safeties clicked in the air, the sharp noise audible between alarm bursts.

"Let's rush these pussies, Z. Come on," Sly said, rocking his weight back and forth on his feet.

"Try it, Sly," Rimsky growled through his mask. "I'd love it."

"Stop fucking around, putos," Belladonna said. "Cover your mouths and noses, use a blanket or a rag, anything."

"Oh, shit," Tubbs yelled. "Look."

We all fell quiet. The low whoop of the alarm continued as the yellowish fog slid into the tent, oozing through the closed zippers, collecting on the floor. The Dream Team backed away from the entrance, afraid to be touched by the gas. Sly and I dropped our makeshift weapons and grabbed rags to cover our lower faces. Tubbs did the same, a wet oval pulsing in and out as he started to hyperventilate.

"Tubbs, breathe even, hombre. Try to relax," Belladonna yelled at him.

The cloud gathered around our ankles. Grits was in the corner crying and shaking. He fell to his knees and began praying loudly.

"Get a rag, moron!" Belladonna screamed, fogging his mask. "Cover your face!"

Grits didn't listen. He kneeled, palms together, looking up and praying aloud as the gas snaked around his thighs. "Dear God, care for my father, my mother and my sister. Forgive my sins and admit me into your heaven."

Sly and I stood there, helpless. I stared at Rimsky over the rag on my nose. He stared back through the curved plastic of his gas mask, eyes vacant. Tubbs had the rag over his entire face now. His breathing made a dry sucking noise.

I was still looking for a way out, but what Rimsky said made sense. Out in the thick of it, wouldn't that be worse? Or was that bullshit? Did it matter?

Grits kept praying. "I'm sorry I stole those candy bars. I'm sorry I cheated on my homework. I'm sorry I lied to Mom."

The Dream Team lowered their guns. Carter and Belladonna looked away. Spitz stared at the floor. Only Rimsky could meet our hopeless gazes.

The gas rose higher. My throat started to burn, or was I imagining it?

"Aw, shit," Belladonna said, not looking up. "Just breathe even, guys, you'll be okay. Stay cool. Keep your mouth and nose covered."

We Four Losers started coughing. Grits continued praying between his coughs, still kneeling in the yellow fog.

"...I'm sorry I stole my sister's cake. I'm sorry I smashed Mister Henderson's window. I'm sorry I snuck into the barn that night and..."

He started to wail and shake.

"...and I was drunk..."

"...and I pulled my pants down..."

"...and I stood behind that goat we had, remember her? Ole Betsy..."

"...and...forgive me, God, but I only did it once." He burst into tears.

We all roared with laughter both genuine and manic.

It was a rare moment of togetherness in our tent. We three Losers gagged as we cracked up, laughing louder because it might be our last time. The Dream Team's masks fogged up. Even Spitz's eyes crinkled, his shoulders shaking.

Grits kept going. "Only once, God, but I did it. Forgive your son. Take me into your heaven." He threw himself face down on the floor, parting the smoke before him, clenching his fists, coughing.

"Don't get low, moron," Belladonna said, still laughing. He marched forward and grabbed Grits' wrist, then tried to pull him up. Grits refused, twisting his arm free. Belladonna gave up and backed off.

"Hey, Grits," Rimsky said, "I don't mean to interrupt your conversation with the Almighty, but did you just say you had sex with a goat?"

It was one of those times I hurt myself laughing. I always hated when that happened, when mid-laugh I'd twist my neck, or pull a muscle in my chest, but I couldn't stop laughing even though each chuckle was followed by a horrible scratching in my throat, a burning in my nose. I didn't care. All I was thinking was the whole situation was fucked up enough to qualify as my death. A normal death would never do. It had to be something like this.

My sight was becoming clearer. I thought it might be tears from laughing so hard, but then I realized the gas was retreating. The sun burned through the tent's windows at unobstructed full-strength again.

Rimsky opened the tent zipper a few inches and peeked through.

"No one else leaves," he said and stepped out, closing the flap behind him. A small wind had kicked up, blowing the yellow smog apart.

Suddenly the alarm stopped. A man's pre-recorded voice spoke over the PA system. "All clear. All clear. All clear."

Rimsky came back into the tent with his mask off. "See that, you big babies?" he said to us. "You're okay. You're still alive."

Grits picked himself up off the floor, wiping at his eyes, sniffling. He flopped down on his cot, sobbing and choking. The Dream Team quietly extracted themselves from their rubber suits.

I rubbed my throat. The scratching was gone. Maybe I had imagined it.

Rimsky broke the silence. "If anyone feels sick, let me know. I'm going to check around the compound. For now, it's just another beautiful evening in Iraq."

I slowly pulled the rag off my face, testing the air with small breaths.

Just before he left, Rimsky turned back into the tent. "See that, Sly? You're fine. Now clean this place up."

* * *

After the chemical attack, everything happened real fast.

Life in the tent was quiet. I'd gotten so used to Sly and Belladonna cursing each other in Spanish, I couldn't sleep without it, but nights now were silent and creepy. I don't know what caused the unspoken truce. Maybe they felt an uneasy camaraderie after facing death together. I guess I should have seen their quiet was a good thing, but the calm made me tense. Something was wrong. I just didn't know how wrong yet.

We did our jobs with much less clowning around. Every time one of us coughed, the rest of us watched and waited. After a week or so, the coughing tapered off. It seemed we had survived.

Why didn't we say something? Why didn't we tell somebody?

It might seem obvious we should have, but we knew we were society's garbage. Hanson's cons-to-soldiers program was just a way of recycling us. We didn't trust going to so-called authority and asking for help. We had all tried that at some point in our lives and knew how useless it was, how we would be blamed for the problem, or whoever we went to would cover up for the person at fault. We had all become good at enduring injustice, not fighting it.

Besides, who could we go to? We didn't know any authority other than Rimsky and he was the problem.

I thought about finding Doctor Love, the guy who touched my balls for the physical. Maybe he could help, but help with what? What was I supposed to say? We're healthy, feeling fine, but I'm scared, can you check us out?

On our rounds, I kept my eye out for any hazmat gear we could steal, but I gave up after a while. No one was coughing anymore. It seemed we'd gotten lucky. The whole problem was leaving my mind the night I realized we hadn't been lucky at all.

* * *

"Get a medic!" Sly screamed.

I jolted awake. The lights were on and the tent was filled with a crunching sound like someone stepping on a soda can repeatedly. Tubbs was bucking on his cot. He looked like he was trying to do sit-ups at a rate someone that fat couldn't possibly do them. It took a second for the sleep fog to clear, for me to realize he was having a seizure. Sly stood over him.

"Tubbs, you in there? Tubbs? Aw, hell no."

He was covered in sweat, his dark skin a sickly slick yellowish brown. His eyes were rolled up like he was looking back into his brain.

"Oh, shit," Sly said, "he's bleeding out his ears." Dark blood spit onto the white sheets whenever Tubbs' head smacked down.

The whole tent was waking up. Belladonna shoved Sly and me out of the way. He turned to Carter. "Tell Doctor Love to get his ass here now!" Carter ran off. I followed him. I don't know why. I just felt like I could be more useful that way. Plus, it was better than watching Tubbs. He had started bleeding out his mouth, too.

I ran, following Carter through the dark rows of tents, barely keeping up. We pounded on the door of the medical trailer. Doctor Love yanked the door open, blinking, wearing only jockey shorts.

"What the hell?"

"One of our guys is seizing," Carter said. "Bleeding out his mouth and ears."

Doctor Love jumped out, still in only his underwear. "Show me."

The three of us ran back, where we found Belladonna saying a prayer over Tubbs' still body. Grits was sniffling, rubbing his eyes. The doctor rushed to the body and started checking his vitals.

"He's got some faint signs. Can you carry him?"

Using the cot as a stretcher, we remaining three Losers and Belladonna carried Tubbs to the medical trailer. Damn, he was heavy. He twitched occasionally along the way. We set him down in the emergency area and backed against the walls as Doctor Love slapped a button, setting off an alarm. Two other medics rushed in.

They buzzed around Tubbs, calling out jargon. Doctor Love turned to us.

"Get out. Now."

We stepped into the sectioned-off area serving as the waiting room, listening, but it was all doctor-speak.

"Come on," Belladonna finally said. "Nothing we can do here."

We followed him out. On the short walk back, Sly turned to him. "Gracias, puto. You're the only one of the Dream Team that's not a complete asshole."

"De nada," Belladonna said. "I might think you're a screw-up, but I do the right thing. Except when your mama's around."

Sly mumbled something in Spanish.

We were back at our tent barely a minute when Rimsky scolded us. "Come on, people," he said. "You're late. Work to do today."

"We've got a man down. Sir," Sly said.

"We've all got casualties, son. We don't stop soldiering because of it."

When Rimsky turned his back, Sly gave him the finger. Even Belladonna smiled.

* * *

The rest of that day, Grits mumbled prayers to himself. It was annoying, but what really made me edgy was how quiet Sly was. We picked at our lunches in silence and went through the motions of our janitor work like robots. We were cleaning the cafeteria when Rimsky showed up with Doctor Love and they called us together.

We sat around a table I had just cleaned, the streaks of the bleach wipes still visible. The three of us sat across from Rimsky and the doctor, both dressed in camouflage.

Doctor Love took a deep breath. "I'm sorry to tell you. The man you brought me this morning. What was his nickname?"

"Doesn't matter now," Rimsky said. The doctor turned and glared at him, slowly and deliberately. Then he looked back at us.

"Tubbs," Sly said. "His name is Tubbs."

I thought I saw Sly's hard eyes get harder. Maybe he was holding back tears, or just bracing himself the way a tough life had taught him.

"I'm sorry," Doctor Love said, "Tubbs passed away an hour ago."

Grits gasped, the only one at the table that the news took by surprise. He mumbled a prayer.

The doctor went on. "Did he ever mention he had cancer? Ever say he was in pain or felt sick? The tumors were very advanced. It's incredible he was up and walking around. He had to have known."

Grits, Sly and I shook our heads no.

"No mention of it? Maybe he was exceptionally tough. Anyway, I thought you should know, that's all. I'm sorry about your friend."

He rested his hands palms-down on the table, like he was eager to get away.

Sly spoke. "Could the cancer have been caused by a chemical weapon?"

"You mean a couple weeks ago, when the camp got hit?"

"Yeah," Sly said, getting louder, "that's what I mean."

"If that was the cause, everyone would have it, but the protective gear did its job."

"We didn't have any gear," Sly answered. "Tubbs neither."

"Shit," the doctor said, looking at Rimsky. "Why didn't you tell me that?"

Rimsky's face boiled red. "We stuck to protocol. Everyone stays inside the tent."

"It would have been nice to have known that. None of you had suits?"

"Tubbs and the three of us," Sly said, "we had nothing. Just rags on our faces."

We all looked at each other.

Rimsky's cheeks pulsed as he clenched his teeth, his eyes bulging slightly. Sly was pushing his luck. Pushing all of our luck. I had visions of Rimsky knifing us in our sleep, but I loved the look of powerless fury on his face.

"This was advanced cancer, so I doubt it," Doctor Love said. "There's no chemical weapon I know that moves that quickly, at least like that."

"And you," he said, turning and pointing at Rimsky. "You're supposed to file a report for an incident like that."

"We stuck to Redfire protocol. You're U.S. Military. No jurisdiction." Rimsky snapped. He then looked at us. "Any of you feel ill?"

We were clearly supposed to say no.

Sly and I said nothing. Grits opened his mouth and closed it without speaking.

"You let me know the moment you do, all right?" the doc said. He glanced at Rimsky then back at us. "Come straight to me." His cell phone rang. He looked at the screen. "I've got to go. Sorry about Tubbs. We tried." He jumped up and jogged from the room, phone to his ear.

We slowly picked up our mops and got back to work. Rimsky sat at the table alone, his huge arms folded, his face bright red, staring into space. After several uncomfortable minutes of quiet, he pounded the table with his massive fist, sending a boom throughout the whole cafeteria. He stomped toward Sly.

"You speak out of turn like that again," he said, "you're fucking dead."

"Yeah," Sly said. "Just like Tubbs."

I wasn't even sure I saw what happened next. Rimsky was so fast, it took me a second to realize he'd punched Sly in the stomach. Sly crashed to the floor, curled up and stayed there. He didn't make a sound. Rimsky left without a word.

Grits and I ran over and helped Sly up. He bent to pick up his broom, wincing.

"I'm all right," he said, coughing. "Let's just finish cleaning this shit."

* * *

I was next. Sort of.

I woke up in the dark, covered in sweat. It wasn't a thin filmy sweat like after a nightmare, I was soaked and dripping, like I had just taken a shower and hopped into bed. Even weirder, the wet was unevenly distributed. My arms were drenched but my head and face were completely dry. It didn't make sense.

I wiped myself off, using my blanket. I still felt slimy and sticky, so I staggered outside toward the showers, wearing only my underwear, looking for a towel.

When I stepped into the light of the latrine hut and saw myself in the mirror, I knew I was fucked.

My tattoos were gone.

Mostly gone, I should say. My art was one big smudge. Purplish stripes ran from my shoulders down to my wrists, where I had tried to wipe away what I thought was sweat, but was actually ink.

I spun around in silence, looking my body up and down. I looked back across the floor of the shower room. Black footprints marked where I had walked, watery blue handprints rested where I touched the counter.

I took a towel and wiped across my chest. The ink swept off like soap, revealing unmarked white-boy skin. All the symbols and pictures and words that made up my life, my memories, my identity, me. It was all gone.

It took a while before I realized I was whispering to myself with terrified awe.

"Oh, my God. Oh, my God," I said each time I ran the towel over my skin and another blurred patch of images vanished. Even the lizard that started it all had left his perch high on my right shoulder.

Zerd was history.

My heart was racing. I saw spots in the air. I sat down on a bench and put my head between my knees, trying not to faint. I tried to scream but couldn't. My mouth opened and closed like a fish gasping as it died. I sat like that for a long time, yelling silently into the mirror, watching my life drip onto the floor.

I don't know how long I sat there, but eventually I stepped outside into the night. I walked without direction, the full moon making my blank skin glow.

I had no idea what to do, so I wandered back to the showers.

I sat on a toilet and looked at my legs, my arms, my chest, all lines smeared, melted or vanished. I cried hard. I covered my mouth with both hands and finally found the strength to scream.

I pounded the tops of my fists into my eyes. When I finally pulled back my hands, I realized how truly lost I was. Steve's two rules of fighting, his two rules for life, "Expect pain" and "Stay calm," were no more.

There were no rules anymore.

What had defined me was gone. I was worse than dead. I was nothing. With my history gone, I never had been anything.

* * *

I stared at the floor until the tiles turned pink from the sunrise, the faint light turning the ink smudges on the floor light blue.

When I staggered back to our tent, I was trembling like a baby during a thunderstorm. The Dream Team was stirring from sleep.

"Wrong tent, dude," Rimsky said, glancing up from cleaning his assault rifle.

"It's me. I need to see Doctor Love."

"Huh? Who are you?"

"Zerd. I've got to see a medic."

"But," he looked to my empty, wet black cot and back to me. "Holy shit."

"My tattoos. They're all gone." I held out my arms.

"I can see that," his voice was rising. "Damn. You're blank."

The Dream Team and the remaining Losers crowded around.

"That is fucked up," Belladonna said. "Did you use cheap ink or something?"

"Look at his sheets!" Carter squealed. "Boy sprung a leak!"

"Maybe he had his period," Rimsky said, shrugging.

"Well, fuck me with a switchblade," Sly said.

"Oh, this is not good," Grits said, and he flung himself to his knees, praying.

"If he tells us again about how he fucked a sheep," Carter growled, "I'm going to kick his ass."

Spitz stared at me like this whole thing was my fault.

"Jesus is coming to claim us all!" Grits cried.

Rimsky grabbed my arm, letting go quickly, looking at his purple-stained fingers. He wiped them on his pants. "You feel okay?"

"A little light-headed."

"This is messed up," he said. "Let's go see Doctor Love, so he doesn't give me shit for not reporting it like he's my fucking boss."

I was stunned. For a moment, I was tempted to think of Rimsky as a nice guy. He seemed genuinely concerned.

"I'm going with you." He grabbed the stained sheets. "Rest of you, carry on."

We walked together in silence. I was glad to have someone telling me what to do, even if it was an asshole like Rimsky.

Doctor Love was standing inside the medical building entrance, reading a file. Forms stacked on his desk were weighed down with bullet casings.

"Check this guy out," Rimsky said. "His tattoos are gone."

The doctor looked up. "What?"

"Remember him? Con-soldier covered in tattoos?"

"You're that guy? No way. I didn't recognize you. You've got his face, though."

Rimsky held up the blanket. I could almost make out the reversed images of my back piece.

"Shit."

"You ever hear of anything like this?"

"If you get cut deeply enough, the ink can leak out, but over the whole body? Like this? No. How do you feel?"

"Okay. A little light-headed. Hungry. Very hungry."

"Did you get into anything? Anything wash over you?"

"Just the chemical weapon," I said. My voice was still shaking.

Rimsky scowled, but I didn't care.

"And you feel fine?"

"I'm hungry." Now that I mentioned it, my stomach was burning. Like I hadn't eaten in days.

"I'm going to do a whole check-up."

"Just let me know what you find," Rimsky said. "I don't want to stay here while you anal probe him."

He left.

"Now, with that jerk gone, tell me everything," Doctor Love said.

I told him. I told him about the chemical attack and how we thought maybe Tubbs got that speedy cancer because of it.

Doctor Love took notes while he talked. "I did some research. Rimsky was right about one thing: staying inside the tent is the procedure. So is covering your mouth, but you said there wasn't enough equipment?"

"There were only four protective suits, but eight of us were in the tent. Shouldn't someone get reprimanded at least?"

Doctor Love sighed. "They should, but it's not going to happen. Redfire handles their business, U.S. military handles theirs. We stay apart, except when they need our help. Right now, let's worry about you."

A half-day later, he had taken my blood, checked my heart, my lungs, and every other part of me. I was starving the whole time, but I didn't say a word. I didn't want to cut the tests short.

Before he let me go he said, "Normally this is good news, but... you seem fine. I can't find anything. I'll do some more tests and poke around in the research, but everything looks good for now. I don't know what to do other than let you go. You feel sick at all, you come back immediately."

"I'm really hungry."

"You don't need to be a doctor to know the cure for that."

* * *

I found Grits and Sly mopping a bathroom, just before they were heading out to lunch. I told them the news.

"We have to tell someone," Grits said.

"Tell who? Tell them what?" Sly said.

"About the chemical attack."

"Doctor Love knows," I said. "I just spent half the day with him."

Sly laughed. "And you just said the doc confirmed they followed procedure. That's the defense right there. No one is going to care about a few cons. We're not even ex-cons yet. The only ex we are is expendable."

I thought about what Dad would say. Something about people being so beaten down they don't complain about injustice. My stomach was growling, roaring.

When we got to the cafeteria and I sat down to eat, Sly pointed to my tray. "You get any vegetables with that meat?"

I looked down. All I had was ham and chicken. No vegetables, no rolls, not even dessert.

"Hey, I'm hungry," I snapped. "Fuck off."

Sly was quiet for a minute. Then he said, "I'm sorry, brother Z. Things are getting more fucked up by the minute. I'm just trying to keep a sense of humor."

As I started stuffing meat in my face, I realized that was the first time I had ever heard Sly apologize about anything.

* * *

After the loss of my ink, I felt fine except for one thing: I was starving all the time. Even after I ate, stuffed my face, the hunger would leave me for at most an hour. Every time I went to the cafeteria, I got the meat. I had to remind myself to try other foods I liked. They tasted as good as always, but I'd end up pushing them around with my fork and wolfing down the protein.

The real messed-up stuff came later.

We had to unload a truck into a warehouse. As usual, the rig pulled up, its driver and armed escort took off, leaving the three of us to empty the huge trailer all by ourselves.

The container was a tangled mess of partly dismantled scaffolding. Metal pipes were bent or broken from having flexed or twisted too far. The construction guys were either in a hurry or had no clue what they were doing.

Taking it all apart was slow, dangerous work. When we finally untwisted or unbolted a few, a bunch more would come crashing down.

To add to the misery, it was blazing hot, which made the pipes hot to touch. Sly and Grits kept complaining about how they couldn't hold them for more than a few seconds. For some reason I didn't have that problem, so I thought they were just being pussies.

Grits and I were taking our turn inside the truck, handing the pieces out the back to Sly for transfer to the warehouse. He was moving even slower than usual. I figured the heat was really bothering him.

Several hours into this horrible job, when I stepped on a bunch of pipes to unscrew a bolt, I lost my balance. I went flying forward, crashing into a knot of metal.

"Dang it," Grits asked, helping me up. "You okay?"

"Shit," Sly called from the back of the truck. "Need help?"

"No," I said, "I'm all right."

I pulled myself up and got back into position, ready to try again when Grits groaned and pointed at me.

"Your arm," was all he said, and turned away.

I looked down. A thick tongue of skin, torn from my wrist to my elbow, was sagging off my forearm, exposing bone. Blood was drooling down the flap onto the truck's bay. Weird thing was, it looked a lot worse than it felt.

"I'm gonna be sick," Sly said. He turned away and vomited, holding the loading ramp for balance. Grits whipped out the towel he used to wipe his sweat and gently laid it under the hanging slice of skin and muscle.

"Man, oh, man," he said, squinting, as he slowly pressed the flap back into place.

The whole time I watched it was like it was happening on TV. It made me ill to look at it, but I didn't feel much at all.

"Doesn't it hurt?" Grits asked.

"Feels like a rug burn."

"A rug burn? Oh, Lord. Oh, Jesus. Hold this towel in place, okay? Let's get you to the med tent."

We staggered over the pipes, trying to keep our balance. I held the towel, waiting for the pain to arrive, dripping blood as I went.

We were moving slow, stepping carefully as we moved to the back of the truck where Sly was still puking.

When I got near the ramp, following behind Grits, my foot landed on a pipe, I stumbled again and dropped the towel, falling to one knee.

The wound wasn't bleeding any more. The hideous gash outlined an upside-down ragged V across my arm, in faint blood. The skin was no longer falling off. My arm looked like I had drawn on it with a purple marker.

Grits was at the bottom of the ramp. "Oh, dang. What happened?"

"I fell."

He rushed to my side to wrap my forearm again. Sly was still bent over, coughing and spitting.

"Hold on a second," I said, showing him my arm.

"What the heck? Did you push it back?"

"Yeah."

"It looks like- Oh, Sweet Virgin Mary."

I took my water bottle and poured it over the wound, washing away the blood and gore. I wiped it clean with the towel and all that was left was a bright pink scar.

"Oh, no," Grits said, fingering the crucifix around his neck. "No. No. No."

"Maybe it wasn't as bad as we thought," I said.

"Not bad?" Sly said, turning from his puke-stance, his voice rasping, "That was the nastiest goddamned thing I've ever seen."

He fell to all fours in the sand. Dry heaves racked his body.

"I'm okay," I said to Grits. "Let's help him."

Grits ran over to Sly, kneeling next to him, hand on his back. I checked out my arm again. The wound had healed almost entirely, the scar lines now faint pink.

"Maybe it's the heat," I said, "making us nuts. We're seeing things."

"I didn't imagine that shit," Sly croaked. "I saw what I saw."

"Me too," Grits whispered to him. "Me too."

Sly coughed violently. Drops of pink fell from his glistening lips.

At that instant, Rimsky showed up. "Why aren't you retards working?"

We ignored him.

"You faking again, Sly?"

"Just a little sick, massa," Sly said, standing up weakly, his eyes bloodshot.

"Listen up," Rimsky said, "I'm spreading the word. We've got a V.I.P. coming sometime soon. Senator Hanson is visiting us for an inspection and assessment. So, be on your best behavior. Got it?"

My stomach growled in the silence as he waited for an answer.

Sly's eyes rolled into his head and he toppled over backwards. He twitched in the sand, saliva and blood foaming from his mouth.

"Damn," Rimsky said, "he couldn't even wait until I was gone. Come on, you idiots, help me with him."

* * *

That night Rimsky told me and Grits to take ten minutes to visit Sly in the infirmary. It was a surprising gesture of compassion. I should have suspected something.

"Just a few minutes, okay?" Doctor Love said as he led us through the tight corridors of the med ward. "He needs rest."

Sly was lying on a bed with a tube in his arm, light brown stains on the white sheet under his chin. He was sleeping, each breath a strained wheeze. Grits retreated to a corner of the curtained-off area, bent his head and began mumbling prayers. I watched Sly's chest rise and fall.

"Come on," I finally said to Grits. "He's out."

Sly slid his hand forward and grabbed mine. It was a weak grip but his hand shook like he was using all his strength.

Eyes closed, he spoke in a breathless, scratchy tone. "They're shipping me out."

"Oh, man," I said. Grits went back to praying.

"Spots on my lungs. Cancer."

"Shit. Well, they've got all kinds of treatm-"

"And in my brain."

"Shit."

"Yeah. Shit."

"Worst part? I'm going back to the big house. Not home. I couldn't even make it as a con-soldier."

"Don't-"

He coughed violently, each racking of his body painful to watch. I looked away. He left fresh red stains on the sheet on his chest. He leaned back, eyes still closed.

"Fuck," he gasped. "I'm going to die."

I said nothing. He was right. We both knew it.

"That chemical weapon jacked us up, Z."

"Yeah."

"First Tubbs, now me. What about you?"

"I'm a fuck up. Just lost my ink, I guess."

"Once a white boy, always a white boy, try as you may."

I laughed. "I try to fight it but-"

Sly smiled weakly. "You take care, all right?"

He growled something in Spanish and seemed to fall asleep. I let him hold my hand. We were like that a long time. Grits stayed in the corner, but at least he was quiet now.

Suddenly, Sly opened his eyes, a wild panicked look on his face. He wheezed as he inhaled, then spoke quickly. "Make them pay for this, Z. I don't want to be lonely in Hell. Send me a friend."

"I will," I said. I tried not to cry, but the tears pushed through.

"Hope you do, brother." His voice quieted as he ran out of air. He lifted his hand and formed a shaking thumbs up. "To Zerd, king of the losers," he coughed. "Patron Saint of Fuck-ups."

"Yeah," my voice gurgled as I spoke.

"Diablo blanca," he whispered, turning his head to the side, closing his eyes again. "Diablo blanca."

His face relaxed. He was definitely asleep now. His breathing was quick, shallow.

"No need to worry," I whispered. "You're not going back to jail, buddy."

* * *

Grits was blubbering all the way back to our tent. "I'm going to die."

"We all do eventually, Grits."

"No, I mean soon. That chemical weapon got us and there's nothing we can do, is there? Each one of us had something go wrong. I'm next."

"Look, Grits, I'm still alive. We might make it."

"You might have cancer. I might, too. We could die any time and I don't have any tattoos to spare."

"Grits, the ink did not protect me."

"That's my point. We're going to die soon. You too."

"Grits? Shut up."

I hated being cold, but I didn't want to talk about it, especially since I agreed. Plus, I was starving. I didn't want to be thinking about food then, but my belly kept demanding to be fed.

* * *

The next morning, Grits was still.

The Dream Team had left early and I was alone with him. I thought he had died in his sleep, but I called the medics anyway. They said he still had some faint vitals before they took him away.

After another trip to the hospital, Doctor Love took me to a private conference room and closed the door.

"Look. You got to talk straight with me. Tell me everything. I mean everything. What the hell is going on here? Three guys from your tent end up with cancer, and you lose your tattoos. What the fuck?"

"I've got nothing more to tell," I said. "I can only guess it had something to do with the chemical attack. There weren't enough protective suits. What do you want me to say?"

"I want you to say why you're okay and the others are dead or dying."

That confirmed my suspicions on how Grits was doing. "I don't know."

"Is that all? You're sure you're okay?"

"I'm hungry all the time and my tattoos bled out but other than that, I feel fine. You're the one who did the tests. Can you do more?"

"It helps if we know what we're looking for."

"Can you test for cancer?"

"If we know where to look. So far you don't show any signs of anything. Your tattoos washed away and you're hungry. That's weird, but not a lot to work with."

"Make me a lab rat. Shove a probe up my ass. I don't care."

"I'm also going to check with my doctor pals and my Redfire contacts. I'll be doing some poking around, but not in your ass. I know you were hoping, but, sorry."

We shared a weak laugh.

He took a blood, urine and skin sample from me right there.

"Let's schedule some x-rays to see if there's anything in your lungs."

"Fine."

"The machine is a premium so I have to book the time. If you don't hear from me in the next couple days, stop by and remind me."

* * *

I can't quite remember much after that because that's when my stomach started growling non-stop. The cramping was so bad I was walking hunched over. Even while eating, I felt hungry. Maybe I was going crazy, but I swore I could feel the acid sloshing around in my belly.

The Dream Team returned that evening, took off their gear and ignored me. All except Rimsky, of course. He stood in the middle of the tent, watching me sweep, hands on his hips.

"Hey, Z. Where's your friends? Permanent leave? Back in the slammer? They missed the ass-pumping so much they had to go back for more?"

"Grits was bad off this morning. He's with Doctor Love."

"Shit. One of you came up with the idea to call in sick, now you're all doing it."

I looked up at him, then went back to sweeping.

"Don't stare at me like that. If you knew what I just did to some hajjis, you'd suck my dick just so I didn't turn your way. You think that ink you used to have made you a badass? Without them we see the real you. Just a pale hairless white pussy on a little girl. Am I right?"

Look down at the sand, I reminded myself, keep your head down.

"Yeah, that's what I thought," Rimsky said. He spit on the ground in front of my broom. I covered the saliva with sand and pushed it away.

* * *

"You," Grits groaned from his intensive-care bed as I stood beside him. His complexion was paler than ever, red rings circling his swollen eyes.

I was thinking of what to say but was interrupted by a commotion behind me. A small crowd was trying to get into the room. Two burly guys in suits forced their way in.

"Who the hell are you?" I said.

"Move back," one of them answered. I was about to tell him to fuck off when in walked Senator "Hands-on" Hanson himself.

I always wondered what I would do if I met the guy. If he was as evil as I thought he was, shouldn't I strangle him? Or at least call him an asshole? Something that would make Dad crack up? Instead I just froze. I couldn't believe it. There he was, real enough to kick in the balls, and I was too stunned to move.

The doctors were crowded behind him. I met Doctor Love's gaze for a moment, but he turned away quickly. A cameraman followed Hanson, practically attached to his back. Grits looked around at the suddenly crowded little room. His eyes widened for a moment, then were dull again.

The bodyguards squeezed me into the corner, right past Hanson. He was taller than I thought he'd be. His bulk did make him look like a hands-on guy. He smelled a little on the pretty side, though.

He stood by the bedside and placed his hand on Grits' forehead. He closed his eyes tightly and whispered a prayer to himself. When he opened his eyes, they were moist with tears.

"It's going to be all right, son," Hanson whispered, sliding his hand to Grits' shoulder. The camera's red light blinked, capturing the scene.

I was starting to think maybe Dad was wrong about Hanson. Sure there were reporters around, but he was a U.S. Senator taking time to visit a political nobody.

Hanson whispered to the camera.

"This brave soldier was hit with a chemical weapon and now he has terminal cancer. I want those cowards in Congress to look at this young man and see what we're up against. Imagine if we left and the terrorists followed us home. I know some of my colleagues are saying we didn't find weapons of mass destruction in Iraq, but the evidence that those weapons exist is right here, this fine young man is the living proof."

Grits rolled his head to the side. He looked drunk. He gazed up at the senator with eyes that couldn't focus.

That's when the cynicism Dad gave me kicked in. Hanson was using my dying friend to support his war. How sincere could he be with a camera crew in tow? I should do something. But what?

"Senator, can you be sure it was a chemical weapon that caused the cancer?" asked a man with a bulletproof vest. A glossy badge marked "Press" hung around his neck. His helmet kept falling over his eyes.

"Quiet!" Hanson hissed. "Show respect for those who serve our country." The reporter blushed. Hanson clasped Grits' left hand and whispered, "A grateful nation thanks you for your sacrifice, son." Cameras flashed. Hanson walked out of the room with his head bowed, reporters, bodyguards and doctors following.

If only Dad had been there. He would have known what to say, some brilliant question to shout to dismantle the whole show. Not me. I just watched them head out.

As quickly as they came, they were leaving.

Doctor Love was the last to go. "All right. Everyone out," he said as the entourage moved on. "He's a patient, not a goddamned prop."

* * *

That night, the juices in my stomach were churning so painfully I couldn't sleep. I didn't know what my body was trying to tell me. Was I hungry? Did I have a stomach ache? Was I constipated?

I left the tent and locked myself in one of the portable toilets for maximum privacy. I sat there for at least an hour, trying to crap, pushing as hard as I could, but nothing happened. I leaned my head against the plastic wall and nodded off.

My growling stomach woke me. I was dreaming of food and something smelled good. Really good. Whoever had used this chemical toilet before me had eaten hamburger. With each breath it smelled better. Before long it smelled awesome.

My nose was focused. I could smell the shit and the chemicals, but I homed in on the hamburger among that cocktail. It was cooked black, greasy and delicious.

I stood up and turned, sniffing the bowl. Resting on the lumpy liquid below was a pile of poorly-digested beef. It smelled so good I didn't care about anything else. My belly had overruled my brain. I reached down into the slime, scooped up the burger bits and smashed my face into it, stuffing it into my mouth.

Glorious, delicious beef.

My throat burned as if a mix of lumpy tequila and mouthwash was going down, but when the burger-filled sludge hit my stomach, it felt fulfilling. My belly digested the meat and rejected the chemicals.

My whole body started bucking. The chemicals burned going down, and they burned worse coming up, but there was nothing solid among the watery puke. My famished stomach had grabbed the raw protein and used it that fast. My tongue was scorched, all the taste buds mercifully gone. All that mattered was being full.

There are times when life is so bad you think to yourself, if there's a God out there, he'll kill me for mercy's sake. "Just kill me now," you pray, and you mean every word of it, even if you don't believe in a higher power. There's just no one else around to ask.

That was one of those times.

* * *

I woke up alone in the tent. The Dream Team had left.

I wandered in circles, delirious. What was I supposed to do again? My memory was messed up. I paced around, unsure. I knew I had to wash up, so I started there, thinking I'd remember what to do eventually.

During the quick, cold shower, my stomach started cramping again. The hunger was back. Doubled over, I headed straight to Doctor Love's.

By the time I got there, I was practically crawling. He was at his desk, his head in his hands. He looked up. "I was just getting ready to look for you."

"My stomach is killing me," I said, almost crying. "I'm hungry all the time. I can't get full. You've got to help me."

"Oh, shit," he said and I knew I was done. Nothing says bad news more clearly than when your doctor says, "Oh, shit."

"Look," he said, "I don't. I, um. I did some looking with my contacts in Redfire, like I promised. A couple computer nerds helped me out too."

"What did you find? Am I going to die?"

He didn't answer. He scribbled a note on scrap paper and beckoned me deeper into the maze of trailers and tents that served as the mini-hospital. My stomach roared as I followed him. I had to lean against the walls to keep from falling over.

"You got here just in time," he whispered. He led me into a small study for the medical staff. He held a finger to his lips, pointed to a clock, handed me the note and closed the door.

I was alone, thinking, What the fuck?

I read the note.

"Read. Remember. You have ten minutes. I'll stall. I'll destroy the papers later. Eat this note."

I stuffed the tiny note in my mouth and swallowed it without chewing.

Papers were stacked before me. They looked like print-outs of emails. The top part of each one was taken up with computer lingo like "encryption successful" and "decryption key accepted" then a whole page of garbage characters followed by a few words at the bottom of the page. There was so much encoding going on, only one or two sentences fit per sheet of paper. Doctor Love had used a yellow highlighter on the text that wasn't gibberish. I turned the pages, eavesdropping on a conversation one decoded line at a time.

Project report.

Next page.

75% success. Manifest rapid, terminal cancer. Control group unaffected.

Next page.

Status remaining 25%?

Next page.

Subject tattoos vanished.

I stopped and looked around. The situation was so heavy I sat there like an idiot who, on top of being a dumbass, just got lobotomized. "Tattoos vanished" made it obvious. They were talking about me. I kept reading.

Elaboration necessary: subject tattoos vanished?

293

Next page.

25% non-fatal result of DNA alteration caused by product release. Advise.

Next page.

Objective remains 100%. Test failure. Execute complete scrub and retry.

Next page.

Understood. Will terminate.

I skipped science class all the time, but I got the idea.

The chemical attack was an experiment, but by who? That Arab dude I saw in the storage building? Was Rimsky a part of it? Had he hidden our chemical resistance suits? The 75% success meant three of four something. Tubbs, Grits and Sly. But not me.

Rimsky was a psycho but he wasn't crazy enough to allow an experiment that put him in danger, even with protective gear. He'd have to be stone cold nuts to do that.

Was he?

It wasn't enough to be unpaid working stiffs for Redfire. Why not lab rats, too? Why not test chemical weapons on us, and then blame the enemy? They get free research and can keep their war going. Who cares if a bunch of cons end up dead in a land where our beloved troops were dying every day?

It was a slick plan. Evil, but ingenious.

Dad was fired for being a paranoid crank, but his mistake wasn't that he was paranoid. He wasn't paranoid enough. Whoever was behind this was hiding far past where anyone could point and still be considered sane.

The problem was the truth really was that insane.

Dad was a lousy father, but he was right on about war: it's a scam in a million ways, and a lot of people with nothing to do with it do all the suffering.

Holy shit.

I heard talking and looked to the clock. Time was up. As Doctor Love approached, he raised his voice to alert me. "This is the research library. We are-"

He pushed open the door. "What are you doing here?" he asked, trying to look surprised.

Our eyes met. There was so much I wanted to ask him.

"Come on," he said, "I know it's hot out but you can't stay here."

"Sorry," I muttered, keeping my head down. My stomach roared.

He stepped aside so I could clearly see he was with someone else. The guy looked like a kid to me, and I was practically a kid. He was wearing a white polo shirt with the Redfire logo tucked into tan shorts. He looked like he was going golfing, not to a war zone.

"Pete," Doctor Love said, freaking me out by using my real name. "This is my replacement, Robert Campbell." We shook hands.

"Doctor Robert Campbell," the kid said, emphasizing the word "doctor" like he was really Doctor Asshole.

"You're leaving?" I asked Doctor Love.

"As soon as I clean up and shred some confidential records," he said. "Redfire was awarded the contract for the medical work at this base, so my skills as a lowly US serviceman are no longer required. I don't know where Uncle Sam is sending me next, but Doctor Campbell will be taking over here. Now, move out."

I paused at the exit. "Exactly when are you leaving?"

"Within the hour."

Something was being said as we stared at each other, but I didn't know what. Doctor Love turned and led Doctor Campbell into the study, closing the door behind them.

Alone in the hall, for one instant, my thoughts were not about food. I was thinking about the end of the decoded exchange, the final word.

Terminate.

* * *

Somehow I kept going, doing my chores. I'd stop and bend over when pain lanced my stomach. Then I'd run to the mess hall for a pig out. That kept the cramps away for a while. Then I'd repeat the whole thing.

I kept thinking of trying to contact my dad, but I had no idea how. He would know what to do.

At dinner, I ate as much as I could stand, crept onto my cot and pretended I was asleep while The Dream Team talked about their latest mission.

Panicked questions were flooding my thoughts. Did Doctor Love expect me to do something? Could I escape? Was my life going to be one long stomach cramp until I was 'terminated?'

Finally, The Dream Team turned in. Whatever I was going to do, I had to do it quick. My insides were burning all the way from my throat to my asshole. I sat up on my cot and looked up to the tent roof.

"Make it stop, please," I whimpered.

A gentle breeze pressed against the tent and my nose twitched, teased by a scent. A meal waited in the distance. Like a dog, I sniffed the air, following the smell of food.

I crept out of bed. The Dream Team was sleeping soundly. Quietly, I grabbed one of the Redfire combat knives they left lying about. I wasn't planning on coming back and I needed some kind of weapon. The knife was the only one I really knew how to use.

I stepped out into the faint glow of the camp's dimmed floodlights. I was still in my underwear, but something smelled so good, I couldn't be bothered getting dressed. I had to get to it now.

I started jogging, raking my hand over my face to wick off the saliva. Something smelled delicious, like half-burnt hot dogs covered in chili sauce. I followed the aroma to a closed tent and slid along the fabric, finding the entrance in the darkness by locating where the odor was strongest.

The camp lights dimly lit the interior.

I was in the morgue.

Body bags were folded in the corner. Wooden coffins full of human remains were stacked on metal shelves.

I was so fucking hungry, I was breathing out loud. They weren't dead bodies to me, they were meat. I smashed my fist against the wood, using the Redfire knife's spiked knuckles to hack away at the coffin's lid. The wooden shards made my skin tear, bleed and then tighten up as they healed.

The lid finally popped off. Resting in a foam bed lay a man's body positioned as if he were whole. His leg was torn off below his knee, the bone showing through. The remainder of his leg (including the foot) was placed where it would have rested if it were still attached.

Where some violent explosion had severed his leg, the flesh was burnt black and that char smelled goddamned delicious.

I wasn't thinking. I was simply hungry. I reached in and grabbed the severed lower leg and foot and took a huge bite out of the calf where the flesh was ragged. I kept chewing, my teeth clicking against the exposed bone as I twisted the leg in my hands.

It was a little cold but thoroughly cooked. My stomach attacked the protein as I swallowed, thanking me with silence.

I fell back against a metal table and slid down to sit on the ground, gnawing and tearing like a dog. Like a starving man given a life-saving meal. Some of my teeth loosened and came free against the tough grit, but I couldn't stop.

As the hunger pangs vanished, what I had done hit me. I made damn sure I didn't look at the coffin's name tag, or the body's face.

"What's happening to me?" I whined. I started to vomit, but only saliva came out. My greedy stomach had already taken the flesh.

My bowels were gurgling and I felt a burning in my ass. I ripped off my boxers a split second before a stream of diarrhea squirted out of my cheeks.

"Just let me die," I cried.

Once I gave some guy a tattoo and he told me about being seasick, how he had puked and shit at the same time. He said it was the lowest point in his life.

I definitely had him beat.

After my body expelled what it could, I was a dripping mess. I felt around in the dark until my hand rested on a folded cloth. Using it, I wiped my mouth and my ass dry.

Suddenly, the single light bulb hanging from the tent's peak came on, and there I was, half-naked, a partially-devoured human leg in one hand, and in the other, an American flag with a massive turd skid perpendicular to the stripes.

The military police officer who had flicked on the light gaped at me, trying to absorb what he was witnessing. We stared at each other for a moment, each of us shocked.

"Look what they've done to me," I said, choking, crying, my voice gurgling.

"What the fuck?" the MP screamed. His reached for his pistol. I dropped the flag and the leg, grabbed the knife and slithered under the tent's edge, bolting into the darkness. A single shot exploded. The MP screamed something.

I had no idea where I was going. I ran and kept running, charging toward the main gate. The guard on duty yelled, but I was done with that place, done with life. I ran through the gate, my bare feet churning the sand, tearing around the barrier.

The yelling faded behind me as I disappeared into the black moonless desert.

They didn't follow. Somehow we all knew that I belonged beyond the lighted safety and sanity of the camp.

Monsters like me belonged in the darkness.

* * *

I walked away until the sun rose behind me. In all directions the world was a featureless, sandy, yellow-white. I didn't notice the cluster of homes until I was practically on top of it. Its bricks were the same color as the sand.

The largest of the single-level buildings was partially destroyed by bombs, but some of the structure remained and offered shade. I sat down inside and prepared to die.

My belly growled again. I ignored it. Let me starve to death.

I leaned against an inside wall and nodded off.

* * *

My twitching nose woke me. I followed where it led, almost against my will. I knew what I was going to find.

Whether from bombs, gunshots, or dehydration, I'd never know. All I knew was that they had died here, their arms around each other. A man, a woman, a child.

I resisted as long as I could, but eventually hunger always wins.

I turned over their brittle bodies so I couldn't see their shriveled faces. The knife cut through the jerky-strength flesh easily.

The first bite was difficult. After that, they were just food.

JAMIL

IRAQ

2007

"Hello, mister boss sir!"

Omar saluted as Jamil parked his car alongside the lot where a pickup football match was in progress. Three tall boys followed behind the hobbling Omar, who gave them a quick command. The boys slapped their hands to their sides and stood with their backs rigid.

Omar pivoted on his prosthetic leg to face Jamil. "I have secured the fastest and most tight-lipped boys I could find, boss sir. I have devised a rotating schedule among other volunteers so all boys interested may share in the work. All of this is committed to my memory, nothing is written down, as I anticipated you would prefer and for quicker reference."

Jamil smiled, folding his arms and leaning against his car. "You gathered couriers for me?"

"I did, boss sir Jamil. To save you time. Simply pull up in your car and I will have runners ready. You pay me their fees and I will take a small manager's percentage. Then you may be off to your other business ventures. The work has my guarantee. Full refund if the job is not completed to your liking." He stood as straight as he could, all his weight on his natural leg, his artificial one hovering off the ground.

Jamil laughed. The sensation felt strange. How long has it been since I casually laughed? he wondered.

"You are clever, Omar. And bold. But I don't need help today."

"You don't?" Omar blinked rapidly, glancing at the boys behind him. Their postures sagged. "You said I could earn the money you gave me."

"Today I work alone."

"I promised these three you would have work for them. Where are you going?"

"I have a special assignment."

"Then why are you here?"

"I like to watch the football games. You shouldn't ask questions."

Omar's face tightened. "I promised I would earn the money you gave me. On my honor. You must allow me." The boys behind him nudged each other and started laughing. Omar turned and glared at them. They half-heartedly resumed their attentive posture.

"Omar," Jamil said. "Today, I cannot."

"You must! I am a proud Muslim man. I do not need charity." His three recruits dispersed onto the playing field. Omar's lower lip trembled.

"Omar-"

"You must!" He stomped his good foot and nearly fell. Tears snuck out of his squinted eyes.

They stared at each other in silence.

"All right," Jamil said, throwing up his hands. "You may come with me. Only if you stay by my side and do exactly what I say. And don't ask questions. Ever."

"Thank you," Omar whispered, wiping away his tears. When he looked up again, all trace of anger was gone. "I will be your best worker, boss sir Jamil."

"I know you will," Jamil said. "Now let's watch the game together. Since you are my assistant, you may lean against my car."

Omar's eyes widened. He turned and brushed his hands across the bottom of his pants before leaning against the car. They both stood there with their arms folded, watching the match like an older and younger brother.

* * *

Jamil shouldered the pack and led the way, Omar at his side, chatting incessantly. It was obvious Omar was lying about the family he was supposedly supporting. First he was caring for his mother, then his father, then his sisters, then three grandparents.

Jamil made his own deductions. Omar had no family and lived on the street. The relatives lived only in the boy's imagination, for his survival or, more likely, for his sanity.

"So, we pull the string and leave the pack?" Omar asked.

"Yes," Jamil said, the small dense burden poking against his sweaty back.

"Then we have ten minutes to escape."

"Yes, we move quickly but not obviously. And you must no longer talk about it."

"Or ask questions, yes?"

Jamil didn't answer.

As they approached the target building, the city's usual crowd thickened, but not so much that they could not push on. At the back of the throng, everyone was standing on their toes to see the platform and podium erected inside an open-air courtyard.

"You must be important," Omar said, "having to make so many deliveries."

Jamil stayed silent. Omar was content to talk to himself.

LARRY NOCELLA

Jamil was not surprised to find minimal security. Rimsky either
knew it would be that way or had arranged for it. Snipers were visible
on the rooftops, but there was not a single metal detector to get into
the area to hear the speech. A low fence and a line of armed security
guards separated the mass of people from the platform. Beyond the
fence was a moat of empty space wide enough to drive a car through.
Another layer of security personnel stood leaning against the stage.

"There sure are a lot of guards," Omar said.

Jamil pressed his way forward, protecting the pack.

"Mister Jamil. Let me carry the parcel. I want to do it. I have done
nothing to earn my money."

"You are with me, talking to me about things."

"How does that help?"

"You keep me company. We blend in."

"Please. I am at your service," Omar said as he snapped to attention
and saluted.

Jamil grabbed the boy's hand and pulled it down.

"Please stop saluting me."

"Yes, sir. I'm sorry, boss sir."

"When I say, we must move quickly, but do not run."

"I cannot run, so I am a help already."

"Yes. Exactly," Jamil said, trying to hide a tone of exasperation.

Suddenly the crowd around them pressed forward, cheering. Several
men walked out onto the stage. Jamil recognized Senator Hanson from
the television. Tom Rimsky followed behind him, his expression grim
and partially hidden under his ever-present reflective sunglasses.

Senator Hanson stepped to the podium and tapped the microphone,
causing a gentle squeal through the public address system. He leaned
forward and spoke.

"Freedom-loving citizens of Iraq, I bring you greetings from the
United States!"

The crowd buzzed with excitement and condensed forward. Once
the movement stopped, Jamil flipped the pack off his shoulder and set
it at his feet. He massaged his neck with both hands.

"I want to help," Omar said. "I want to do more."

"You have done enough," Jamil said. He stood on his toes to see
the stage.

Hanson's voice boomed through loudspeakers. "My name is
Senator Wayne Hanson. I hope you don't mind my surprise visit. I am
here to assure you that your friends in the United States, who love

freedom and law and order as much as you do, will not abandon you. I know you have heard cowardly statements from some in America who want us to leave your country in chaos, leave you to your fate. I promise that we will stay until your great nation has stabilized. You still have enemies. We will fight them with you! Together, we will achieve victory!"

The crowd was cheering. Best to do it now and be done, Jamil thought. He looked down for the bag.

It was gone.

He spun around, frantic, shoving the people around him out of the way.

"Omar!" he called. "Omar, where are you?"

He could barely hear himself over the senator's voice and the crowd's cheers. The crowd shifted and swayed all around Jamil, sharing in the excitement of a personal promise from a U.S. senator.

"Omar!" Jamil called, trying not to be too loud, sound too frantic.

Through the waving hands, just for an instant, Jamil caught a glimpse of the small boy, several yards away, standing over the pack, the cord in his hand.

"Omar!" Jamil screamed. The crowd closed up again. Jamil shoved his way forward.

Stop panicking! Jamil scolded himself, You're drawing attention. Rimsky had said that, after arming, the detonation would occur in only ten minutes, so there is still-

The blast threw him.

He had only an instant to duck his face against his forearm before he was hurled against the people around him.

A thought lanced across his mind before everything went black. The bomb had been rigged for quick detonation, and Rimsky had insisted that he plant it himself.

Rimsky wanted him dead.

* * *

Jamil had become used to the noise of the blast, the gust of heat that swept past, the warm draft flowing in the opposite direction to fill the vacuum, the gently drifting dust afterwards.

It was the wailing he had never grown accustomed to. Hideous crying born from agony, as fear and rage erupted all around. Pieces of concrete and flesh in sizes from grain to chunk covered him. Jamil pushed up against bodies and body parts, checking himself for injuries. Except for the high-pitched ringing in his ears, he felt complete and damn lucky.

He kept his head down, walking in any direction, staggering as he went. He worked his way to the edge of the carnage, struggling to keep his balance as he stepped on debris, some of it still bleeding. Several large black SUVs with darkened windows rolled up before him, crunching over brick and flesh.

He froze as enormous men who appeared to be a cross between soldiers and businessmen leapt out of the vehicles and ran towards him. They were wearing buttoned shirts and ties with bullet-proof vests over them, as well as desert-camouflaged pants and mirrored sunglasses.

The word "Redfire" was stenciled neatly on the left breast of the bullet-proof vests. Jamil sagged. He was too weak to run, too shocked to fight. They had to know he was behind the bomb. They were coming to kill him. It was all part of Rimsky's plan, kill him or blame him. He closed his eyes, hoping for a quick end.

They ran past him, shouting to each other in English.

"Where is he?"

"Over here!"

"Clear a path!"

Iraqi ambulances rolled up, their sirens blaring. The parked Redfire SUVs prevented them from getting closer.

Bristling with guns, the Redfire men stood in two rows, creating a rough gauntlet for Senator Hanson to walk through to the edge of the ruin. The Senator staggered along, coughing, carrying a bleeding child. Another man followed closely, a hand-held camera pressed to his eye. Behind the cameraman, Rimsky followed, pistol drawn.

Jamil hid his face.

"Got one here!" someone called, standing near the ambulance.

The arriving medics leapt out of their ambulances, surprised by the Senator running at them, carrying the limp, bloody body to the back of their vehicle. They took the child and thanked him as it was all caught on camera.

Rimsky and Hanson's other bodyguards followed, surrounding him, knocking against rescue workers carrying a body on a litter. The rescue workers were cursing in Arabic. The Redfire men cursed back in English. The cacophony was backed by the gut-wrenching shrieks of the dying.

Jamil still wasn't free of the mayhem. He was knocked flat as the Senator plunged into the pile of the wounded, the protective circle of his bodyguards moving with him. The camera's gaping glass eye watched as Jamil tumbled onto the debris, then turned away quickly while the Senator staggered through the mist of pulverized brick, helping a weeping man to his feet.

Several people were yelling commands. Senator Hanson emerged from the dust with a woman, her forearm dangling by a strip of flesh. The Senator fumbled at his waist and quickly pulled loose his belt, tightening it around the woman's arm between her shoulder and elbow.

Where he had stopped to care for the victim a bottleneck formed. The Iraqi paramedics were blocked from the rescue effort as his entourage swirled around him.

"Stay back!" the guards shouted in English to the Iraqi ambulance crew.

Jamil crashed against a building and slid down, sitting heavily as he spit up dust, catching his breath. Two of the Redfire mercenaries were guarding the vehicles.

"You believe this fucking circus?" one of the men said.

"I told you. He's a genuine badass. Hands-on Hanson lives up to his name."

After delivering the woman to the ambulance, the Senator jumped into the back of the lead SUV. Jamil watched as Rimsky jumped in to drive.

Jamil looked around for another car. One sat nearby, idling. Its driver had leapt from his vehicle and was wailing, hands in the air, "Why? Why has this violence been brought to us? When will it stop? Merciful Allah, save Iraq!"

Jamil stepped quietly into the man's car and drove away, chasing the SUV with Senator Hanson and Rimsky inside.

* * *

The black SUV rounded turns sharply, scraped against parked cars, and even clipped the leg of a boy crossing the street, sending him rolling away. Jamil leaned on his car's horn, trying to stay close behind, but it was futile. First one car got between them, then another, then he lost them. He pulled over and turned on the radio.

"Breaking news. A suicide bomber has just detonated near American Senator Wayne Hanson during a speaking engagement in

Baghdad. Several are dead but there is no official count. Details are scarce at this time and Hanson's whereabouts and well-being remain unknown. We will-"

Jamil shut off the radio and punched the steering wheel furiously, crying as he did.

He searched his pockets, found his cell phone and dialed.

"Salaam," his mother answered before one ring was complete. Jamil knew she must be sitting by the phone faithfully. He said nothing.

"Hello," she said. "Whoever my silent friend is-"

"Mother?" Jamil said.

"Jamil?" she whispered slowly, awe-struck.

"Yes, mother. Jamil. Your son."

"I know. I know your voice. Even all these years gone. Oh, my darling boy. My sweet child. Where are you? Wherever it is, anywhere in the world, we'll come get you."

"Mother, I have something to do. After that, I am coming home."

"But Jamil! You don't have to do anything. We will come to you."

"Mother. I will be home in the next week or not at all. I wanted to tell you I love you and Father and Uncle and my sisters."

"Please, Jamil. Just tell me where you are."

"Goodbye, mother. I will see you soon, or never."

"No, Jamil, don't hang up! Please!"

Jamil stepped from the car and into the street. He dropped his phone under his foot and crushed it, grinding it under his heel.

* * *

Jamil drove to the outskirts of the city, taking the freeway to where it whittled down into a simple black strip across an endless expanse of sand. When he could see nothing in all directions except for the road and desert, he pulled over.

He popped the trunk and stood at the front of the car, looking down on its steaming interior. He reached forward, feeling the heat of the engine on his palms, like someone warming himself before a fire. He drew his hands back. He was right-handed, so he reached forward again, hesitantly, with only his left hand. The heat scorched his palm bright red. He drew back unconsciously.

Jamil took a deep breath, and when he opened his eyes, he smashed his left palm on the scalding metal of the engine block. He screamed, looking up to the sky. The smell of burning meat wafted across his nose. Fighting his instinct to pull free, he ground his hand against the metal harder. His skin smoked and burned, the heat and agony traveling up his arm. Blood dribbled out from under his palm and boiled to pink steam. He leaned in, pushing into the pain, yelling to redirect it.

His plan worked.

He popped loose and shot toward the sky, looking down on himself looking up screaming. In this state he could hear nothing, but he could see the agony on his creased face as his body shuddered. He directed his attention out to the horizon, forcing himself to rise. To the east was Baghdad. To the north, mountains. To the south, the sea. To the west there was desert and the base that Rimsky had taken him to. Just beyond that, a plume of dust rose where a lone SUV pulled to a stop before the ruins of an old settlement.

He didn't care what they were doing. He just wanted to know where they were.

To the west.

He took one last look around from this bird's-vantage point before willing himself to return. He fell from the great height, crashing into his body, into his open, screaming mouth.

He yanked his hand free, leaving a black hand-print of his flesh on the engine. He tumbled backwards into the sand, bleeding.

The pain was so great he could not yell, only hiss. Using his right hand, he wrapped his wounded left with a rag from the car's back seat. Even the gentle touch of the fabric felt like a blade raking his hand. He pulled his gun from his jacket and set it on the passenger seat.

Clenching his teeth, using only his right hand to drive, he headed west.

ZERD

IRAQ

2007

While I was waiting for The Dream Team to come kill me, I re-inked myself. Using the point of the Redfire knife, I cut my skin, tracing what I could remember of the lines, sketching Zerd in dark red instead of black. The lines were sloppy since I had to hold the blade close to its tip, the larger part of the knife sticking way above, its weight throwing off a balanced stroke. I didn't care. I'd be dead soon.

The crazy lizard was reborn deformed, right where Steve had first drawn it. Then I drew the symbols that defined Tracy and Charles: the butterfly-dragon lady and the pink triangle with the middle finger. I re-did them all, dragging the blade-tip roughly across my flesh, drawing them as close to their old homes as my faltering memory and my flexibility allowed.

Steve's mantra, "Stay Calm. Expect Pain," reappeared in tiny bloody letters as best I could on the tops of my fists. I even did one for Dad: the hammer and sickle of the workers and farmers.

One last redraw summed it all up neatly: the grave, the skeleton's hand reaching up through the dirt, giving the entire world one last middle-finger, the letters P.S.F.U. on the tombstone. I wanted to draw more but my memory dropped off after those few.

All that was left to do was die or maybe say a prayer. Why not?

"Religion is the opiate of the masses" was engraved under one of the ceramic heads on Dad's bookshelf, but my current situation wasn't very traditional, so maybe he would have found my prayer a refreshing change.

* * *

Ever since I landed here in the sand, I've been thinking of Iraq, this nation that's being trashed. Actually, I've been thinking of the Middle East as a whole, this giant desert where much of human civilization began, where many of humanity's gods were born. Why? Why were so many gods born here? I think I have an idea.

Here in the desert, the sun bakes your brain, makes you hallucinate and drives you insane. At that extreme edge of existence you pass beyond what is human. That's where you find gods.

Just as people are born and left behind, cast out by society or by nature, so there must be gods who never were honored. They were born from humanity's heat-stroke lunacy, but ignored, abandoned and outcast. Like me.

It is those rejected gods that I call upon. I know you are out here! Reveal yourselves and help me. I accept into my soul any higher power, any ignored spirit wandering this desert in search of someone to worship them. Malicious or kind, good or evil, you can be my god. I need all the help I can get.

Hear my prayer, my fellow outcasts! In the coming battle, I ask that you help me kill at least one of my enemies before I die. That is my one request. In exchange for my life, I ask to claim one of my enemies.

I call to any rejected god, any fallen angel. My blade is your blade. My vengeance is your vengeance. Help me strike back at the favored, the powerful who have used us, smothered us, sought to obliterate us all.

Forgotten gods, hear your patron saint.

Guide my hand.

ZERD AND JAMIL

IRAQ

2007

Strange.

How would they know where to find me? Did they follow the direction I ran to the only possible shelter? That couldn't be. My footprints would have been erased, even any ink I dripped would be covered by the wind and sand.

The knife.

I twisted the handle and after some effort, it unscrewed from the blade. Inside was a small circuit board. A GPS unit. Shit. I pulled out the device and crushed it under my foot, but it was too late. The hulking SUV was already parked outside the compound, its engine idling as The Dream Team spilled out.

An older man jumped out of the back seat and into the driver's seat. Damn if he didn't look like Senator Hanson. He couldn't be that hands-on, could he?

The Dream Team crouched low and ran against the wind toward the building, their handguns out. They were going to crash in, two on either side, and trap me in the middle. I buried myself in debris, pulled one of the corpses over me and gripped the knife, making sure the spiked knuckles were aligned for maximum damage.

Just one. If I can take out one before they kill me, I'll accept that.

Instead of footsteps, I heard a heavy clanking noise as a grenade bounced off the sandstone walls and rolled through the building. There was no boom, just a pop and a hiss as white smoke billowed out and filled the rooms.

Nice try, assholes. This place is riddled with bullet holes.

I put my cheek against the brick and sucked in clean air.

You're going to have to come in and get me.

One of them burst through the fog, wearing a gas mask. Carter. He slammed his back against the wall, swept his gun around the room from corner to corner, the muzzle tracing over the body I hid beneath.

If he saw me this would be over in seconds.

I held my breath.

Finally, he gestured behind him and moved deeper into the home. Spitz followed, crouched and moving slowly, walking backwards, watching their rear.

I jolted at the sound of a gunshot followed by a heavy thud from the next room. Spitz vanished into the smoke.

Voices muffled by the masks yelled at each other.

"Fuck! The prick wasted Carter!"

"He went the other way!"

"No, he's over here!"

"Shit!"

Another single shot and another body fell.

"I can't see!"

"Spitz? Spitz! He got Spitz!"

"Where did he get a gun?"

Belladonna crashed against the wall of the room I was hiding in, followed by Rimsky. Belladonna crept low, kicking aside debris with his boot.

"He's hiding. The floor's slippery here. Looks like blood."

Yeah, my blood and soon yours, amigo. Sorry it has to be this way, you were the one I hoped I wouldn't have to kill.

Belladonna kept talking. "We've got some old dead bodies here, Rimsky," he said. "Really fuckin' old and really fuckin' dead."

Through the smoke and behind the junk, he couldn't see me staring right at him. I could hear his breathing through his mask, see his eyes. I tightened my hand on the knife.

Back off, Belladonna, don't make me do this.

From my viewpoint, I saw Rimsky step up behind him and calmly put his pistol to the back of Belladonna's head.

Boom.

Belladonna's brains sprayed the inside of his gas mask as he collapsed.

Rimsky stepped backwards and waited, waving away the smoke. He pulled off his mask, pulled out his cell phone and pushed a button.

Why the hell was he killing his own crew? I knew the guy was a dickhead, but that big of one?

"Scrub complete," Rimsky said, turning to look into the other room.

I gently pushed my way out, emerging from the ash and bodies.

"Taken care of," Rimsky said.

I stepped carefully over Belladonna's body, his hand still twitching.

"Yep," Rimsky said. "We should be safe for another trial."

Wait or go for it? Wait or go for it?

Fuck it.

I crept forward.

I couldn't make out the words, but I could hear the other voice on the phone talking.

I was standing so near I could see the hair on Rimsky's neck.

He hadn't reacted to my presence at all. I raised the knife.

Die, motherf-

Something exploded in my chest.

Rimsky spun around and kicked with his massive boot, catching me in the mid-section. I felt ribs break as I flew backwards across the room, scraping along the floor, and hammering into the wall, as a raisin-dried corpse and rotted piece of furniture broke and fell over me.

I started to black out. No. No. Don't. Don't black out.

Please.

"Nice try, Z. Really nice," Rimsky said, slapping his cell phone closed and waving away the last of the smoke. "I didn't think you had it in you."

I was in too much pain to answer, but I managed to groan, "Asshole."

"Do you believe these fucking rag-heads? They killed my whole team. Wasted good Americans."

He pulled a metal pole from his equipment. I thought he was going to beat me with it, but then he pulled it apart to form a tripod. He fished in his pockets and pulled out a card-sized camera and took pictures of Belladonna's exploded head close up. Then he screwed the camera into the tripod and set it to face me.

Pain was stabbing my insides. My broken bones were knitting back together, a thousand shards tearing me as they melded. I wanted to tell my body to just leave the ribs broken because that had to be less pain than this, but my body wasn't normal now. It wanted to be in pristine condition all the time.

My chest rattled, not like the airy rattle of a cough shaking loose phlegm. This was actual scraping, rocks in a bag.

Rimsky pushed some buttons on the camera. "Wait until the pussies back home see this. Chemical weapons used in Iraq. More Americans killed and put on display. They're never going to want this war to end."

I started to cry. I tried to fight it, but tensing up to hold back the tears was just too painful. Crying was painful, too, but at least I couldn't fight anymore.

"That's good, Z. Perfect," Rimsky said. "Cry like the baby you are. We'll do audio later, so that thing you're doing with your shoulders shaking? Perfect."

I wasn't listening. I just cried. The world was cruel. My life was shit and it was going to end like shit. I would never get home. For all those reasons and so many more, I just cried.

"Hell, Z, you don't need to blubber. It's not all bad," Rimsky said. "Ever hear of that website Real War? The ones Hanson and the other war-supporters talk about? You're going to be their new star."

I was bawling. I didn't answer.

He looked at me through the viewfinder, laughing. "Work it, baby! Work it!" he yelled, like he was filming a fashion model. He smacked the camera. "Come on, fucking uplink. Transmit already."

"Just kill me," I croaked.

I couldn't find my knife. It had flown somewhere when I was kicked across the room, or I would have used it to kill myself.

Rimsky kept talking. "You know, Z, when I was a kid, some child psychologist said I was showing sociopathic traits: sadism, lack of guilt, all that shit. I thought I was just being honest, you know? My parents tried to fight it. Shit, my mom gave me all kinds of drugs. I crushed them and put them in water bowls for the neighbors' pets. Killed three dogs and one cat. Never caught."

He pushed a button on the camera. "Don't tell anyone that, all right?" he laughed.

"Fucking. Asshole," I choked.

"Exactly. Why fight nature? You'll lose. The key is finding an environment where your nature works. That's common sense. Shit, just because someone's a little different doesn't mean there's no place for them. Play to your strengths, right?"

I tried to push myself up. I was getting impatient waiting for the end. If I rushed him, maybe I could get him to shoot me.

"Now look at you," Rimsky went on, "You never found a way to make fucking up work for you. I guess that makes sense, though."

"Why are you telling me this?"

"I want to make your death as painful as possible. Sadist, remember? It's got to suck knowing that you tried with all your might to make a life for yourself but still couldn't. It makes my dick hard to know you're in pain. Not just physical pain, but spiritual pain. Existential pain. Fuck yeah!"

He grabbed his crotch and dry-humped his hand while he kept talking.

"You'll live on in video, though, as an advertisement for the war effort. The folks back home, they'll see you cry on the Real War site. Hanson will say, 'Look what they did to these fine Americans.' Then he'll give Redfire another sweet no-bid contract. You should be happy we found a use for your sorry ass. People don't need heroes, Z. They need victims."

He pushed some buttons on the camera.

"Now let's try some audio."

He cocked his gun, took a step back out of the camera's view and started screaming at me in Arabic.

I thought about yelling something to mess up his video, but I was crying uncontrollably. He stepped backwards again.

Steve once said, You don't get to choose how you die. I tried to calm myself with that thought, but it was useless.

Goodbye, Steve.

Goodbye, Dad.

Goodbye, Charles.

Goodbye, Tracy.

Goodbye, Zerd.

Rimsky was still yelling in Arabic when he kicked forward violently. I winced. I thought he was going to boot me in the head.

Instead he flew backward, was horizontal in the air for an instant before landing hard, flat on his back. His head knocked on a brick with a wet smack, his chin driving into his chest.

It was a spectacular fall, the kind people take while walking on ice, when they completely and utterly have their legs whisked out from under them. It was the kind of fall that, in a different context, turns out to be hilarious, even if the person gets hurt.

Especially if the person gets hurt.

The stupid bastard slipped in the pool of blood I left on the floor when I was trying to tattoo myself.

No time to waste.

I dragged myself to him, a broken snake slithering for its immobile prey, my ribs grinding together. I shoved Rimsky's head back with my palm on his forehead, exposing his neck.

All that time I spent here nibbling on corpse-flesh did me well after all. My jaw muscles had developed strength like a steel leg trap. I opened wide and snapped down on his Adam's apple, bit into it until my teeth connected together again inside the flesh of his throat. He instantly regained consciousness, thrashing, struggling. I ripped upwards, tearing a hole in his windpipe, his torn, sweaty neck muscle salty on my tongue, stubble raking the inside of my cheek.

I chewed.

His scream was windy and hollow. He shoved me off, dropping his gun, both hands flying instinctively to the gaping wound in his neck. His blood gurgled between his knuckles.

His eyes were wide, the whites as prominent as his icy pupils. With one hand over the wound, he staggered to his feet. He stumbled toward his gun, but I kicked it across the cement floor and under some rubble.

I'll say this for the prick, he was as tough as he acted.

He fell back against the wall and held both hands over his neck. The lack of air was draining his strength fast. He slid down, fought to stand back up, then slid down again, finally releasing the wound, leaving it free to leak breath and blood.

His body sagged and was still. I stared into his eyes until the focus left his gaze.

Dead.

I limped around the room, my body taking its time knitting me back together. Rimsky's boot-print was smeared into my half-dried blood puddle. All that blood I spilled trying to get my tattoos back ended up helping me out.

Maybe sometimes fucking up is good for something after all.

Rimsky sat against the wall, the hole in his throat staring at me.

It hurt to laugh, but I did it anyway.

* * *

Senator Hanson tapped the steering wheel, the engine running.

He was finishing a conversation on his phone, staring at the compound that Rimsky and the other three men had entered.

"Excellent," he said, folding the phone closed.

He didn't notice the approaching figure with the gun until the man stood next to him and fired. The bullets lodged in the driver-side window, crooked snowflakes appearing in the bulletproof glass.

"Holy shit!" Hanson squealed, dropping the car in gear. Jamil continued to shoot, the bullets bouncing off the well-armored SUV. Hanson accelerated.

Jamil sprinted for his car.

Hanson pushed a button to redial and yelled into his phone. "Rimsky, I've got a problem. I'm heading back to the base."

The senator kept an eye on the GPS directing him to the nearest camp. The pursuing car closed in.

Hanson screamed.

The small car rammed the SUV from behind, damaging itself more than the much larger vehicle. Hanson looked in his rearview. He didn't recognize the driver. The smaller car rammed him again. He tried to maneuver, but the sand gave and the SUV fishtailed, taking another strike from the other car and bouncing up on two wheels.

"Goddamn bastard!" Hanson yelled.

He shifted into the lowest gear. A bass tone vibrated the cabin as he pointed the car toward the base. Thin smoke was rising from the smaller car's hood, wafting over the windshield as it fell further behind.

Hanson's SUV leapt over a ridge. He could see the camp on the horizon. He pressed the accelerator to the floor, smirking as the smaller vehicle fell back, continuing its futile chase.

Hanson kept his eye on the car fading in his rearview. He shook his fist.

"You missed out, asshole!"

He looked up just as bullets ripped into his SUV, popping the trunk, shredding the tires. The truck lost its traction and tipped, rolling in the sand, tumbling off to the side, skidding to rest parallel to the base entrance.

The soldiers opened fire on the second vehicle. Bullets sparked against its side as it turned and sputtered back into the desert.

 The soldiers at the checkpoint converged on the overturned vehicle.

"Hold your fire! It looks like one of ours. I think it's a Redfire vehicle."

"Then why was it coming in top speed?"

"Keep your distance."

"Everyone knows to approach the gate slowly."

"It might be stolen. Stay back. That shit's probably wired."

After several hours of tentatively approaching the vehicle, the body was pulled from the SUV.

Soon after, the Redfire base commander locked his top advisors in his office. He stood behind his desk, scratching his bald head raw.

"I know what you're all wondering, so I'll tell you what I know. He's unconscious, but stable. Thank every damn god you believe in that he's going to live. Now, there's only one question and someone in this room better have an answer or make up a good one. What the hell is a U.S. Senator, the same one who is dodging an inquiry into alleged improper dealings with our company, doing out here driving one of our vehicles?"

* * *

Looking back on what little I can remember of my life, it's obvious there's not a lot of reasoning going on. I do what I do. It's Mom's impulsive streak, I guess.

So, I can't say exactly why I decided to tattoo Rimsky's corpse. Tats faded from my skin, but I could use his. He wasn't going to need it anymore, so why not?

I dragged him out into the middle of the slippery floor, took off his vest, tore open his shirt, and started carving names into his flesh. It seemed a good way to remember the people lost to the war he so much wanted, and as I had just learned, worked so hard to keep going.

What were all the connections between Rimsky, the Real War website, Senator Hanson, Redfire and the chemical weapon? I'll never know. Like Dad might have said, we don't know how far down the hole goes, but we know for sure it stinks down there.

So I set to work inking his corpse, using the blade and his blood. After I was done, I looked up and realized his camera was still on, its red light still blinking, filming me and sending the image who knows where.

Oops.

That's when the stranger appeared.

* * *

Jamil held his gun before him as he stepped over the corpses, stopping as he came upon the strange scene.

A camera was set up on a tripod. Text flashed on the camera's screen: "Uploading video." Beyond the tripod, a naked man was using a knife to carve letters into the chest of Tom Rimsky's corpse.

The naked man's skill was impressive. Even using such a peculiar medium and tool, the writing was legible.

The man turned around.

"What are you doing?" Jamil asked in Arabic, lowering his gun.

The man sat back, admiring his work, silent.

"Who are you?" Jamil said in English. "What are you doing? Answer me."

"Just writing some names," the naked man said. "People that are... lost."

"Do you know who that man is?"

"He's an American soldier. A mercenary. He was."

"Why is this camera on?"

"I just noticed that myself."

"It's not yours?"

"No."

Jamil thought for a moment, then spoke. "Leave."

Zerd started to push himself up. "Fine. I'm done."

"Wait. Can you carve another name?"

"Sure."

* * *

So I did it. J-A-M-I-L.

"Who's Jamil?"

"Me. Now leave."

I didn't argue.

I waited outside by his smoking car and watched my wounds heal. My skin, where damaged, was flaking off to reveal healthy flesh beneath. My bones stopped rattling as they became solid again. I stood there for a long time in the sun, just listening to the quiet, until my stomach started growling again. My body needed protein to finish the repairs, I guess.

The Jamil guy came out of the building, a sack made from Rimsky's shirt in one hand. Inside was something roughly spherical, about the size of a volleyball. The pouch was stained dark at the bottom.

"What's in the bag?" I asked.

Jamil stopped and looked at me with a weird smile.

"You're never supposed to ask that."

He unlocked the passenger side door of his car and set the round package gently in the seat. He closed the door firmly but not too hard, as if the package might break.

"You know," he said as he came to the driver's side, "I never liked when people refused to answer a simple question. You ask 'What's in the bag?' and they would not tell you. Why? Surely they were hiding something, but perhaps they refused because they felt you already knew the answer."

I tried to pay attention, but I couldn't help noticing the stain on the bottom of the satchel was expanding. Jamil leaned against the driver's door.

"So, my strange friend," he said, "you ask what is in the bag. I will tell you."

"Okay. Tell me."

"It is a present for my mother."

"That's not really an answer."

"It's the only one you are getting."

He got inside the car and started the engine.

"Do I know you?" I said. "You look familiar."

"Yes, I thought that of you, but the man I saw had many tattoos."

"That was me. The tattoos are gone. I have these things I scratched into my skin, but they'll be gone soon too."

"Gone?"

"It's a long story."

"How does a tattoo vanish?"

"Now who's asking the questions?"

He chuckled drily. "Fair enough. I am certain now. I see it in your face. We have met before, briefly."

"I think so."

Jamil looked forward through the windshield. He sighed, then looked back at me. "So you will understand."

"Understand what?"

With one smooth motion, too fast for me to dodge, he raised his arm and shot me through the heart.

JOHN

USA

2008

John Abbott pulled off his gloves and safety goggles, set down his hard hat and walked through the warehouse. He punched his card and headed out to the loading dock, saying good night to no one, as was his routine. He stopped for a cigarette, quietly standing near but not too close to his fellow smokers, so he could more easily ignore their inane gossip. He stared out across the parking lot before heading to the bus stop.

He hadn't cleared the loading dock area when a large black SUV with tinted windows rolled up. Two bulky men wearing suits and sunglasses exited from the truck. Each man had a curly wire running from his ear, disappearing under his suit jacket.

One of them approached the dock and called out.

"We're looking for a John Abbott."

John whipped his head around.

"Any of you know a John Abbott?" the second man asked loudly.

"Who wants to know?" one of John's co-workers asked.

"We do."

John backtracked. "I'm John Abbott. Who are you?"

"Federal agents. We need to speak with you."

"About?"

"Come with us."

"Hey. Don't you need to show him some papers?" someone else asked.

"Come on," the men insisted.

"I want an attorney," John said.

"We'll get you one."

"Show him your badges, your official identification," another smoker yelled. A small restless crowd was gathering.

The agents flipped open their wallets and handed them to John. He studied them for a long time.

"No joke, Mister Abbott. We're for real."

John turned back to the onlookers. One of them pointed to the corner of the building where a security camera was aimed at the SUV.

"Thanks," John said, nodding.

He slowly got in the back of the agents' truck.

"Where are we going?" he asked as they drove off.

"To the local police station," one of the men said. "We'll talk more there."

They didn't say another word the whole half-hour drive.

* * *

When they arrived, the local officers cleared out of an interrogation room so only John and the agents remained. The two men stood while John sat down at a table across from them.

"Where's my attorney?" John said.

"He's on his way," the agent snapped. "Mister Abbott, your son Pete had a nickname, am I correct? He was called 'Zerd' by his friends, is that right?"

"Yes. What's that-"

"When was the last time you spoke with him?"

"I haven't spoken to him in years. Last I heard he was joining the cons-to-soldiers program. I went to wish him well at the jail before he left, but he refused to see me. The last few times we talked we mostly argued anyway."

"So you haven't seen him. Have you visited the popular website 'Real War' lately on your computer?"

"No. I don't own a computer."

"No computer?"

"No computer. I'm familiar with the site, though. It pretends to be a site for voyeurs but I think it's more of an informal propaganda arm."

"We don't need your opinions. You say you have no computer? Really?"

"I read books. You may not be familiar with them."

"Don't be a smart ass. Please look at these photos."

One of the agents pulled several folded eight by ten photographs from his inside jacket pocket. He slid them across the table.

"These are recent pictures from the Real War website."

The grainy color images showed a naked man lying on his side. Words and names were scratched across his muscular chest, the letters dripping blood. John read aloud. "In Memory Of. Sly. Grits. Tubbs. Belladonna. Spitz. Carter. John Abbott. Zerd. Jamil."

"This guy has my name carved into his skin," John said, looking up. The agents looked at him blankly. John glanced at the photo again. "Where's his head?"

The agent snatched the pictures back. "Most of the people, ah, written there, are confirmed dead or missing, except for you."

John swallowed hard. "My son?"

"Your son's whereabouts are unknown. He's missing in action. Actually, he's more likely absent without leave."

"Con-soldiers get leave?"

"Mister Abbott, I hope to impress upon you again that this is extremely serious. It's not in your best interest to clown around. Especially if you care about your son. Has he attempted to contact you?"

"Do you think he did that? Carved names into some guy's skin? Beheaded him?"

One of the agents leaned on the table, casting an enormous shadow over John. "All we want to know is, have you heard from him? Do you know where he is? That's all we're trying to find out. We just want to talk to him. We want to help him."

John folded his arms. "And I want to talk to a lawyer."

"Sir, we can throw you in jail and hold you there indefinitely. Lawyers are not an obstacle any longer."

"Okay, look," John said, raising his voice, "I've cooperated so far, but now I'm annoyed, so let me get this straight: You're American federal agents threatening me, an American citizen on American soil, with indefinite detainment, without access to a lawyer and without explaining the charge."

"Yes."

"Will I be allowed to read?"

The agents looked at each other. John continued.

"Because look where you picked me up. You think that dump I work in is some kind of paradise? If you wanted to throw me in a jail cell where I get my food delivered daily and I can read books, I would be glad as hell to take you up on that offer."

One of the agents turned around. "Christ," he muttered.

John kicked back in his chair and crossed his feet, banging his dirty work boots on the tabletop. "I know you boys probably aren't into intellectual pastimes, but this is where I say 'checkmate.'"

The agents left the room without another word, closing the door behind them. John was alone.

An hour later the local police chief entered.

"They said you can go now."

* * *

Professor John Abbott saw his reflection in the library's glass doors and frowned at the baldness taking over his scalp. He shook off the cold and entered. After wandering around for several minutes, he was still unable to find the microfilm machines or card catalog.

"Figures," he groaned as he came across a bank of computers.

He sat down at a terminal and watched a ball bounce around the screen. He pressed the space bar and the ball vanished. A rectangle requested his password.

"Sir, can I help you?" someone asked.

"I'm trying to use the computer, and um, I don't know how." John stared at the screen, then looked up.

"Really?" The pale, tall thin man was dressed in skin-tight black pants and a black turtleneck. He seemed out of place in the library, an unnatural transplant from an art gallery. "Well, I can get you started," he said, "but I'm supposed to check you in if you're using the computers. May I have your library card?"

"Sure." John fished it out of his wallet.

"Professor Abbott!" the man yelled as he took the card. Everyone in the library looked up annoyed before going back to their work.

"I don't teach anymore. I'm just Mister Abbott now. Were you a student?"

"I didn't recognize you," without your hair, he left unsaid. "I was a friend of your son! Oh, my God, it's been so long. My name's Charles. I'm not sure you remember, there was ah, an incident once..."

"Oh. Oh," John said, frowning weakly. "Yes. I remember." He waited a moment. "I can be such a jerk."

"Well, we weren't exactly innocent, and I must say that was the most unique scolding I ever received. So how are you? I haven't heard from your son in forever. I've lost track of him. How is Zerd? I mean Pete. How's he doing?"

John shrugged. "We haven't spoken in years."

"Oh. Oh, no," Charles said. He sat down at the computer next to John. "I'm sorry to hear that. You're not alone with family troubles, believe me."

"He's the reason I'm here. I'm looking for information about him."

Charles turned to the computer and began typing briskly as he logged on. "What are you looking for?"

"I'm trying to find a photo."

"A photo of?"

"Well, it's something that is, um."

"We're not allowed to look up pornography," Charles winked, "but I'll make a special exception for an old friend."

John didn't laugh at the joke. "It's a picture from Iraq. Of a man. Beheaded."

"Beheaded? Oh, my God. Not-"

"No, I don't think it's Pete. In fact I'm sure it's not. Um, that site, Real War. Is that still up? I had my teaching assistants print pages from it when I discussed it in class those years ago. I only knew about it from reading my political journals."

"Sure, it's still up."

John watched as Charles typed and controlled the on-screen arrow.

A red window popped up. The text "Unauthorized!" flashed in bright yellow.

"Damn," John said.

"Oh, don't worry. Most sites with disturbing content are automatically blocked by our system, but I'll get us through. After all, I do work here."

Charles' fingers swept over the keyboard with a light tapping. In seconds, the Real War website was up. The screen was bright red, offering several cropped thumbnails of gory photographs and a headline that promised "Live Terrorist Footage!" Animated blood dripped down the screen. The colors made John's eyes hurt.

"It's funny you came in here," Charles said. "I was thinking of you recently."

"You were?"

"Of course. Your old friend, Senator Hanson. He's all over the news."

"He is? For what?"

"You haven't heard? He went to Iraq and was supposedly injured when a suicide bomber detonated near him. The story has lots of holes because there is also footage of him walking around after the blast. But then there are also reports that he's laid up in a hospital on a Redfire base. His office keeps putting out contradictory information about where he is, who he was with and what he was doing. No one's heard from the man himself. Some say he's just ducking the hearings into his connections with Redfire. The congressional committee is screaming for answers, threatening to drag him in to testify. Every day there's more dirt. No one knows what's really going on. I can't believe you don't know all this."

John shrugged. "I stopped following the news. I'm mostly just reading the classics. I've lost my political fight these days. I gave it up to be a good father a few years too late."

Charles tapped John's arm compassionately, then turned to the computer. "Maybe you just needed a rest. Okay, let's see. The Real War website. Yuck. Videos and still images. Dismemberment, dead bodies, executions by shooting, executions by stoning, firefight videos. A beheading, you say? Here's the recent ones."

"That one. Right there. The guy with the carvings in his chest. Zoom in there. What's that say?"

Charles moved a magnifying glass across the screen. The beheaded corpse, names carved into the torso, filled the monitor. The image caption read: "Beheaded American found outside Baghdad, tagged by sicko rag-head graffiti artists."

Charles squinted and moved his face closer to the screen. "It says… In memory of… Holy shit!" Charles screamed. The other library patrons looked over at him again. The librarian behind the desk hushed him. Charles brushed her off with a contemptuous wave of his hand.

"It's your name," he whispered. He continued panning across the picture. "Who are these other people? Tubbs? Grits? Oh, my God. There's Zerd."

John leaned in. "Someone had to know him. It couldn't be a coincidence. Who has a nickname like 'Zerd' and why is my name there? Whatever happened, my son was there."

"Well, the body can't be your son. There's no tattoos."

"I know. Whoever did it knew my son. Or he did it himself."

"But he wouldn't cut a man's head off."

"I don't think so, but… it's been a long time. Who knows what happened to him over there. Some friendly men from the government stopped by my job and asked me about all this. I don't know a Tubbs or Belladonna or anyone else named there. Never have. I only know my son's nickname used to be Zerd. The G-men said most of the people named there on the body were dead."

"Including…?"

"Except for me and my son. He's not… confirmed. They don't even know where he is. At least that's what they told me. If they did know, I don't think they would have sought me out. I have to think he's still… somewhere."

They sat in silence, staring at the gory photo for some time. Finally Charles shook his head and rested his hand on John's shoulder. "I know your son and he's a resourceful guy. I'm sure he's all right."

"Thanks."

The silence returned, uncomfortable and awkward.

"Do you mind if I click off of this?" Charles said, referring to the picture of the beheaded body. "It's gross."

"Hm? Sure. I've seen enough. That was all I needed."

Charles logged off the computer. "You should stop in more often. Your class was the only one that really stuck with me. My major was languages, but I became a librarian because I believe in free access to information. I picked that up from you."

"You did?"

"I did. And look, here I am."

"Well," Professor Abbott said, "at least someone was listening."

UNKNOWN

IRAQ

2008

The lone nomad guided his two camels and herd of goats across the desert, moving away from the rising sun.

Something rustled under the sand. He stopped, whistling so the herd reared up and began milling about, bleating. The man's eyes were old, but still sharp. Was it just a dune? A light wind? It was too large to be a snake.

It shifted again, the sand moving as one bulk.

Something was there, definitely. Something large.

He waited and watched.

There was constant war across this land. He and his ancestors had never gotten involved and knew to stay away from the unknown. That tradition had saved his life more than once. Whatever was buried there could be a landmine or an unexploded rocket shell, a still active bomb, anything. He had all the supplies he needed so there was no reason to investigate for salvage.

He watched the lump while steering his herd around it in a wide arc. His aged heart stuttered as the sand suddenly heaved upward and separated. The shape of a man rose, sand pouring from his naked body as if he were being born from the earth. He stood and let the grains fall from him in trails, lifting his hands, spreading open his fingers and observing them as though he was seeing them for the first time.

The herd sensed their leader's fright and began to scatter. The nomad calmed them with his touch and whispers, keeping watch on the strange figure as it stretched like one who had just awakened. The nomad slowly pulled his rifle from over his shoulder. He didn't aim it, but kept it in front of him, ready.

The sand-man was not armed. He brushed the grime from his body, turning, finally noticing the nomad.

Their gazes met. The one born from the sand smiled and tilted his head slightly. His skin was pale, unmarked.

"What are you?" the nomad asked. "Djinn? Efreet?"

The sand had completely fallen from the man. His white skin and fair eyes matched that of the most recent invaders to this land. The man looked at the nomad but said nothing.

The nomad called out again. "Are you all right? Where did you come from?"

The man grinned stupidly. The nomad suspected he was dealing with a mentally ill person. He had seen it before, those who appeared normal physically, but they could not remember things or they spoke in loud grunts and had difficulty learning. But how would such a man get here? Why would he be here? Such people needed constant care. There was the abandoned structure a few thousand paces back, but nothing else. A man with diminished mental capacity could not possibly survive out here alone.

The nomad guided his flock around the naked man and continued walking.

The sand-man watched him but did not move.

"You'll burn," the nomad called as he passed by. "Your skin is fair. You should get out of the sun."

The naked man followed him silently, keeping his distance.

The nomad looked over his shoulder as he walked mile on mile, the sun creeping along with him. The naked man still followed, neither threatening nor retreating. When the sun was at its highest, the nomad rounded up his herd to rest in the scant shade of a small clutch of palm trees. The naked man stopped and stood in the sun.

Finally the nomad beckoned to him. With one hand on his rifle, he held out his canteen at arm's length with the other. The naked man approached, finally close enough to take the flask. The nomad pantomimed drinking from it. The naked man tilted it, letting the water splash over his mouth.

"You seem harmless enough," the nomad said. He retrieved some old rags from the bundles on his camels, wrapping a turban around the sand-man's head and covering him to protect his skin. The rest of the day they walked together in silence.

In the evening, the sand-man clumsily helped the nomad round up his herd, then watched, catatonic, while the nomad lit a fire. They stared at each other across the flames.

"I've been on my own for a while so I'll drop you off at the next village," the nomad said. "Someone there can care for you."

The sand-man spoke for the first time in an alien tongue. "I don't remember much," he said.

"I'm sorry, I don't understand you," the nomad said.

"I'm sorry, I don't understand you," the naked man replied.

Each speaking his own language, they shrugged at one another.

The sand-man continued speaking. "I remember the basics," he said. "How to walk, how to talk. I can still breathe. That stuff I know." He paused. "Everything else is like," he waved his hand out toward the night desert, "just a flat surface covered in darkness, I know there's something beyond but I don't know what. So if you're asking me what came before, what I'm doing here, who I am, those things I can't answer."

After that, they quietly studied each other through the fire.

Finally the sand-man leaned to the side and absently ran his fingers through the sand around him, tracing lines through the grains. The curves reminded him of the shape of the nomad's chin. He turned back to the grooves and continued to sweep his fingertips lightly across the sand, drawing more lines, looking up at the nomad for reference, then back to his work.

"What are you doing?" the nomad asked.

The sand-man didn't reply. He was stroking both hands across the top of the sand, his motions fluid, confident.

Finally the nomad rose, walked around the fire and stood over the stranger.

The sand-man said something and leaned back, smiling. He swept his hand, palm up, over the lines he had made. A drawing of a face, expertly crafted, stared up from the ground. The portrait was made out in stunning detail. The nomad recognized it as his own face and couldn't help but smile.

"Well done," he said. "Incredible."

He patted his hand on the sitting sand-man's shoulder, and grinned down at him.

The sand-man looked up, his face full of pride. Then he blinked as if a thought occurred to him. He shook his head, said something the nomad couldn't understand and leaned over to continue his drawing.

*** THE END ***

A NOTE TO READERS

Dear Reader,

Thank you so much for taking the time to read *Loser's Memorial.* If you have a moment, you can help independent publishing by leaving a fair and honest review on Amazon.com or your favorite reading website. Reviews help authors reach more readers and assist those authors in improving their craft.

So thanks again for reading *Loser's Memorial.* I hope you found it time well spent. All the best to you.

Larry Nocella

* * *

PROOFREADING HELP

Many thanks to Tom Demi for his proofreading assistance. Any remaining errors are mine. - LN

* * *

ABOUT THE AUTHOR

Larry Nocella sold his first article at age fourteen, and has been writing ever since. He lives in the USA. Visit www.LarryNocella.com.

Where Did This Come From? a novel

Based in the fictional South American nation of Palagua, the novel Where Did This Come From? follows the Huapi tribe's desperate struggle for survival. When American tourist Joe Vera saves the life of the Huapi chief, he is rewarded with a rare and beautiful crystal unknown to the outside world.

Back in America, Joe gives the crystal as a gift to the terminally-ill son of his ex-girlfriend, but it isn't long before the crystal attracts the interest of a leading U.S. toy manufacturer, MajorCo Toys. In an instant, Joe is rich and the crystal is selling like crazy. MajorCo stock is skyrocketing, just before the Christmas shopping season.

The news from Palagua is much more grim. Mining operations are tearing apart the Huapi land. Civil war erupts as factions battle for control of the huge wealth suddenly found in this once-poor nation.

The Huapi find themselves and the jungle that supports them on the brink of annihilation. Joe struggles to stem the forces of desire he has unleashed. How do you fight want? How do you fight greed?

Can Joe and the Huapi hope to resist the hunger of those who never bother to care Where Did This Come From?

* * *

It Never Goes Away (short story)

Author Larry Nocella terrifies readers with a suspenseful struggle for survival in the short story "It Never Goes Away." The lone survivor of a mysterious catastrophe awakes to find himself buried alive in the ruins of his home. Every attempt to escape only buries him deeper. Facing starvation, thirst, and a lack of air, his odds of survival diminish with each passing second. As he pieces together the true nature of the disaster, it seems beyond imagining. Will he live long enough to find out the truth?

Includes an essay by the author about the story's real-life inspiration.